Also by PETE RAWLIK

*Reanimators*
*The Weird Company*

# REANIMATRIX

## AN ARKHAM ROMANCE BY

## Pete Rawlik

NIGHT SHADE BOOKS
New York

Night Shade books may be purchased in bulk at special discounts for sales promotion, corporate gifts, fund-raising, or educational purposes. Special editions can also be created to specifications. For details, contact the Special Sales Department, Night Shade Books, 307 West 36th Street, 11th Floor, New York, NY 10018 or info@skyhorsepublishing.com.

Night Shade Books® is a registered trademark of Skyhorse Publishing, Inc. ®, a Delaware corporation.

Visit our website at www.nightshadebooks.com.

10 9 8 7 6 5 4 3 2 1

Library of Congress Cataloging-in-Publication Data

Names: Rawlik, Pete, author.
Title: Reanimatrix / Pete Rawlik.
Description: New York: Night Shade Books, [2016]
Identifiers: LCCN 2016018015 | ISBN 9781597808804 (softcover)
Subjects: LCSH: Murder—Investigation—Fiction. | Paranormal fiction. |
    BISAC: FICTION / Fantasy / Paranormal. | FICTION / Horror. | FICTION /
    Mystery & Detective / Hard-Boiled. | GSAFD: Fantasy fiction. | Mystery
    fiction. | Horror fiction.
Classification: LCC PS3618.A948 R43 2016 | DDC 813/.6—dc23
LC record available at https://lccn.loc.gov/2016018015

Print ISBN: 978-1-59780-880-4

Cover illustration by René Aigner
Cover design by Jason Snair

Printed in the United States of America

for
Bob and Wilum and Joe
who showed me how

The most dangerous and frightening of mankind's emotions is love, and the most dangerous and frightening kind of love is not love lost, but love of that which we cannot have. The unconsummated love festers in a man's mind, becoming cancerous, crowding out all other affections that might find home there. Rare is the man who can battle such a malignancy, and rarer still is the man who can overcome it and remain free from the hungering emptiness it leaves behind.

—Robert Blake

## PART ONE
# Robert Peaslee
## 1919–1924

# CHAPTER 1

# "Revenge of the Reanimator"
## From the Letters of Robert Peaslee
## May 5 1919

My dearest Hannah,

You must forgive me for dispensing with the usual pleasantries; I promise to send you a more formal letter at a later date, but for now you must make do with this haphazardly written missive. Under the circumstances, it is the best that I can do. So much has happened in the last few hours; I have so much to tell you about that I can hardly keep myself contained, and yet, at the same time, I am hesitant, for what I have seen defies the bounds of common decency, and borders on the absurd, and likely wanders into the realm of pure madness. It may all be simply too much for a simple boy from Arkham to take in. That, in itself, is amusing, for it was because of Arkham that I was drawn into the strange events that have so disturbed my mind, but I get ahead of myself.

Paris is a madhouse. I thought perhaps it was because of the end of the war, that the Peace Conference had drawn not only the great powers of the world to the city, but the madmen as well, but I think it is simply the nature of this place. As a member of the security detail attached to our mission, I must, on a daily basis, sift through the reports generated by the locals, constantly searching for evidence of some threat that might disrupt the conference or endanger the staff. Each day brings a new revelation, a new wonder, or a new horror. Last month, the authorities arrested a man they suspected of murdering dozens of women. Criminal geniuses joust with the police. Masked vigilantes armed with super-science haunt the streets, doing battle with infamous thieves, murderers, and nefarious organizations. It is not uncommon to see strange inventions roll down the streets or glide past amongst the clouds. Such things had become routine, so it was a surprise when my commander ordered me to the outskirts of the city to help the gendarmes. He wouldn't tell me much, but the words "Arkham" and "Miskatonic" had been uttered. He knew I was from Arkham, knew our family history, and decided I needed to be the one to take a more detailed look.

Montmartre is an odd little part of Paris. Before the war, it was home to a thriving artistic community, but now, it has slowly become home to a rather unsavory element that needn't be discussed here. Hidden within this labyrinth-like neighborhood are several small estates of several acres each, some of which have been turned into private sculpture gardens for the more well-to-do members of this community of eccentrics. One of these was named the Locus Solus, and was the playground of the prominent Dr. Martial Canterel, a scientist and inventor whose fame in Paris rivaled that of Edison, but whose eccentricities rivaled those of Tesla. Although I have no direct knowledge, rumor has it that Canterel was responsible for the so-called "Miracle of the Marne," which used taxi cabs to transport reserve troops to the front lines: an absurd proposal to be sure, but one that worked, and changed the course of the battle. This, then, was the nature of Canterel's reputation and work: the adaptation of one invention to another use that seemed absurd or completely impractical, but in practice worked, and produced what could be thought of as scientific romances or engineering art.

As I left the street, the gateway to the estate was not-unexpectedly bizarre, consisting of facsimiles of teeth from some titanic beast that curved into the air to form a kind of arch. Normally such a thing would be considered macabre, or perhaps outré, but the fact that each immense tooth had been painted in splashes of various pastel colors made the thing simply laughable. I may have been walking into the maw of an immense beast, but it was candy-colored, and that made it somehow acceptable.

The pavers upon which I trod were equally as whimsical, for each one was connected to a pneumatic system that responded to each step. In essence, as I walked from the street to the house, my gait provided its own processional beat, until I at last reached the door and was announced by a rich contralto bleating. The door, which was a thick steel thing colored purple, swung open to reveal a familiar face, one of my colleagues, a man who like me had served in the war, but was found to be too useful to ship home, at least just yet. Gatsby had a way with numbers, and with people, so the Brass had kept him on, though not for much longer. He had been accepted to one of the upper-crust British universities, and was just days away from starting his life over as a student.

Gatsby ushered me inside and in a veritable whirlwind of activity moved down the corridor to the library. He sat me down in a chair shaped like an octopus, looked at me oddly, and then smiled. "In a few seconds a man, Dr. Martial Canterel, is going to come through that door," he said, pointing at a fragile-looking panel of glass and lead. "When he does, he is going to talk to you as if he knows you. You need to play along, and follow him when he moves. Whatever you do, don't try to stop him. Do you understand?"

I nodded my affirmation as Gatsby backed away.

As soon as he was clear, the door swung wide and a suave man wearing a ridiculous green-and-purple paisley suit walked in. He was thin and well groomed, and walked with that odd way of carrying himself that told me he wasn't an American. He smiled as he approached and greeted me warmly, taking my right hand in both of his.

"My dear Doctor, I am so glad you could come," he said as he vigorously shook my hand. "It has been so long since we last spoke, twenty years I suppose. Has it really been that long since I was in Arkham? I heard that you had some trouble with the faculty at Miskatonic?"

I was utterly confused. "I'm sorry, I'm not a doctor. I think perhaps you have mistaken me for Professor Nathaniel Peaslee; I'm his son, Robert."

I looked around for help, but Gatsby had vanished.

Canterel let go of my hand. There was a smell, actually two odors, one of perfume; an attempt to mask the other, a stench that hinted at rotting food.

"Of course, still, what do those old fools know?" he replied. "If it weren't for men like us, those milksops would still have us in the Dark Ages shaking bones and muttering incantations." He spun around and seemed to be listening to something. "Yes, but I assure you, my friend, there is no need. I have a demonstration set up in the garden, and I brought a suitable specimen, and a sample of my reagent." He paused once more. "Yes, it is derived from the one we worked on so long ago, but I've made a number of improvements since then. It may not produce the exact response we are looking for, but the results are consistent, reproducible between subjects."

He turned back toward me and leaned in to where I was sitting, so close that I had to slouch back into the chair. When he spoke again, it was in a sly, almost secretive whisper.

"Come into the garden, my dear Herbert, let me show you what my Resurrectine can do."

From his pocket he produced a small glass vial of fluid so green that it nearly glowed, and flecked with small grains of purple. Doing as I was told, I rose from my chair and followed Dr. Canterel into the garden. As we strolled down the hall, Gatsby was nowhere to be seen.

Outside in the garden, free from the bonds of architecture, Canterel's work was awash in the nonsense that has infused the art movement known as Dadaism. The whole landscape was surreal, and I was reminded of the worlds described by Lewis Carroll, and in some ways L. Frank Baum. There was a tree hung with lunch pails, which when Canterel touched them would bark like schnauzers. There was a grove of books, chiseled out of marble, with the pages attached and moveable using great stone rings, themselves carved out of the stone.

He pointed to a goggled-eye light fixture. "When I was a young man, I found that on the beach. I believe it to be part of Nemo's Nautilus. Some kind of death ray I suppose. For me, it is my favorite lamp, which I keep lit using a small jar of glow bugs." He paused suddenly. "You have no interest in such things, do you, Dr. West?" He shook his head and went *tsk tsk* through his teeth. He pointed at a large empty space. "Not even in my giant diamond aquarium? You see that cat? And the head?"

I looked, but there was nothing there. I could not understand why I could not see it. He paused and seemed to be listening.

"Yes, it is the head of the famed politician Danton. I reconstituted it and administered an early version of Resurrectine. The head still speaks, but it needs motivation. Thus the cat will occasionally stir the thing. Ignore the dancing girl, she was an afterthought, but now that the piece has been installed, I find it too difficult to alter it." It was as if he was seeing something that wasn't there, or had been once, but was no longer.

We wandered down the garden path a little ways before Canterel stopped once more. "Indulge me for a moment, my friend," he pointed to a bas-relief map of Paris, upon which a small red light was slowly moving about. "Throughout the city I have placed a net of radio receivers tuned to capture the regular signal of a small transmitter which I attached to a feral dog. By using the signal strength from each of the receivers, I can estimate the location of the dog almost instantaneously on this map. By recording those locations, I can create a history of the dog's movements, a kind of travelogue if you will."

I looked at where he was gesturing, but again the space was empty.

"It is an amusing little project, but I cannot for the life of me find a practical use for it. It could be used to track people as they move through the city, and perhaps direct police or reroute traffic as needed, but I find it hard to believe that we could convince the masses to wear my devices in support of such a cause." He paused and his face took on an annoyed expression. "Please, my friend, there is no need to be so angry. What you wish to see is just around the corner, come follow me, and you shall see what I have done with your reagent. It is truly a masterpiece."

Once more, he waddled down the path, and I dutifully followed, but, this time, as we came around a hedge, I was greeted by the most astounding of sights. There were eight enclosures; glass cubes each about ten feet on a side. Inside were people, one per cube, all different, and all doing different things. There was a woman rocking a child to sleep, though the child itself was a doll. She just sat there rocking the doll, singing to it, over and over again. She made no deviation from her pattern, made no attempt to acknowledge our presence.

More disturbing was the marrying man, a man dressed in a tuxedo in front of a dummy dressed as a priest. Beside him was an articulated mannequin on wheels dressed in a wedding dress. A speaker mounted on the side of the priest dummy would recite vows, which the man would acknowledge. There were pauses were the mannequin would supposedly speak as well. At the end of the ceremony, the man would kiss the bride and then run down an aisle. After about thirty feet, he would suddenly stop. A hidden cable would drag the mannequin back to the priest, and the groom would join them. I thought it was a kind of performance art, but the precision with which it was repeated was disturbing. I might even say unnerving.

Canterel motioned me down the path in a way that made me think he was trying to be quiet, but as I approached he started giggling and then addressed me in a normal tone.

"I'm sorry, I tend to forget that they don't acknowledge our existence, so it doesn't matter how we speak or act. They are so lifelike, a magnificent *tableau vivant*, all thanks to my reagent, my Resurrectine. It brings the dead back to life, and then they continuously reenact the most important event in their lives, at least from their perspective. It is not perfect, mind you; there is still the matter of decay. The decomposition may have been slowed, but they do rot. And of course there is the matter of nutrition, but the less said about that the better."

He smiled, and I stared at the young man who was acting out fishing in the river and pulling up a rather large, but wholly unidentifiable fish. "Perhaps *tableau vivant* is the wrong way to describe them, *tableaux mort* might be better."

He stepped away and then turned quickly. "My secret ingredient, of course it is the Vril energy. I infuse it into the reagent during formulation. It affects the mind, you see."

Suddenly Canterel spun around and looked at his arm. "Sir! Just what do you think you are doing?" He reached for something that I could not see. Whatever it was, he found it. He twisted left and right, and then spun around. "I haven't corrupted anything," he yelled. "I haven't made a mockery of your work; I've turned it into an art!"

He suddenly spun around and screamed, "*DOCTOR WEST!*" His voice gurgled and his back arched. I saw the light in his eyes grow dim as he crumpled to the ground. He lay there for a moment, still as the grave, but only for a moment. Without warning, he was convulsing and screaming. Canterel's body was flopping around on the ground like a dying fish. He screamed again, and then went quickly silent. Without a word, he stood up and in silence he walked away, passing me and returning to the house.

I did not follow him, for as he stood, I saw what lay beneath him. I ran instead, ran from Canterel, ran from the estate called Locus Solus, ran through the streets of Paris, and took refuge in the American Consulate, where I could drown away what I had seen with French wine and Kentucky bourbon. I didn't need to follow Canterel back into his house to know what was going to happen next. I had seen enough, seen what had happened, and I knew I didn't need to see it again.

Canterel was going back inside, back to the library, where he would once again act out the last few minutes of his life, the moments during which he had met with the man who had invented the reagent, the basis for his own Resurrectine, and during which he could at last boast of his achievement to the one man whom he respected. It was an encounter that Canterel would consider the greatest of his life: one that would end with one man attacking the other, and Canterel being murdered.

If only he had stayed dead, but whoever had killed him, a man, a doctor by the name of Herbert West, had found it amusing to dose Canterel with his own creation, his own version of the reagent, his so-called Resurrectine. Canterel was trapped, not alive, but not dead either, at least until he succumbed to starvation, or rotted away.

Until then, he was no longer Doctor Martial Canterel the artist; he had become what he cherished the most: a work of art.

Your dearest brother,
Robert Peaslee

# CHAPTER 2

# "The Sepia Prints"
## From the Letters of Robert Peaslee
## June 24 1919

My dearest Arthur,

My apologies, I did not mean to scare you. Most mornings I wake screaming. I have bad dreams, but those dreams, they help keep me sane. The fact that such things still terrify me, in an odd way I find comforting. My sister likes to say that I came back from the war changed, others nod and whisper words like "shell-shock," but it wasn't the war that did this to me. It was something worse, something far worse.

It was just after the war, but at this point what isn't—I was still in Paris working as security for the American delegation to the Treaty of Versailles. I was on leave following a disagreeable turn of events involving a strange estate on the outskirts of the city and a rather disreputable doctor who, like me, was from Arkham. The Major had given me some time off and I had squandered most of it by wandering through the streets of the city, searching for something, though what exactly I cannot say. There was a sense of ennui within my soul, a longing that cried out to be fulfilled, but try as I might I could not find what I needed. Unable to satisfy myself I instead indulged in more earthly delights.

It was thus that I found myself one night on the balcony of the hotel that many of our mission had laid claim to. I was intoxicated, but not incapacitated. I was enjoying the view—the balcony was five stories above the square, and provided an excellent point from which to observe the comings and goings of those below, without being too close to those sometimes-maddening crowds. As I have said, I was intoxicated, lost in the drink and the beauty of the city, for suddenly I was no longer alone at the ledge. There was a woman standing next to me, staring wistfully out at the city lights and its people. She was an attractive young woman, in a European way, but she was also disheveled. Her clothes were ragged, some of her hair had broken free from where she had pinned it, and three of her fingernails on one hand were broken.

She was uncomfortably close, and when I cleared my throat to gain her attention she stared at me with such a wild look in her eyes, such madness and fear, I was suddenly taken aback. I recognized her, a girl from Guernsey, a singer, or at least a student of the art. She was fluent in both English and French, and therefore had been useful to us in the past. Her name was Evelyn—it seemed to me most girls from Guernsey were named Evelyn—and she looked at me with a touch of madness in her eyes.

Her voiced cracked as she spoke. "Have you seen the prints?"

I stuttered out a puzzled, "I beg your pardon?"

There was a book in her hand, a folio of some kind. She offered it to me. "The prints, have you seen the sepia prints?" The book slipped from her fingers and tumbled to the ground, its contents, photographs, spilled out and scattered across the stones of the balcony, like dry leaves in a light breeze, falling to earth, but with no intent of staying there.

My eyes caught hers, and there was a tear. "The prints," she whispered.

"Not to worry," I said, kneeling down to gather up the images and the book itself. They were indeed sepia prints. As I crouched there by her feet I saw her weight shift. Her feet rose off from the ground. A shoe, black, shiny but scuffed, fell back down. I put out a hand to catch it and as I did rose up as well, offering the errant shoe to the young lady like some prize, as if I were a conquering knight.

She was gone.

I was alone.

I searched the balcony, but to no avail.

A puzzled word slipped through my lips. "Where?"

I stood there, a woman's shoe in one hand, and half a dozen prints in the other. At my feet the folio blew open and more of the sepia-tinted prints leaked out. I was staring at the space where she had been, where she no longer was, and could see nothing but the spot on the railing that had once been covered with a fine growth of ivy, which now was torn and broken.

Then I heard the screams from below, and with a casual glance saw what had caused them. Evelyn was there on the square below, her arms and legs at impossible angles. Her other shoe was rocking back and forth on the masonry like a ship tossed on the sea. Her head had caught the garden fence and had been impaled with such force that it had been torn from her body. It stared back up at me with wide open eyes; eyes that I swore were still filled with fear and madness.

I didn't wait for the authorities. It would take time to deal with the local police, and they had no love for us Americans. They would have questions, but I had no answers. I didn't really know the woman, barely knew her name, had barely spoken ten words to her—was it even ten words? They would want to take the book, the folio of prints, but it was the only clue I had, and I needed it. If I were to figure this thing out, I would have to start somewhere. The book was as good a place as any. I cannot even today say why I did this thing. I just did it. As I have said, I was searching for something to fulfill myself, and this girl's death, or more importantly, understanding the impetus for her death, seemed to provide a taste of what I needed.

I gathered up the loose prints and the thin book that had once held them. I sprinted down the winding stairs, down the hall and out the back door. Leaving the alleyway, I slowed my pace and merged into the pedestrians who were moving along the street. The Mission had another house, a place several blocks away that we used to lodge dignitaries or visitors. I knew it was empty and made my way there, trying not to draw attention to myself as I weaved through the crowd.

In the safety of that anonymous townhouse I held the book and in the dim light examined it and tried to put it in order. It was bound in black leather, but that was faded in spots, frayed at the corners, broken in places along the spine. Traces of gold inlay revealed that there had been stamped letters on the cover once, but the majority of them had been worn away, leaving only a few specks of precious metal here and there. Even the letters themselves had nearly faded completely away. At first glance I thought that the repair of the book would take a significant amount of time, but I was mistaken. While the prints were all the same size, the stains and stray marks that rimmed the edges made matching each to the correct page much easier, and within hours the book was in order and intact once more, and I was able to examine it in its original state.

Investigations begin in odd ways, and no two are alike. The exact way to start is driven by the antecedent conditions, the style of those investigating, and the available clues. I only had two pathways to follow: I could investigate the woman, delve into her personal life and her work, or I could begin with the book. Reasoning that any conversation with family, friends, or coworkers would eventually be tied back to the book, I decided to begin there. It was, after all, already in my possession. It was perhaps the best place to start, and so I began my examination in earnest.

Though the letters on the cover were gone, the title page made it clear what the collection of photographs was. I did not even need to translate from French, for the title was repeated in English.

*The King in Yellow*
A Souvenir Collection of Images of the Cast

On the Occasion of its Premier
The Sixteenth of February, 1899

Palais Garnier
Paris, France

I knew the Palais Garnier by its more common name, the Paris Opera House, a magnificent edifice, a cornerstone of Parisian society, albeit one that was occasionally drenched in a little blood. Since the building had been completed there had been rumors that it was haunted, and these rumors came to a head in the early 1880s with the strange affair of the Opera Ghost. That phantom was not the only scandal that had befallen the opera house, for there were still rumors of strange figures haunting the halls, balconies, and alleyways of the edifice. Indeed, I recalled some mention of a fire that had taken the lives of an entire cast, and even some audience members.

Below the title there was a stamp in blue ink that identified the book as part of the collection of the Bibliothèque-Musée de l'Opéra, a library with which I was not familiar. I consulted a guide book and learned that the library-museum was attached to the Paris Opera

House and served as an archive of both the opera house itself and of opera in general, holding thousands of scores and librettos, as well as costumes, props, and memorabilia of performances themselves. This book, it seemed, was part of their archive and documented a lavish performance that had occurred almost two decades earlier.

Lavish was an understatement.

The costuming was magnificently decadent and purposefully grotesque. I had heard stories concerning the Opera's production of Don Juan Triumphant, but I could not imagine that it was any more extravagant or ostentatious than what was in these images. First, the set was intricately detailed, with great banners and glass chandeliers hanging in the background, while the foreground was reminiscent of the art deco style of designer Erte. There was hedonism rampant in every set piece, and through it all ran a hypnotic triple spiral motif that drew the eye and threatened to make me dizzy. That design, which was a kind of triskelion but only in the most abstract sense, continued into the costumes for each character. It could be found in the lace that trimmed the gowns of the twins Cassilda and Camilla, and in the crown of the regent Uoht, and his wife Cordelia's headdress. Aldones's spectacles were three-lobed, and Thale's staff bore a triple spiral. It could even be seen in the pale cloak of the Phantom of Truth, and the bindings that held together the Pallid Mask. Only The Stranger seemed to be without any influence from the weird design, and this served to set him apart from the others, to make him an outsider amongst a society of the strange.

Each character was photographed in two costumes, one in a kind of formal attire, and then again in a kind of masquerade, each with its own mask, one simple, one ornate. Heavy makeup had been applied to all the actors which suggested that beneath their masks they were all horrifically scarred. The only exception to this was The Stranger, who had one simple costume and appeared to have only one mask, or perhaps none at all.

As I progressed through the images I began to develop a strange idea, a suspicion really, one that was confirmed with a single ensemble photograph. For each character there were two actors, one in common costume, and the other in fancy masquerade. The resemblance between actors playing the same part was astounding—indeed I suspected that some of them were twins or at least siblings—but there were subtle differences. There was a facial mole in one photo that was absent in another. One actor for Uoht had very different earlobes than the other. The actor playing the fancy Aldones was missing the tip of his left index finger. The girls playing the twins Cassilda and Camilla were no doubt sisters, or perhaps cousins, but certainly part of the same family.

All except The Stranger, of course—he seemed to be played by just one actor.

But then there in the photograph I saw something that suggested that my conclusion was mistaken. There was in that ensemble photograph of the entire cast in costume a plethora of arms. One arm too many to be precise, it was off to the left, and nearly hidden behind the cloak of one of the Phantoms, but it was there. It was right where it should have been if one were to balance out The Stranger on the far side of the photo. An errant arm existed, one belonging to an actor who had been cropped out.

I flipped through the pages more carefully this time and sure enough I found suggestions of him throughout the other images: a shadow figure in the background, a hand that didn't belong, and a boot that seemed out of place. It was then and only then that I realized I was missing a page. It had been excised, I could see where the leaf had been cut, and the line was smooth and tight to the binding. I had seen other books, rare manuscripts that had been vandalized, and those looked similar to this. Whoever had done this not only wanted to take the images, which could have been done by simply taking the prints, but to erase all trace of their existence and hide what had been done.

Reviewing the images and the death of Evelyn must have had a profound impact on me, for that night my dreams were invaded by the wildest of images. I was sitting on a stage, surrounded by the set from the images. The actors, or more precisely the characters from the prints, were walking around me, and seemed to be engaged in some great undertaking on my behalf, though what it was exactly was unclear. Aldones, the dwarf, seemed to relish what was going on, dancing around me to some strange staccato beat. The twins used me as a maypole, effectively binding me to the chair with ribbons. The giant Thale brought me coffee in an ornate silver cup, but when he saw I couldn't drink it, my hands being bound by the girls, he sighed and lamented about what he would have to do with the pie he had made.

It was the actions of Cordelia which most disturbed me. She paced nervously, gnashed her teeth, and clenched her fists as she did so. That she wanted to tell me something was obvious, for she started toward me on more than one occasion, but then seemed to think better of it and turned away. The Phantom of Truth, a gauzy thing with only the hint of a face, haunted her. It had eyes with which to see and ears with which to hear, but no mouth with which to speak.

If the phantom haunted Cordelia, then The Stranger stalked her, or perhaps he stalked the whole family. He lurked in the background, moving amongst the shadowed curtains. He had the run of the stage, and would disappear from one spot and then suddenly appear in another. These actions were most disconcerting to Cordelia and Uoht, but for the twins Camilla and Cassilda it seemed more of a kind of game. The two girls screamed, but then as they ran their screams turned to giggles, which caused Thale to frown.

Eventually, in a sudden rush, Cordelia overcame her hesitancy and ran to my side. It was only then I realized that I was wearing the Pallid Mask. She looked into my eyes, grabbed me by the shoulders, and brought her face up next to mine. I could smell the rosewater that she used as a perfume, and the sequins on her own mask nearly blinded me with their scintillating reflections.

Her breath was hot in my ear and her voice was panicked as she whispered softly and desperately the same words Evelyn had said to me before she killed herself. "Have you seen the sepia prints?"

I woke in a cold sweat, my heart pounding in my chest.

The next day I made my way through the crowds to the Bibliothèque-Musée de l'Opéra, which was on the western side of the theater. I carried with me the folio, secured inside a leather satchel. From the outside the library was impressive, a kind of pavilion that was attached to and mirrored the design of the main structure. However, as impressive was the exterior, the interior was ghastly, for it was not only poorly lit, in a manner that only libraries seem to manage and the French have taken to an art form, but also unwelcoming. It was cramped: great shelves and cases lined the walls and extended up beyond the lamps into the darkness. There seemed to be a plethora of spaces at which one could work, but these were covered in manuscripts, papers, and dust. As far as I could tell there were no other patrons. The library was empty save for me and the man behind the great reception desk.

He was old, perhaps an octogenarian, bent with age, smartly dressed, and by all evidence a well-educated man. He asked me if I needed assistance. His request was odd in that it came in English, and he laughed at my obvious surprise. "You Americans think that you look like us, or at least the British. You don't. Your clothes are cut differently. You're overfed. You walk oddly. You stand differently. You may look like us, but you aren't us, and we can see that."

I smiled at his candor and recalled how I talked the same way about European women. "I was hoping you could tell me about this?" I opened up my satchel, took out the folio, and handed it to him.

"Young man, I am Moncharmin, I am the curator here. If I cannot help you, no one can." He flipped through it, and though he did his best to conceal it, I could see that he was genuinely thrilled to be handling the object. He paused at the title page and made a hissing noise, presumably at the stamp that identified it as property of the library. This was followed by a disappointing *Tsk*, when he almost immediately saw the missing pages. With a flourish he closed the book and raised his eyes to mine. "Where did you get this?"

"A girl I knew had it," I said. "A girl named Evelyn. She killed herself yesterday. The book, the photographs, seemed important to her."

The old librarian nodded. "I knew Evelyn, a girl of some talent vocally. She came here often to read, and study the archives. I am sorry to hear that she is dead. Though given what she had been studying, her death is not surprising."

"Why do you say that?"

He closed his eyes and pursed his lips, obviously mulling over how much he was willing to tell me, if anything. "Please. You will follow me."

He stood up and pushed his way past me. I don't know why I followed him, but as he moved through the door and down the hall I seemed to have no choice. The old man had mesmerized me. Through the stacks we went, winding through the shelves and cabinets of books and papers. There was a door, a thick wooden thing with clasps of black iron. He unlocked it with a thick brass key that he pulled from his vest pocket. Beyond, in the flickering light, there were stairs leading down into the depths of the basement of the opera house. Great stones formed the walls and the steps, and the only signs that anybody had been down here in decades were the electric lines and lights that had been strung up using hooks pounded into the masonry gaps. As we descended he spoke, and I listened.

"Those were dark days. 1898 was a bad year for the Opera, for all of Paris, but for the Opera in particular. The excesses and scandals of the Third Republic had culminated in the Dreyfus Affair and public sentiment had slowly turned away from supporting the arts and literature. The Opera and its managers did things, and allowed things to happen that were not made public. The Opera was used for unsavory productions."

"Like this play, *The King in Yellow*?"

He nodded slowly. "You must remember that this was just three years after Jarry's *Ubo Roi*, an exercise in what he would later call pataphysics, the study of the laws of exceptions and the universe supplementary to our own. It was nonsense, of course, a first step into the absurdism and surrealism. The crowd on that first night, they rioted. There was a man, a poet of some renown in the crowd who wrote, 'After this what more is possible? After this, do we bow to the Savage God?' The authorities banned the play and Jarry had to flee Paris."

We were descending deeper. "*The King in Yellow* made *Ubo Roi* look tame. The authorities, the censors of the Third Republic, banned it before it was ever performed. They ordered all copies of the text destroyed."

"Then these photos were of a production that never happened."

"I wish it were so." There was shame in his voice. "It was a private production, rehearsed and staged in secret. None of our regular performers would participate. We recruited players of ambiguous morals. They were easy to find. Zidler was dead, and his successors at the Moulin Rouge had no use for freaks and deviants. Once Toulouse-Lautrec would have been their voice, but he had gone mad and been confined to a sanitarium, and with him had gone any hope of reason or human compassion. Do you think it odd that I consider that little syphilitic dwarf as the voice of reason, as the voice of morality?"

"There have been stranger sources of laws." I had not missed that he had inserted himself into the story.

"As you say. We were decadents, willing to do whatever in the name of pleasure, in the name of art. It was not the first time such ideas had played out in this theatre. We all knew the stories, the legends; concerning the chandelier, and the Phantom. We wanted to bring some of that madness, some of that grand theater, that gothic majesty back to life; to challenge the Parisian authorities with a morbid spectacle; to show them all what they should truly be fearful of."

"Which was?"

"The Phantom of Truth. The Pallid Mask. The Stranger."

"Death?" I offered.

He laughed. "Bah! Death is just the end of flesh. Men have so many other things to be fearful of. We are cattle being led blindly to slaughter, but that slaughter is not our death. The King and his tattered robe dull our senses, and for that we are eternally grateful."

"I thought *The King in Yellow* was just a play."

"A sonnet, a play, an opera, these are just manifestations of his divine symphony, vehicles for his infectious melodies. We are his chorus and must learn his book, one way or the other."

"You are mad!" I whispered. I thought perhaps of turning back, of fetching the authorities, but I was driven by some strange force to follow him deeper into that chthonic pit.

"Is it madness to speak the truth? Is it madness that the song remains the same? Our President Felix Faure thought so. He saw our performance, and died that same night. Come with me and I shall show you the truth, and then we shall see who is mad."

Down we went, further and further, and as we did Moncharmin continued to speak, but whether it was to me, or just to hear his voice, I was not sure. "The architect Garnier planned four basements, but the builder did more, many more. There are vast chambers that most never know of. They are used for storage, scene changes, and the like. One entire level houses the machinery that helps move the stage. Most people think there is only the one stage, but beneath that there are innumerable others. An entire separate production could take place in the under theatre, and those above would never know it." His voice had become odd, almost theatrical. "There are so many stages; some of them have been completely forgotten."

We were deep when he finally stopped descending and instead led me down a hall and threw open yet another door. "Behold," he proclaimed, "the 1899 production of *The King in Yellow*!"

Beyond that door I saw things, things that should not have been possible, not in the twentieth century. I stood there entranced as the old man donned that aged costume, as he placed that crown of antlers upon his brow, as he rose into the air, into that darkened space amongst the rafters. He danced there and I recognized him as the character who had been excised from the photographs, and I knew that the actor who had played him had been Moncharmin himself!

Even now, all these years later, I can still hear him reciting his lines with poise and bravado. "The Yellow King is dead," he shouted, "and who shall take his place? Shall it be the White Queen, the Crimson Cardinal, the Black Man, or perhaps the Green? The White Knight still guards the gate, but the scion is already within the walls. The exile returns and he seeks his rightful throne!" He floated down and took his place amongst that horrific tableau. He was a maestro, a master puppeteer; he was the spring amidst clockwork bones and flesh. "Kneel before me," he commanded. "Kneel before the Sepia Prince!"

They say I went mad, that these things did not exist. The Parisian authorities deny all of it. There are no reports concerning what was down there, and the officers I knew to have been involved are now scattered across the country. They claim the fire, the one that three days later consumed that old rehearsal hall, was an accident, bad wiring, but I know better. What they couldn't understand, what they couldn't comprehend, they burned away.

But I know what I saw, and I know what I did.

Here is the truth. The old librarian floated there surrounded by his machine, a demonic construct of ropes and wire, of pulleys and desiccated corpses that danced to the sounds of an infernal barrel organ. He floated there, bearing the mantle of the upstart, the exile, the Sepia Prince. He was a terrible thing, the counter to the madness of the Yellow King, but just as mad. He floated there and demanded my allegiance, demanded that I take my place amongst those decayed and corrupted mannequins, demanded that I willingly accept him, and by doing so be corrupted by his dark influence.

I did what I thought was right, what any true man would have done.

I took my pistol from my jacket and I shot him. I shot him once, through his left eye. One shot was all that was needed.

His death is well documented. They could not erase the truth of that. I have seen the report. My name is on it, they acknowledge that I shot the man. They say that none of this happened, but if that was true tell me why was I not charged? If I shot that man, and he was just that, a man, and not the Sepia Prince, why was I not charged? If I was mad, why was I not hauled away to the asylum?

Sometimes I wish they had taken me to the madhouse. Then, at least, I could have had the illusion that I was mad. I could have let the tattered veil of the King in Yellow fall back across my eyes and be blind once more. Instead I see what others will not.

The worst part is my dreams. Moncharmin lies on the floor dead. The others are there as well, dancing; their arms outstretched, begging me to join them, to take Moncharmin's place.

"Have you seen the Sepia Prince?" they cry out.

"Yes," I tell them. "Yes, I have!"

Then I reach out for that pale brown coat, and the crown of horns. I reach for them with intent.

And then I wake screaming.

It is not the screaming which terrifies me. That I still scream at the offer gives me comfort, it tells me I am still a man. The night I no longer scream, when I no longer fear accepting the mantle of the Sepia Prince; that is what I fear the most.

Not my screaming, but when my screaming stops.

# CHAPTER 3

# "The Ylourgne Accords"
## From the Journal of Robert Peaslee
## July 30 1919

By early July, I was no longer in Paris. I wish I could say that I had finally given up on the city, or that it had given up on me, or that the local authorities had demanded that I be reassigned. None of that happened. The truth was that regardless of what I had seen, of the maddening things I had witnessed at Locus Solus and the Paris Opera House, I had remained mostly unaffected. My nervous condition seemed to be controllable, mostly through liberal administration of spirits. If my work suffered, my superiors said nothing. I did my job, insured the security of the delegates, and made sure that nothing unseemly happened to any of them. I assumed that on the day the treaty was signed my services would no longer be needed, the Major would pat me on the back and that I would soon be headed back to the States like so many of my fellow agents, like Chan, Charles, and Vargr.

But Major Reid had other plans.

There was a conference, a meeting of scientific minds to discuss how some of the recent advancements in medicine were going to be dealt with in the future. Like any such conference there were concerns, and while the French were in charge of overall security, each delegation, including those from the defeated Central Powers, was bringing its own protection. Our delegate, a man I had never met, had requested me personally. Despite how it was expressed, as a request, I really had no choice in the matter; I knew, as any good soldier did, that it was an order, no matter that it was framed in pleasantries.

The meeting was to be held in the South-Central part of France, in the province of Averoigne, an area dominated by a dark virgin forest that few have penetrated. The territory is sparsely populated, with the only city being Vyones, the foundations of which had been first laid during the Dark Ages. Vyones would have been a scenic destination, but I was not to be so fortunate. The conference was to be held in the ruins of the ancient fortress Ylourgne, amidst crumbling walls and fallen masonry. The place had a weird reputation and the locals shunned it. There had been a catastrophe once, a horror that I could only find the vaguest of references to. The woods were said to have been haunted by werewolves and worse. There was a reference to the "Beast of Averoigne" which, right or wrong, I took to be another werewolf story not unlike the more recent tale of the Brotherhood of the Wolf which had plagued Gevaudan. The ancient, dark forest had done its best to reclaim the ruins of Ylourgne, but there were areas where nothing would grow, and only dead barren soil remained.

The French had found a use for such a place, and had already begun laying the foundations and earthwork for what would become the L'Ossuaire d'Ylourgne, a memorial cemetery for those who had fallen during the Great War, regardless of nationality. The work was being done primarily by a firm out of Paris, but with so many partners and sub-contractors it seemed like a veritable army of architects, masons, and carpenters had descended on that ancient site. It was an international call, a rallying cry for those who cared about such things, and it seemed the charitable and popular thing to donate to. Even my client, the enigmatic Meldrum Strange, had contributed to the building fund.

Meldrum Strange was an affable man, rich would have been an understatement; he dealt in information by profession, but was also an industrialist. He was Carnegie, Vanderbilt, and Morgan all rolled into one, with triple the ego to boot, but without the haughty superiority complex. On the drive through the countryside he actually talked with me, he had a deep melodious voice and seemed genuinely interested in what I had to say. As we conversed we discovered that we knew people in common. Strange had even studied briefly at Miskatonic University, where he had earned his undergraduate degree before moving on to study business abroad. He had a soft spot for Miskatonic and was proud that his son Hugo was studying medicine there. As affable as he was, Strange seemed tinged with regret. There was work to be done, important work, Strange was engaged in some great undertaking that he implied would be a boon to all men, but the President had asked him to attend this conference personally, and when the President asked you to do something, Strange suggested, it wasn't really a request.

"There are duties, responsibilities a man must accept," Strange said, "regardless of his wants, no matter what they cost him professionally, or personally." When he said that, I took it to heart, for it reminded me of my own sentiments, and I knew that this was a man worth knowing.

The conference village, including a great reception hall, had been built in the last few months by the assembled legions of workmen who were now busy rebuilding the fortress, transforming it into a great memorial chapel. One day these outbuildings would serve as the offices and homes of the resident caretakers, but until then they would serve our purposes. The great hall had incorporated stones from the ruin itself and in the archway above the entrance was carved a phrase I supposed was meant to inspire unity amongst the fallen, the mourners, and even perhaps the delegates. It was written in medieval French but was easily translated as,

THEY THAT COME HERE AS MANY
SHALL GO FORTH AS ONE

It was beneath this inspiring motto that dozens of delegates, professional diplomats, men of science, and even men of business gathered. Dr. Astrov had come from Russia, General Mazovia from the Polish Republic, Dr. Lorde and General Duval represented France, the Austrians had sent von Schelling and Dr. Miklos Sangre, while the British a man named Richard Steadman. The Germans had suffered during the war, many of their best and brightest had been lost or fled, the man they sent to represent their interests was known to everyone else as a cruel and vicious man, a criminal who would have been arrested had he not been traveling under diplomatic papers, Dr. Cornelius Kramm, whom the more sensational of journalists called "The Sculptor of Human Flesh."

When Strange saw Kramm he warned me to be wary of the man, but also to keep a close eye on him. "He's a dangerous man, ambitious, manipulative. He ran his own crime syndicate in New York and Paris, The Red Hand. It took an entire team of adventurers to bring him and his brother down. He had been assumed dead."

"In my experience," I declared, "dangerous men have a habit of not staying dead."

He looked at me incredulously, as if I had said the most important thing ever. "Do you know what this conference is about, Lt. Peaslee?"

I shook my head, "I don't have clearance for that."

He thumped me on the back as if we had been boyhood friends. "You have what clearance I say you have, and right now I need you to understand why we are here, what has happened, and what we hope to do about it."

It took me hours to read the files that Strange gave me, and even then I didn't want to believe what they revealed, but I knew it to be true, I knew what could be done to the dead. It was possible to give the deceased a semblance of life, to give them motion and some sense of self. They could be given purpose, tasks, even played with. I know this because I had seen it done, not once but twice. Of the men described in the files I was familiar with one name, that of Doctor Herbert West, who had been involved with the events at Locus Solus. The files had a picture of West, a mousy man with a shock of blond hair. They had pictures of his colleagues as well, including the nondescript Daniel Cain and the stoic Canadian Major Sir Doctor Eric Moreland Clapham-Lee, who had died tragically and then been victimized further by West himself. I stared at that photo of Clapham-Lee; his piercing eyes and strong nose seemed so familiar. I had seen this man before, but where I could not recall.

The next day the purpose of the conference was made plain to me when General von Schelling opened up with a plea to the other delegates for a sense of human decency. "This science of reanimation, this thing that was released on the battlefields of Europe, we must put a stop to it. I do not deny that we ourselves are guilty of exploring the procedure. Our agents have obtained Herr Frankenstein's notebooks; we have carried out our own experiments." His voice became proud and frightened at the same time. "I tell you this path leads not only to abominations, but endangers the very balance of world power. If this technology were to fall into the hands of the Persians, Chinese, Japanese, or even one of our own rebellious colonies, it could be the end of European dominion of the globe, and could potentially cast us back into a new Dark Age."

This little speech set the delegates ablaze and the room exploded into a cacophony of accusations and excuses. The delegates quickly fell into old political alliances, and familiar lines were drawn. The chairman, General Duval, motioned for security to take action and several guards moved from their stations, their hands going for their guns.

I tapped Strange on the shoulder and suggested we withdraw. Instead, Strange stood, slammed his fist onto the table, and bellowed out at the others. "Are you fools? Have the last few years of war taught you nothing? Millions lie dead and you still bicker. Your precious alliances and treaties have led you to war and the brink of destruction. Your nations lay wasted and your landscapes ruined and still you cling to old ideologies and familiar patterns. If we are to survive, as men, as nations, as a species, you must find a new way of thinking, for all our sakes."

The crowd was stunned into silence, and the room grew still. Duval raised a finger and his agents paused. Something electric was passing through the crowd, something contagious. I could see it in their eyes, and in the way they stood. They were ready, ready for change, they just needed a leader, someone to show them the way, a way forward. Was that man Strange? Looking at him as he stood there, the bulk of him, his great grey beard and powerful eyes, he was like some Old Testament prophet. He was Moses ready to lead his chosen people to the Promised Land.

Then the lights went out.

It took an hour for someone to find the fault. By that time the delegates had left the hall and wandered out into the gardens. Strange and I had taken refuge in the shade of an old oak. Together we watched as German Kramm and Austrian Sangre talked furtively. They kept looking over their shoulders like they were afraid of being watched, which of course they were. We ourselves did not go unnoticed and were soon joined by the French and British delegates, General Duval and Richard Steadman.

"A rousing speech, Mr. Strange," commented Steadman. He wore a tall, black hat, rectangular glasses, and an ascot to accent his suit. His hair was neat and blended into a thick dark beard. His voice was accented but not one I recognized; he was obviously a member of the Commonwealth but beyond that I knew nothing about his origins. "Tell me, do you think it will make a difference? Do you really think you can change human nature?"

Meldrum Strange took a drag on his pipe. "Explain yourself, if you would?"

"Our history, our legends, our myths, they all suggest that any time we develop a new technology, a new idea, a new invention, we tend to succumb to its most deleterious of effects or uses. Eve, Prometheus, Pandora. Innovations tend to have disastrous beginnings, and men never seem to learn, or change."

"I take your point, sir, which is why I intend to at least try. Would you have us do nothing, and let history run its course? Should we leave well enough alone?"

Steadman made an odd noise that seemed to express his displeasure. "Would that Frankenstein, West, Cain, Hartwell, and Tsiang had left well enough alone."

Strange nodded. "You forget Clapham-Lee, Mr. Steadman; surely he was as much to blame as all the others?"

The British delegate turned and walked away. "I assure you, Mr. Strange," he called back, "Clapham-Lee has not been forgotten, least of all by me. But I do not blame him for any of this. He is as much a victim as anyone else."

Duval gave a strange little salute and said, "Be seeing you," before trotting off after Steadman.

That night, while Strange slept, I reviewed the files once more and familiarized myself with more of the men that were documented within. I had of course known about Victor Frankenstein, who had meddled with the dead in the 1790s, but I was not familiar with the exploits of his descendent Henry, or those of the mysterious Dr. Pretorius. Nor did I know about those other children of Frankenstein. As for the name Tsiang, it was in reference to an unfortunate event that had occurred on the Franco-Austrian front. Tsiang had been a priest of Siva who in his attempts to please the French had created undead soldiers, nearly invincible things that only stopped moving when the enemy forces reduced them to ash.

No matter how many files I read, I kept coming back to Doctor West and his colleagues. West had used the war as a source of subjects for his experiments in perfecting his own method of reanimating the dead. Like West, Cain and Clapham-Lee were graduates of Miskatonic University. There was another man, a doctor named Hartwell who had done something to soldiers as well, but the details were vague. Looking at their photographs, these men didn't look mad, or even dangerous. Yet they were just that, not only to others, but to themselves. Major Doctor Sir Eric Moreland Clapham-Lee had by all accounts died when his plane was shot down, but West had claimed the body from the morgue, a body which had by all accounts never been returned to Toronto for proper burial.

This information was classified. The British knew West, Cain, and Clapham-Lee had served in their forces, but the other allies didn't, and neither did the Central Powers. They knew that the dead had been brought back, but they didn't know by whom or how. Strange and I intended to keep it that way and if possible put the genie back in the bottle. The other factor we had to contend with was the civilian angle. West and his followers had not confined their work to wartime. They had experimented at home, amongst unsuspecting townsfolk, and they had not been as discreet as they thought. Despite the risks, military intelligence had decided to keep the activities of these men a secret from local authorities and even other federal agencies. It was, as Meldrum Strange suggested, the only way to keep the knowledge from spreading across the world and disrupting the natural order of things.

The next day came early, when one of the security men woke me before dawn; there was a man outside the gate who was asking to see me. I suggested that I meet him at one of the smaller rooms off the hall, but the officer shook his head. The stranger refused to come any further down the road. If I were to see him I would have to go to the gate. As reluctant as I was to leave the comfort of my bed, I dressed and allowed the officer to drive me out to the edge of the property, where the dark forest swallowed the road.

The man waiting for me there had all the trappings of an Indian mystic, the sash and his turban, the great, bushy black beard that covered his face all suggested this, but his skin and his eyes betrayed his Western origins, as did his voice: his French was tinged with an accent that suggested he was from Brittany. "I am Sar Dubnotal, the Great Psychogogue. I come bearing a warning."

I lit a cigarette and invited him to come with me to the village, but he refused. "This place is a necropolis, a city of the dead. I am too sensitive to journey any closer."

"You are mistaken," I told him. "The construction has just begun, there are no dead yet interred here."

Sar Dubnotal shook his head. "You are mistaken, sir; the dead have held sway here for centuries. The construction of the ossuary is merely a formality. You sleep in a grave for thousands."

I was frustrated with his mystic mumblings and vague inferences. "Your warning, sir, what is it?"

His tone betrayed that he was equally annoyed with me. "I know what you and the others do here; the voices of the dead have told me. They say you are a good man, that you might do the right thing, and let the dead rest. There are others who do not share your sentiment. They would seek the power for themselves."

"Kramm and Sangre?"

"I cannot say. The dead do not say the names of the living; it is unseemly. I beg you do what you must, prevent the spread of this madness. If you do not, our world and the next will suffer."

"Why didn't you find me in Paris, tell me this there? It would have saved you the trip."

"Indeed," said Sar Dubnotal, "but then it would not have been nearly as dramatic, and you would not have taken me seriously." With that he bowed, turned, and began to walk away.

I called after him, "Where is your car and driver?"

As he marched, he looked back. "I need no car, Mr. Peaslee. I walked here from Paris. I shall walk back."

"That's more than two hundred miles!"

"One can always use more time to think, Mr. Peaslee. To reflect on what one has said, and what one has heard. You should try it some time."

I took a drag from my cigarette and watched as he disappeared beyond the first curve in the road.

Strange was waiting for me when I returned. "Anything I should know?"

"According to a very odd mystic the dead think I am a good man. They are counting on me to do the right thing, and let them stay dead."

Strange harrumphed, but whether it was at me being a good man or the dead having an opinion I didn't know. "Anything else?"

I nodded. "I think Ylourgne has secrets that we haven't been told. I think there is a reason the French have decided to build the memorial here. I also suspect that Kramm and Sangre might not be our only concerns."

"Of whom do you have suspicions, and why?"

"When Steadman spoke of Clapham-Lee he used the present tense. The man was supposedly killed, twice at that, but I suspect that he is still alive, or at least no longer dead. I think he might even be here in Ylourgne."

Meldrum stewed for a moment and then gave me instructions. "I'll be in committee all day; we're supposed to be drafting an accord making the use of the reanimated as soldiers a war crime. Most of the delegates should be there. Do what you can to learn more about our opponents, both those we know about and those we don't." With that, my massive employer left me, assured that I would carry out his orders to the best of my ability. It seemed that the dead were not the only ones who had faith in me.

It has been my experience that if you want to go through someone's things, it is best to make sure that your target is occupied. In this case I made sure that Kramm's security was busy going through my room, leaving me free to go through Kramm's apartments. I spent twenty minutes opening drawers and skimming files. In the end I learned that Kramm knew less than Strange and I. He had files on the Frankensteins which were slightly more robust than ours, but his files on West and Cain were weak, and as for the others, those files were little more than single pages. Kramm may have been the enemy, he may have had an agenda, but from what I could gather he wasn't the player that the strange mystic had warned me about. The only thing of any interest that Kramm possessed was a photostatic copy of an ancient book written in German. While my reading of that language is satisfactory, this volume had been printed using a black letter type I was unfamiliar with, and thus could not immediately ascertain the book's contents. I took the book, assured that neither Kramm nor his security would report it missing out of embarrassment.

Once I was secure in the quarters I was sharing with Strange, and had assessed the covert search that Kramm's man had done, I settled in to review the book I had taken from Kramm. Now able to peruse it leisurely, I found it to be entitled *Von Unausprechlichen Kulten* and attributed to Friedrich Wilhelm Von Junzt. After only a few pages I discerned that its contents consisted of accounts of the rites, practices, and beliefs of secretive cults and unsavory orders scattered throughout the world. Von Junzt had apparently traveled the globe collecting what knowledge he could on these heretical religions, and in some cases even participating in certain ceremonies amongst those believers which still remained extant. It was a compendium of horrors detailing the most fiendish of sorceries and necromancies. So terrible were the things written and hinted at that I dare not mention them here, save for the one section of that grimoire which was most pertinent to my own tale, for there was in that hideous book an entire section on Ylourgne.

Indeed, there were two entries for the ruined castle, which apparently had been built by a line of marauding barons who had been exterminated by the Comte des Bois d'Averoigne. The first chapter related the tale of Gaspard du Nord, a would-be wizard who did battle with a monstrous creation of his former master, the Necromancer Nathaire. In the spring of 1281 Nathaire and his ten disciples, fearing a Church-led purge against sorcery, fled Vyones for the ruins of Ylourgne. Not long after, there came to the cemetery of Vyones and all the other boneyards of Averoigne a plague in which the newly buried dead, chiefly those stalwart men who had died in misadventure, would simply not stay buried. Not even the pious Cistercian monks were immune to the fiendish call. The source of this necromancy was of course Nathaire and his followers, who used the reanimated bodies to construct a titanic golem of flesh and bone with Nathaire's face and his voice that strode across the countryside attacking peasants and nobles alike. Only through du Nord's limited knowledge of necromancy was the creature stopped and laid to rest in a shallow grave by the River Isoile, not far from Vyones.

The second section dealt with a legend that grew up in the area almost two centuries later. In 1476 shepherds reported that an area along the Isoile had been disturbed and great holes had been rent in the earth. Investigators sent out by the Comte confirmed that the riverbank had been disturbed, and that something large, perhaps many things, had been removed. A trail of damp clay led from the riverbank through the woods to the road. The road itself was disturbed, for whatever had traveled down its path had not been carried by horses or cart. Whatever had been moved down the road had been dragged to the ruins of Ylourgne, where even the Comte's men dared not follow.

There then grew up around the ruins tales of lights and noises emanating from the crumbling stones, and in the months that followed rumors of witchcraft, more specifically of a coven that drew their power from the evil that had been done at Ylourgne. Some say it was Nathaire and his disciples who had returned as a cohort of liches who haunted Ylourgne. Others suggested that this was the work of L'Universalle Aragne, the deposed Louis XI, who was still resorting to necromancy in his war against the Duke of Burgundy. Whatever the truth, by the time Von Junzt visited the area he found little evidence of occult activity. There were lights and sounds but the sources could not be discerned and Von Junzt left after a week, disappointed and as perplexed as he had been when he arrived. Though he was insistent that someone had inscribed in the ruins a quote in medieval French from Nathaire, perhaps as an epitaph:

THEY THAT COME HERE AS MANY
SHALL GO FORTH AS ONE

It was the same saying that decorated the great hall, but in this context it was no longer a message of peace, but rather of the dark and twisted necromancy that had allowed Nathaire to transform hundreds of the dead into a single titanic golem of flesh, the Colossus of Ylourgne. The thought that the memorial cemetery was being built in such a place, and that the conference, a conference focused on the science of reanimation, was being held in such a place seemed too much of a coincidence for me. I stood and made for the door, fully intent on taking my suspicions to Strange, but I barely made it through the entrance. Someone was waiting for me on the other side, someone who had something large and heavy. I was knocked unconscious by a man I never even saw.

When I finally regained my senses I was handcuffed to a chair. The room was dark except for a single bare bulb swaying back and forth from a dangling cord. It was such a cliché that even in my semiconscious state I was forced to chuckle. As I did there was movement in the dark, several forms shuffling about beyond the range of my sight.

"Is that you, Kramm?" I managed to mumble. "Or is it Sangre? Perhaps both of you? Not that it matters. Show yourselves, or do you prefer to skulk in the dark like rats?"

A match was struck and a flame sputtered to life, illuminating a man whose face I knew, a face with a beard accented by a fancy cravat, the British envoy, Steadman. He took a drag from his cigarette and smoke filled the air. It seemed to billow up around his head like a fog. "We are sorry, Lt. Peaslee. We hadn't meant to be so heavy-handed, but you had obviously put some things together and put our timetable in jeopardy. We needed to remove you from the playing field before you got yourself hurt, before you could spook the enemy and put them on guard, before we could flush them out into the open."

"Them being Kramm and Sangre?"

A second figure stepped out from the darkness; it was, as I suspected, Dr. Kramm. "The Austrians aren't capable of such deviousness; with the loss of the war they have been placed in a most difficult position. They no longer have any desire to possess the reanimation technology, nor do they wish to see any other nation possess it. It is a terrible power, Lt. Peaslee, one that the Austrians fear could reshape the globe, and wrest it from European control. It is a childish fear, but one that cannot be ignored. But where are my manners, I must echo my ally's apology for your poor treatment."

I stared at these two men and despite the questions running through my head I voiced only one. "Can someone please take these handcuffs off me?"

As Kramm undid my chains, Steadman opened the curtain and let in the fiery light that roared outside. The conference village was on fire, and a long line of cars was slowly making its way out of the gates, carrying the delegates to safety.

"Am I to understand that you blew up the conference?"

It was Steadman who supplied the answer to my question, and many others that I was thinking. "We warned everybody anonymously first. I realize that it may be somewhat anticlimactic, even rushed, but I saw no reason to drag things out. Whatever the greater plan was for this place, whomever was behind it, this brings it to an end. It has accomplished at least one task."

"Which was?"

Kramm smiled. "The players have been revealed. They have made themselves known. This in itself has changed the game. The field has been leveled."

The heat was getting to me. "What of the memorial, the confer-ence, the accords?"

Kramm's smile turned into a chuckle. "The French can build their memorial cemetery someplace else. This place will be left as a ruin. As for the conference and the so-called Ylourgne Accord, the lesser nations have already signed it. Though for various technical reasons France, Great Britain, and the United States have refused to endorse it."

"Strange won't stand for this."

"Meldrum Strange has been bought and paid for with what he holds most dear: information." Steadman spewed as if the idea was bitter in his mouth. "He is not the idealist you thought, Peaslee, he is a realist. The conference is finished; despite the fact that the Ylourgne Accord has been signed, it is for all intents, pardon the word, dead, or at the best, useless."

My head was swimming.

"Reanimation is the future, Peaslee," exclaimed Richard Steadman. He took off his coat. "There will be no restrictions, and the nations of Earth will be free to pursue whatever studies in reanimation they desire." He took off his cravat. "General Duval, Strange, Sangre, and the others like them can do what they want. And they will, and one day the undead shall outnumber the living and they shall rule the world." Then Steadman took off the last of his disguise.

I ran, fleeing the awful thing that Steadman had revealed. I fled toward the cars fleeing the conference. Meldrum Strange found me and took me back to Paris. I was discharged a week later. My discharge was honorable, but my nerves were destroyed; it took years of therapy before I could sleep easily. Though I will admit even now I carry certain scars from those events.

After all these years, what Richard Steadman did still haunts me. It was a little thing really, almost nothing compared to the other things I had seen, but perhaps it was all that needed to happen to push me over the edge. Perhaps it was the fact that Strange had struck a black, unholy bargain with the man, or that Kramm stood there laughing. Regardless, when I close my eyes, I can still see that face, Steadman's face as he took off the false beard and revealed his true face, a face that I had seen amongst Strange's files, the face of Major Dr. Sir Eric Moreland Clapham-Lee, the decapitated man who Herbert West resurrected in

Flanders. He was there standing before me, his disembodied head in his hands, and he was laughing; he and Doctor Kramm were laughing.

And I knew that I had witnessed a new and terrible terror, and I was too weak to do anything to stop it.

# CHAPTER 4

# "The Awakening"
## From the Journal of Robert Peaslee
## January 8 1921

I still recall how the snow was falling that morning; it seemed so peaceful, so calming as it floated out of the sky. In the background the mountains had turned gray and at times it was hard to tell where the Catskills ceased and the sky began. Tempest Mountain, the peak wrapped in clouds, was like a shaft leading up into unknown heavens. It was December 23, 1920, and I was stateside for the first time in years. My commanding officer, General Sternwood, had asked me and another agent, Hadrian Vargr, to spend our last few days of service with him at a Christmas retreat. It was supposed to be an honor, a reward for our service during the negotiations of the Versailles Treaty. At least that is what we were told. The truth was something entirely different.

Sternwood and I had taken the train up from New York to Kingston and then transferred to the Ulster and Delaware line to reach Leffert's Corners. From there, a picturesque horse and sleigh had taken us up the mountain along snow-covered trails to the resort. Kellerman's was a picture-perfect winter getaway that brought back fond memories of my own childhood holidays. It was an opportune time for me to reunite with my sister. It had been years since I had seen Hannah, but unlike the estranged relationship between me and my father and my brother, we two had maintained a pleasant correspondence for many years. Indeed, when I learned that her graduation from The Hall School in Kingsport was imminent, I heartily regretted my oath never to set foot back in my native state. Likewise, when I learned that she had been offered, and accepted, a position as an instructor at that same venerable institution, I was doubly proud and regretful. So when General Sternwood had asked Vargr to come from Boston, escorting Senator Lowe to the resort, it was a minor request to ask him to do so for my sister as well. Vargr readily agreed, and Sternwood saw no fault in our plan. Even when the party grew by one more, a charge of my sister, my colleagues simply smiled and expanded our reservations accordingly.

As I sat in the lounge, the main building was bustling that morning; the owner's son Max was desperately trying to get Christmas decorations up, drafting the resident physician, Doctor Lawrence Houseman, and his ten-year-old son Jake into covering the hall with boughs of evergreens and ribbon. A small army of deliverymen were moving through as well, making sure that supplies were laid in, not only for the Christmas Day feast, but for the potentially long winter as well.

In the hotel library, a bookman by the name of Geiger and his associates were busy evaluating the contents of the shelves. The volumes occupying the room had been cobbled together from the contents of various dilapidated estates surrounding the resort and included texts in Latin, Greek, and even Dutch. While the selection might have been exceptional for an antiquarian, it failed to pique the interest of either the staff or guests of the hotel. Consequently the Kellermans had called in Geiger and his team to evaluate the contents, sell what they could, and update it with more modern fare. In this endeavor Geiger was aided by a team of three experts: the gaunt and taciturn Toht was an expert in Germanic and Nordic literature, while the garrulous and fawning Cairo, who always smelled of geraniums, was an expert in the Levant. The third of Geiger's assistants was Dr. Chet Copperpot, a man whose work I was familiar with because he had studied under my father. His thesis, concerning the economics of New England privateers, had stirred much debate amongst professional and amateur historians. I do recall my father mentioning that he had obtained a position at Faber, in Oregon. How and why he had come to be employed by Geiger I could not say.

The academics and holiday decorators weren't the only people milling about the building. In the theater the Italian trumpet player King Leopardi and his band were rehearsing, desperately trying to hear themselves over the banging of carpenters, masons, plumbers, and electricians. There was a surfeit of tradesmen in the area, at least according to Max Kellerman. Work on the local Ashokan Reservoir had finished a few years earlier, and the process of moving buildings and constructing new towns and the reservoir itself had brought hundreds to the valley. When the work was finished hundreds remained behind, and, combined with many of the unfortunates displaced by the reservoir, had settled into squatters' villages, and were willing to work a great deal cheaper than those from Leffert's Corners or Chichester. The result had been a flurry of work at various resorts which could often get by on paying the men little more than a hot meal or two a day.

Also in the lobby with me watching the snow fall was a young lady who spent a considerable amount of her time at her sketchbook by the name of Winifred Lefferts. She was a distant relation to the Lefferts for whom the local hamlet was named, all being descendent from an early Dutch settler named Piter Lefferts, of whom she was quite proud.

"The Lefferts' house in Brooklyn is a museum now, run by the Daughters of the American Revolution." she told me proudly. "It used to sit on Flatbush Avenue in Brooklyn, but after the family donated it to the city it was moved six blocks into Prospect Park. Have you been to Brooklyn, Lt. Peaslee?"

I informed her that I had not.

"Oh, you simply must go. It is a beautiful city, made all the more wonderful by Prospect Park. They say that the president of the Park Commission was instrumental in the creation of the park, but the truth is he never could have done it without Frederick Law Olmsted, who did most of the designs. It was Olmsted that had designed Central Park in Manhattan as well. It's early times yet, but as an artist I can recognize what Olmsted was able to accomplish, and maybe someday he'll be recognized as a premier landscape architect. He already has a name amongst the painters and sculptors. If you have a chance, see John Singer Sargent's portrait of the man. Never will you ever see a better characterization of an old man in love with his work. Why, it is as much a landscape as it is a portrait." Amused by her talkative nature, I inquired as to the content of her own work. The young woman blushed and admitted that her own work was still in a formative stage, but she hoped one day to find employment in graphic design or perhaps with magazine work. She showed me a page from her book and I must say I was quite impressed by her rendition of the trees outside the hall that were now more than just dusted with snow.

Just as she opened her mouth to speak once more, which was exactly when I realized that I had perhaps made a mistake in opening a conversation with the girl, Geiger and Copperpot burst out of the library, each with a small stack of books in their hands. Geiger was quite animated and speaking at a frenetic rate. "Mycroft's *Commentaries on Witchcraft*, Poe's *The Worm at Midnight*, and *The Qanoon-e-Islam* go to the MacDonald's in Glenbogle; Von Junzt's *Uber das Finstere Lachen*, Vallet's *Le Manuscript de Dom Adson de Melk* go to Old College in Oxford; and most importantly Marks and Co. are to get the *Histoire d'Amour* by Bernard de Vaillantcoeur. You'll find the addresses in my book." He handed his pile to Copperpot. "Make sure they make today's train, I don't want them to be stuck here over the holiday."

As Copperpot nodded there was a sudden braying from outside, announcing that the horses and sleigh had arrived. The beasts stamped as they pulled beneath the awning and an avalanche of caked snow fell off of their harness and legs. The wooden sleigh was larger than I expected, and varnished bright red with brass trim. It was piled high in places with packages and luggage, including trunks, some of which were likely the property of my sister. Not counting the driver, the sleigh was occupied by five passengers, all of whom were either guests of General Sternwood, his employees, or guests of my own. Knowing this, I made a move to help the travelers unpack themselves from the sleigh, but was quickly halted by Geiger's arm on my shoulder.

"Lt. Peaslee." His grip was firm and his voice cloyingly pleasant. "My associates and I are throwing a little party this evening. Nothing too extravagant, I assure you, just a gathering of like-minded men who enjoy each other's company." He handed me an invitation printed on heavy paper embossed with a time and place. In the lower left corner, a green carnation had been stamped. Suddenly I understood. "I do hope you'll join us." His hand slid down and lingered too long at the small of my back.

Our eyes caught each other's, and below his well-manicured mustache I thought I caught a sudden flash of his tongue between his teeth. He was an attractive man, refined, educated, well dressed even, but there was something about him that made me suspicious. "Perhaps," I said in a noncommittal tone. "I have other obligations that must be tended to first."

He smiled, nodded, and turned sharply to march back into the library. Outside, my colleague, Hadrian Vargr, had emerged from the sleigh, and was helping the other passengers climb down onto the icy ground. First to exit was a man whom I was vaguely familiar with, Senator Henry Paget Lowe, who was a vocal member of Congress often in opposition to President Wilson. He was a large man, rumored to be fond of his food and of expensive clothes. His traveling outfit consisted of a finely cut charcoal business suit with a mink-lined overcoat and a fur-trimmed top hat. As he dismounted the sleigh, there was a noticeable groan, but whether that was from him or the sleigh I was not sure. In his wake came a much smaller, round-faced man with a balding head and black rimmed glasses. Though I had never met him, I knew this had to be Doctor Geoffrey Darrow, scion of the Darrow Chemical Corporation, and yet another graduate of Miskatonic University, though in this case it had been from the Medical School. While not as famous as some of the others, Darrow was considered a hero, serving through and helping Arkham survive the plague that had ravaged her in 1905. He stumbled as he climbed out of the cabin, but Vargr caught his arm and guided him down to the frost-covered brickwork.

A gust of wind cast a dusting of snow across my line of vision, causing me to temporarily lose sight of the sleigh. I thought it was only a moment, but it must have been longer, for when it finally cleared, Vargr was arm in arm with two of the loveliest ladies I had ever seen. One I was partial to and recognized immediately. It had been years since I had seen her but I would have known Hannah Peaslee anywhere. She had blossomed from the gangly girl I had known as a sister into a charming and delicate thing that reminded me of my mother in both poise and grace.

As they crossed the threshold, Hannah broke ranks and dashed forward to great me, throwing her arms around me and nearly bowling me over. "Robert!" she exclaimed with gleeful exasperation. "You have no idea how much I've missed you." She pulled back and grabbed my collar with both hands. "Look at you, such a fine-looking man you've grown into." She kissed me on the cheek. "A little thin, though. What have they been feeding you?"

"Always the same Hannah," I laughed, "more my mother than my sister." A faux pout appeared across her face. "Still, where would I be without her to take care of me?"

She daintily pushed against my shoulder. "Still trying to learn how to properly dress yourself." There was a sudden laugh that swept through the small crowd, and I caught the dulcet tones emerging from Hannah's young charge. Hannah realized she hadn't yet introduced the girl to me and in flustered sentences did so. "Robert, may I introduce you to Megan Halsey-Griffith, a first-year student at The Hall School. Megan had no plans for the holidays, so I suggested she come along to this lovely mountaintop resort as my traveling companion."

As the young lady removed her snow-covered hood I was instantly enraptured. Her skin was pale white and she had large blue eyes with long lashes. Her lips were full and wine-dark red. Her hair was wispy and cut in a most wild fashion, though I admit this may simply have been my own lack of experience with recent American styles. The snow melting off her coat and hood caught the light and framed her in a scintillating aura that made her almost angelic in appearance and reminded me of the image created by the artist Richard Upton Pickman in his early canvas, *Eurydice Descending*. She was perhaps the most beautiful woman I had ever seen, and she moved me in a way that no woman ever had before. Yet I took Hannah's subtle hint that she had concealed in her introduction. Despite her appearance, this ravishing beauty before me was no woman, but still a girl; first-year students at The Hall School were usually under fifteen years of age. Not that I had any romantic interest in the girl; Hannah knew of my proclivities, and was more than likely providing me that information so that I could protect her from the advances of others who might take advantage of the girl. The invitation to Geiger's party came to mind, as did the prominent green carnation that decorated it.

As a reflex I gently took her hand and spoke in a most polite and caring manner. "A pleasure to meet you, Miss Halsey-Griffith." My words brought an odd stare from Vargr, who knew that I normally despised meeting new people, particularly women.

She giggled at my formality. "Please, sir, call me Megan, or Miss Halsey. I have never been comfortable with being a member of the Griffith family." Her tone was frightfully frank and it seemed she was going to speak, as young women often do, of family secrets better left unspoken.

Hannah spoke up and offered details that seemed to diffuse whatever the young woman was going to say. "Megan joined us just a few months ago. She's the daughter of the famed Doctor Allan Halsey, and the stepdaughter of David Griffith, who was lost when the Lusitania went down. Her mother sent her to us after it was realized that the schools in Arkham weren't going to be able to fulfill her needs." She turned and looked lovingly at the young lady. "You see, Megan is something of a prodigy, a genius really. At least Wingate thinks so."

At the mention of my brother's name I flinched, a reaction that my friend Vargr noticed and thankfully took action on. "Robert, the ladies and I have been traveling all day; perhaps it would be best that we take them to their rooms and allow them to freshen up. We could meet for lunch at one o'clock. I am told the chef here, a man called Bremmer, makes the most magnificent confit de canard." He leaned in closer and whispered in my ear, "The driver has also told me that there is still a supply of beer on the premises, something I have sorely missed since we have left Europe."

"Of course." I nodded and patted my Montenegrin friend on the shoulder. "You show the girls to their rooms and I shall see to General Sternwood and his guests."

From behind me came a gravelly voice, "I think we can see to ourselves, Peaslee." I turned to find Sternwood approaching from the stairs. He was a tall man; thin as a rake, but with an air of authority that went beyond the uniform. He was a commanding presence with deep-set eyes that seemed to bore into you and demand obedience. He had been a hard man to work for in Paris, for it was he who had been in command of our security team during the treaty negotiations. Ultimately, it had been Sternwood who had sent me to Locus Solus and Ylourgne, where I had learned that which had driven me to the brink of madness. He had, in his own manner, apologized, but the time in Ylourgne had damaged me too greatly, and I had lost respect for the man. I still followed his orders, but the number of days for which I would be obligated to do so were rapidly diminishing.

"I beg your pardon, sir?"

He waved his hand dismissively. "You and Vargr go spend time with your sister and her friend. I can meet with Lowe by myself." He waved me off again, and this time I didn't argue and ran to catch up with Vargr,

Hannah, and the charming Megan. A quick glance back and I saw Lowe with his hand on Sternwood's back while Darrow shook the General's hand vigorously. It seemed so very odd, for in my experience Sternwood was not fond of being touched. He was, in his way, adverse to the presence of most human beings, and instead preferred being alone. That the General had let both Lowe and Darrow touch him suggested that they were all well acquainted with each other, more so than I had previously thought. These were fleeting thoughts, and soon I was preoccupied with catching up with Vargr, my sister, Hannah, and her charge, Megan.

The threesome had already taken the stairs and by the time I reached the upper floor, the girls had disappeared from the hall. Only Vargr remained, struggling with some crates the porter had left there. A dozen or so of the roughly hewn wooden crates remained, all carefully marked as to the manner in which they were to be transported. Unbidden, I grabbed one of the packages and walked into his room.

As soon as I opened the door to Vargr's room I was hit with a wave of heat and humidity. Inside there was a Franklin stove with a low fire in it surrounded by several pots of water, all of which were giving off a low steam. Arranged farther out, away from the fire, were about a dozen potted plants, orchids of great variety in tones of fleshy white, pink, and striking yellows. Each of the crates that we were bringing in from the hall seemed to contain yet another specimen of orchid.

"They're a gift from General Sternwood," explained Vargr. "I made the mistake of mentioning how much I liked his collection in Paris." My puzzled look elicited an explanation. "He had a small glass house on the roof of the mission building. Kind of odd, don't you think, an oasis of tropical plants on a roof in the middle of a major city? The funny thing is he's going to do it again. He has an estate out near Los Angeles, he's building a greenhouse. I've seen the designs, the thing is going to be grandiose."

I looked at the plants. "A rather expensive hobby, don't you think? Where does he get all the money?"

"You remember Gatsby? He went into business for himself, import-export or some such thing. He and the General have some sort of arrangement, a partnership of sorts, something to do with manufacturing. I should know more, I admit, but the General has been very secretive of late, and I am not paid to pry into his affairs."

"At least not yet," I snickered.

"I don't think the Bureau would have much interest in the business affairs of retired generals."

I nodded, humoring him, knowing that his usual suspicious and inquisitive nature was often suspended when it came to military men. "When do you start in Washington?"

"Boston, actually, and at the end of January. I have just enough time to see Sternwood to California."

Just then the young Miss Lefferts wandered through the hall and rather than continuing on her way, paused to admire the flora that crowded Vargr's room. "What lovely flowers," she exclaimed, "such colors and textures." She spun about the room slowly so as to take in the whole of things. As she did so, her pencils and sketchbook fell from her hand and tumbled to the floor. Vargr went down on his knee and nearly collided with Lefferts as she too knelt down. Their eyes caught and locked. "Please may I sketch them, Mr. . . ."

"Vargr, Hadrian Vargr. Of course, young miss, but you must promise me to not touch them, and to keep them warm. They are fragile things and must be cared for in the most precise manner, and you must promise me one of your sketches."

"Of course, Mr. Vargr." She picked up one of the pots that was overflowing with succulent stems and flowers. "My name is Winifred Lefferts, I'm in number 5 at the end of the hall." With that she strolled down the hall, the delicate orchid and pot floating before her like some sacred object awaiting reverence.

As the door to number 5 closed, that of number 4 swung open and Hannah and Megan flowed out into the hall. They had changed clothes and now wore dresses and warm sweaters that bore the crest of The Hall School. They were giggling as they came into the corridor, as girls will do when they have been speaking of something that they do not want others to know of, usually men. Together the four of us made our way down the stairs to lunch and the hope of reestablishing relations with my dear sister.

I will not bore you with the details of our meal, but will say that the conversation between Hannah and myself continued long after we had finished our food. Indeed, we took coffee in the lounge and chatted as the snow fell, coating the grounds in a thick white blanket. While

Hannah and I renewed our relationship, I could not help but notice the way that Vargr was looking at Megan. For some strange reason I felt a pang of jealousy, an emotion that I had only rarely experienced before. It confused me, for I had never before considered Hadrian Vargr as anything more than a friend. That I should suddenly be envious of a young girl filled me with confusion.

It was a state that my face must have betrayed, for Hannah took my hand and asked me about Hadrian. "Have you known Hadrian for long?"

"Eh? What? I've known Hadrian for years, since we were both assigned to the security detail in Paris for the treaty negotiations. Sternwood wanted a cosmopolitan team, quite smart actually, given the diversity of people we had to deal with. He recruited agents from all over. Hadrian is from Montenegro. Chan is Chinese, well, he's from Hawaii but he's first generation. Charles is from some town not far from here called Sycamore Springs, but he's Greek on his father's side. We even had a Belgian, a funny little man named Achille who was the most excellent cook. He taught Hadrian how to make a proper omelet. It takes a bit longer, but it is well worth the wait."

"Doctor Lydecker says the treaty is nonsense. He says that a second war in Europe is inevitable. That the negotiations and reparations will be the root cause."

"Who is Doctor Lydecker?"

"Roman Lydecker is a new addition to The Hall School. He serves as both a physician and an instructor of sciences, biology, chemistry, and the like. He's quite an intelligent man. He was injured in the war, needs a cane to walk around, and speaks rather hoarsely due to a throat injury." She smiled. "The conversations we have in the staff lounge have become quite lively since he joined us."

"Your fellow instructor seems quite pessimistic," I retorted. "President Wilson and the rest of the Peace Conference have worked hard to negotiate the treaty and make it fair for all involved, not just the victors. I'm sure once it is ratified, the treaty and the League of Nations will help form a roadmap to a new age of peace and prosperity for the whole of the civilized world."

"Not if Senator Lowe has his way," chimed in the precocious Megan. She carefully watched to see how we would all react to her suddenly joining the conversation.

Vargr scoffed, "That blowhard, why would he oppose the treaty?"

"From what I've read in the papers," Megan spoke hesitantly at first, but picked up steam as she found a rhythm, "he fears limiting the powers and independence of the United States. He is something of an Imperialist, and an adherent to the Monroe Doctrine. He wants Europe out of the Western Hemisphere, and wants the States to have a free hand to deal with Central and South America as we see fit. Binding ourselves with the treaty and the dictates of the League of Nations would prevent that. It might also limit our military prowess, and force us to rely on allies such as Great Britain and France to bolster our forces. In the Senator's opinion these allies have not proven themselves reliable. Finally, and perhaps most importantly, the proposed alliances and automatic military support might in the future create another chain reaction like the one that started the Great War. Some minor offense between two nations with unpronounceable names might draw in greater powers aligned with both and then escalate out of control, plunging the world into war."

"Surely there are men wise enough to prevent such things from happening," proffered Hannah.

Megan shook her head. "There are always men wise enough to prevent such things; they tend to be executed or imprisoned or banished by others who would rather rush headlong into conflict. It would be nice to let calmer heads prevail, as they say, but often there is little time for such things and louder, more passionate voices rule the day."

"Perhaps," Hannah interjected, "what we need are fewer men in power, and more women."

Vargr dismissed the concept with a wave of his hand. "There are some things that I have found to be true in my time. First, when it comes to food, there is such a thing as too many cooks; second, when it comes to work, there can be too many clients; and, finally, though many would disagree, no matter what the issue, there can always be too many women."

Megan pressed the issue. "Are you really that much of a throwback, Mr. Vargr?"

A wry smile came across his face. "You must understand, in my home country of Montenegro, women are raised to be harridans. It is a country with a rich culture and history rife with difficulty. To survive, and to see their children thrive, the women must be strong and ruthless, as strong and ruthless as men. It does not endear them to the opposite sex, nor does it allow for the development of what Western society calls 'a ladies' man'. It is not that I dislike women, but rather that I find no need for them, and that things would be simpler if they weren't around."

"Professor Higgins once expressed similar ideas." Megan snorted. "He's married now, with three daughters."

Hannah raised her glass in a sarcastic toast. "To Hadrian Vargr, unapologetic misogynist."

Hadrian raised his own glass, one that had somehow been filled with beer instead of tea. "Present company excluded, of course."

"Of course," nodded Megan, smiling as she sipped her water.

"Just one question," said Hannah as she put her glass down on the table. "If General Sternwood was working for the staff putting together the Versailles Treaty, and Senator Lowe is opposed to it, why are Sternwood and Lowe meeting?"

I looked at Vargr, and he at me. We both realized that we didn't know the answer to that particular query, but we wanted to find out.

It was a short time later, our extended luncheon finished and the four of us strolling through the hall, that Max Kellerman, in a heavy coat covered with a dusting of snow, burst through the front doors and shouted for the desk clerk to fetch Doctor Houseman. Our interests piqued, we all made our way to the entryway and watched as the sleigh arrived back from its afternoon trip, but instead of Kalley, the regular driver, at the reins was Doctor Copperpot with Kalley slumped over to one side.

Ignoring the cold and what appeared to be a startling accumulation of snowfall, Vargr and I ran out the doors and with Kellerman met the sleigh. We gently picked up Kalley's limp body and carried him inside to the couch in the lounge, where a roaring fire was going. I stripped the man out of his winter coat and gloves and tried to rouse him, but with no success.

Copperpot came in just a moment later with an explanation on his lips. "We were about halfway up the mountain when he just slumped over. I'm not sure why. He's too big for me to have manhandled into the passenger compartment, so I just left him there on the seat and held on to the reins. The horse did most of the work."

Kellerman dashed back out to tend to the horse while Vargr and I searched for a pulse. By the time Doctor Houseman arrived his only act was to confirm what my friend and I already knew: Mr. Kalley was dead, most likely from a heart attack or stroke; his body was already cold. With Houseman and Kellerman on one end and me and Vargr on the other, we carried the lifeless corpse from the resort's main building to a small wooden cabin nearby. The building was a poorly insulated summer home, and therefore sufficiently cold enough to preserve the body. The county coroner would come, claimed Houseman, but with the snow continuing to pile up when he would arrive was anyone's guess.

Back at the lodge we found the girls in the lounge, talking with Copperpot, who was trying to warm up with a sandwich and a cup of coffee. He was regaling them with tales of the legends of the surrounding mountains and valleys and I saw no reason not to join them. He spoke of the stone house that sat on the storm-beset Tempest Mountain, and the Martense family that lived there. About how they cut themselves off from the world and then vanished from it entirely. He mentioned the Howe Caverns, which were said to honeycomb great portions of the mountains in the area. He even mentioned the tale of Old Man Zumpe, who wandered the hills around Bishop's Falls and spoke of a treasure hidden in a hollow. He had disappeared years ago, but the legend of the treasure lived on. Some said it was gold, others a meteorite that had fallen in the area centuries earlier, even fewer claimed both. Dozens searched the valley for Zumpe's treasure, but no one ever found anything and when the area finally flooded, the chance of finding Zumpe's gold became just about zero.

He then told us about Joe Slater, a murderer who was confined to the asylum in Albany back in 1901. He suffered from weird visions of unearthly vistas and related them as best he could using words far beyond his normally feeble mind. Imprisoned, the doctors monitored his madness, which seemed to be inexplicably linked to his deteriorating health, a situation no one could explain. One young intern took an unhealthy interest in Slater, and one night in a lapse of judgment connected Slater to a machine of his own design, one that he had built years earlier while at college. It relied on the theory that thought itself was a form of radiant energy and could be transmitted from mind to mind—a radical theory, but not unlike the work being carried out by Nikolai Tesla. Unfortunately, the intern and his friend with whom he had experimented were unable to get it to produce any results. All that changed when he hooked it up to Slater.

Copperpot paused and took a sip of his coffee. "In his official report on Slater's death, the intern described communicating with a being of pure light who was engaged in a conflict with another entity near the star Algol. Slater's prosaic descriptions were actually the poor man relating messages from the alien itself." He let that sink in. "Of course, nobody believed him. He had no evidence, and only cited the discovery of the star GK Persei as corroboration. He was censured by the medical community, and nearly lost his license to practice. Thankfully, the intern's mentor stepped in, pulled a few strings, and found for him a position as a doctor in an isolated community that didn't care so much about his past indiscretions."

"And how is it that you know about all this, Doctor Copperpot?" There was a tone of incredulity in Megan's voice.

Copperpot lit a cigarette. "How do I know this, Miss Halsey? How is it that you don't? I know this because I went to school with that young intern, I was the friend on whom he experimented, and it was your father, the famous Allan Halsey, that was his mentor and who found him a place to work when no one else would hire him."

Megan chuckled. "So where is he now, this disgraced physician? Someplace in Alaska? Florida? The Hawaiian Islands?"

The cigarette turned to ash as he took a long drag off of it. "Nowhere as severe as that. In fact, the poor man only had to relocate fifty miles." He smiled knowingly. "That young intern is here in this hotel. He's worked here almost two decades, tended to staff and guests alike, without any of them knowing his secret past."

"You're talking about Doctor Houseman!" Hannah exclaimed.

Copperpot put a finger to his nose and smiled. "Hard to believe, isn't it?"

Vargr looked at me, knowing what I had been through, but I couldn't bring myself to say much about my experiences. "No," I finally stuttered out, "I don't find it hard to believe at all."

With that we bid Doctor Copperpot farewell for the evening and went in search of better company, or at least less puerile conversation.

The hours passed quickly and soon the four of us along with Lowe and Darrow were all gathered around a single table as guests of General Sternwood. He made a perfunctory speech and then dazzled us with an assortment of courses all prepared by the Kellermans' fine staff. There was even a wine, though nothing worth mentioning compared to the selections we had sampled in Paris. Vargr raved about the meal, and called the chef a genius, and as he finished his coffee he stood up, and marched into the kitchen and congratulated the man personally.

Despite my expectations, Lowe and Darrow were actually quite charming, but we avoided politics and the treaty negotiations. Darrow it seems had been a student of Halsey as well, which seemed highly coincidental to me. That Darrow and Houseman had both been students of Halsey, and Copperpot had been at Miskatonic, coupled with Megan, Hannah, and I with our links to the university, all seemed too convenient. As I realized this the wheels in my head began to turn, and I realized that we were being played, manipulated, like puppets. We had been brought here, all of us, not just myself, Vargr, and the girls, but Geiger and Copperpot and the others. I just couldn't figure out who was pulling the strings; was it Sternwood or Lowe?

Or was it both of them?

After dinner the girls and Vargr retired for the night. I couldn't blame them. It had been a long day's travel for all of them. Kalley's death just added to things. I, on the other hand, was being fueled by suspicions. I found the invitation that Geiger had given me, ran my thumb over the green carnation that was stamped on it. I thought about what that symbol meant and how in some ways I despised it. I thought about Paris, and about London, and about Arthur Valentine, the man who took care of me after Ylourgne, the man with whom I had fallen in love, the man whom I had left behind. I went back to my room, shaved, showered, and dressed.

By nine o'clock I was in the lobby looking for the Buchanan Room, which turned out to be a rather innocent-looking cabin a few yards behind the lodge. The inside, however, was something entirely different, as there was a complete bar stocked with a selection of fine liquors and expensive cigars. Milling about were some two dozen or so men all smartly dressed, but not overly so. This is not to say that they were all dressed the same, indeed the style of dress was as varied as the men themselves, who ranged from the relatively short to the tall, from the thin to the corpulent, from the pale to the swarthy, and from the masculine to the effeminate. They were as varied as the flowers in the fields, which is the thing I, and the rest of the men, had in common, for we all wore the green carnation, and because of it we all knew what we were.

At the bar I ordered a glass of white wine and smiled as the bartender overpoured and emptied the bottle. Geiger was at my side, his hair slicked back and his mustache waxed. He wore a gray silk suit in a European cut with a thin burgundy tie. He looked at me with deep blue eyes; I hadn't noticed those before, and they smoldered as he looked me up and down.

He put a hand on my arm in a gentle but not—altogether—casual manner. "I'm so glad that you could join us, Mr. Peaslee."

"Call me Robert," I offered.

"Robert, yes of course," he stuttered, "and you should call me Arthur." As he said this, I quickly swallowed my surprise at him having the same name as the man I so cared about. "Have you been to one of these before?" I admitted I hadn't, and he offered to explain things to me. "Everyone is wearing a carnation; some are on the left side, some on the right. This is not by random chance and actually symbolizes orientation."

I was just about to ask him to explain what he meant by that when a bloodcurdling scream pierced the night. It was distant, but not that far, and it brought the entire party to a halt. It was a sound I had heard before; it was the sound of a man being killed. I took a swig of my wine and turned to apologize to Geiger. Before I could say a word his mouth moved toward mine. For a moment I wanted to respond—to greet his gesture with one of my own, but only for a moment. He wasn't Arthur, and no matter how much I wanted this to replace what I once had, that simply wasn't going to happen. I pulled away, apologized, and dashed out the door.

The snow slowed my pace, but the whimpering cries that carried through the night drew me to the source, a cabin not far from the lodge, a cabin that I had been to earlier in the day. It was the cabin in which we had placed poor Mr. Kalley's body. As I approached I noticed that the freshly fallen snow had been disturbed by the passage of several different boots. Closer still and I saw that the door to the cabin was wide open, and not just open but unhinged and with a shattered frame as well. Another set of tracks, these leading away from the cabin and into the woods in a wild and strange manner that seemed as if a man had stumbled or perhaps loped out into the night.

Inside the cabin there was a whimpering sound, in a voice that I recognized, a voice that had for years issued me commands and demands. There on the floor was the body of General Sternwood, bent and broken in a manner that was unnatural to the human anatomy. His legs were twisted almost completely round and blood was weeping from a gaping wound on his thigh. I ran to his side. He was barely conscious; the pain must have been overwhelming, and he was crying and begging for help. I bent down and tried to stop the bleeding.

As I did a shadow suddenly appeared, a thin and frail form stood in the doorway blocking the pale light of the moon. She was a slip of a girl and wore only her nightclothes and a pair of boots. What Megan was doing there I didn't know, but she stood there in a daze, her eyes glazed over and staring out into the void. The wind was blowing from behind, her hair swirling about her head, and her nightgown like a sail caught by a breeze. She was an angel, a Muse, a Grace, a goddess of the night, but why she had come to me here and now I could not understand. Still, she was here and I could use her help.

"Megan," I called out, but she just stood there entranced and entrancing. "*Megan!*" I yelled, and that got her attention. She snapped out of whatever daze she was in. "Go back to the hotel and tell them we need Doctor Houseman in cabin number six immediately. When you're done go wake Vargr and send him here as well. Then go back to your room and lock the door."

She faltered, hesitated really, and then in a confused voice spoke. "I thought I heard a baby."

"There's no baby here, Megan, quite the opposite really. Now focus and go get Houseman and Vargr."

She left, but it seemed to me that there was no particular speed or motivation to her movements. She moved like she was in a dream, like a gossamer thing tossed about on the currents of a fairy breeze. One moment she was there, and the next she was gone, and I was left alone with the dying General Sternwood.

I kept him still and tried to quiet him down while I kept pressure on his wound. In the darkness, as I waited, I looked about the cabin and surveyed the damage. There were signs that men had come to see Kalley's body, to sit with it, for there were now two chairs, or at least what was left of two chairs, arranged around the bed where the body had once lain. I assumed one of those men was the General, and from that assumption leaped to the conclusion that the other was either Darrow or Lowe. Given the relatively small size of the chair I thought Darrow for sure.

It was then, my mind wandering, that I noticed the faint phosphorescence that seemed to be providing a dim illumination. With my bare hand I reached out toward what my eyes perceived as a patch brighter than the rest and wiped the surface of a side table. My hand suddenly tingled, and holding it palm up I saw a fine layer of oily liquid radiating a vibrant green light. It was a fluid I had seen before, and read about in detail. There was no doubt in my mind that this was a sample of material considered classified and dangerous by the men who ran the mission in Paris. This was Herbert West's reagent, or a variant of it, a fluid capable of reanimating the dead.

I had first encountered the victims of this dread compound in Paris at the estate known as Locus Solus, which Herbert West had turned into a kind of macabre diorama. Later I had traveled to Ylourgne, where the Great Powers attempted to find some diplomatic solution to the new science of reanimation, one that would forbid the use of it during war time. It was here that I encountered the mad genius Sir Eric Moreland Clapham-Lee, himself a decapitated member of the reanimated. It was my encounter with Clapham-Lee that had driven me over the edge and forced me to retreat with Arthur to a sleepy little seaside village in Cornwall by the name of Portwenn. It was there, after much soul-searching amongst the green fields and rolling waves, that I decided to request reassignment from the mission.

Officially, I worked for the American Commission to Negotiate Peace, but no one ever called it that: it was always the mission, or The Mission. Occasionally, and with some trepidation, we who had been part of the organization for years referred to it by its original designation, The Inquiry, and those of us who went back that far still thought of ourselves as Inquisitors, though that designation came with baggage, as pointed out by Head of Research Walter Lippman, and was formally removed from use. Now both the Mission and the Inquiry were defunct, General Sternwood was retiring, and Vargr and I were assigned to make sure he had whatever he needed during his last few weeks of service. When the General completed his service, so did we.

Now, as the General groaned beneath my hands, it looked like that service might be coming to an end a little bit sooner than expected.

I heard Vargr and Houseman before I saw them, their boots crunching through the snow and their breath ragged from running. I heard others as well, and as the four of them came through the door, the fact that Kellerman and Darrow had accompanied Houseman and Vargr not only did not surprise me, but seemed almost inevitable. As the two doctors knelt down beside Sternwood's body I took a moment to confer with Vargr and Kellerman.

"Someone has attacked the General, he's wounded quite seriously." I gestured toward the scene of carnage. "Whoever did this also took Kalley's body. There are tracks leading off into the woods." I was being deliberately vague so as to keep Kellerman in the dark. He didn't need to know the truth, at least not right now; there was still a possibility that this could be contained.

Kellerman looked stunned. "We've had problems with bears getting into the garbage and breaking into some of the remoter cabins."

I nodded at his serendipitous suggestion. "This bear seems to have a taste for more than just garbage. We need to secure the lodge, reinforce the doors, and make sure that this thing can't get to anyone else." I paused as Houseman and Darrow seemed to be arguing. "We'll also need to bring the General back to his room and make provisions for his condition. He'll need a lot of clean linen, towels and sterile dressings, and boiled water."

Kellerman seemed shaken but more lucid than Megan had been. He dashed from the room at a brisk pace, following orders given from a voice of authority. Later, when he had time, he might question that authority, but now in the heat of the moment he was happy just to be given something to do, even if it was just an illusion. It was what most people wanted, not the truth that they could do actually very little that was useful, but the lie that what little they did was extremely helpful.

The argument between Houseman and Darrow grew louder, and it instantly became plain what the issue was. They had managed to stem the blood loss, but were now focused on the injury to Sternwood's back.

Houseman was resigned to the fact that the General was going to die, while Darrow was urging the use of an experimental treatment derived from the transplant studies of Carrell and Guthrie, which Darrow had in his medical bag. Houseman opposed using the drug on the grounds that it was still experimental, and that results were likely to be poor.

"What choice do we have, Houseman," sneered Darrow. "Would you see this man die? How will that impact your reputation? You're already considered a nut, an outcast from the medical community. When they find out what has happened here, you'll likely never practice again."

"Just exactly what are you implying?"

"It's obvious, isn't it? Kalley was in some kind of catatonic state, maybe even in a coma, but he wasn't dead. You misdiagnosed that. When he came out of it he must have been in a state of mania, a kind of psychosis. Sternwood must have come along and become a victim of that rage. What's happened here is a direct result of your incompetence." Darrow paused. "But this wouldn't be the first time, would it?"

Houseman was flabbergasted, stunned for a moment to the point of speechlessness, but not to a point of inaction. He gathered his tools, closed his bag, and stood up to leave. "Mr. Peaslee, it is my professional opinion that this man is going to die. There is nothing I can do for him but make him more comfortable. Doctor Darrow, on the other hand, has access to some unproven drug that he claims might heal the man. I'm not going to try and stop him, but I'm not going to be party to it either." With that he left Vargr and me alone with Doctor Darrow.

The little physician didn't wait for either of us to approve of his actions. As Houseman left, Darrow plunged a syringe into Sternwood's spinal column, and then wrenched the poor man's body back into a more normal position. Sternwood screamed and then fell into a kind of rhythmic panting that could not have been in any way natural or healthy. Darrow took out his watch and a small notebook and began to record what I assumed to be his observations.

Five seconds and I saw no identifiable change to his breathing or status.

Ten seconds and Sternwood's breathing remained erratic, almost bestial.

Fifteen seconds and I could tell Darrow was becoming nervous.

Twenty seconds and Sternwood's breathing had suddenly become shallower. Darrow checked his pulse.

Twenty-five seconds and Sternwood stopped breathing; Darrow tore the man's shirt open and tried to find a heartbeat. The look on his face was one of panic.

Thirty seconds and Sternwood reared up off the floor, screaming and flailing about. His erratic movements threw Darrow into the wall and the little man curled up into a ball to protect himself. Spittle and foam poured out of Sternwood's mouth, and his eyes glowed with mania. For all the thrashing about, it was only Sternwood's arms and torso that were moving. Everything below the waist was still motionless. Sternwood had become something monstrous, and even without his legs he was extremely dangerous.

I grabbed a sheet and wrapped it around itself into a crude rope. In a swift motion I looped it over Sternwood's head and then cinched it behind his back. I did it so quickly he didn't have time to respond. Then I twisted it clockwise, tightening it down and pinning his arms against his body. Any struggles toward freedom were to no avail. I tied a crude knot behind his neck and sat him upright on the floor. He snarled at me, snapping his teeth at my face like a dog.

"General!" I yelled, as I slapped him across the face. He responded to that. He shook off the blow and I saw some sense of recognition in his eyes. He ceased to be an animal and suddenly his whole body relaxed. His breathing became regular, controlled even. Darrow came out of his shell and carefully checked the General. Darrow found a pulse, and a heartbeat, then looked into his eyes. The General remained calm for the whole process, even while Darrow checked the man's wound, which seemed to have ceased bleeding altogether.

"Cold," mumbled the wounded old man. "So cold."

Vargr and I grabbed some blankets and sheets, slid the man onto them, and while Darrow steadied him, we carried Sternwood back to the main house. Kellerman had prepared a new room for receiving the General, a large spacious suite on the first floor. We slid him into the bed, wrapped the blankets around him, and made sure the fire was stoked. Then Vargr and I departed, leaving our commanding officer in the hands of Doctor Darrow, a man I suspected of having access to Herbert West's reagent, a reagent I also thought may have turned

Kalley into a horrific undead thing, but at the same time may have saved General Sternwood's life.

Vargr went to check on the progress made on securing the building, while I went upstairs to change out of my blood-stained clothes. As soon as I had reached my floor, I was accosted by the presence of Arthur Geiger, who had apparently just been knocking on my door. As he saw me, the look on his face was one of frustration, and he opened his mouth to say something, but then he saw the blood that soaked my shirt and sleeves. His look changed almost instantly, converting to one of concern that reminded me of my mother.

"They've shut down the party; I suppose you have something to do with that?"

I nodded. "General Sternwood has been attacked. There may be a madman on the loose." I turned the key in my door and went inside.

Without permission he followed me in. "Are you injured?"

"No, this is all Sternwood's blood." I took my left arm out of my coat— the dried blood had welded the sleeve of my shirt to that of the coat and I had to slowly pull them apart.

"Here, let me help with that," said Geiger as he came up behind me. With two hands he separated the two sleeves and then helped me off with my coat. With care he laid it on the overstuffed chair by the door. "We'll have to get that cleaned, this shirt, too." With a deft hand he turned me around and began undoing my tie.

"Mr. Geiger . . ." I began to protest.

"I told you to call me Arthur. Now let's get this tie and shirt off." The tie slid off my neck and fell to the ground. His fingers went to work on my buttons, gently popping them out of their holes one after another. I felt his breath on my neck and chest as he worked his way down. I slid one arm out of my suspenders, and then another. He pulled the shirttail out of my waistband to finish what he had started. I kicked off my shoes. As he unfastened the last button, the shirt, and my pants, fell to the floor.

I took my hand and gently raised his chin, staring into those big beautiful eyes. I kissed him, gently, and then as I pulled back I stroked his hair. "Arthur," I whispered, not knowing whether I was referring to him, or to my lost love Valentine. As he led me to the bath, I wasn't exactly sure that it even mattered.

It was close to midnight when I once more left my room. I'll admit to some discomfort with leaving Geiger sleeping in my bed, with access to all my personal items, but the truth is I had little in the way of possessions, having over the last few years lived a rather Spartan lifestyle. If he wanted to steal what little I had, so be it. Besides, we were all snowed in, where would he go? I let the man sleep and went about with a task I had meant to do earlier, before I was distracted, namely checking on my Hannah and Megan.

As I made my way down the hall I became aware of a sudden drop in temperature. A creeping cold was working its way across the floor and with every step toward my sister's room it grew more noticeable. By the time I reached my destination it felt as if I was already outside, and if it weren't for my night clothes and robe, I would surely have been subjected to a significant chill. Indeed, I could see my breath fogging up and small patches of condensation forming on the metal fixtures.

I had thought to force the lock, but found that course of action was unnecessary: the door to the room occupied by my sister and her charge was unlocked, and swung open with barely a sound to disturb the occupants. Little light was streaming in from the hall, and the curtains were mostly closed, but the glow from the wood still burning in the fireplace was enough for me to take note of the slumbering form nearest to the door, and identify it as my sister, Hannah. I will admit that I felt a little sigh of relief at the realization that my sister was safe, but that feeling was short-lived.

As my eyes adjusted to the weak light, I saw the face and form of Megan Halsey-Griffith sitting upright in bed, her pale skin glowing in the moonlight, her eyes full of that vacant faraway stare that I had seen earlier. At the foot of her bed stood another form, that of a man, or at least a semblance of one. It was naked and bent like an animal, its tongue lolling out of its mouth in an odd bestial manner. Its skin was covered with dirt and debris, and in places dried blood, most of which I suspected was not its own. Small twigs and leaves were embedded in the thing's hair and its eyes were glassy and pale. I recognized it, of course, even as a parody of a living thing. I recognized it as what had once been the resort's coachman, Christopher Kalley. Now he was barely human, more simian than man, and driven by base desires to feed and propagate, desires that were, given his lack of clothing, plain for anyone to see.

The thing was muttering, not any words I could understand, but the rhythm was such that I knew what was being implied. The undead thing was praying to her, offering up homage to the girl; she was, as I have said before, angelic in appearance and nature, and this sad, twisted monster had chosen her as his own personal divinity. It was sickening to watch it drool and worship her—not that I couldn't understand how that had come to be, but I still found it revolting.

That feeling of revulsion grew and festered inside me, speeding from one emotion to another at lightning pace. One minute it was revulsion, and the next it was compulsion and I was driven to act. I burst into the room, grabbed the poker from beside the fireplace, and lunged at the creature, fully intent on smashing in its skull with the iron rod. It dodged and hissed in anger and pain as the hooked end came down on its shoulder and dug into its flesh. There was a crack as something broke inside of it, but the thing took no notice, grabbed the poker, and tried to wrench it from my grasp. As we struggled, the hook tore out of its shoulder, leaving a gaping wound that oozed a black viscous fluid that was more oil than blood. With all my might, I pulled and pushed against the creature and with a single Herculean tug, ripped the end of my makeshift weapon out of its hands.

Instead of fighting to redirect the poker, I used the momentum and directed it in a wide arc that brought the weapon back into play and crashing down on the unprotected head of my foe. It was a glancing blow, but one that was enough to knock the thing off of its feet and send it whimpering to the floor, clutching its face with both hands while small geysers of foul blood erupted, spraying the room with a thick and noxious mist.

The battle woke Hannah, who began screaming, and from the corner of my eye I saw her rush to Megan's side. As much as I wanted to, I couldn't whisk them out of the room, but Hannah was doing her best to drag the child from her bed and away from danger. Megan, on the other hand, was still entranced, almost catatonic. Her eyes glazed over and her mouth was slack-jawed. She was in no condition to help Hannah in her own rescue, but she was in no condition to resist either.

The pause to check on the girls was all the inhuman creature needed to go from being a prone victim to an attacker. It tried to spring up from the floor, snapping with powerful jaws full of bloody fangs. I swung the poker and smashed it across the face. Spittle and broken teeth flew across the room as the inhuman thing spun and hit the floor. Something in my mind snapped and I came up behind the wounded thing, my weapon held high, and with a mighty blow I plunged it into the back of the thing's skull. It whimpered and gasped what was likely its last breath, but I didn't care. I wrenched the poker out of the oozing gray matter and in a swift motion brought it crashing down once more. I did it again and again and again. I brought my makeshift weapon down upon that creature's head so many times I lost count.

I could hear Hannah crying behind me, but it was a distant thing, like a dog howling in the night. I could see nothing but the monstrous thing that was beneath me, could feel only the soft thud of the poker in flesh, could hear only the delightful crack of bone. Everything else was just noise to be ignored. At least until the light came on. Whether it was Hannah or Vargr that finally flipped the switch I don't know, I only know that it was done and it brought the entire room into view, and I caught sight of myself in the mirror that hung on the wall.

I was a monstrous thing to behold, covered in blood and bone and brain, a gore-soaked weapon in my hand with bits of scalp and hair dangling from the tip and hook. My eyes were wide and held a wild, almost crazed look. My face was locked into a kind of grin, a risus sardonicus that completed my transformation. Somewhere in the last few seconds I had gone from champion to maniac, from hero to madman, from righteous to monstrous. In the mirror I caught the faces of Vargr, Hannah, and Geiger, and could see the terror in their eyes. Vargr had his gun out, but whether he planned to use it on the thing at my feet or on me I wasn't sure. I dropped the poker; let it fall haphazardly to the floor. It had served its purpose, but now it was a haunting reminder that I had lost control and instilled in my friend, family, and lover the knowledge of what a monster I could become.

I fell to the floor, and watched as Hannah handed over Megan to Vargr and then rushed to my side. As she used a sheet to wipe my face, Geiger slipped away. There had been a look of shock on his face, one that I felt assured was a betrayal of a state of disgust. In Vargr's arms Megan began to rouse; she awakened slowly, mumbling something about dreams that made no sense.

"I had the oddest dream," she casually announced, clueless as to what had just occurred. "There was a child, a newborn who came to me mewling and crying, such a beautiful child."

I closed my eyes and composed myself. "Hadrian, get her out of here." My friend nodded and carried the delirious child down the hall to his own quarters, leaving me alone with my sister, Hannah.

"Are you all right?" she casually asked, knowing the answer. I nodded, and she nodded back. "You have Father's temper."

I was silent for a moment, contemplating the implications. "I suppose that is true. I had forgotten his rages, forgotten most everything about him before he . . . changed."

"Mother calls it 'The Episode,' and he's better since he came back. He's more humble, less demanding. I think whatever happened to him changed him, gave him some perspective, made him less of a monster, more vulnerable." She wiped some blood out of my eyes. "You're a lot like him."

"You think so?" I looked at the blood-soaked room and the still-twitching corpse of the twice-dead thing that I had beaten to a final death. "I hope not; that would be terrifying."

I spent Christmas Eve day in bed, sleeping. It was a fitful sleep, full of nightmares and awakening in cold sweats. As I tossed and turned I still on occasion caught the scent of Geiger where he had rested his head on a pillow or blanket. I ached a little inside at the thought of him, but I yearned for Valentine more, and tried desperately to remember the days we spent visiting the quaint little towns of Midsomer. Yet each time I closed my eyes and tried to force the memory I failed. Something else intruded—I would have thought it was Geiger, or Hannah, or Hadrian, perhaps Sternwood, or even my father, but surprisingly it was Megan Halsey-Griffith. Each time I drifted off to sleep she was there in her gossamer nightclothes, looking radiant and angelic, dominating the scene. She was standing there staring at me, reaching out with her hand to caress my cheek. She was smiling at me in a childlike way, one that expressed nothing but love and innocence, but each time she spoke I awoke screaming.

I emerged in time for dinner, a sumptuous feast hosted by Max Kellerman with performances between courses by King Leopardi.

General Sternwood was not present; he was confined to his room, attended by Darrow, who reported that he was lucid, that everything below the waist was not entirely paralyzed, but extremely weak. He had also developed an extreme sensitivity to cold, and was only comfortable if the temperature was above eighty degrees or so. Vargr had informed his family of the change in his condition and they were making the necessary preparations for his arrival in California.

Vargr had also developed somewhat of a friendship with the young Miss Lefferts, who had, as promised, taken good care of the orchids and produced stunning sketches of the strange-looking plants. Vargr was quite pleased with her compositions and Miss Lefferts was absolutely beaming with pride. The two exchanged addresses; Vargr had some strange reason he wanted to stay in contact with the girl, nothing lascivious, but rather for some future project he had in mind. He said that one day he might write his memoirs, and Miss Lefferts's work might do as a cover art.

From the book appraisers there were few words, although I did overhear a short conversation between Geiger and Megan. He was an amateur photographer and wanted to know if she would pose for him. Hannah nipped that idea in the bud, reminding her that she was a lady of standing. The rest of Geiger's team, Toht, Copperpot, and Cairo, seemed content to chat amongst themselves. They had come to a formal agreement with Kellerman concerning the final price for the library, and were going to spend the first few days of the New Year scouting books in New York so as to replace and update the selection for guests. They seemed pleased with the outcome of their venture, as did Kellerman.

The other guests, including Doctor Houseman and his son, Jacob, seemed to enjoy the celebration, but it was clear that the subject of Kalley and what I had done to him was off limits. I did catch a few stares coming my way, but nobody lingered too long and I was even asked to dance once I had shown some competency with my sister, Hannah. It shocked me somewhat when my waltz with Mrs. Houseman ended and I was suddenly faced with young Megan demanding a turn.

As we spun and twirled our way to Leopardi's trumpet she made it clear that she had no memory of what had occurred the night before. "They tell me you saved my life."

"I hadn't thought of it that way, but I suppose so."

She stared at me in the most curious fashion. "I am not the easiest woman for men to get along with, Mr. Peaslee. It comes from my upbringing. My father died before I was born. My stepfather, a truly horrid man, most pedestrian in his thinking, was rarely around anyway, and died when I was nine. My mother and my spinster aunt, my father's sister, are withdrawn from public life. I would not call them reclusive, but they are the only adults I've had in my life for many years. Consequently, I've not developed any level of social etiquette; this coupled with my precociousness has made meeting members of the opposite sex difficult."

"Surely you've attracted some suitors? Not all men are put off by an educated woman."

"There was one man, a doctor whom I met in Boston at an art gallery. I found him fascinating. I thought perhaps he felt the same way. He said he knew my father." She looked wistful. "He disappeared and I never saw him again."

"Megan, you are only fourteen."

"Mr. Poe married Virginia when she was thirteen and he was twenty-six."

"And it was considered something of a scandal," I retorted. "You are a brilliant young woman with a great potential. You should be thinking of things other than meeting boys."

In the middle of the dance floor, she stopped and took a step back. "You confuse me, Mr. Peaslee. I saw you that night in the cabin, I saw you wearing the green carnation. I know what it means. Yet I see the way that you look at me. How your eyes follow my movements. Did you notice that as we danced, your hand drifted downward across the small of my back? You didn't, did you?" She saw the look of bewilderment in my eyes. "I think perhaps you are more confused than I am."

With that our conversation ended and we ended the evening opening presents and wishing each other a happy Christmas. We then retired for the evening. In the morning, at breakfast, Kellerman announced that the road down the mountain had been cleared and that a special train had been scheduled to help evacuate the area. By midmorning I was back in Lefferts' Corners and by noon we were all in Kingston. Vargr and General Sternwood, accompanied by Doctor Darrow, were heading south to New York City, while Hannah and Megan were headed north to Albany and then east to Arkham. Senator Lowe was traveling that way as well and although he promised to keep an eye on the girls, his oath left me with no sense of comfort.

As for me, I was in no rush to go anywhere. I was discharged, a free man, able to wander the country at will for the first time in years. Still, the events of the last few days had left me shaken and whatever plans I had for the rest of my life were still undecided. What I did need to do was think about what had happened. I found a quiet hotel with a decent café and pondered over the details of my time at Kellerman's. Had it been a plot to bring all of us together? If so, who was pulling our strings? Sternwood and Lowe seemed the most likely of candidates, and it was clear they had some business interest. I suspected that interest was somehow linked to Darrow and a version of Herbert West's reagent, but I had little proof to substantiate that, and even less to take to the authorities. Besides, what authorities would I go to? Who would believe me? The whole situation made my head spin, and I eventually collapsed in the hotel room bed and succumbed to the nightmares that waited in my sleep.

Megan was there, wearing her nightgown. In the background King Leopardi blew his trumpet in a sad, lonesome tune. A small dwarf in a burgundy suit danced while an old man sat in a red velvet chair watching him. I could place neither of these weird images, and when Megan asked me to dance, I forgot all about them.

Megan felt good in my arms; she was warm and smelled like roses. Her hair tickled my chin. I loved the way she moved as I caressed the small of her back. I could feel her heartbeat, and found that its rhythm matched mine, and provided a fine counterpoint to the wail of the trumpets and the black-dressed ingénue that had joined the King on stage. Her song was sad and haunting, about love found, and lost and remembered. The old man in the chair was crying and the dwarf was trying to comfort him.

Megan spun out of our embrace and twirled across the dance floor. The song became a moan, and then a cry. As she glided across the marble, the trumpets and vocals were gone, and only a screaming remained. She fell into my arms and looked up at me with those glassy, empty, soulless eyes. She wrapped her arms around me and put her cheek next to mine. As she whispered in my ear, I strained to hear what she was saying. As her words became clear, I woke screaming, the sheets covered in sweat, my legs cramped. I fell to the floor and curled into a ball, trying desperately to protect myself from what that beautiful and charming and horrific avatar of Megan Halsey-Griffith had asked of me.

It was only one question, asked over and over again, but it drove me mad and shook me to the core.

"What happened to the baby?" she asked.

But that's not true, if she had asked that it wouldn't have been so terrible.

"What happened to the baby?" That's what I wanted to hear, what she actually said chilled me to the bone, though why I cannot say.

"What happened to our baby?" she pleaded.

*"What happened to our baby?"*

*"What Happened To Our Baby?"*

*"WHAT HAPPENED TO OUR BABY?"*

Where her whispers began, where the screaming trumpet ended, where the crying vocals echoed, and where my own sobs started, I couldn't tell.

CHAPTER 5

# "The Tillinghast Inquiry"
## From the Files of Joint Action Committee-K
## September–October 1923

CENSORED ACCORDING TO JAC-K PROTOCOL SIX

*3rd September 1923*

"Well, what d'ya think?" Agent Flynn McGarrigle demanded in his thick Irish accent.

I was in no mood to talk, let alone answer McGarrigle's questions. I had been in the room for an hour, and had possession of the file for less than that, and he wanted to know what I thought about a case that was more than three years old. What I thought was that somewhere along the line I had made a terrible mistake. I was back in New England, a region I had hoped never to return to. Arkham, the place of my birth and where my brother and father still lived, was less than a hundred miles away. I had done my best to avoid family obligations for the last decade or so, and being in Providence was too damn close for my comfort. Somewhere part of me wished that the war were still on and I and my unit were still in Europe.

The unit, however, was no more. We always talked about what we would do after the war. The plan was to stay together, and form our own security agency. It just didn't turn out that way. As soon as we were released, my friends and I scattered across the country. Charlie went home to Hawaii, Nick got his position with Continental back, and Hadrian took a high-level job with the Bureau. I kicked around for two years, living off my savings and the family trust fund. I thought about college, looked at Barden and Faber, and even Horlicks, but in the end I called Hadrian and asked if he could find me a position. Not because I needed money, but because I needed something to do. The memories of what had happened in Paris and Averoigne were still eating away at me. My need was to be occupied, not have an occupation. Hadrian and the Bureau set me up in Palm Beach; lots of millionaires who needed to believe that they were being protected. I spent most of my time enforcing the Mann Act, chasing gigolos from lonely wives, and drinking gin.

My little stint came to an end in late August with the arrival of orders and tickets for the train. I was to make my way to Providence where my assistance was needed on a suspicious death. Normally the Bureau didn't get involved with anything of that sort, leaving such things to the local authorities, but the victim had been the son of real estate tycoon Alfred Tillinghast, and he had raised a stink. Apparently the elder Tillinghast had not been satisfied by the work of the Providence cops and, being a man of wealth, had asked the Bureau to investigate. How I fit in wasn't clear, and as reluctant as I was to head anywhere near my home state, I packed my bag and headed north.

I looked at the file and then back at McGarrigle. "Are we sure that this man **REDACTED** just didn't kill Crawford Tillinghast?"

"Leave him out of it," McGarrigle barked. "He's a dead end. His bullet only hit the machine, causing it to shatter into several pieces. Alfred Tillinghast isn't interested in pursuing murder charges. He wants to know if this statement about the machine is true. Did Crawford Tillinghast's machine allow him to see and interact with creatures from another dimension, or was **REDACTED** just bonkers?"

"There are other possibilities," I offered. McGarrigle motioned for me to explain. "**REDACTED** could be lying about the whole thing; there is nobody who can confirm or deny any of this. Alternatively, both **REDACTED** and Tillinghast could have been delusional, *folie à deux* as the alienists term it. Tillinghast could even have invented a machine that made him and others think that they were in contact and interacting with things from another world."

"What about the servants? How do you explain their disappearance?"

I shrugged. "Murdered, either by Tillinghast or **REDACTED**, or by both, either because they undermined the delusion, or their deaths served to support it." I flipped through a few pages. "I do have one question, though."

McGarrigle chuckled. "Just one?"

I tossed the file across the table. "Why am I here? There's nothing in this to suggest I needed to be part of this investigation. Why bring me up from Florida?"

McGarrigle pawed through the file. "Sorry, the father's statement is missing, we'll get that for you. You don't recognize the name Crawford Tillinghast? He worked for your father doing odd jobs about the house. His father, Alfred, insisted that he work his way through college. Anyway, according to the father, Crawford got the idea for the resonator from something he saw in your father's house back in 1913."

I sat there for a moment trying to gather my thoughts. Finally, with nothing else to do, I reluctantly told the truth. "When I was a kid, my father had some sort of breakdown. He lost his memory, and his personality. He became someone, something . . . else." I let loose a heavy sigh. "My mother couldn't take it. She took us to live with relatives. Years later, his memories and old personality came back. He had lost five years, woke up right in the middle of giving the lecture that he had collapsed in. I tried to reconnect, the man was my father after all, but my memories of him weren't of the man he was, but of the emotionless stranger he had become. Five years may not seem like a long time, but to a child, to a son, it's a lifetime."

I paused again, but McGarrigle wanted more. "During his episode my father was capable of things that I still don't understand. If Crawford saw something in my father's house that inspired the resonator, I'm inclined to believe it. Though I'm not sure that matters. My father is still around, still teaching at Miskatonic University, but I doubt he'll be able to help us; not that he wouldn't, he just can't. His memories of that time are simply gone. Besides, I haven't seen or spoken to my father since before the war, but I would advise leaving him out of this. According to letters from my brother and sister he can be somewhat maniacal about what he did during that time. You tell him this and he'll drag you down a rabbit hole and have you working for him instead of the other way round."

"You're sure about that?"

"Dragging my father into this is a dead end." I paused in frustration. "Is that why I was asked up here, because of my father?"

McGarrigle stared at the table. "Partly, mostly it was because Vargr said you were familiar with these kinds of cases, that you could handle this kind of work, and yourself. Said you were wasting your talents in Palm Beach. Said he didn't want to see you going soft, that left to your own devices you would end up marrying some debutante and become Robert and Erica Peaslee of New York, Palm Beach, and Beverly Hills. He didn't want that for you, that you should apply yourself to the greater good, and not end up solving crime as a hobby with your wife and dog in tow. He also thinks that you should speak to your father."

I pushed my chair back, my anger held just in check. "Hadrian Vargr doesn't want me wasting my talents! Did it never occur to him that I might have been happy in Palm Beach, or that being married to a debutante might be exactly what I need? Don't I get a say in the way my life goes?"

"Did you ask him for anything?"

I closed my eyes and tried to calm myself. "I asked him for a job."

"And how long have you known Vargr?"

"We worked together for three years."

"So you know how he is?" I nodded. "Then you're in his debt. As far as he's concerned, you owe him, and he won't stop manipulating you until he feels that debt is paid."

I sat back down and looked at McGarrigle. "He's got you, too, doesn't he?"

The red-haired detective snorted. "You and I are just the tip of the iceberg."

I threw my hands up on the table in a gesture of futility. "So what does he want us to do?"

McGarrigle gathered the papers from the table. "Solve the case. Prove that Crawford Tillinghast wasn't mad, or conversely that he was."

"How do we do that?" The frustration in my voice was thick.

"You're the one who is supposed to know about this stuff."

I sat there mulling it over in my mind, turning the case over and over again. There was a way to do what Alfred Tillinghast wanted, a very obvious and simple way, a way that was possibly very, very dangerous. "We need to rebuild the Tillinghast Resonator."

McGarrigle used words I never heard before; some of them weren't in English.

We called Alfred Tillinghast and made arrangements.

*17th September 1923*

Tillinghast and Company sat at the end of a private spur on a rail line in Vermont not far from Red Bud and Townshend. It was a massive, rambling facility of utilitarian warehouses, dour, brick office buildings, and large machine shops from which the sound of timbers being cut, metal being bent, and rock being chiseled rung out incessantly. Part of the compound functioned as a lumber yard and was filled with local trucks and horse-drawn carts from the nearby towns including Townshend. There was a kind of hierarchy to the backwoods folks who had come to buy from the mill. Those with trucks clustered together and cast looks of scorn at their less-sophisticated cousins with horse-drawn carts. In turn, these cast their own foul glances on a single ram-shackle wagon with a lone downtrodden horse and its two queer occupants. The older man, who was easily beyond his sixtieth year, wore strange robes and carried an odd walking stick, both decorated with queer symbols that echoed designs found amongst the Mennonites. His bald pate and gray beard set off his deep-sunken eyes that seemed filled with suspicion and animosity. His companion was a giant, a man easily over seven feet tall, with thick, wiry hair and a fat, goatish face. He moved slowly, carefully, and leaned on the cart for support. It was obvious to me that the man was wary of his surroundings, and that while he was able and strong, it served his purpose to appear anything but capable. By seeming to be physically inept, he appeared to be weak and therefore not a threat to those who seemed to despise his presence. I had seen similar behaviors elsewhere, and I knew that no matter what time these two men had arrived, their social standing meant that they would be the last to be served, and then only after everyone else was gone.

Amidst this slice of country life and the dozen or so old buildings and worn shops was a queer and new addition to the landscape, a thoroughly modern building in the art deco style, marked with an ornate sign that identified it as the Tillinghast-Yutani Radio, Electrics, and Light Laboratory. This was where Alfred Tillinghast had, on our behalf, commissioned his staff to rebuild his son's machine, based on plans McGarrigle and I had liberated from the evidence locker in Providence. Those plans were not for the original machine, the pieces of which were lost along with its blueprints during an estate sale of the furniture and contents. Instead we were working with designs prepared by Crawford for an improved version for the next phase of work. Thus the engineers at TYRELL, which is what those who worked there called the lab, were working to create something that no one, not even Crawford Tillinghast, had ever seen before.

Despite this, the scientists seemed sure that the design for the resonator would produce the sonic waves specified, though they admitted that they could not guarantee that they would have the same, if any, effect on the sensory perception of a human subject that Crawford described.

The lead engineer on the build was a man named Henry Annesley, a former professor whom the firm had lured away from Miskatonic University to head their new venture. The Tillinghasts had made their money in real estate and construction, but Alfred Tillinghast was looking forward into the future, and what he saw there was the infiltration of radio, electronics, and optics into the everyday lives of ordinary people. Annesley was assisted in his work by Doctor James Xavier, a medical man, also from Miskatonic, who was researching a field called biophysics, the reaction of biological systems to various forms of energy including heat, electricity, radiation, sonic vibrations, and light. Together, Annesley, a short, rotund man with receding hair and horn-rimmed glasses, and Xavier, a British subject, tall and debonair with a commanding voice, were determined to revolutionize the future and fill it with electro-mechanical marvels to benefit all of mankind. According to Xavier, X-rays were just the beginning of the future; a universe of electro-mechanical and chemical miracles were waiting to be discovered or invented. All this explained why they were working on rebuilding the Tillinghast Resonator, or at least allowed them to justify why they were working to do so.

"Would you look at that?" McGarrigle whistled at the resonator. It was large, taking up the majority of a fifteen-by-fifteen room with a dozen metallic prongs, essential electric tuning forks, and the equipment that allowed for their control and manipulation. Above the forks was suspended a large copper ball pierced with abstract shapes that seemed intuitively linked to the concept of sound propagation. Bulky cables ran from the steel boxes to a control room, a cinder block cube with a small window comprised of thick glass. Annesley had said the room was soundproof, a precautionary measure that he hoped wasn't truly necessary, though it had been in the past.

"We've been experimenting with various botanical extracts and preparations from South and Central America," explained Xavier. "And the chemists have isolated some interesting compounds that might be useful for treatment of psychosis. There's a drink they make, Ayahuasca, that contains a compound we've designated 'dimethylytriptamine' which has some very interesting effects on human perception. We thought at first it was a psychedelic, but after reading the Tillinghast report, we suspect that it and the resonator both stimulate the pineal gland in similar ways. We built the box after several experiments that left the researchers feeling unsafe with the test subjects. We thought they were just paranoid, but we're reconsidering that position."

"How does a real estate and construction tycoon become involved in research on hallucinogenic plant extracts?"

Annesley seemed suddenly nervous. "The corporation is in the process of diversifying their interests. They are currently building a radio tower, and are researching various other applications of that technology. The broadcasting of voice and music is likely just the beginning. We're experimenting with static images, books, documents, and photographs, converting them into patterns that can be broadcast and then reassembled. We've found that some individuals are sensitive to these transmissions and can detect them without any equipment at all."

McGarrigle was incredulous. "You're saying that you can turn a photograph into a radio signal, and that some people can see that image without any kind of receiver?"

Annesley fidgeted nervously. "Not exactly, we're still in early stages of study here. We can broadcast the image, and in controlled studies some subjects are able to tell us when that is happening, and DMT seems to improve those results, but as for what that image actually is, no, they can't do that. Not yet, anyway. At least not in any way that makes sense. Then of course there were the accidents."

My eyebrows rose, but before I could say anything Xavier cut in. "As I've said, some of the test subjects made the research team nervous. Their behavior can sometimes be extreme, and to the untrained it can be unnerving. Some of our more reactive subjects have incurred injuries, died, or just simply disappeared. Given the current economic troubles I'm not surprised that some of the men have drifted away."

"Disappeared," mumbled McGarrigle, "just like Tillinghast's servants."

I put a hand on my partner's shoulder and he took my meaning. We had stumbled into something here, but whether it was Bureau business or not would have to wait for later. Right now our focus was on the resonator. I steered the conversation in a new direction. "Are you ready to demonstrate whether this thing works or not?"

Annesley nodded and the four of us made our way inside the control booth. I had expected Alfred Tillinghast to be there, but apparently he and his business partner, the enigmatic Daisuke Yutani, were away on business in Costagauna. This was a common state of affairs, and I suspected that while Tillinghast's name came first on the masthead, it was Yutani who was really in control. I knew that such situations never sat well with the Bureau, which, while willing to use immigrants and recruit foreign agents for its own needs, was generally unhappy when American corporations became dominated by those same people. It was unnatural, or so the internal screed went, foreign control of corporations was a parasitic relationship, and one that was alien to the conservative thinking of those in power. The more McGarrigle and I dug into the people surrounding this case, the more I disliked it and them. In the back of my mind I was already building a case for a return trip to investigate the finances and practices of this little operation that Tillinghast and Company had hatched in our midst. That, however, was to be future business; this day I was still trying to figure out whether Crawford Tillinghast was a genius, or a madman, or perhaps a little of both.

The control booth was cramped, and I was forced to stand behind and above Annesley, who was giving off an odd odor, a combination of sweat, grease, and ozone that made my nose wrinkle in annoyance, if not quite disgust. For some reason, it reminded me of a week I spent stationed on Erin Island. He had that kind of salt air, dead fish, working class stink to him. It was the kind that never washes off, the kind of stink that tells people where you've come from, the kind of stink that keeps you from moving up in the world. He was methodical in his movements, going through a checklist of preparations that confirmed that a series of circuits, circuit breakers, fuses, and the like were all in working order. Xavier was equally methodical, working through his own list of recording devices and esoteric sensors. A whole series of recording pens jumped to life and began tracing lines on rolls of paper that turned off spindles and slowly folded into trays. The room was filled with humming electricity, the whirring of wheels and gears, and the chattering of machines.

"Here we go," announced Annesley as he flipped a switch. The lights in the room dimmed as most of the power was shunted to the resonator. The weird machine jumped to life and the great forked prongs began to vibrate, each in its own specified way. "We can control the amplitude and frequency of each of the rods from in here. It will take us a moment to reach full operation." He tapped a dial and watched the needle waver and then steady. "Everything seems nominal on my end—James, how are the recorders?"

"Fully operational and ready to proceed when you are."

Annesley nodded and began resetting levels on a series of knobs. "According to his notes Crawford was achieving his best results by blending three distinct harmonic frequencies into a single sympathetic vibration, while at the same time layering in a series of subharmonics." He turned a dial and the air in the room suddenly changed, grew more electric. "He called this arrangement the Zann modulation, though why, he never says. It's not a single, sustained sound though; rather, it's a progression. Once established, the harmonics and subharmonics tend to interact in an odd way. The individual parts of the resonator still put out the same frequency and amplitude, but as they progress through time they move in and out of phase, changing the way they are perceived by ourselves and any sensors."

Xavier ripped a sheet from one of his recording devices. "We're progressing through the first series; if this is going to work we should be seeing something soon."

McGarrigle leaned forward and searched the room for some sort of response. He stretched and craned his neck, pressing his nose up against the glass. "I don't see anything." His breath left a fog on the surface and as it spread I felt something needle-sharp spike into the space above and between my eyes. I wasn't the only one, for we all seemed to be reaching for our foreheads. I winced and bowed my head. I wanted to leave it down and let the sudden pain disperse, but McGarrigle cursed, "Mary Mother of God!", and I snapped my head back up.

They were in the air, swimming like jellyfish and eels and fish, but they weren't any of those, they were something else, something not of this world, something never meant to be a part of it. We could all see them as they moved through the spaces around us, and it instantly became apparent that they could see us as well. They moved at the booth, but whatever weird properties allowed us to see them were negated by the walls and glass. Annesley and Xavier seemed to take comfort in this, and I too seemed to accept our security, but McGarrigle didn't. I could see him becoming more and more nervous. Beads of sweat were forming on his head and his eyes became frantic. I reached out a hand to steady the man, but as I touched him something snapped and he screamed. He pushed his way through the three of us and threw the door open and ran into the lab, screaming.

"Shut it down!" I yelled as I went after my fellow agent.

"It's not that simple," shouted back Annesley. "We have to cycle down, it'll take time."

I didn't stop to argue with him, but instead followed McGarrigle through the lab and down the corridors to the front door. I careened through the reception area, knocking over a dark, curly-haired man and his bald assistant. I had no time for apologies. Whatever Tillinghast's machine had done to us had obviously affected McGarrigle more than me. I had hoped, or at least thought, that the effect of the resonator would have been confined to the laboratory, but alas I was mistaken. All around me the strange creatures swarmed and darted in great shoals of unearthly colors and weird, unnatural pulses. Larger things, obviously predators, whirled and arced in pursuit of extradimensional prey. I myself dodged and weaved past a congress of weird spherical things that pulsed and twisted in response.

As I broke into the yard I realized that no one else could see what McGarrigle and I could. The brief exposure to the resonator had done something to our perception of reality, but had not impacted those outside of the lab. Still McGarrigle was running, fleeing in terror at what he had seen, and I had to stop him before he hurt himself, or in his panic someone else. He had a head start on me, and I was at a disadvantage for I had no choice but to follow his lead, but it soon became apparent that his mad dash was simply that. He had no destination, he was merely running blind, and I was following. I caught a glimpse of him as I rounded a building and he turned the corner of another in the distance. A flash of light made me realize that his madness had progressed. As I ran I opened my holster and took out my gun and let the word "Please" roll off my lips. I didn't want to shoot the man, but he had already drawn his gun, and I suspected his madness was progressing in ways I didn't understand.

As my feet pounded against the hard ground I heard the sound of men and horses panicking, and picked up my pace. As the blood coursed through my beating heart, I focused on the task at hand, and as my time dilated in response to the stress, the things that stalked and fluttered and banked through the aether around me began to fade. They shuddered as I ran, phased in and out of my view, disappearing from my perceptions and then reappearing until they were little more than shadows cast against a wall fading as the sun rose. At least for me.

McGarrigle was screaming, yelling at the top of his lungs. "What are ya? Ya filthy . . . God help me! Ya stay right there, ya filthy thing. So help me! Sweet Jesus! Get away from it, old man!"

I rounded the corner and saw McGarrigle on his knees, cowering and trying to crawl backward across the ground. His gun was out and was pointed at something I couldn't see, something that the building blocked my view of. He was shaking in terror and crying in fear and madness. I drew a bead on him with my revolver and called out "McGarrigle!"

He snapped his head at the sound of his name. He saw my gun and that triggered a switch and then his training took over. His arm followed his head, the great big gun in his hand changing its angle, closing in on my position. I saw something in his eyes, just briefly, some flash of rationality, an acknowledgement that something had been set in motion and that neither he nor I was in a position to stop it. His gun barrel was arcing toward my direction and mine was already pointed at him. Just like him, I let my training, my instincts, my reflexes take over.

I don't even remember pulling the trigger. I don't even remember the sound or the smoke or the kick of the gun in my hand. I don't remember running to him. I only remember McGarrigle lying in my arms, the blood soaking into my clothes, and the ground around me. His eyes were still wild, and as he lay there drowning in his own fluids he tried to speak, tried to tell me something. He pointed at the road and at the horse-drawn cart that was slowly winding away from Tillinghast and Company. The cart driven by the old man and the giant, the only people who had been in the lumber yard when I had shot my partner and brought him down.

"Not a man," McGarrigle had whispered, "not a man."

## Addendum
## From the Journal of Robert Peaslee

*8th October 1923*

The Bureau cleared me, but made sure I was whisked out of there and sent back home to Florida as quickly as possible. Alfred Tillinghast was apparently pleased with the results, but realized that whatever his son had created, it was too dangerous; he had Annesley and Xavier disassemble it. Then both of the researchers were reassigned, as was most of the staff. I'm told they were dispersed to facilities in either Chicago or Denton.

I still hear Flynn's words, and I think about them at night, when I wake in a cold sweat, and the spot above and between my eyes aches, and I have to drink a bottle of rotgut bourbon to get to sleep again. I think about those words and I half-remember the flash of what I saw as I rounded the corner and surveyed the yard. The old man was there, and so was the giant, but those of the air, the things that swarmed around us, were in a panic, as were the great predatory things that stalked amongst them like sharks and eagles. For just for that brief instant, so brief that my conscious mind didn't acknowledge it, there was something else there in the giant's place. It was something massive, something monstrous with tentacles and hooves and pulsating gills that flexed and contracted like the wings of a bat. It was an inhuman thing that I saw only for an instant, but McGarrigle, I think he could see it clear as day. I think it drove him mad. So mad that he was no longer a man, but rather a terrified animal capable only of fear. It is a terrible thing, I think, to live in fear.

I think it is time I stopped.

# CHAPTER 6

# "The Reservations of Senator Lowe"
## From the Journal of Robert Peaslee
## May 27 1924

Senator Henry Paget Lowe was interred today; the service was closed casket. His long-time assistant will be buried later this week. Their deaths by fire in a hunting cabin near Aylesbury were reported by the press as a tragic loss to the state and his constituency. I, however, disagree. The man was dangerous, and while I may have set in motion the events that led to his death, I regret nothing. Certainly it may have been unethical of me to have used my position at the Bureau of Investigation to my own advantage, to claim a position that was not mine by achievement alone. Of this I am guilty. That Lowe and O'Meara are dead is not my responsibility. Still, some explanation, some record of my actions must be made. So for that reason and that alone, I am making this record, making this account, so that someday if needed, my involvement in these things can be made clear. I hope it never comes to that; there are some things that men are better off not knowing.

It was the morning of Friday the sixteenth of May, and it was raining when I finally reached Bolton. The train ride from Boston had passed through Arkham, and I was tempted to disembark there and explore the locale that dominated my adolescence, but something held me back. I must admit that I have had doubts about this course of action, and on several occasions have pondered turning back, forgetting what I have deduced, and resigning my commission. Yet as much as those thoughts have wandered about in my mind, I still made my way to Bolton and disembarked in the cold and dreary rains that are typical of the region in May.

The streets were empty; smoke from the mills hung low over the town, and seemed to stain the rain gray with soot. The discolored torrents gathered in the gutters, which were insufficient to the task and overflowed across the walkway and streets. It made trudging up the hill past the company-owned row homes more difficult than it should have been. I should have come on another day, one with better weather, but my appointment had been made weeks ago, and the man I was meeting wasn't likely to reschedule. It is no easy task to make an appointment with a United States Senator, particularly one as senior as Henry Paget Lowe. It was only because I had once worked with Lowe, in Paris, that I was granted an audience. Normally my skills would be applied in service to men like Senator Lowe. However, on this day, my only concern was using my talents for my own benefit, no matter how inappropriate that may have been.

The Eckert Building dominates the central city block of downtown Bolton, and towers a mighty five stories over the rest of the town. Only the smokestacks of the various mills and factories rise higher, and then not by much. This is where the vast majority of commerce for Bolton is carried out, the Eckert serving as the business offices of the firms that reside in the village. The manufacturing centers, the mills, and other factories are in general dirty and unseemly places; they are not places where genteel merchants are wont to meet with their suppliers. It is best to keep the men buying the product away from the men and women and children who spend their days manufacturing it. Thus the lower floors of the Eckert are home to corporate offices and the like, while the upper floors house lawyers, accountants, and the offices of Senator Henry Paget Lowe.

Despite its height, it is a rather unassuming building, almost utilitarian in design, a simple brick box with plain windows and entryways that does nothing to either cheer or sadden the surrounding neighborhood. Indeed, in a larger city the entire building might have been entirely nondescript, unnoticed amongst the more ostentatious or cleverly designed offices found in New York, Boston, or Providence. Indeed, as I reached the main entrance there wasn't even a doorman to greet and direct me. There was a building directory, and I noted that Lowe's office was on the top floor. Also catching my eye was the headquarters of the Delapore Chemical Manufacturing Company, which had offices on the second floor. I hadn't known that before, but it made a kind of perverse sense, and made me slightly more cautious. My business with

Lowe concerned Delapore, and I feared that one might leverage the other once my intent was made clear.

The interior of the building was just as plain as the exterior, and after shaking off the last of the rain I made my way up the simple, cut-granite stairs. Each of my steps echoed through the great central well of the building, filling it with what must have sounded like the footsteps of giants. Like the town itself the interior of the building was devoid of inhabitants. It was an eerie state, one that could easily have triggered my fears, but I knew from my investigation that this state was very common. During working hours most of the residents of Bolton were in the mills, the few children too young held in care centers staffed by elderly women who were too slow or infirm to be on the manufacturing floors. Elderly men were employed as cooks, janitors, and the like. It was, in the mind of the industrialists that ran the place, a perfect, almost utopian town. Still, it left the streets and office buildings empty and eerily quiet. It was not until I reached the top floor that I encountered another human being.

The door to Lowe's office was flung open and from it emerged a rather angry young man whose red face contrasted with his formal, white shirt. I recognized him immediately as a local attorney of some notoriety named Arnold Schiff. He huffed as we passed each other and mumbled something about how no child of his was going to grow up in a town that didn't know the meaning of law and order. I turned to say something to him, but he was already stomping down the stairs. If my footsteps had echoed like giants', then his were not unlike those of a fallen angel tumbling from heaven. I caught the door before it swung shut and then politely introduced myself to the receptionist who sat behind the desk. She was a young woman, with dark auburn hair that flowed around a rather shapely face above a torso that had curves in all the right places. She was, I suppose, rather attractive, the kind of girl my buddies would call a dame, if you were into that look, but far too feminine for my tastes. A sign across the front of her desk said that her name was O'Meara.

I cleared my throat and she bore down on me with large piercing eyes magnified by sharp-rimmed glasses. "I have an appointment to see the Senator," I managed to say without stuttering. "The name is Peaslee, Robert Peaslee. I'm a special agent with the Bureau of Investigation."

I offered my hand and she took it—it was a reflex, and one she regretted almost immediately. Her grasp was dainty, gentle, and soft, but her fingers and palm were cold, barely above room temperature. She pulled her hand back and seemed annoyed. She pursed her lips and wrinkled up her nose at me, those dark eyes seeming to smolder, but whether it was with desire or contempt I couldn't say. She rose from her desk, never unlocking her eyes from mine. When she spoke, her voice was husky and made me feel small. "Wait here." She turned slowly and sauntered off through a door marked private. I stood there for a moment watching the door slowly swing shut, but before it could close and latch Miss O'Meara had returned and was ushering me in with those come-hither-but-stay-away eyes. "The Senator is ready for you, Agent Peaslee." With that and a few steps I was through the door into the senator's office. It was only when the door was fully shut that I took my eyes off her, removed my hat, and wiped my brow.

"Don't you worry son, she has that effect on a lot of people." Senator Lowe's voice was gravelly and hinted at a Boston upbringing. It had been years since I had seen him, but he hadn't changed much. He was still a large man, both broad and stout with a shock of gray hair that reminded me of an aged raccoon. His eyes were clear but the skin around them was old, sagging like wet bags. He smelled vaguely of cumin, always has, never bothered to ask him why. His smile was that of a man who was powerful enough to worry about nothing, nothing at all. He motioned for me to sit, pointing to a red, upholstered monstrosity of leather, brass, and oak that was obviously not designed for comfort.

As I found my seat, Lowe took the opportunity to reminisce. "How is civilian life treating you?"

"I'm doing fine, right as rain." I lied, and he knew it, but we both let the pretense pass.

"That's fine, Robert. I haven't seen you in a long time, since dinner at the Café d'Ys. Do you remember that place, Robert? They served such a magnificent version of ratatouille there."

"I remember the restaurant, Senator; you ate there quite a bit. A rather exclusive place, if I recall. I tried to take a girl there once, but couldn't get in."

Lowe nodded as he reminisced. "They were always packed to the gills; I made reservations six or seven times a week. Didn't use them all, of course, but that was the only way to make sure you had a table." He paused, still smiling. "You didn't come here to talk about the old days."

"No, sir, the reason I'm here is because of the Versailles Treaty. I have some questions. There are some things I don't understand."

Lowe leaned back in his chair; the gray light coming through the window behind him transformed part of the great man into a shadow. "Is this an official visit, Robert? Are you here on Bureau business? Because if you are . . ."

"No, sir," I cut him off. "I'm here strictly on my own business. In the wind, as we say." He nodded his understanding and I continued. "We spent all that time negotiating the treaty, and I went to Ylourgne for the accord. All that work, and then after President Wilson made his points concerning why the treaty was a good thing, you and other members of the Mission convinced Congress to reject the treaty, because you had reservations. May I ask why? What reservations could possibly have been so important as to cause the rejection of the treaty we had all worked so hard on?"

Lowe leaned forward and rested his hands on the desk. He was studying me, assessing how much of the truth he could tell me, and trying to figure out how much I already knew. "Do you know what the Triple Entente was, how about the Triple Alliance?" I nodded. "Then you know that these agreements between the great powers of Europe were essentially a powder keg that started the Great War. The Europeans were so entwined with each other that it only took a small match to set off a chain reaction. The Versailles Treaty was like that as well; it would have tied us to our allies, forced our hand when anything went against one of them, regardless of when and where or why. It would have set up another chain reaction, one that we could not have avoided." He paused. "It also would have prevented the United States from acting on its own, and would have forced allied states to act against us."

"I don't follow."

"The old order of things is falling apart. The Great War has forever altered the map of the world, and not just for those who lost. There are grumblings in London and Moscow and Paris. Things are changing; the colonies have seen that the empires have grown old and weak. When they fall, and trust me, they will fall, there will be a power vacuum, and I intend to have the United States ready to fill it. The Imperial

Dynasty of America will rise to fulfill its destiny and take its rightful place amongst the nations of the world, not as a nation of farmers, but as warriors and leaders of a new world order!"

There was something frantic in his eyes—madness had taken root and corrupted his brain. "This explains so much." I reached into my coat pocket and tossed a satchel of papers onto his desk.

He snatched at it and tore it open like a rabid dog. "What is this? What do you think you have?"

It was my turn to ease back into my chair. "I've learned quite a bit, working for the Bureau. You've done a good job of covering your tracks, but I've learned a bit about accounting and receipts and bills of lading, and shell corporations. For example, those documents in the blue envelope show that you are the primary owner of Delapore Chemical, having taken over after the founder died in Anchester last year."

"Is that a crime?"

"In itself no, sir, but the yellow envelope contains documents showing Delapore Chemical purchasing over the last six months, which has strangely shifted to unusual quantities of arsenic trichloride and acetylene, the primary ingredients in the manufacture of lewisite, also known as M1, jokingly referred to as the dew of death, a gas, one that smells like geraniums, that blisters the skin and irritates the lungs. Delapore is making chemical weapons, Senator Lowe. You know it, I know it, and these documents prove it, and you and I both know that the federal government is attempting to ban the use of chemical weapons. The Washington Naval Conference may have failed, but certainly the Geneva Protocols will not. President Coolidge is quite certain."

"Coolidge is a fool, and he will do nothing but weaken this country and betray her destiny." There was venom in his voice. "What, pray tell, is in the green envelope?"

"That is evidence of your involvement with Darrow Chemical and the transfer of an old farm and several acres of the local potter's field to them so that they can expand their facility. I find it curious that while a great deal of earth has been moved, there has been no actual construction. The property was once occupied by Doctor Herbert West, about whom I know enough to be suspicious of these activities. I'm also concerned that Dr. Geoffrey Darrow himself has relocated to the farmhouse. If I'm not mistaken, Darrow, like West, studied at Miskatonic

University. They were in the same graduating class. I've been watching the farmhouse for a month now. What does he do with all of those cats? It is so very odd, so many cats, dozens each week, and a furnace that only runs at night, and so many strange smells and sounds. A curious state of affairs, it really should be investigated. Aren't you at all curious, Senator Lowe, or do the boxes of product marked *Reserved for HP Lowe* make you turn a blind eye?"

Lowe's composure suddenly fell. "If it's a game of secrets we're playing, Agent Peaslee, are you sure that you don't have anything to lose? What was that man's name, the one in London? Valentine, wasn't it? How inappropriate of both of you. It would be a shame if that information made its way to the Bureau. Your friend Hadrian Vargr might develop some reservations concerning the quality of your work."

I half-smiled and laughed a bit. "Vargr already knows about that, and frankly I'm looking for a way out of working for him. You, Senator, are that way out. You see, with Coolidge moving forward with his plans, you and your little operation here in Bolton are a liability. If what you are doing here were to become public knowledge, the repercussions would be devastating, and believe me, if I can figure this thing out, there are sure to be others who can and will too. That would be bad for Coolidge. So you are going to shut Delapore down, and then you are going to shut down whatever is going on at Darrow Chemical and that farmhouse. Then when everything is taken care of you are going to retire, quietly, peacefully. You've earned it. And in return you will be left alone."

"I'll not be put on a reservation without knowing why. What do you get out of this?"

I leaned forward. "That is not your concern."

"With your experience, your knowledge, you could have been an Army colonel. There's another war coming, Peaslee. The terms of the Versailles Treaty all but assure it. We need to be prepared. We will need weapons, weapons that kill entire platoons in an instant, and soldiers that are stronger and more powerful than normal men, soldiers that are resistant to disease, and injury, and even death. We need soldiers who can be shot and still fight. You know this is coming; you were at Locus Solus, and Ylourgne. We need to prepare." He reached into his desk and grabbed a small ampule. The liquid inside was radiant green and cast sick shadows against the walls. "This is what Darrow is working on.

It's a chemical that makes men resistant to death itself. There are side effects, certainly, but that is merely a matter of dosage. Some subjects retain all of their faculties and functions. You could join us."

I smacked the ampule out of his hand. "And some subjects are reduced to mindless, ravenous beasts that attack and kill everyone in sight." The small glass vial tumbled through the air before crashing to the floor and shattering against the tile. "We are supposed to be the righteous, Senator Lowe. The defenders of the weak and downtrodden. You and yours would make us conquerors, using monsters and madness to create an American Empire. Is that what you want, Lowe, an empire? Have you forgotten why we set this country up in the first place?"

He repeated his question, making it a demand. "What are you getting out of this, Peaslee?" He was on the verge of rage.

"I told you that was none of your concern." I retrieved my hat and coat and stood to go. I gestured in the direction of the envelopes that were on his desk. "You can keep those. I've got copies. So do a few other people. They're not a patient bunch, Senator, so I would suggest you start closing up shop as fast as possible."

With that, I walked out of the senator's private office and stalked past the desk of Miss O'Meara, who glared at me like I had spit in her soup. I paused, put my hands down on the desk, and got right up in her face. "The Senator's retiring in the next few days. I suggest you cancel his appointments and reservations for the next week or so." I smiled triumphantly, "You're out of a job too, but not to worry. Someone of your qualifications should have no problems finding a position in a library or bookstore. I think I saw an opening in Arkham, at the historical society. Maybe you could work there, organizing shelves, setting up book clubs for little old ladies." With that I hightailed it out the door and down the stairs. I swear I could hear the two of them screaming at each other all the way to the front door.

Outside, the clouds had partially broken up and the sun was starting to peek out. I reached into my breast pocket and took out my badge: not my Bureau badge, but my new badge, the one that identified me as a member of the Massachusetts State Police. The position was a gift from Governor Cox, earned for blowing the whistle on Lowe, and of course delivering the message that he was done. I whistled a happy tune on my way to the station.

As I said, that was on the sixteenth. Three days ago, the news came out of Bolton: Lowe was dead, along with his long-time assistant Miss O'Meara. They had been at his hunting cabin near Aylesbury when a fire had broken out. At least, that is what the papers said. I used my contacts to get the official report, and that told a slightly different story.

A routine visit by a state game warden had found the cabin door open. Suspecting a break-in, Officer Sams found two bodies: Miss O'Meara had been shot at close range with a shotgun which had created a gaping hole through her torso. Lowe's body was sitting in a chair nearby, a shotgun cradled in his lap. In most cases this would have made Lowe the most viable of suspects. In this case that was unlikely, for while Lowe's body sat in the chair, his head sat on the table, eyes wide, blood pooling beneath the neck and dripping onto the floor.

Officer Sams was a veteran of the war; he had seen death before, this was nothing new, but something had made the officer run from the cabin and slam the door behind him. He was methodical in what he did next. He blocked the entrance and then soaked the porch and perimeter of the house with a store of gasoline he kept in his car. He lit the fire and then retreated to a safe distance. He stood outside for two hours, making sure that the entire cabin and its contents were reduced to ash before radioing for assistance in preventing the fire from spreading to the surrounding forest.

When pressed by the investigating officers and the coroner as to the cause of his actions, the young veteran was at first reticent to speak. Eventually, however, under threat of criminal prosecution he revealed the impetus for his pyromania. There in the dark of the cabin, the fire burning and casting long shadows over the dead, he had made to leave and call in the murders, for surely this could not have been an accident or suicide. Decapitated men don't shoot people, thus the scene had been clearly staged.

It was then that the body of Miss O'Meara began to twitch and moan. It rose up off the floor and from its mouth issued a wailing scream. The scream slowly faded and was replaced with a wet, gasping cough. Blood and gore dripped from the open wound and the once-lovely Miss O'Meara seemed to survey the damage with a sense of disbelief. "I can't believe you shot me!"

This was followed by a deep, gurgling response from the head on the table. It was plain to Sams that words were being mouthed, but because there were no lungs to drive air through the vocal cords nothing more than a sick, bubbling whisper was possible.

There was something ghoulishly funny about the situation, and Sams admitted to letting loose a guffaw at the whole thing. This sound apparently enraged the headless senator's body, which once more pulled the trigger on the shotgun, narrowly missing the officer's own head. As Sams retreated out the door his last vision was of O'Meara leaping like some deranged hell beast toward the head and body of her former employer.

The preliminary report recommended that Sams be placed on medical leave and be evaluated for a psychiatric condition. The fact that the coroner's report found the two badly charred skeletons, one headless, locked in what appeared to be mortal combat, does provide certain mitigating circumstances that will likely prevent the dismissal of Officer Sams. Hell, they might even give him a medal.

The report also notes that the head of Senator Lowe was not found amongst the remains. Today's service was followed by a cremation of what little remained of Senator Henry Paget Lowe. His ashes were entombed in the family crypt in Arkham. The funerary urn was larger than it needed to be. A precaution on the part of the mortuary in case the head is ever found.

I hope that is Senator Lowe's final reservation.

PART TWO

# Robert Peaslee
## April 1928

# CHAPTER 7

# "The Man on the Train"
## From the Journal of Robert Peaslee
## April 9 1928

Coming back on the train from a long weekend in Manhattan, as usual I can't sleep. Writing this at least keeps my mind busy, keeps me from woolgathering. The weekend with Philo was simply horrible. He had ditched Van and we spent our time in his aunt's brownstone, vacant while she is in London. We wandered through Central Park and then made our way down to Red Hook to buy shellfish from that market he likes. We brought some wine and cheese up from the cellar and had an entirely decadent Friday night. Saturday we dressed, put on our green carnations and went out on the town with Cranston and that rather entertaining Rowan woman. The food at Rusterman's was exquisite, and we ended up at Dundee's club until well after two in the morning.

There is something simply magical about New York. The buildings, the lights, the people, it is almost in a way a fictional place. It is as if some writer decided to create the quintessential metropolis, filled with everything you could conceive of, and therefore ripe with possibility. Boston pales in comparison, and Arkham is little more than a quaint little hamlet, full of mostly small-minded people. If it weren't for these weekend getaways I would simply go mad. I suppose that the time I spent in London and Paris has corrupted me, that I will from now on be lost in the romance of the big city, as opposed to the small towns that dot both the American and European countryside. Where else can you find the mélange of people and things that produce such a rich canvas to paint your own landscape?

Philo himself lends support to my argument. Where else could a man of his background and temperament not only find tasks worthy of his highly refined, albeit esoteric skills, but such that he might become something of a minor celebrity? His ability at the art of deduction is staggering, with only my friend Nick being any real rival, not that either would notice. It's a big pond and there are plenty of murders, kidnappings, and thefts to keep a dozen master detectives employed. Indeed, Philo spent a good portion of Saturday night regaling us with a case of his from the previous fall, the murder of a nightclub singer, and a most curious alibi. Though I will admit that while Rowan and I were fascinated, Cranston looked downright bored.

Yet as the night progressed into early Sunday I became annoyed and then eventually peeved by the whole situation. The entire evening was spent talking about Philo, and while that might be fun for some time, it soon became apparent that the man was simply relishing in his notoriety and that Van was an integral part of this. I, on the other hand, was little more than an appendage to be rolled out on weekends. In many ways I have come to think of Philo and Van as simply two sides of the same coin. One without the other is simply a shadow of the whole. They belong together, though they might not realize it.

Sunday was a lazy day spent around the fire, reading a slim volume of poetry by Edward Derby. Philo had wanted to go see a play, a piece featuring the Yiddish comic Boris Thomashefsky, but we both decided that we were too drowsy to even leave the house during the day. We finally ventured out after the evening had wrapped the city in her dark skirts, strutting through the streets like two cocks on a fence. We finally wandered into Montagnino's for dinner before making a dash to get me on the midnight train back to Arkham. By this time Philo had deduced that there was some tension between us and he made an attempt to probe for details, but I rebuffed his advances. I think it is time to pursue new directions. I can't live in Philo's shadow, and I shouldn't have to. If Van wants that job, he is more than welcome to it. There is enough darkness in my life, in Arkham.

When I joined the Massachusetts State Police I had expected to be assigned to Troop B, in the western part of the state. Instead, after reviewing my record the Colonel assigned me to Troop X, which wasn't even a cohesive unit. The members of Troop X were scattered across the state, embedded into the police forces of smaller metropolitan areas where they could supplement the locals. Against my very vocal objections I had been assigned to Arkham, reporting to Chief Nichols. Ostensibly, Nichols was my direct supervisor: I was his to order about as he seemed fit. At the same time, on paper I wasn't part of his payroll, so he had no incentive to keep me happy. Inevitably, I got the cases Nichols didn't want his own staff to handle, dirty jobs with questionable outcomes. Police work isn't always black and white; there are gray areas. Sometimes, to obtain justice cops need to bend the law. I was Chief Nichols's crowbar, and if I fouled up he had almost complete deniability. It was a shit job, but for one reason or another I couldn't find a way to quit it. I belonged in Arkham. Somehow or another the situation made sense, a sad man in a bad job.

At the train station I saw a rather sad-faced man, dressed for traveling, by which I mean he was adorned in comfortable clothes and shoes. They were still finely made, and I recognized some of the fabrics and styling as originating in some upper-end shops to be found in Manhattan and Chicago. He did not carry himself as a local, and seemed utterly confused by the station itself, asking on at least three occasions for directions. During one of these queries I came to understand that he too was bound for Arkham. Being concerned for his welfare, mostly because I didn't want to see the man suffer some misfortune at the hands of a ruffian, either here or on the train—either of which situations would have involved me professionally—I flashed him my badge and offered to guide him to the train and stay with him until we reached Arkham.

To this arrangement the stranger wholeheartedly agreed, and introduced himself as Edwin Dennis of Chicago, in New York to see his sister, Mame, on family business, before moving on to Arkham for more of the same. He was an older man, fit and muscular but not overly so. In a way he reminded me of Philo, whose weekend trips to the Athletic Club were balanced with afternoons of drinks and canapés. The effect was a strong frame with a layer of softness around it. Yet, there was also something delicate about the man. He walked carefully, slowly, with a cane draped over one arm in case he needed it. There was a gray cast to his face and his eyes seemed to hold some secret sadness that yearned to be spoken and explored. I said nothing, having learned long ago that such men will speak of things when they need to, if they need to. My patience was not tested for long.

We were in the same car, sitting across a table from each other. The waiter had brought us coffee, and hinted at the possibility of something stronger, which we both declined. As the amicable server walked away my companion lowered his eyes and whispered, "Keep it down, kid, the old man's hung." There was a tinge of regret in his voice, a soupçon of sadness, a spoonful of longing, and a healthy dash of melancholy. I let him wallow in it for a moment and then, as our cups arrived, the moment was past. His composure quickly returned; it was one thing to slip in front of a stranger, but entirely another thing to do so before the help.

After a few minutes I finally broke the silence, making small talk more than anything else. "Do you have family in Arkham, Mr. Dennis?"

The look I received in return was one I could not categorize, for it was equal parts hope and despair. "Apparently I do, though I didn't know it until last week." He took a sip of his coffee; his hands were shaking, and the motion of the train added to his unsteadiness. "Tell me, Mr. Peaslee, have you ever been in love? I mean, have you ever loved a woman so much that you ache for her; not just a dame who you spent a weekend with, but an honest-to-goodness woman who you cherished, and can't ever forget?"

I looked him square in the eye, careful not to look down or up, my interrogation training kicking in, a reflex really. I looked him square in the eye and lied just a little. "I've had my share. In Paris there was a nurse, we thought we were in love, but in the end it was only the war, and the aftermath of war. There was a blonde in Palm Beach, an heiress; she bought me a coat with a fur collar. Can you imagine? Ninety degrees in the shade and she buys me a winter coat. True love, the kind you're talking about? No, not even in the Catskills."

I had slipped and he had caught it. He smiled and let me slide. "I've loved the same woman for the last fifteen years, and for ten of those she's been dead." He fumbled with his coffee cup. "Tell me, Mr. Peaslee, is it wrong to love a dead woman more than the living son she gave you?"

I went to speak but he waved me off, and with a gentle shake of his head withdrew the question. "Her name was Laura, Laura Horne, a daughter of a fine old Boston family. I met her while I was on busi-ness; I was working with her father, an hotelier who wanted to expand his family business to the west coast, a fool of a man who had married a woman eight years his senior to gain in both standing and wealth. Laura had joined us for lunch; she was everything her parents weren't. She was young, vivacious, outgoing, and oddly attractive in an exotic kind of way. Her features reflected neither of her parents'. Her face was round, with a slightly flattened nose, and wide-set, sloe eyes of an enchanting color that was not green, hazel, brown, or black, but almost of a violet hue, though even this was not right. Her hair was black and straight and fashionably styled. Her figure was lithe, almost tiny, for at times her head seemed much larger than it should be. Her arms were thin but muscular with delicate hands and deft fingers that danced across piano keys with accomplished skill. To hear her speak, and her voice was melodic, she had been offered a spot at two prestigious music academies, but her parents refused the notion of training her talent beyond that of simply a skilled amateur. Her deftness was suitable for entertaining friends and family; it would be unseemly to pursue it any further, or so her parents told her."

He paused and sipped his coffee. "We would go for long walks. She loved the waterfront and the ocean. She had learned to sail. She knew the tides and winds, knew the shells that washed up to decorate the Cape. Somewhere along the way she had learned to filet fish, a task that was certainly beneath her status, but one I found endearing. The fishmongers all knew her name, and she knew their names as well, and wasn't afraid to call them out when the offerings weren't fresh. She knew what foggy eyes and pale gills on a fish meant, and why clams might gape. She could spot a bad oyster or sour crab without even picking it up. When I held her she smelled of the sea, and the beach, and the wharf. Her kisses tasted of salt. Her hands caressed mine and danced in my hair like the breeze coming off the bay. It took me two years, but I eventually won her heart, and she agreed to be my bride."

"We married in June, 1915, a seaside service, everything as Laura wanted it. We had wanted to honeymoon in Fenwick, but the war made those plans untenable. Instead, we spent two weeks on a boat cruising the Caribbean. When we finally flew home from Sulaco it was with much regret, both of us having fallen in love with that port and the wonders she provided access to." He sighed, a long, happy sigh. "My business kept us in Bangor during the week, in a little three-room apartment above a bakery, but on weekends we drove down to a small cottage we had bought on the road overlooking the ocean between Cabot and Crabapple Coves. We were happy together, and nothing seemed destined to interfere with that state of affairs."

"Funny how things change." The light had left his eyes. "In the spring Laura had a miscarriage. I hadn't even known she was pregnant. I came home to find her collapsed on the floor, her hands and legs covered in blood. She didn't take the loss well. We went to the cottage to recover, two weeks alone. I pushed work aside and took care of my wife. I eventually returned to Bangor, she never did. She could never find the courage to return to our apartment; it reminded her of death, and of failure. She stayed in the cottage while I worked, which may have not been the best of ideas. She began suffering horrific nightmares, about unborn children rising out of the sea to ravage the coasts. The doctors called it a kind of hysteria, where once the ocean had given us so much comfort, now it generated fear and despair. By the fall things had progressed to such a state that my hands seemed tied. I sold my business in Bangor, sold the cottage on the road overlooking two coves, and moved Laura and myself to Chicago; as far from the sea as I could reasonably get and still find suitable employment. My partner, John Gilbert, and I had an office near the offices of the Independent News Service, which was of no small benefit to our firm. Most importantly I got to spend each night and morning with Laura, and slowly nursed her back to her old self. It took time, but eventually it was she who suggested that we take a stroll along the lakefront. On that day with the wind in her hair, I knew that my Laura had finally come home to me."

He took a long sip of coffee, and motioned for a second cup. He noticed that I had barely touched mine. "Laura liked her coffee cold as well. But late in August of 1918 she stopped drinking it. She said she had developed a sudden distaste for the stuff. She began getting sick after breakfast. A few days later the doctor confirmed what we had suspected: Laura was pregnant once more. It was a joyous occasion, but we both knew that there were risks. Laura was confined to her bed, her diet was controlled, and all excitement and stimulation beyond that of the radio, a good book, and an occasional visitor were forbidden. Laura's nanny, Norah, still employed by the Hornes as a housekeeper, was sent for to once more tend to Laura's needs, and to those of the baby when it came. Strangely, though it didn't even cross my mind, neither Laura's father nor her mother offered to come and visit with her. They had grown distant after our marriage, and their letters to their daughter became fewer and farther between. This second pregnancy seemed to be a final impetus. They sent Norah, gave up a good domestic servant, wasn't that enough? At least that was how it seemed. There was an explanation, of course, but I had no time to investigate it then. With each passing day Laura's health seem to deteriorate. The dreams, those awful nightmares concerning the ocean and ravenous hordes of the unborn, had returned. At first they were isolated, perhaps once a week, but by the time Christmas came around, they were nightly occurrences. They took their toll. Laura ate little, and her skin seemed to sag and fade to a pale green. A rash had broken out on her neck, and on the back of her arms. She lost her hair in clumps. There were daily shots of vitamins and tonics of all sorts, but they did nothing to ease her burden, or slow her consumption. There were whispers amongst the nurses, they said cancer, but the doctors said no such thing. The results of every test they came up with simply left them more confused. In January she was moved to County General, and three days later went into labor. It was not an easy delivery. There were screams and moans, and not just from Laura. Three nurses had to be replaced owing to exhaustion, and perhaps overactive imaginations, but after eighteen hours she finally pushed out the child. It was a boy, strong and healthy with a mop of sandy hair. As we had agreed I named him Patrick. He's nine years old now. He never knew his mother; I'm the only parent he's ever had. Of course, Norah helped, but she wasn't his mother, was she?"

"We told the boy that his mother, my wife, Laura, died giving birth to him. That wasn't true, of course, though perhaps it is better that he thinks that way. No child should know that their mother ran from the delivery room, madness in her eyes and voice, screaming about dreams, about monsters, about giving birth to monsters. No child should know that their father had to plead with their mother to come down off a bridge, the icy wind whipping through the thin linens that she was wrapped in, blood and fluid and something else clinging to her leg. No child should know that his mother jumped into the nearly frozen river and that try as they might the police were unable to recover the body. No child should know these things, and so we have never told him."

I stared at him in disbelief as he paused but for a moment, and then once more began to speak. "I raised him as best I could. We moved into a residence hotel, me, Patrick, and Norah. He's a smart boy, goes to the Latin School. I worked hard, made sure the boy was provided for, perhaps too hard. A few weeks ago I had a heart attack. The prognosis is not good. The specialists have given me a year, maybe two, no more than that. Patrick is going to be a very rich young man, but I wanted to see if I could give him more than that. He should have a family, people to look after him."

"I was in Boston last week, to see Laura's parents and to try to make arrangements for them to become Patrick's guardians." His eyes became puffy, and his voice started to break. "They wouldn't even meet with me. They had their lawyer handle the discussion. They had no interest in seeing Patrick, none at all; in fact, they were offering a sizeable amount to have me keep the boy away. I was stunned, confused, and disgusted. I demanded an explanation, and was provided one, much to my chagrin. The Hornes were not Laura's biological parents; she had been adopted. The lawyer showed me a certificate from The Ward Home for Children in Bolton, Massachusetts. I shrugged, what difference did that make? Apparently it made a significant amount, at least in the minds of the Hornes. They had been told that Laura had been the daughter of a Swedish millworker, and that her features were common amongst those people. It is true that dark hair and sloe eyes are often a Scandinavian feature, and so the Hornes adopted the child, proud of her Northern European ancestry, which was similar to their own. In the last few years, however, certain irregularities concerning children at The Ward Home had come to light. Paperwork was falsified, and ancestries often simply created out of nothing but fancy. According to one matron who could no longer tolerate the situation, many of the children weren't from Bolton at all, but rather from farther east. It was suggested that many of the infants were from villages on the coast, where seafaring men of questionable morals often came back from voyages with wives of exotic natures. The implication was plain: Laura was not of Swedish descent, but rather was probably a child of a low-born shipmate and his swarthy Pacific island bride. The Hornes wanted nothing to do with her, or her child. They had no proof, of course, there was no proof either way, but the rumors were enough, and the embarrassment had driven the two elderly and genteel Bostonians into seclusion until the whole matter was forgotten. They would be leaving for an extended stay in London, and having Patrick with them or waiting for their return was too much of a reminder that they may have been played for fools. I took their bribe; it didn't matter to me that it was blood money: Patrick might need it one day. I took it and went immediately to Knickerbocker's and set up a trust."

"Patrick will be well looked after. My sister is a spoiled child who never grew up, but I know that she will take care of Patrick, and make sure that he grows to be a fine man. She'll have oversight, of course; Knickerbocker's has assigned a man to administer the trust, to make sure the boy is not taken advantage of. It isn't what I wanted, but it'll have to do. I just wish I could do more."

He paused and settled; this time I was able to speak. "But why travel to Arkham?" As soon as I said the words I knew the answer, for I had read the reports concerning The Ward Home myself.

He harrumphed. "Arkham is merely a waypoint, Mr. Peaslee. I will do some research there, and then I will make some inquiries, some demands in Bolton. The Hornes' lawyer didn't just give me money; he also gave me the paperwork that he had uncovered concerning Laura's birth and adoption. There is a curious notation on those forms. A note I don't understand. One that has disturbed me, and scratched at the back of my mind for the last few days. It won't let me go, so I'm going to pursue it. I'm not long for this world, but there is a mystery here. A mystery concerning the woman I love; a woman who has been dead almost a decade, and whom I still love more than my own life. I have to know. I have to know who Barnabas Marsh of Innsmouth is and why his name is written on my wife's birth certificate!"

This last outburst seemed to drain the man and he fell into a fit of wheezing and coughing. He clutched at his chest, and I made a move to call the waiter, but he waved me off. "Just too much excitement, Mr. Peaslee, I'll be fine after a short nap."

With that the man seemed to shrink back into his coat, laid his head in the corner where the window met the seat, and closed his eyes. I had been dismissed, without even a word. This, I suppose, is the pre-rogative of the dying man. I wished him well, and he softly muttered his gratitude. I wish I could sleep on trains, I spend enough time on them, but it is a skill I never acquired. Instead I've sat down and filled my journal with these words, the tale of Mr. Dennis, or, The Man on the Train. Why I bothered I wasn't sure, but an investigation of The Ward Home and the involvement of Barnabas Marsh might be in order. There was a warrant out for Barnabas Marsh, the Feds had raided Innsmouth some months earlier for rum running, and hints of worse. Barnabas had been identified as a ringleader, but had escaped capture. In my mind I hoped that a dying man might have the drive to find and expose the fugitive. I had learned the hard way that dying men have peculiar, nearly supernatural motivations, and to whatever dark and hidden place Barnabas Marsh had fled I supposed it mightn't be far enough to hide him from the prying eyes of Edwin Dennis. After all, who or what could stop a dying man in love with a dead woman?

# CHAPTER 8

# "The Loss of Megan Halsey"
## From the Journal of Robert Peaslee
## April 9 1928

They were waiting for me at the station, Copper and Bacon, patrol-
men who worked the river. They stood there on the platform like two
shadows in the fog waiting for the sun to burn them away, but dawn
was hours away and the lamps of the train, as bright as they were, were
insufficient to the task. As I stepped off the train they came for me
and mumbled something about being ordered to fetch me by Chief
Nichols. I didn't ask how Nichols knew that I was out of town, or how
he knew on which train I was returning. I accepted it as just another
quirk of living in a small town. I grabbed my travel bag and with as few
words as possible fell into step behind the two beat cops. Bacon had the
odor of cigarettes and cheap perfume about him, while Copper reeked
of garlic; a byproduct of his Italian wife's cooking. Neither one was
pleasant to smell, but compared to the rest of the boys who worked the
harbor, they were a regular bouquet. I didn't need to ask why they were
there and they didn't say. When the chief sends two men to meet me at
the rail station in the wee hours of the morning it can only mean one
thing: someone is dead, and Chief Nichols would rather have me deal
with it than have it fall on his shoulders.

I can't say I blame him. Given that choice I would do the same.
It's not as if I didn't have a history, didn't have the experience. This
is the job I signed on to do; no sense in whining about it when it has
to be done. I never planned for this to happen. I never woke up and
said, "Today, I've decided to become a detective, but only work on
the truly bizarre cases." I never set out to do this, but somehow or
another, the crimes that no one else would touch became the norm in
my life. My brother, Wingate, always the psychotherapist, would trace
my attraction to these odd cases directly to what happened to Father.

I will admit there may be some truth to his suspicions, but in the end the why doesn't matter, it won't change what needs to be done, or that I need to do it.

I thought Bacon and Copper would bundle me into a car. Instead we continued on foot, turning south on Garrison, crossing over the soot-stained viaduct over the rail, and then made our way over the Miskatonic River itself. The wind whipping off the water was bitterly cold, and tore through my coat and wormed its way down my neck and across my back, making me shiver as I crossed. The river reflected back the amber lights of the bridge and the streets. The dark waters made the reflected light pale and gray and played with the reflections and shadows of the warehouses that lined the other end of the causeway. As we made our way north on River Street I watched shadowy figures step back into darkened alleyways and doors. The Docks have a well-deserved reputation for smuggling and other less-savory activities, and I'm sure my presence made the men here nervous, just as I was sure that Copper and Bacon represented no threat to the factions of crime, organized or not, that had taken root there.

I was led past the waterfront, and I could feel the following eyes of old men haggard from age and wind and the salt of the sea. They were preparing their boats to head out at first light. Fishing takes a toll on men, more so than other professions, I think. That there were even fishing boats in Arkham was odd, but ever since the local shops had severed ties with Innsmouth another supplier of fish had to be found, and while Kingsport would have made more sense, that town had long ago turned most of its harbor over to pleasure craft. Consequently, despite the Miskatonic being a treacherous waterway and not one to be traversed without caution, a ragtag fleet of fishing boats had come to thrive in Arkham.

At Dock Twenty-Three, we turned and moved out over the river. This was a cargo pier, and still vacant of workmen, but piled high with barrels and crates and the turns of ropes that were the stock of life on the docks. As I walked down the creaking boards, gulls, annoyed by my presence, cackled as they waddled out of my way, and I was not sure whether they would continue on their slow walk away from me, or on a whim turn and attack my ankles with hard beaks, sharpened on the boney carcasses of cod and tempered in battles with blue crabs and wayward clams. The dock was a lonely place, cut off from the others by distance and darkness and the hulking ships that clung to the pilings like spiders in the wind. As we reached the end of the pier I saw there were three men huddled there around a single weak light, two fishermen and another patrolman, whom I knew, by the name of Roberts. They were standing over a large indistinct mass that glistened in the light. I could see the tangle of worn and tattered ropes and torn netting that had wrapped themselves around a body. Of course it was a body; why else would I have been summoned. As I drew closer Roberts flicked on another light and played it over the victim so I could see what I was dealing with.

"Watermen found her floating in the river about three hours ago," explained Roberts. "The nets got tangled round on the pylon." I nodded. I didn't believe that to be the whole truth, but whatever the two watermen were hiding likely had little to do with the body. The looks on their faces told me more than I needed to know. They had found it, made the mistake of fishing it out, and then had further compounded their error by reporting it. Busting them for smuggling, or poaching or whatever they were doing, wasn't going to help solve my case. I let them keep whatever secrets they were hiding.

The body was that of a young and fit woman. She was dressed in a heavy coat, over men's trousers, shirt, and a pair of leather boots, but all of this was covered with filth, mud, detritus, and the like. In fact, there was amidst the material a large quantity of red clay, which I recognized as originating in the upper reaches of the river past Dean's Corners near Aylesbury. The implication being that the body had entered the river miles upstream, and then taken days, perhaps even weeks to work its way past Arkham and Kingsport. Days in the water, but as I moved the body it showed no signs of being waterlogged. It was not bloated, nor did the skin show the discoloration I expected. There was no damage to the body either; one would expect a body moving downriver to accumulate wounds through simply colliding with the river bottom, rocks, and branches, but no such injuries were present. Also absent were any scavengers; I saw no leeches, no crayfish, and no crabs. Nothing at all had seemed to worry the body or take an interest in it. It was all very unusual. As I continued to examine the corpse I found no evidence of rigor, suggesting that she had been dead for more than two days.

However, as I lifted her shirt I found there was also no postmortem lividity, no purple or red bruising indicating where the blood had settled in the body. The lack of rigor or lividity suggested that she was newly dead, perhaps only two hours, but the accumulated material suggested otherwise, and it had been more than three hours since she had been hauled up. It was all very strange, but I was sure that once the coroner took a look at the body he would have a logical explanation for all of these contradictions. Perhaps the water temperature along with the constant motion of the body in the water had somehow retarded the normal postmortem processes.

It was then, my examination nearly finished, that I turned my attention to the face. Even in the darkness, her face and hair covered with filth, I could see that she was still as beautiful as she was when I first met her. I knew who she was instantly, and I suppose I startled Roberts and the others when I gasped and then cried out. It was unprofessional of me, and Bacon chuckled at my reaction, but I shut him down with a glance and a raised finger. There on the dock was the body of Megan Halsey, the young girl who had intrigued me so many years ago in Leffert's Corners. There was no doubt in my mind and as I cleared the muck from her eyes I remembered how intelligent and full of life she had been. I also remembered how she had endeared herself to my sister, and how I was going to have to break the news of this girl's death not only to her family but to Hannah as well. I swallowed my emotions and forced myself into doing things by the book, falling into the routine that helps men in my position get through difficult situations. Even so, as I looked at the still and cold form of the girl I once knew, it was all I could do to keep from breaking down, and I found it necessary to focus on the curious and contradictory state of the body to keep me distracted enough to reign in my emotions.

I was not the only one to recognize her: Roberts knew her from the files. Her mother was Elizabeth Halsey-Griffith, who had been widowed twice, but had herself vanished from Arkham back in the spring of 1921. To hear Roberts tell it, the only family the girl had left was a spinster aunt by the name of Amanda who had served as Megan's guardian until she came of age and inherited the combined fortunes of both the Halseys and the Griffiths. She was a member of society, related to families that weren't quite founding fathers, but were close enough to cause trouble.

I took the three beat cops to the side and told them to keep their mouths shut, especially to the *Advertiser*. I had Copper go call for a wagon while Roberts took me home in the patrol car. Bacon gave me some guff for having to stay with the body but I pointed out he had the easiest of jobs; if he would like he could drive me home and then over to French Hill to speak with the aunt, followed by the rest of the day at the Coroner's Office. After that the complaints stopped, and the three men started following orders.

Roberts and I proceeded in silence through the streets of Arkham, letting the drone of the engine drown out any stray sounds while I concentrated on what I had seen and tried to figure out what it all meant. It only took a few minutes to reach the eight hundred block of Sentinel Street, but by then the sun had started to rise and the bakery over which my apartment sat was already in full production. Normally landlords would look poorly on my unconventional hours, but the Silvermans were well aware of my position with the State Police, and were accommodating enough to let me come and go as needed, and always had my choice of day-old breads and pastry. In return I put up with early mornings full of old men yelling at each other in Yiddish. It wasn't the best place to live, but it was mine, and I had grown to love lox and corned beef and schmaltz, though I still missed breakfasts with bacon and sausage.

As I fumbled in my coat for my key ring I dismissed Roberts, who gave me a puzzled look. "I don't expect you to drive me around all day. I just needed to put Bacon in his place. I'm going to go get cleaned up, eat something, and take a quick nap. I'll be at the morgue by nine. After I talk to the Doctor I'll head on over to the Griffith House and talk to the aunt." Roberts still looked at me as if I was doing something wrong. "The girl is dead, telling the aunt now or a few hours from now won't make much of a difference. Now go home to your wife." And with that, I trotted up the walk to my home and assumed Roberts went on to his.

Someday, someone will write a book concerning the mistakes we make when we assume too much.

As I walked through the door and up the stairs I fell into a machine-like routine. While my body took care of necessary maintenance, my mind was preoccupied with the case; at least that was the delusion, the reality was that I had become preoccupied with the victim. I remembered the precocious teenager whom my sister had brought with her to that Catskills resort and how she had charmed me with her intelligence, wit, and innocence. That she had been threatened by an inhuman thing, which I had rescued her from, probably had something to do with the way I was feeling. There was a fire in my belly. I was irrationally angry that Megan Halsey was dead, and I wanted to make sure somebody paid for what they had done to her. That I had no evidence that she had been murdered was irrelevant. Someone had to be held responsible for extinguishing this beacon of light and innocence, and I was determined to be the one who brought that person to justice. Something rational reared its head and made me briefly question why I was so hell-bent on solving this particular death. I had only met her once, but that cool bit of reason was no match for the emotions that were broiling inside me. To all outward appearances I was merely going through the motions of a normal day, but inside I was seething with a desire for vengeance.

It was an hour later, and I was showered and shaved and slathering schmaltz over a thick chunk of bread from downstairs and savoring their fresh-ground coffee, when the knock came at the door. It was a sound I knew all too well; I think they teach it to beat cops on the first day of the job. It is a knock that says I'm not here on a social call, but neither am I here on business. It is a knock that conveys both a sense of trepidation and urgency, and fills the occupant with a sense of unavoidable dread. I have grown to hate that sound, the soft *rap-rap-rap* of bare knuckles on wood, for I more than anyone else know what it might bring. There are times when I would just like to ignore that dread beat and side with my paternal grandfather on the issue. He was a staunch old solicitor, fond of debates concerning what was legal, what was permissible, and what was polite, his favorite saying being, "There is no constitutional imperative to answer the door."

But he wasn't a policeman.

It was Roberts, and as he stood there, fidgeting in his wide size-10 shoes, I knew that the news was not good, that things had somehow gone from bad to worse and that somehow or another I was at fault. I shoved the pastry into my mouth and chased it with a gulp of perfectly brewed java. Like Copper and Bacon before him, Roberts was taciturn, barely saying hello as I grabbed my hat and coat. He had left the car running, and I barely had time to notice that the cold winds of the night had succumbed to the morning sun and it was turning into a rather fine spring day, before I was whisked away.

I would like to say that I was surprised that we were retracing the route we took early that day, but I wasn't. Nor was I surprised to see three police cars at the entry to Dock Twenty-Three. Even the presence of the ambulance and Chief Nichols' Nash didn't seem unusual. I was in it deep and was going to have to bat for the whole nine yards. The dock had been roped off and the coroner was there doing his job while Nichols was screaming at the coroner. The body at the end of the pier wasn't wrapped in a net and rope, and it wasn't a young girl anymore. Lying there on the salt-washed wood was the body of Officer Lyle Bacon, his head lolling off to one side in an entirely unnatural way. There was a bulge in his neck where his broken spine was pushing up from beneath the skin.

The moment I caught Nichols's eye his verbal assault of Copper ceased and he stalked toward me in a fury. "You're supposed to be smarter than this, Peaslee! What the hell were you thinking?"

I tried to stay calm. "I was thinking that Copper was only going to be gone a few minutes. I was thinking that Bacon was competent, that the scene was secure, and that no one could or would be coming down the dock to interfere with a veteran beat cop and a dead body."

A vein on Nichols's neck was beating to its own high-speed drum. "Well, Copper stopped for coffee and to chat up some waitress. By the time he got back Bacon had been killed, his neck snapped by two very powerful hands. Looks like he got a shot off before he was killed, but the weird thing is he was shooting toward the end of the pier and down toward the deck. It's possible that our suspect came out of the river, surprised Bacon, dodged the shot, snapped the man's neck, grabbed the body, and disappeared back into the river, all without being seen by anyone."

"Hell of a thing, coming up on a cop like that, killing him, and losing the body. Very embarrassing to the department."

Nichols harrumphed. "No, not embarrassing, not at all, because no one's ever going to find out. Officially, Bacon was killed when he and Copper came across some rum runner who had just raped and murdered the Halsey girl." He eyed me, wondering if I would play ball. "You got that, Peaslee, or do I have to explain it again?"

I nodded. "I got it. So whoever killed Megan Halsey killed Bacon as well. What about the two watermen who found her?"

Nichols took a drag of his cigar. "I'm not looking for a goat here, son. It's clear to me that whoever killed the girl was in the process of dumping the body when he was interrupted. After you left he came back, killed Bacon, and took the girl's body to hide the evidence." It made sense if you hadn't seen the body, and the red clay that had been caked into it. What Nichols wanted, what he always wanted, was a nice tidy package that he could stamp *Case Closed*. It didn't always matter if the truth got bent along the way. "This is your case, Peaslee. The press is going to be all over you. A killer of a beautiful, young society girl and a cop will make the front page. If I were you I would wrap it up as fast as possible." I knew that meant I had a week before he started bellyaching about my performance.

As Nichols pushed his way past me and marched back toward the street I looked at Bacon and the muddy handprints that had been left on his neck. They seemed small, too small to belong to a working man, and I wondered what kind of monster could take an innocent girl like Megan and kill her. Not the same kind that could kill a cop like Bacon. Nichols thought he was doing me a favor, tying the two cases together, making it clear that if I found one, I had both. The truth, per usual, was more complicated than that. Standing there on the dock I thought about how Lyle Bacon had lost his life, Megan Halsey had lost that and her innocence, and how Chief Nichols had somehow lost his moral compass. If I wasn't careful, I might lose either my job or my need for the truth.

I didn't need to ponder which was more important.

CHAPTER 9

# "The Madness of Amanda Griffith"
## From the Journal of Robert Peaslee
## April 9 1928

Everyone said that Amanda Griffith was mad. She hadn't always been that way. Once she had been quite respectable, but that had been before Megan had come home, before Elizabeth Halsey Griffith had disappeared. If I were to meet Miss Griffith, tell her about Megan, and then proceed to investigate her family, I wanted to know more about her and them. Which meant I had my work cut out for me. From the docks I walked through the city, my collar turned up and my hat pulled down, mulling over what had happened and how I was going to pursue this particular case. I don't consider myself a good detective, I'm not deductive like Sherlock Holmes, or intuitive like Father Brown, or even sly like the Belgian that Hadrian Vargr talks about. I'm not even manipulative and commanding like Vargr; if you gave me a room full of men to command I wouldn't know what to do with them. I'm a bloodhound, pure and simple. You set me on the trail of somebody and I'll lock onto that scent and follow it till the quarry is treed or I'm too bloody to go on, sometimes both. My methods aren't pretty or fancy or even fast, but I get the job done, and the people in charge rarely complain, mostly because the cases I'm assigned are too dirty or dangerous or weird to give to anyone else.

This means I've got to work at being smart, and when it comes to learning about the ins and outs of what goes on in Arkham there's only one place to dig up the dirt. In other towns it would be the city newspaper, but here in Essex County I've found that the Historical Society tends to stick its nose where it doesn't belong and keep files on the more prominent families. Consequently, after slipping the curator a dollar I spent a good part of the morning in the archives, reading the fragile pages and notes accumulated by men obsessed with Arkham's past, familiarizing myself with the life of Megan Halsey. By all rights I should have been over at the Griffith House first thing, but I had chosen instead to learn a little more about the family I was about to devastate with the news that Megan was dead. Imagine my surprise when I discovered that through a series of unfortunate tragedies, the family had dwindled down to a single member.

Those tragedies began long before Megan was born. Her grandfather, Doctor Augustus Hoag, had died in the summer of 1899 when his horse threw him and he tumbled down against the footings of the Garrison Street Bridge. Her grandmother, Honoria, was a daughter of the Kingsport Pikes, a family which had over the years dwindled from greatness to near-destitution, and through despair had reduced its numbers to a single female member. Honoria and Augustus had only one child, Elizabeth, born in 1885, who, shortly after her mother's death in a 1904 Manhattan subway accident, married a friend of her father, the physician Doctor Allan Halsey, a man several decades her senior.

There was some talk about that, gossip mostly, particularly when they extended their honeymoon in New York, but all idle talk was snuffed out when they returned and were greeted by the start of the epidemic. Elizabeth was banished for her own safety, sent to Halsey's cabin in the hills around Dunwich. Allan died, a victim of his fervor to save those who had succumbed to the plague. He was buried swiftly, like so many others, even before Elizabeth could return. She stayed in Arkham for a while, even volunteered at the asylum in Danvers, but then suddenly fled back to Dunwich. When Elizabeth Halsey returned in 1906, she brought with her the infant child that she named Megan, after Allan's mother.

It was only two years later that Elizabeth married the man whom she had hired to handle her financial affairs, the brother of Elizabeth's childhood friend, Amanda; a former suitor by the name of David Griffith. David had a rather stained reputation in Arkham, but after Elizabeth and Megan moved into the Griffith home in South Hill all that changed. Within a few short years David Griffith, his wife, Elizabeth, and Amanda Griffith were central figures amongst the upper crust of Arkham. Sadly, it was not to last. Always a keen businessman, he left Arkham in late April bound for England. He had booked passage on the RMS *Lusitania* and on May 7, 1915, it was targeted by a German U-Boat, killing all on board.

The loss of her second husband must have been too much for Elizabeth Halsey-Griffith, for in 1916 she bundled the ten-year-old Megan off to boarding school in Kingsport. By all accounts Megan was an exceptional student, though she was reported absent from the school on more than one occasion, and was once even picked up on the streets of Boston. This was about the time that Hannah came into her life and brought her to meet me. The papers called her behavior unladylike; I would have called it a result of boredom. Given what I knew of her, and The Hall School where she was enrolled, I found it hard to imagine that she found any satisfaction in the curriculum there. Still, it seemed a better home for her than the Griffith House.

It was in May, five months after I saw Megan in Leffert's Corners, that Elizabeth Halsey-Griffith vanished without a trace. The police in Arkham did what they could, searching the countryside for any trace of the woman, but to no avail. With little recourse, the courts assigned Amanda Griffith as Megan's guardian, and the administrator of the combined Griffith and Halsey estates. One would have thought that Miss Griffith would have comforted her niece, but instead she left the girl enrolled at The Hall School and left for a tour of Australia, Tasmania, New Zealand, and Papua. Amanda Griffith did not return to Arkham until the fall of 1923, and did not rejoin society, but rather became isolated in that great house on South Hill, shunning all visitors and apparently roaming the streets at odd hours of the night.

In May of 1924 Megan Halsey came of age, and with that came a reversal of roles. Suddenly Megan Halsey was in control of the estate and Amanda Griffith was relegated to the role of dependent. Unlike her aunt, Megan seemed to have some sense of the value of things. Certainly she had her fun, but she also made sure that the house was maintained and her social obligations were met. Once, she even took Aunt Amanda with her, but the woman had become such a doddering embarrassment that Megan made sure that she was never seen in polite society again. Even when she left town, which seemed to be often, old Aunt Amanda was left behind.

That was the extent of what I could glean from the files: she had dead grandparents, a dead father, a dead stepfather, and a missing mother. The only person left to mourn for Megan Halsey was appar-ently her crazy Aunt Amanda.

And it was my task to go tell Amanda that her niece was dead.

The Griffith House, 507 West High Street, stood near the top of South Hill, a Victorian masterpiece from the middle of the last century surrounded by manicured lawns that separated it from the wide road, with the boughs of majestic elms casting shade over yard and house alike. It was a neighborhood I hadn't been in for years, but I could recall being here as a child, when my father would bring me to faculty functions. A few blocks one way was the home of the university's librar-ian, Henry Armitage, and down the hill I could make out the copper roof of the Wilmarth ancestral home, and in the other direction the sprawling Georgian mansion of the architect Daniel Upton. Just being on this street brought back memories of my childhood, my family, and my father; these were things I wasn't yet ready to deal with, or perhaps had been dealing with all my life, just in a rather indirect fashion. I opened the gate to Griffith House, and as it closed behind me, I shut my mind to any further thoughts about my own family.

As Victorian mansions go, the Griffith House was rather small. To one side, a long wing capped with a peaked roof jutted out from the front and joined the carriage house to the main structure, while off to the other side a squat tower of one and a half stories brought to mind storybook romances of princesses. Between the two a third tower clung to the structure like a small parasite, with a huge window looking out over the city and the river. This feature I knew to be a cap-tain's walk, and supposed it dated back to when the Griffiths were once involved in shipping. Up the flagstone stairs and onto the gray slate porch, I found a magnificently carved wooden door depicting the face of a sundial. With some trepidation I raised my hand and knocked on the door, using the ominous *rat-a-tat* I had come to loathe. I waited for a moment, but when there was no answer and I could detect no move-ment within, I rapped on the door again.

There was no response.

Undeterred by the lack of answer to my knocking, I cast furtive glances over each shoulder and then confidently proceeded to walk around the squat tower and head toward the backyard. As I did so, I took the opportunity to peek into the tower windows and discovered it contained a small but serviceable library. Once past the tower I found myself under the elm tree and moving along a straight wall with many windows, all of which had drawn curtains through which I could detect nothing. As I moved toward the back of the house the land sloped down, dropping away. This elevated the ground floor beyond my reach, but at the same time presented the cellar level for easy access. Facing the garden, the cellar boasted a large bay window through which I could see a quaint parlor with fine furniture all orientated to take advantage of the view. A door off to the right seemed to be the only access, but also served as a divider, for farther to the right the elegance of the bay window vanished to be replaced by dreary stone walls lacking any windows at all.

Once more I sought entry to the Griffith House, and this time I rapped on the plain wooden door of the cellar. The ancient worn boards swung open with a long and ominous creak. It had not only been left unlocked, but also not even closed properly.

Sheepishly, I peered inside and called out, "Hello, anyone home?" To my left, the parlor room sat unmoving in the dim light. To the right, an open door revealed a root cellar lined with canned produce, with a thick table in the center where, from the implements and fat cookbook that it bore, apparently most of the canning was done. In this room an oil lamp burned, providing some light, but also suggesting that someone had been about, and quite recently. Again I called out, hoping my voice was loud enough to penetrate the depths of the house.

There came a response, but not from the direction I had expected. Instead there came from the garden a rustling in the hedgerow accompanied by the huffing and puffing sound of someone struggling through the brush. The woman who emerged from the overgrown garden was wearing a thick cotton dress and a pleated jacket that both had once been white, but with age and filth had turned gray with flecks of green and brown. Her hat was no longer even identifiable as to style and had faded into the same smear of color that her dress had become. I had thought, I had hoped, that this was merely some form of ancient overdress that had simply become the most comfortable thing to wear while out working in the yard, but it soon became apparent that this was not the case. As she moved out of the garden and into the sun, I saw that she wore nothing underneath and hadn't changed out of this particular outfit in some time. The smell was palpable, and as she approached I had to suppress my desire to gag; how the small dog that she cradled in her arms could stand it I didn't know.

As she entered the clearing she looked up, and for an instant glanced in my direction. "David, dear, come help your sister, would you?"

Despite her mistake I moved to comply and with a few steps was at her side, holding her arm. "I'm not David, Miss Griffith, my name is Robert Peaslee. I'm with the State Police. I need to speak to you about your niece."

"Megan?" The older woman's voice broke. Closer up, she wasn't that aged, not much older than me. "Megan's away at The Hall School."

I shook my head as she shuffled around me through the back door. "She graduated years ago. She has been living here, hasn't she?"

Amanda Griffith paused to stare at me. "Megan? She comes and goes. She's like her mother, never could stay comfortable in one place. Restless."

We passed to the right and she set the dog down on the table next to the book. It was a small thing, a spaniel of some sort, I thought, damp and shivering from the cold. She had the dog by the scruff of the neck with her left hand while she leafed through the book with her other. The pages were ancient and I could see that it had been printed in Latin with extensive woodcut illustrations. She caught me eyeing the volume and smiled.

"This book has been in my family for generations. We thought it lost when my Great Uncle Cyrus's house was struck by lightning back in '86. No one had seen it, or Uncle Cyrus, for fifty years, then I'm cleaning up some old trunks in the attic and there it was, as if it were waiting for me. Of course, I had never seen it before, only heard stories, but I knew what it was right away; there are few books that could be confused with Pigafetta's *Regnum Congo*."

The title didn't sound familiar. "I'm afraid I've never heard of it . . . a cookbook of some sort?"

Suddenly Miss Griffith was chuckling. "You could say that. I wouldn't, but you could." Her hand grabbed something long and sharp. It flew through the air in a swift motion that set me stumbling back in fear. The dog yelped. Something hot and wet splashed onto my face. I fumbled with my holster and pulled my pistol out. The dog was kicking, its throat cut, kicking and gasping, desperate for life. The book on the table was suddenly pointed in my direction. I could see the picture that Amanda Griffith had been looking at. The image was centered about a primitive butcher shop, but one that could only have come from a nightmare. Human limbs and quarters hung on the walls while two naked women haggled, hoping to trade a string of pearls for a torso. At a table, two men flayed another, and a third held a severed head while gleefully sucking the meat off the fingers of a dismembered arm. In the foreground, a small child lay roasting on a grate over a fire pit.

She looked at me with a gleam in her eye and the knife dripping blood. "They say meat makes blood and flesh, and gives you new life. Have you ever wondered what would happen if that meat was more like your own?" I was panicked, my eyes darting around, searching the root cellar for options. There in the corner I saw the net and the rope still wet from the river. She noticed that I had found what she was hiding. "Megan brought that home this morning. She's always bringing home the strangest of things." There was a sudden look of realization on her face. "Well, she won't be doing that anymore."

She took a step forward and I panicked. I suppose in a way I had been threatened. She had the bloody knife in her hand, there was the book, with those awful pictures, and of course the suggestion that she had done something, something horrible with Megan's body. Without even thinking I let thunder and lightning erupt from my hand, not once but multiple times. The room filled with the smell of gunpowder and death. Amanda Griffith was cackling as the first three bullets carried divine retribution into her body. The fourth one caught her in the head and spun her around, leaving a trail of blood and brain and bone arcing through the air, painting the walls. She hit the floor and blood spurted from the holes in her back where the bullets had passed through. I watched as she twitched violently and then went still.

I dropped the gun to the floor, trying to separate myself from the action and the cause, but at the same time knowing that it was all over, or almost. On the table, the dog was still gasping, drowning in its own lifeblood, which was now running across the table and onto the floor where Amanda lay. It wasn't right, what she had done to that poor animal, but at least I had avenged it. At least it had lived longer than her. I wrapped both hands around the dog's head and snapped its neck, ending its suffering, ending its pain.

Just as I had ended the madness of Amanda Griffith.

# CHAPTER 10

# "The Haunting of Griffith House"
## From the Journal of Robert Peaslee
## May 1 1928

It was twelve days after I killed Amanda Griffith that I moved into her house, and just four days later that I realized the place was haunted.

It was only minutes after I had fired my revolver, ending the life of Amanda Griffith, that a police car arrived to investigate, called no doubt by a neighbor startled by the sound of certain death breaking the quiet in the normally sleepy South Hill. They found me standing over the body, cradling the dead dog, blood running down my suit. For a brief second I had a gun pointed at my head, but thankfully somebody on the force recognized me, and cooler heads prevailed before another shot fired in panic ended my life. At first they thought me mad, but then they saw the dog and the book and the knife still clutched in her hand, and they knew that I was anything but.

We spent three days going through the house and the garden, but besides the rope and nets we found no sign of Megan Halscy. Still there was no shortage of bodies. By some estimates we recovered more than three dozen skeletons of cats and dogs, and what appeared to be squirrels, raccoons, and even opossums. Interviews with the local butcher and grocer found that deliveries to the house had been repeatedly canceled by Amanda only to be reinitiated by Megan a few days or weeks later. I guessed that Amanda had been living off of neighborhood pets and wild animals off and on for several months.

Her diet, however, could not account for what was found during the autopsy. The cause of death was without any doubt the bullets I put through her chest and head. However, as the coroner, Doctor Morton, assisted by the Griffith woman's personal physician, Stuart Hartwell, discovered, I only hastened her death. Inside her skull they found that her brain had suffered some sort of organic degradation, and had shrunk or been diminished by almost half. So startled were the two physicians that they both took extensive samples and photographs and fully expected to collaborate on a publication detailing what they called an Arkham variant of something called Creutzfeldt-Jakob Disease. I found the whole exchange between the two medical men extremely morbid.

A brief hearing was held in which the District Attorney, supported by the Chief of Police, argued that Amanda Griffith had been responsible for the death of Megan Halsey and Officer Bacon. Judge Hand pinned the murder of Bacon on Griffith, but attorneys for the family argued that without the body it was hard to prove that Megan Halsey was dead, let alone that her aunt had murdered her. Three of us testified as to seeing the body and making a positive identification, but for Hand and the lawyers that didn't matter. Megan Halsey was declared missing and her estate, including Griffith House, was turned over to the Saltonstall family firm to administer in her absence.

It took me a whole day to work up the nerve to go see Saltonstall. The Chief was busy patting me on the back, congratulating me on solving the case so quickly and cleanly. I didn't have the heart to tell him that I didn't think the Griffith woman had been guilty of either crime. She may have been sick, and she may even have been a maniac, but I couldn't see how a woman like that could have killed a strong girl like Megan, let alone a veteran cop like Bacon, and then dragged the body somewhere to conceal it. It didn't make sense to me. There was a failure in the logic somewhere. Still, I never said any of this to the Chief.

But I told it to Saltonstall.

As an officer of the State Police there were things I couldn't do. I certainly couldn't be hired out as a private investigator to search for Megan Halsey and her killer; that would have been viewed by the Chief as undermining his authority. However, the law firm had just become responsible for the Halsey-Griffith properties and would need a caretaker for the house on High Street. I could live there rent free, as long as I maintained the place and didn't do any damage. If I chose to go through the contents of the house, and those led me to Megan Halsey or her killer, so be it. It was an odd arrangement to be certain, and I would be regularly visited to make sure I was doing my part, but I could think of no better way to investigate what was essentially a closed case.

It took me less than a morning to pack up my stuff and move out of the room above the bakery. I was going to miss the free stale pastries, but not the caterwauling arguments, and the pots and pans banging together in the sinks. I would also have to get accustomed to other differences. In my old neighborhood everything I wanted was just a few minutes away; now in South Hill I was faced with the fact that the grocer, the butcher, and any diners were blocks away. There were several merchants who made regular deliveries to the area, but the idea of planning a menu for meals several days in advance was entirely unfamiliar to me. I had fallen into the habit of a bachelor, eating whatever struck me as reasonable, depending on what was available and relatively inexpensive. Saltonstall had suggested I hire a housekeeper to handle my cleaning and meals, but this seemed a lavish expense. Surely, I reasoned, I could care for my own needs.

I hadn't realized the size of the house.

The front door of the Griffith House opened to a foyer decorated in dark brown woods. To the right, a short set of stairs led up and into the tower which housed the Griffith library. A little farther down the foyer, another door on the right provided access to a master suite, complete with a private bath and a large dressing room with stairs that led down into the cellar. Moving left out of the foyer was a wide hall that functioned as a gallery displaying portraits of the family, but also a wide variety of statuettes and wall hangings. To the left, with windows facing the street, was a tastefully appointed salon, while opposite, with French doors opening onto a balcony, was the formal dining room. Continuing down the gallery hall, there were stairs leading both up and down, and then a door leading to the carriage house. A large pantry and store room occupied the corner of the house, and also functioned as a tradesmen's entrance. As the hall curved to the right it opened up into a large keeping room with worn but comfortable furnishings arranged around a central fireplace. Beyond the fireplace, with doors on either side, was a conservatory filled with tropical plants including fruit and spice trees. Opposite the fireplace, the back of the keeping room connected to the spacious kitchen, which included a small nook suitable for informal meals. A small butler's pantry connected the kitchen to the dining room.

Going up the stairs, at the first landing, a set of double doors led to a covered porch on the roof of the carriage house. Taking the stairs to the next landing placed one in the middle of a central hallway, at either end of which were large suites with private baths. Between them, overlooking the garden, were two smaller bedrooms which shared a bath. On the front of the house there was a comfortable office, and next to it a captain's walk, which also doubled as an upstairs library.

Down in the basement, the stairs offered two choices. To the left was a billiards room, complete with an ornate bar that would have been more at home in a speakeasy. A whole wall of spirits remained, but judging from the accumulated dust, hadn't been touched in years. To the right was the sitting room with the large windows looking out over the garden. Near the door was the access way to the root cellar where Amanda Griffith and I had encountered each other. On the far side of the sitting room was a door that led to a small but quaint apartment, complete with bedroom, bath, and small kitchen that I assumed functioned as a quarters for a live-in domestic. Toward the back of the sitting room, set behind the stairs, was an alcove full of crates and spare chairs which concealed a set of glass-paned doors. Beyond these was a room with large tubs and running water that appeared to function as a private laundry. A door along the wall led to a large wardrobe with stairs leading up back to the dressing room of the master suite.

While the layout of the house seemed straightforward, and I could discern the functions of most of the rooms quite easily, some things perplexed me. The master suite had clearly once been occupied by a man, and some photographs and papers suggested that it had been David Griffith, but he had been dead for eight years and in all that time it appeared no one had touched the room. More so, the furnishings and accoutrements of the room suggested that only David had lived in this room. It led to the question of why were none of Mrs. Griffith's affects present. I found the clothes and personal items of Elizabeth Halsey-Griffith in one of the smaller bedrooms upstairs, the one that shared a bath with the other small bedroom, in which I found what assuredly were the belongings of Amanda Griffith. As for the two large upstairs suites, I determined that one had been used as a nursery for the young Megan Halsey, while the other had apparently been transformed for her use as an adult, once she had returned home and become master of the house. The sixth bedroom, the one in the basement apartment, had not been used for quite some time, and, while still furnished, showed no signs of any personal items that might identify a former occupant.

For several reasons I decided that I would occupy the master suite on the ground level. While such a decision might seem straightforward, it being the largest of the rooms, this actually did not factor into my decision. David Griffith had been dead for years, and was unlikely to be a player in my investigation into Megan's death, thus I could safely pack up and move his belongings without rigorously going through them. Additionally, I could move those belongings down into the basement quite easily by using the private stairs in the dressing room. This also allowed me to close off the upper level and limit the amount of area I had to routinely clean and heat. Finally, as I was going to go through the effects of all the women who had dwelled in Griffith House, Megan, Amanda, and Elizabeth, it would be easy to use the office and the captain's walk as a place to organize materials that I either wanted to examine, or had finished doing so. All the actual work could be done in the library on the main floor. In this manner the clutter of my work would be contained and kept from the eyes of any visitors. Thus, my first day was spent cleaning out the rooms that had once belonged to David Griffith.

It had been my plan to use a number of trunks from the basement, mostly steamer and cabin trunks made by the Seward Company, but some from Leatheroid Manufacturing, to store all of David's clothes. However, as I began to pack these things away I realized that not only had he and I been of similar builds, we also had the same taste in styles, and much of what had once been fashionable dress a decade ago, was still in common use in 1928. So as where I only had brought with me a handful of shirts and pants, and a single jacket, by using David Griffith's wardrobe I suddenly had more than a dozen options of each. There was, however, the problem that the clothes had not been cleaned in some time, and I went about organizing them for delivery to a laundry. This proved somewhat enlightening about Mr. Griffith as his pockets were full of the most unusual items, including betting stubs, IOU markers both in his name and others, and a number of matchbooks, often from restaurants or clubs, and often with a woman's name and number written on the inside. This itself was not damning, but I knew several of the locations from which the matchbooks originated and also knew that they had not been in existence before David and Elizabeth had been married. All of this set my mind in motion and I quickly concluded that David Griffith had not only been a frequent gambler, but was also likely a philanderer.

As I moved the materials about I noticed the inevitable: I was not the sole resident of the house. Behind crates and trunks, in the back of drawers, and in forgotten corners there was the telltale sign of mice, something that I had fully expected. Not content to share my home with such vermin, I found a box full of traps in the cellar and set them about in key locations, most in the basement, but others in the kitchen and pantry, and one in my bedroom, under a dresser. Thankfully, the linens had been properly stored, and I found David's oversized bed joyously comfortable.

Everything was tidy by early evening and just after six I put on my coat and walked down the hill into the next neighborhood to a little Italian restaurant that I knew. Not a particularly fancy place, but they make meatballs with a touch of sausage, Parmesan cheese, and a liberal amount of oregano. They also had, available to select customers, some very fine Calabrian wines, which they served in a back room, far from the prying eyes of the other diners. I will admit that on that night I may have overindulged, both on the food and the wine, but I had reason to celebrate, even if it was just moving into a new home. I cannot recall exactly, but I may have finished off an entire bottle, perhaps even two. It was near midnight when I finally stumbled out of the restaurant and back onto the streets of Arkham. The night air was cool, but it felt good as I climbed the dark and empty streets of South Hill.

This part of Arkham was so different from the tenements of French Hill, or the university, or even the merchant district of Northside. The slope let me look out over the city and the river that ran through it and for a moment the rows of streetlights and the bridges and the dark empty stretch that marked the Miskatonic reminded me of Paris and the Seine. It had been a decade since I had first seen that wondrous metropolis, and I could still remember walking through the winding labyrinth of its rues and avenues in the company of my fellow agents. Our guide that first night had been a local detective, Frederic Belot, an affable man who was rather annoyed at being assigned to chaperone a party of foreigners. Thankfully, Chan, always the most empathic of our coterie, noticed the distress of our host and was able to steer the conversation toward police work, and thus put Inspector Belot at ease. That night, like this one, I consumed too much wine, and in our revels ended up in a strange little club where we indulged in a brandy tinted with extracts of stygian black lotus. It was a powerful narcotic and hallucinogen, and the visions I and the others endured that night were both wondrous and terrifying. The liquor had heightened our senses and altered our perceptions of the world and our place in it. The effects lasted only for a few hours, but the resulting understanding of certain esoteric mysteries lingered for days; even now it seemed that I could see more, understand more, and conceive of more than the average person. Whether that was a result of my tragic upbringing, the tainted brandy, or of the experiences that I had endured through the years I could not say, but I recalled that I still had a small flask of that tainted brandy, hidden inside a hollowed-out copy of De Sade's *Justine*, secreted away in case I ever needed it again. It was something I hadn't thought of for years, and I was suddenly struck with an ominous feeling that I might soon have no choice but to partake in a few drams of that mysterious liquor.

As I made my way down High Street all such woolgathering suddenly vanished, as what I saw set my heart beating at an anxious pace. There, just above the surrounding trees, I could see the upper story of Griffith House, including the prominently octagonal window that marked the captain's walk. It was there in that weird cyclopean aperture that I saw an unmistakable flickering light moving back and forth in the room. Despite my elubriation my mind jumped to the obvious conclusion: someone was in my house, in the very rooms where the clues to Elizabeth's disappearance and Megan's death were possibly hidden. My hand instinctively went to the holster that I wore beneath my jacket and I broke into an unfettered run.

My boots slammed out a rhythm as they pounded down the sidewalk. I took the ancient wrought iron gate at a run, slamming through it. It let out a loud screech followed by a terrific clang as the metal crashed against the stone pillar that held it in place. As the gate reverberated, the light in the window suddenly stopped moving. The intruder had heard me coming and I assumed he had set his lamp down as he fled, not that it mattered; there was only one way down from the upper level and I was most certainly going to be waiting at the bottom of those stairs.

I burst through the front door and cleared the foyer in bounding but sure steps. I took the corner fast and careened off the far wall before sliding into position at the base of the stairwell. It was only then that I remembered the door that led to the covered porch that sat atop the carriage house. I cursed my poor memory and dashed up the first flight to the landing. The double doors were closed and locked, and I turned to face the second flight of steps that led up into the uninviting darkness of the second-floor hallway. Cautiously, I crept up the stairs, feeling along the wall for the switch that controlled the electric lights. It took a moment or two but I finally found the control and in an instant the lights sprung to life, banishing the menacing darkness and allowing me to see to both ends of the house.

To my left, all the doors were closed, but to the right, several doors were ajar, including the ones that led to the captain's walk and Megan's adult bedroom, and from the former room I could see the weak amber light of an oil lamp. I took a careful step forward, but try as I might the old floor creaked under my weight, revealing my position, as if turning on the light hadn't done that already. Frustrated with my own ineptitude, I dashed down the hall and without a hint of caution threw myself into the captain's walk, my gun leading the way.

It was perhaps the most idiotic thing I had done in years, and thankfully it didn't cost me my life. Except for the dying flame of an oil lamp, the room with the great octagonal window was empty. Still fearful, I stuck a hand into Megan's room and turned on that light as well. Like the hallway and the captain's walk, the bedroom was empty, and a suspicion slowly crept into my brain. I had used that same oil lamp earlier in the day, and in the captain's walk where the sole electric light was terribly positioned, and I was certain I had left it right where it now sat. Could I have left it lit? It was possible. I had no recollection either way, nor could I remember looking back at the house as I walked to dinner. What, then, could account for the flickering movement of the light I had observed as I had approached? Just then I heard the gentle breeze rustle through the great elm that occupied the side yard, and as my eyes shifted I saw the branch outside the window shift slightly, and the streetlights beyond vanished momentarily. Even in my drunken state I realized, however belatedly, that the same movement coupled with the flickering light might generate the illusion of a moving light. If the observer was intoxicated, the possibility of misinterpretation would be even greater. I thought back to how many times I had interviewed witnesses who had ultimately turned out to have embellished their accounts, and realized that like them I was suddenly narrating a story in which I saw only what I wanted, and reported inferences and supposition as fact. I had become the entirely unreliable narrator of my own account. Frustrated, I extinguished the oil lamp, wandered down the hall and stairs, turning the lights off as I went. I found my bed, the bed that I had never before slept in, and collapsed into it. Within moments I was asleep, I wish I could say peacefully, but that had not happened for years. But at least I slept, and for me that is often solace enough.

I woke the next morning to the sound of church bells and a hangover. One I could ignore, the other I could not, but I hoped to banish the latter with coffee and sausages and an elixir purchased at the local pharmacy. It amazed me that despite prohibition the number of headache cures available continued to rise. I had always been told of the effectiveness of the Prairie Oyster, but had, while in Britain, discovered Dr. Vesalius's Restorative and had been completely convinced of its effectiveness. Stumbling around in the kitchen, I noticed that the mousetraps had been sprung, but had failed to catch anything.

After breakfast I lounged about for half an hour and then committed to spending the day going through the papers in Megan's room, though the first order of business was to make both the office and the captain's walk habitable. This entailed removing the old books and taking them down to the library, and boxing up family papers that had lain untouched for years, if not decades. Most of this consisted of ledgers and correspondence between the Griffith family and their various business partners. Also here were files concerning the health and welfare of each family member, including birth certificates, medical records, school diplomas, and the like. While it may have been less than ethical on my part I perused each file at length and discovered some puzzling facts. In one file, I discovered a note from his psychoanalyst detailing the extreme breadth and deep entrainment of David

Griffith's aquaphobia. In another I found that the same therapist had diagnosed Amanda Griffith as suffering from female hysteria, including bouts of chronic sapphism. In Elizabeth Halsey's file I discovered an array of notes concerning numerous minor injuries including bruises, bites, and cuts, all of which had occurred in the time shortly after her first husband's death. Attached to these was a letter from the director of Sefton Asylum asking that she cease her charitable visits to the hospital. There was a vague threat that if she returned, the director would have no choice but to notify the authorities of her indiscretions. There was even a file for Megan, and in it a birth certificate, albeit in poor condition with the date of birth obscured but her name clearly spelled out, as was that of the man who had delivered her, Doctor William Houghton of Aylesbury.

After a few hours of this I had accumulated a rather large pile of trash consisting of unintelligible receipts, boxes, and water-damaged papers which as best as I could determine had no value to my investigation or to anyone else. Wanting to dispose of this refuse, I wandered down to the cellar where a barrel was kept for storage of combustible items. It was the simplest of tasks and should not have created controversy in any manner. Yet as soon as I took the lid off the barrel I discovered the most startling of things. There in the bottom were the bodies of three mice, still fresh, their bodies pinched in that queer manner that comes from being caught in a trap. I quickly raced about the house and discovered that three of the traps I had set had been sprung, but there were no bodies pinned beneath the arm. Confounded, I reset the traps, all the time wondering how and who had disposed of the bodies, for it certainly had not been me.

This was but the first of many events that I could not rationally explain. Of course, I tried to rationalize it. Perhaps Saltonstall had hired a cleaning woman for me, and it had been she who had disposed of the rodents. Perhaps this even explained the oil lamp left burning in the upstairs window. Yet would not such a person leave a note? And if a cleaner had been hired there was no evidence of her work anywhere else in the house. Alternatively, I suspected that perhaps there was an intruder in the place, one who either had a key, or came and went by means of an entrance I did not know about. Yet once again the question rose as to why the traps were emptied and nothing else seemed out of place. It was a conundrum, and I will admit that a sneaking thought concerning my own memory wormed its way into my brain. In the end I laughed it off as a failing of my own memory. Surely I must have been awoken in the middle of the night by the sound of the traps being sprung, and then in a half-awake stupor emptied them, fully intent on resetting them in the morning. Only my semiconscious mind had forgotten the event entirely, and therefore I had not attended to the traps as intended. In a matter of hours I had brushed the whole affair aside, satisfied with what was the most logical of possibilities. Except, deep down in the pit of some dark corner of my mind, something small and insubstantial churned about and whispered doubt into my ear.

The rest of the afternoon was uneventful. I finished cleaning the two rooms, and then began the process of examining the contents of Megan Halsey's room. I gave a perfunctory examination of her wardrobe and the objets d'art that were scattered about the room, but found nothing of real interest amongst these. However, after using a knife to force the lock on her rolltop desk I found myself with an immense number of documents, mostly related to the business of running the family estate, but many of a personal nature as well.

The first thing that caught my eye was a small report written by my brother, the psychologist Wingate Peaslee, being an evaluation of Megan Halsey when she was a child. More specifically, it was a summary of results from various tests he had administered to the girl to evaluate her intelligence and behavior. The details were beyond me, but words such as *precocious, savant, genius,* and *inherited eminence* were all frequently used, as were the terms *psychosis* and *empathic*. It was apparently this evaluation along with my brother's recommendation that initiated Megan's enrollment at The Hall School. That Megan was intelligent came as no surprise to me, but I had not realized that she was considered a genius. That such a life had been snuffed out filled me with a sense of profound loss, and for just a moment I mourned the loss of what might have been.

As interesting as the report was, the most visually attractive was a rather ornate volume with silver tooling and a matching clasp lock. The key was nowhere to be found, but the book popped open easily under application of a knife, and revealed itself to be the diary of Megan Halsey. The pages were full of cramped but neat handwritten notes dating back to the start of her attendance at The Hall School all the way up until earlier this year. This book became one of the first items that I placed into the crate for detailed reading, and marked the beginning of what I soon began to think of as the documents in the case of Megan Halsey.

Rummaging around in the desk, I found several other documents that were of interest, including letters addressed to Megan from her mother and aunt, but also copies of the wills for both ladies as well as one belonging to David Griffith. Also included was a rather large document in an envelope bearing the seal of the Bank of England. Finally, there were several deeds to various properties scattered throughout Arkham and a few elsewhere in the Commonwealth. All of these found their way into my crate for further review.

As the number of documents increased I began formulating a strategy to review them. However, despite the fact that I was formulating an efficient and well-thought-out process for evaluating what I had found, my mind kept wandering back to the diary that Megan had kept. For some strange reason I was drawn to that small volume of private thoughts and though I knew it to be highly unlikely to provide any clues, I decided that this would be the first document I would read. I took my crate of documents into the office and left it there, carrying the diary downstairs, where I could enjoy an afternoon snack and a cup of coffee.

I have called Megan's diary a small book, but the truth is it covered eight years of regular entries, each of quite some length. Surprisingly, the young lady had a most interesting view on life, and had developed a style of writing that seemed to draw me into the rich and lush world that she described. I will not summarize the contents of the diary, that is entirely unnecessary, but I must say that as I read page after page and the minutes became hours and the hours drifted into the evening, I felt in Megan a kind of kinship. This young girl, so wondrously intelligent, had become isolated from her family and instead found comfort in the few equals she could find at The Hall School, namely my sister, Hannah, and a woman called Asenath Waite. It made me happy to know that Hannah had not only been Megan's mentor, but her friend as well, though all three occasionally received a tongue-lashing from the headmistress.

I had become so enthralled by Miss Halsey's writing that I read deep into the evening and only paused when my stomach protested. I had little in the way of groceries, so made do with a rather thick piece of provolone and a sliced pickle smothered with mustard on rye bread. It was not much of a supper but it quelled my hunger and allowed me to quickly return to the task at hand. When the clock chimed nine times I realized that the shadows about the house had grown deep and even though I had taken leave and was not expected at the office, it was time for me to retire. I read a few more pages of the diary by candlelight, but then put the book down on the nightstand and slept. As always, my night was fitful and more than once I woke covered in sweat, my pillow damp and my hair moist. As usual, I flipped the pillow and shifted away from the now-wet blankets and sheets. There was in this an odd kind of comfort. A routine, no matter how unsettling eventually becomes not only accepted but longed for as a representation of the status quo, of normalcy, no matter how strange that may be.

It was late Monday morning when I realized that something strange had happened during the night. I had wandered upstairs to take another look at Megan's bedroom. This time I was more thorough, flipping the mattress, opening picture frames, and flipping through books before once again returning to the rolltop desk. There, amidst the papers that I had yet to go through, I found another copy of my brother's report on Megan Halsey. I thought it odd that she would have two copies of the document, but then I looked again and found duplicate copies of the wills as well. Perplexed, I took the documents back to the office with the full intent of comparing both sets and making sure they were identical. Imagine my surprise when I discovered that the copies I had deposited in the box of documents in the case of Megan Halsey were gone, vanished, no longer in the place where I left them the night before. Somehow, in the night, things, small things, had changed, and I was no longer comfortable believing that I had done it and merely forgotten.

I know there are men who would have left at this point; I'm sure most men would have, but I was not most men. I had seen things, survived things that would have driven others mad, but I was still here, still lucid, and stronger for it, though alienists, particularly my brother, might argue that point. It was true something strange was happening in Griffith House, but I had faced worse, and I wasn't about to scurry away from the task I had set myself. Now that I had read her diary, I was more determined than ever to discover who had killed Megan

Halsey and why, and whatever was happening wasn't going to stand in my way; if anything it only served to steel my resolve.

That afternoon I strolled down the hill to pick up a few things I needed and stopped into a diner for soup and a ham sandwich. On my way back up the hill, I decided to explore my new neighborhood and skipped the turn off Garrison and onto High, and instead tracked down the slope to Saltonstall Street, named for the old family who still served as attorneys for most of the town. I passed the Georgian mansion of the Wilmarth family and a prestigious mansion now operated as a boarding house. Farther on I tramped past the DAR and could just make out the roof of the Miskatonic Club behind it. Crossing West Street I passed a small, well-manicured home which bordered a rather large vacant lot full of overgrown plants and huge trees. Through the great boughs I could see the back of Griffith House and realized that the small gate in the stone wall led to the path that wound through the garden to the back of my new home.

I had not realized the back garden backed up all the way to the other side of the block. I had not entered that part of the property since the day I had shot Amanda Griffith, and had not been part of the team that had scoured the garden for evidence. Still, I knew where the path that lay before me came out, and knew that it led to the cellar door. I don't know why I decided to cut through the garden to Griffith House, but I did. I don't suppose I needed a reason, for it was an entirely reasonable thing to do.

The gate creaked with the annoying metal-on-metal sound that people hate. There was some resistance from the weeds and vines that had grown up and through the frame, but they posed no real problem as the portal swung open and I kicked through the detritus and growth that come from years of neglect. On the sides of the house elms may have dominated the landscape, but here in the back a single, massive red oak stood and spread its branches out to cast shade over the garden. Beneath its boughs shrubs and vines had gone wild and intruded onto the path with various degrees of success. The feral vegetation had climbed up the tree and infested the branches, and between this and the leaves of the oak my sight of the house was effectively blocked as soon as I took a single step off the street.

The path was comprised of crushed oyster shells, common in these parts and cheap to put in and maintain. Some of the better homes use pavers or granite shards, but I have always loved the feel of shell beneath my boots and the sound it makes as it shifts and crushes against others of its kind. You don't get that sound with stones, they're too regular, too apt to settle into place. Oyster shells aren't like that, they rasp against each other, shattering, crushing, crunching, and scraping against each other. It creates a sense of impermanence, of change, of constant motion, not unlike the sea and the beach from whence they originally harvested. I suppose they reminded me of the sea, and the sea has always made me happy.

Farther in, maybe ten steps or so, the oysters became mixed with broken acorns and their caps. The mixture shifted the color and texture of the ground and the comforting crunch of my footsteps became muffled and dull. The path itself was not as straight as I had thought it would be; it curved around the oak, just beyond where the great roots left the surface and disappeared into the ground. It curved around like a hairpin, though once on the far side I could not see through the brambles to where the bend in the trail began. Beneath the tree the spring air was still and quiet. There were no birds flying or singing, no insects either, though given the coolness of the season this was not entirely surprising. There should have been squirrels, though, but maybe they had learned to avoid the area after Miss Griffith had begun her predations.

There was a fork in the path, surprising given the size of the garden, but there it was. I glanced down one direction and then the other. Neither was a straight path to the house, and I could only see a few yards down either before they turned out of sight. I chose one at random, followed it around the curve and past some yews and then some holly. Beyond the holly there was a low stone wall and an open gate. Without thinking, I walked through and found myself not in the yard behind the house, but instead on the sidewalk at Saltonstall, right where I began. Except there hadn't been any holly when I had walked in. I turned back. The holly was gone, as was the path of oyster shell and acorns that had brought me back. Only the oyster shell path remained.

I put my hand on the gate and took a step forward, but then thought better of it. I closed the gate, turned, and strolled down Saltonstall without ever looking back. As I walked, I recalled reports of similar events. There was, of course, the disappearance of Ambrose Bierce, and the temporary loss of Agatha Christie, who to this day still refused to comment on where she had been, and of course the strange events that befell the girls of Appleyard College in Australia. There were other events as well, but these seemed the most poignant, and perhaps the ones that came to mind most readily.

As I entered the house I glanced at the clock and discovered that it was nearly five. Lunch, a trip to the store, and the walk back had somehow or other taken nearly four hours. I fumbled in my pocket for my pocket watch and found that it reported that it was only three in the afternoon. I checked another clock in the house and found that it supported the one in the hall. I had lost two hours while I wandered about in the garden behind Griffith House; the world had spun on, but within the garden things seemed to have slowed down. It was another weird occurrence that would have frightened other men, but for me had become more or less par for the course.

That night over a late supper I let my mind wander about what was happening in Griffith House. The events of the last few days percolated through my little gray cells and rattled around inside the box that held them. I was missing something, there had to be an explanation, but my way of thinking, my reasoning wasn't bringing me any closer to finding it. I needed a new perspective, a new way of thinking, and a new and radical view of the world. As I sat there in the dusk, fumbling with my thoughts and my failures, I hit on a way forward, a way I hadn't thought of before, one that might just help me resolve the issue and discover the truth.

I went to the library, to the box that contained the few books that I had brought with me. There was my copy of *Justine*, and inside its hollowed-out interior was the small bottle of narcotic brandy that Frederic Belot had given me. I tumbled the amber body with the rich murky fluid about in my hands, warming the fluid up to body temperature. I carried it with me to Megan's bedroom and sat down on the bed. I cracked the bottle open and let the heady aroma wash over me. I hesitated for a moment, but only for a moment. Then in a swift and sure motion I brought the small bottle to my lips and drank it dry, letting the liquid drain down my throat and warm my stomach.

I lay back in the bed and let the warmth of the brandy wash over me. I could feel the alcohol working its way through my blood, and with it that strange mélange of narcotic and hallucinogen wound its way into my mind. I could feel the drug go to work on my eyes and ears. My nostrils flared and suddenly I could smell the various distinct scents that permeated the room. They filled my senses, a hint of vanilla from some bit of perfume, some dried cocoa, the intoxicating aroma of moldering books, and even the varnish that had been used to polish the wood. I could smell it all, almost taste it, but not as a single mix but rather as separate streams, as if I could trace each back to its source. The sounds of the house were much the same. I could hear the beating of my own heart, the blood moving through my veins, my breath moving in and out of my lungs. Downstairs, the fire crackled, a log burned, and smoke wafted through the chimney. In the kitchen, the metal of the stove groaned as it cooled and contracted. Somewhere a mouse was searching for a way into the house.

I closed my eyes and concentrated on the events of the last few days, on Griffith House, on the lamp, on the mice and the papers, and the strange garden paths that folded back and then disappeared. I thought of these things and let the idea that perhaps they were connected bubble up out of the deep recesses of my mind. As those bubbles rose they carried me with them, lifting me up out of my body, out of Megan's bedroom, out even of Griffith House. I floated up into the sky, above the property, above the elms and the oak, above the whole town. I saw how the Miskatonic River divided the city in two, and how the bridges connected the two halves of Arkham back together like stitches across a wound. I saw the checkerboard pattern of streets and avenues, and how they had been cut into the hills. I saw all of this and more.

With an extreme force of will I turned my focus back to Griffith House and the secrets that it held. I saw how it had sat in that spot for nearly a hundred years, how the gardens and walls had long ago ceased to be distinct structures, and instead had become a single organic structure. I saw how the roots of that great oak had wound their way through the soil and permeated everything, binding it all together. I saw this, saw how it had grown together and I finally began to understand. Griffith House was a thing in its own right, not entirely alive, but not inanimate either. It breathed and moved in its own manner. It took care of itself, tended to its own needs, and even cleaned up after things. Oh, certainly dust accumulated, as did grime and the other miscellaneous detritus of existence, but in Griffith House books had their place, as did papers and dead mice. There was some force that dwelt there, residing within those walls, making sure everything was nice and tidy.

And this is when I realized that Griffith House was haunted. There was something amiss, something wrong, something alien residing within those walls. It was something that didn't belong. But it wasn't some specter of the dark past, or the revenant of Megan Halsey, or the ghost of Amanda Griffith, or her tragically lost brother.

Griffith House was haunted, haunted by the one thing that didn't belong, the thing that had intruded and disturbed the proper order of things that had existed for years. The disturbing force that I would have to learn to accept, to tolerate, to make peace with if I were to stay in Griffith House, was a phantom of truth and of life.

The thing that had so haunted the ancient edifice was none other than my own self.

It seems that I was the specter that disturbed Griffith House.

And only time would tell if the place would ever come to accept me.

PART THREE

# The Documents in
# the Case of Megan Halsey

# CHAPTER 11

# "Pickman's Marble"
## From the Diary of Megan Halsey
### September 9 1920

I had taken the warm day to wander about the streets of Boston. It really is the most beautiful of cities, much more cosmopolitan than dreary old Arkham, and I must again thank my mother for arranging for me to summer here. The area which I chose to explore was a genteel district comprised of ladies' shops, boutiques, salons, and the occasional antique merchant. Also scattered about were several art galleries, which given my adolescent interests I was immediately drawn to. Finally the caliber of work being produced by American artists has begun to match that done by our European cousins. Beginning to emerge, at least in these Boston galleries, is an overwhelming sense of place and people that I think has been lacking up until now. Particularly notable is the work of Henry Wilcox, whose use of vibrant color in both landscapes and portraits seems unsurpassed in its ability to convey a sense of emotion. I also found the portrait work of Cecilia Beaux to my liking, but to be completely honest I cannot tell you why. Sadly, there are works that I find less than fulfilling. The dark primitivism of Sironi contains no redeeming value that I can see. The free-formed expressions and riots of color produced by MacDonald-Wright, though moving, reveal no real skill. Sime's work shows definite skill, but his content is juvenile and caters to the most puerile of tastes. Angarola seems to handle a similar subject matter but with a wholly more cultured manner. Most stunning were sculptures by Alexander Stirling Calder; I will study the catalog to decide which my favorite piece is.

It was the work of another artist, both a sculptor and painter, that drew me into a strange little shop off the main thoroughfare on a dark little side street, almost an alley. Unlike the other galleries, which took to displaying pieces in front windows to entice potential patrons to enter, the Gallery Giallo seemed to be trying to hide its displays, for the curtains were heavy, moth-eaten, and an utterly distasteful shade of pale yellow. Why would I enter such a place, you might ask? I almost did not, I only stepped down the side street to avoid a rather large crowd coming in the opposite direction, but in that brief moment, in the gap between the curtains, I saw something that intrigued me. A glimpse of gray marble streaked with pink, carved with such mastery that I had to see the entire form.

Stepping inside, I found myself surrounded by the most wild and outré paintings, statues, and crafts I had ever seen. Paintings of otherworldly landscapes crowded the walls, there was an entire case of miniatures depicting charnel rites, pedestals bore strange figurines of clay, metal, stone, and bone, while a low glass case contained strange rings, necklaces, earrings, and tiaras of gold and silver, but proportioned entirely incorrectly for any normal woman to wear. An entire wall was devoted to a single artist, and a small plaque announced that this was Richard Upton Pickman's first exhibition. This young artist's work was both weirdly compelling and disturbing. There were a whole series of paintings set in graveyards, and Pickman's ability to capture the somber dread of such places was uncanny. Yet even more intriguing were the subtle, and in some cases overt, representations of figures that occupied these dreadful landscapes, for their limbs were too long, their heads too sloped, their joints seemed to bend in the wrong direction. Equally frightening was a scene of a surgery in which two physicians were attempting to administer to dozens of patients. One of the surgeons cradled one of the patients, while the other was preparing a syringe of vibrant green fluid. While artistically stunning, *The Waiting Room*, for that is what Pickman had titled it, suffered from some flaws in execution. The dozen or so patients that awaited the doctors were rendered in such a manner that they appeared too still, too inanimate, too lifeless. I understood that the scene was supposed to convey a sense of hopelessness, but perhaps the artist could have added more color to bring a sense of life or animation to the subject.

Turning, I was suddenly confronted by that which had drawn me into the gallery in the first place. It was a statue carved from marble veined in gray and pink, life-sized, or so I assumed, for the subject was a chimera, something ripped from ancient mythology. The head and torso were that of a young woman about my age, with small features and full breasts. Her hair was comprised of dozens of writhing tentacles each about a foot long and covered with rasping suckers. The arms tapered down from the shoulders, and about the wrist suddenly transformed into a pair of large anemones with waving polyps. Below the waist the marine theme continued, for where there should have been some suggestion of downy hair, there was instead a plethora of rough, thorny skin. The lower limbs were fused and the resemblance to the tail of a great gray shark was overwhelming. It was both macabre and beautiful and the artist's achievement was simply magnificent, and magnified by the subtle title Pickman had provided: *The Siren Calls.*

My fascination with the piece must have overwhelmed my senses, for I never heard the man who came up behind me until he whispered in my ear. "Beautiful."

I turned and found myself face to face with an intelligent-looking man, well dressed, wearing glasses beneath a shock of blond hair. "I beg your pardon?" I stammered out.

He gestured toward the statue. "The statue represents one of my greatest achievements." He stepped forward and touched the marble shoulder. "This girl was from Dean's Corners, she was barely sixteen. One of the local boys had become infatuated and took her against her will. When her father found out he called her a whore and threw her out. She was living in the woods when I found her, too ashamed to ask for help. Now look at her, look at what I have made of her."

He tenderly ran his hand through the tentacles of her hair. "I bought these from a fishmonger in Kingsport; the beast they came from was large, easily four to five feet long, and of a species the man did not recognize. It was still alive when he sold it to me, still struggling to survive, teeth rasping, mantle pulsating, tentacles grasping. I was able to sustain it for days, so that I could study it, take notes concerning its movements, understand its anatomy and its beauty." He paused and looked at me for understanding, or perhaps even approval; I smiled and nodded.

His hand drifted down the arms and lingered at the pulpy masses that writhed there. "I found these in the bay on the docks downstream of the pipe where the slaughterhouses discharge their waste. There were hundreds of these anemones covering the rocks. They had grown fat on the blood, bone, and foul entrails that had filtered down the pipe and into the estuary. They had thrived in those waters, propagated themselves amongst those macabre wastes." He wrapped his hand around one of the things and stroked it. "I took that monstrous reality and made it beautiful."

He closed his eyes and lowered his head, resting it on the marble girl's shoulder. "I found the shark on the beach at Falcon Point. It had washed up with the storm the night before and lay gasping on the sand. Even as it lay dying, there was nothing but hate in its eyes. No fear, no pity, no sadness, simply hate. And I took that and transformed it into something else, something entirely different. Something you find beautiful."

I was moved by these words, and by his obvious passion for the work. Never had I met a man who was so moving and moved by the beauty that he saw in life, in all its forms. There was something magnificently powerful about this man and I felt myself compelled to reach out and touch his cheek. As I did so his hand came up and touched mine. There was such a current between us, and my breath suddenly became shallow and rapid. A heat started in my chest and moved up my neck, instantly flushing my face.

He looked me deep in the eyes, and I lost myself as he asked, "What is your name?"

I responded in a whisper, "Megan. Megan Halsey-Griffith."

Suddenly my paramour pulled back. He stared at me as if I had insulted him, and this lasted for almost half a minute before the silence was finally broken. "You are Allan Halsey's daughter," he said, and I nodded to affirm this.

He let go of my hand, and backed away. Another man appeared and handed him his coat and hat. He moved confidently toward the door, paused as he stepped through. "I knew your father." There was a moment of introspection, and then the door closed behind him.

I went to follow him, but the other man stepped in front of me. "Mademoiselle, I could not help but notice your fascination with the statue, would you care to meet the artist, Mr. Pickman?"

A wave of confusion washed over me and I felt my legs go weak. I lost my composure but quickly regained it. "Excuse me, wasn't that the artist I was talking to?" The man politely shook his head. "Then who was he?"

The man ushered me toward the back of the gallery. "He is a friend of the artist. On occasion he supplies models for Mr. Pickman, though this is only, how do you say, a hobby. He is a doctor, a surgeon, I think."

My heart and mind raced. This man, this doctor, what he spoke of frightened me, but he was also magnificently attractive. I had to see him again, feel his hand on my flesh, his breath on my cheek. I had to find him. "Please," I begged, "what is his name?"

The man paused and rubbed his forehead, trying to bring a memory to the surface. Then his eyes went bright and he told me what I needed to know. "His name is West, Doctor Herbert West."

# CHAPTER 12

# "The Inheritance of Megan Halsey"
## From the Diary of Megan Halsey
## May 8 1924

Finally home! Today has been the most frustrating of days. Amanda and I left the house this morning and were in the offices of the family lawyers, Saltonstall and Co., just after they opened. Nice enough people, I suppose, but not ones I particularly want to associate with, very stuffy and officious. I must have signed more than two dozen documents today—the price, I suppose, for being of old money—but I am told that now that I have reached my majority I hold responsibility for the family estate. That estate is both larger and smaller than I was led to believe. That may sound like a contradiction, but it is true, and a source of much friction between me, Aunt Amanda, and a few men who have apparently been drawing funds from the estate without much oversight for years.

I say estate, but the truth is much more complicated than that, now that I am of age and there is not simply a single monolithic fund administered by my aunt anymore. The first part of the morning was spent disentangling me from my aunt. As of today, we each own 40 percent of Griffith and Son, the company that owns a substantial amount of the Arkham waterfront and several cargo vessels. By the terms of my mother's will I own my father's house on Derby Street, the property upon which the Halsey Elementary School rests, Crowninshield Manor, and the Griffith House, albeit with the stipulation that Amanda be allowed to reside there for as long as she so wishes. Besides the real property and corporate holdings, there were also family monies to divide, of which the vast majority was bequeathed to me, and a smaller amount, enough for a handsome monthly allowance, was set aside for Amanda. This, of course, was in addition to whatever funds she held in her own accounts and the monies she would earn from Griffith and Son.

Once my finances and I were distinct from Amanda's she was apparently no longer needed and was politely dismissed. I protested, but it was suggested that what was to come was best first kept in confidence; if I chose to reveal it to Amanda later that would be my decision. Reluctantly I watched my aunt stride out of the office full of pride, but also aware that she was no longer the queen; she had been deposed by the little girl she had watched grow up. For years I had been her responsibility, and suddenly that was at an end; more so, I now owned the house she herself had grown up in. How topsy-turvy things had suddenly become.

After a pause for tea Saltonstall and I continued the disbursement of my financial property and responsibilities. There was a small inheritance from my father, smaller than I had expected, but after going over the account I quickly understood why. Following my father's death, his estate appeared quite healthy and should have sustained my mother and I for the entirety of her life, if not mine as well. Unfortunately, it appears that my mother chose a rather unscrupulous man to manage the account, and in a rather short while the funds had dwindled in stature. That man had been my stepfather, David Griffith. The funds had improved in the years since his death, but I suddenly understood why so much of my family wealth was held in trust, and doled out in small periodic stipends by our financial managers. I think I made the old attorney blush when I saw the extent of the damage and swore in a manner that I had learned while roaming the back streets of Boston.

As flabbergasted as I was by the poor state of my father's legacy, I was further stunned by the presentation of an account that I did not know even existed. I won't talk about the amount, but essentially I have been named the beneficiary of a trust held in the Bank of England and administered by the firm of Utterson and Enfield. The trust has been in existence for more than three decades and was originally established to support the children of an unnamed but prominent physician. Somehow or another I had caught the eye of one of these beneficiaries, who felt that they no longer needed the support, and was named as his legal replacement. It was all very odd and convoluted, and even though I didn't need the funds I had become a beneficiary. Saltonstall wanted to transfer the funds into the Halsey account but I balked at this. Instead, I asked that he investigate the origin of the trust and its beneficiaries, and if I could decline the funds, or perhaps donate them to a worthy cause. The old man went quiet when I said this, but eventually nodded and agreed to see what he could do to learn more about the origin and status of the trust. So strange that someone would just give me money, stranger still to think that my financiers would simply accept it without questioning the source and the motivation.

Afterward, we sat down with some of the staff and representatives of organizations that drew funds from the accounts. There was the genial Irishman, Mr. Kelly Young, who was the managing partner of Griffith and Son, the source of most of the family income. He had been managing partner for the last twenty-five years, and assured me that he had always kept things running shipshape, and intended to do so in the future. I thanked him for his service, and he invited me to visit the main office any time I would so like, and made it clear that if I ever needed anything from the firm I had merely to ask. The Kreitners were an affable couple who were responsible for the care and upkeep of both Crowninshield Manor and my father's old house on Derby Street, where they resided. In reviewing their status I found their remuneration rather pitiful, but this, it was explained, was because they essentially lived rent free. Still dissatisfied, I suggested that the small token rent that the city paid for the property on which the Halsey School sat be used in its entirety to compensate the Kreitners. I also suggested that we look into selling the old Crowninshield Manor, a property apparently bought by my father for my mother and he to reside in, but given his death, never occupied. Why my mother had refused to part with the house, which sat at the eastern end of High Street, far from the more civilized parts of town, I simply couldn't understand.

This time also allowed for a discussion with the two domestics who ran Griffith House, the sisters Julia and Molly, who were both cook and housekeeper, respectively, and who lived in the cellar room overlooking the garden. Holdovers from the days when the house was full, and an entire family needed looking after, Amanda and I were all that were left. As much as it pained me, I suggested that the two begin searching for positions elsewhere. It was my intention to travel, and that would leave Griffith House vacant for extended periods of time. Any work that I needed done could be handled by the Kreitners, or even regular visits by a cleaning woman. When asked what was to become of Miss

Amanda, I responded that it was high time that my aunt learn to cook her own meals. I was not entirely without heart, and created a generous severance package and ordered Saltonstall to assist in finding them new arrangements.

I also decided to review and limit the number of social organizations that the family belonged to. I have no love for the DAR, but Amanda often spends her days at that den of gossiping vipers, so as much as it pained me I agreed to pay the dues for that institution. The Miskatonic Club, however, was easily cut; since I am not welcome in those hallowed halls I see no reason to pay for their upkeep. Another social organization was one I had never heard of, Porgy's Fish House near Hog Island, which I was told was a sporting club. I assumed it was frequented by my stepfather, but was rebuked and told that the membership had been my mother's. Surprised, I deferred making a decision until I could gather some more information on my own. I had always wanted to learn to shoot, and this seemed the perfect venue to do so. Saltonstall tried to persuade me otherwise but in the end I told him I would handle it on my own. I did agree to maintain the family in good standing with Miskatonic University. The cost is really just a pittance, and access to the university library is only one of the privileges granted. Someday, I fully intend to pursue an academic path, and in the meanwhile I would like to partake of the occasional lecture and concert. My tastes, as Hannah tends to remind me, have always run toward the academic, and I do find academic men so attractive. There is something about a well-educated mind that makes me quiver.

That is not to say that such men cannot be off-putting as well. One of the last people I had to deal with today was Doctor Abbott, a semi-retired physician who had been the beneficiary of my mother's charity for nearly two decades. A codicil in my mother's instructions made it clear that after I assumed control of my estate the decision to continue payments to Doctor Abbott would be mine to make, as I would have to deal with the consequences, either way. The whole arrangement was rather obscure and murky, and I suspected that perhaps the good doctor knew something about my parents or myself that would be embarrassing. There was the unsavory stink of extortion, something I had no desire to tolerate, no matter what the secret, but out of respect I met with the decrepit old man and let him make his case.

In rather slow and torturous language, Doctor Abbott explained that many years ago, before I was born, he had been on the staff at Sefton Asylum. During the 1905 outbreak of typhoid fever, in which my father had perished while ministering to the sick and dying, the town was at the same time beset by a more tangible form of death. More than a dozen murders were attributed to the thing known amongst the sensational newsmen of the day as either the Plague Daemon or the Arkham Terror, which had stalked the night streets of Arkham. When it was finally caught, having just killed the parents of Doctor Stuart Hartwell, some thought it more ape than man, for it was a terrifying simian monstrosity that loped about on all fours and grunted and shrieked. Those who examined it came away visibly shaken and spoke in whispers of how markedly it resembled the visage of the poor deceased Doctor Allan Halsey. Some even called for an order to reopen the good doctor's grave to assure that he was still at peace. Such calls were quickly quieted by the newly appointed Judge Hand, who dismissed such superstitious nonsense and reminded more vocal proponents that they lived in Arkham and not Ingolstadt. That the madman, for in the end it was concluded that it was indeed a man, bore some vague resemblance to Allan Halsey was nothing more than a coincidence, and Hand admonished those who believed anything else. In the end, the Arkham Terror was found unfit for incarceration in a prison, and was therefore turned over to authorities at Sefton Asylum. It was here that Doctor Abbott had overseen the care of the thing. While the identity of the Terror had never been established, and most decent folk dismissed the rumored resemblance to Allan Halsey, those whispering innuendos eventually reached the ears of the doctor's young bride, and she, driven by curiosity, took it upon herself to visit the poor creature. Her visit was not an isolated incident and over a course of weeks the visits of Elizabeth Halsey to Sefton Asylum became more and more frequent and, thanks to rather generous donations to one of the orderlies, less and less supervised.

Here the old man paused and smiled lasciviously. He suggested that he had caught my mother in a compromised position with the thing in the cell. What my mother had done was a crime against the laws of both man and nature, and he had no choice but to ban her from the grounds. My mother, Allan Halsey's wife, Elizabeth Halsey, had never returned to the asylum, but not long after semi-annual checks had begun arriving. Even after the monstrous inmate had escaped in February of 1921, and my mother's disappearance three months later, the payments continued, maintained by prior instructions given to Saltonstall. Doctor Abbott expected me to continue those payments uninterrupted, and in return his continued silence, concerning what he saw, would be guaranteed.

I took a moment to mull his revelations over. Mr. Saltonstall was visibly upset and rose to confront the man. I heard the words "Hippocratic Oath" and violation come out of his mouth, but I raised my hand and directed him to remain calm. I followed my own direction, and in an even-handed voice thanked Dr. Abbott for his years of discretion and assured him that I was sure that my mother appreciated it. However, now that my mother was missing, and likely dead, and therefore immune to the embarrassment of titillating knowledge, all such payments would cease. He once again flashed that lascivious smile and in just a few words suggested that while my mother might be immune, I certainly was not, and that if he were to reveal all that he knew my own parentage might itself be called into question. At this affront Saltonstall could no longer contain himself and ordered the man out of the office, citing that he had been friends with Allan Halsey, and I clearly had inherited the Halsey eyes. Furthermore, the lawyer began spouting language and invectives that even I wasn't familiar with and reminded the corrupt physician that if he were to repeat such things to anyone else he would be seen in court charged with slander. Given that he had just admitted to nearly two decades of extortion, Saltonstall was quite sure that the authorities would be very interested in reviewing his personal finances, as well as those of the asylum during his tenure there.

Doctor Abbott stood and left, but as he did, he looked back and stared at me intensely. Finally, as if as an afterthought, he spoke. "You're right, she does have the Halsey eyes. Those steel gray eyes with flecks of green are quite distinctive, and they're the same thing your mother saw when she first looked at the thing that we kept in the cell nearly twenty years ago. 'He has the Halsey eyes,' she said." He put on his hat and coat as he continued spouting vile insinuations. "You've inherited so much today, from your mother, your stepfather, even your mother's husband, the man you think was your father. Are you sure that you've inherited your father's eyes, or is it possible that they come from someone else, someone your mother never told you about? And if you've inherited his eyes, perhaps you've inherited other traits as well. Tell me, Miss Halsey-Griffith, have you ever been ill? Have you ever killed anyone?"

"No, Doctor, and I've never felt the need," I said, "until today."

He nodded and flashed that smile I had grown to hate. "No, I suppose not. The Terror was never sick either. He spent fifteen years half-naked in a cold and damp cell, living in the most vile of conditions, and not once did he ever become sick, nary a cold. Only time will tell if your breeding runs true." With that he left, letting the door creak closed behind him.

Saltonstall immediately began apologizing profusely, but I quickly shut him down. I had dealt with men like Dr. Abbott before, and there was no sense in getting upset over what they said or tried to do. The best course was to stay wary and be prepared. Saltonstall was still fretting about the whole thing when I asked if we were done, and if so could he arrange for a car to take me home. This he dismissed with a wave of his hand and made it clear to me that the two of us were going to lunch together, and then he would take me home himself. We dined at some intimate place not far from his office. The lunch was cordial, and on several occasions my host commented that he had been friends with my father and my mother and that they both would be proud of the woman I had become. I thanked him, but didn't really know whether he was telling the truth, or just being polite. He had been the family lawyer for the Griffiths and the Halseys so I suppose it was possible, but I have no memory of this man ever being at Griffith House before I was shipped off to The Hall School, and Mother certainly never mentioned him.

It was around two in the afternoon when I finally was brought home, and with me came a plethora of documents and paperwork that I was supposed to review and store in a safe place. Frankly I was too tired to deal with it all, and as I came through the door Amanda was there, clamoring to speak about Julia and Molly. Frustrated and exhausted, I made it plain that I was through paying for live-in domestic help at Griffith House, and if she wanted to she was free to pay their salaries out of her own pocket. This seemed to satisfy her and the two servants as well, who were situated just around the corner of the foyer where they thought I couldn't see them. As the three of them all scurried back toward the kitchen I went upstairs and found solace in my bedroom. Strange how this house now belongs to me, but I feel so alienated in it. Amanda likes to say that I grew up here, that she and Molly and Julia were my family. The truth is I have no fond memories of this place, and it seemed that after I turned ten my mother had done nothing but find a way to usher me out the door. She never bothered to keep me around, to teach me how to run things. Instead she abandoned me, leaving me to lock myself in my room and stare at all this paperwork that now lies scattered on my desk.

How very odd. Just now I was flipping through the documents that Saltonstall gave to me and amidst the deeds and contracts and other documents I have found a letter addressed to me, clearly written in my mother's handwriting. Why didn't Saltonstall show me this before? I'm staring at it, my mind racing and overwhelmed with both elation and dread. Perhaps now I shall have some explanation as to why my mother abandoned me.

*Later*

I've read the letter. I remain confused as ever, but I understand a little and now am positive that my mother is alive! My mother, Elizabeth Halsey, missing these past few years, is alive, and she has much to explain to me.

# CHAPTER 13

# "The Satisfaction of Elizabeth Halsey"
## From Her Letters
## May 2 1921

My dearest Megan,

I write this in the hopes that you can forgive me for what I have done. I have struggled with how to convey to you the truth, but what can I say to make you understand the events that force me to leave? How can I explain to you my motivations, my desires, and my needs; and my desperate wish to keep you away from them? I wish I did not have to tell you these things, but I must explain why I now choose to abandon you, I owe you that much at least.

As I write this, I think about how you have blossomed into a powerful and beautiful young woman. I always knew that you were extraordinary, and that your potential was vastly superior to those of your friends and schoolmates. The world is changing, and so too is the place of women in it, and I believe that you might help drive that change. It is for this reason that I sent you to be educated at the finest school I could find. I only hope that The Hall School has served you well. I know that you and your friend Asenath found the place to be an intellectual wasteland, and I know that the two of you often took leave, wandering the streets of Boston without a chaperone; I pray that such adventures have not brought you harm.

My reasons for leaving you have their roots with my father, your grandfather, Augustus Hoag. He was a great man, a pillar of the community and a fine and respected physician. He was also a dominating father, and I lived in fear of his wrath, which was dispensed swiftly through a leather riding crop. Had he not insisted on carrying that damned stick with him wherever he went he might still be alive today, but one cannot always expect a horse to submit to the crop favorably. You would have thought that his death would have brought me relief, but such was not the case. His loss left a strange hole inside me, and I longed for the return of his stern voice, his heavy hand, and his disapproving look. Without him I was free, but I longed for discipline, without it I felt incomplete. I have since read Jung, and I believe that I suffer from his proposed Electra complex. Perhaps someday I shall write the man and ask him to examine my case.

I was eighteen when David Griffith came to my mother and asked for my hand. The Griffiths are a fine family, proud, loyal, of means, but I had no interest in the boy. At twenty, David was a fine figure of a man, dashing in his uniform, well built, well spoken, and with a fine future ahead of him in the family business, which was then, as it is now, banking. A girl would be a fool to turn away from such an opportunity, to reject the man of wealth who offered her a life of luxury and security. Yet that is exactly what I did. I know you must be confused, for David Griffith was for so long the only father you knew, but he was not my true love; that was your father.

My mother found my rejection of David appalling. She suspected that I was suffering from a fever of the brain, or perhaps hysteria, and summoned one of Father's colleagues to diagnose and cure me. Doctor Allan Halsey was decades older than me, a confirmed bachelor, and a man who knew how to handle women. He proved his ability to control our gender by putting my mother in her place when she attempted to interfere with his diagnosis. He was strong-willed, comfortable in his ways, but was not tolerant of nonsense. His manner was caring but forceful, subtle but direct. He praised and punished with equal rapidity. In many ways he reminded me of father, and after several months I grew to suspect that he had intentions toward me. Had Mother not died in a freak subway accident in New York, I am sure that he would have asked her for my hand. Shortly after her death, I became Mrs. Doctor Allan Halsey.

This was at the time somewhat scandalous. Allan was being considered by the university medical school to fill the position of Dean, and in the time leading up to our wedding, many of his peers met to dissuade him from our union. Each went away frustrated. What had raised such strong dissension amongst his colleagues I could not say, but on the day before the ceremony Allan informed me that while the announcement had yet to be made, the board had no choice but to name him Dean; to do otherwise would be their ruin. I did not question my husband, for his confident manner left no room for doubt.

We honeymooned in New York City, lounging for a month in the magnificent Bramford Building overlooking Central Park. The place belonged to Allan's friend, a man who was away on business. It was a magnificent home, filled with the most stunning of architectural details, charming furniture, and an extensive library of works in Latin, French, German, Arabic, and even Hebrew. The library had a profound effect on me, for in many ways it reminded me of Father's study. The rich cloth and leather bindings, offset by the equally fine furnishings, the silk divan, the calfskin chair, drew something sensual out of me. I ran my hand along the brass, felt the heat of the sun-warmed metal and smooth leather, and reveled in it. That night, surrounded by the books and furnishings of that room, Allan took me, the smell of old books, linseed oil, leather, and brass filled my senses as Allen filled me. He made me a woman, and I knew then that, for this man, I would do anything he ever wanted me to. For the first time, I had a hint of what it meant to be satisfied.

My education, my seduction, began the very next day. I have read Cleland's *Memoirs of a Woman of Pleasure*, the works of Von Sacher-Masoch, and those of de Sade, including *Justine* and the *120 Days of Sodom*. If you think such writings to be the imaginings of a perverted mind, I can assure you that such women exist, and that they are capable of delivering to others the greatest of pleasures. I know this because I saw these women, saw what they did to and for men. I met with them, spoke with them, and with Allan's permission, I became one of them.

We spent a month in New York, and during that time I immersed myself in the study of the erotic arts. I learned patience, the art of seduction, and the skills to use my hands, my hips, my mouth, and my whole body to bring pleasure to another, while subverting my own needs. I learned how to use and take the tools of the trade; feathers, bindings, chains, gags, the whip, and the riding crop. I ached as the feel of the crop brought the memory of my father back to me. Every such woman must eventually find her specialty. For me, it was submission, the complete surrender of my body and soul, the leather crop caressing my buttocks and stinging with leather kisses. My sex would swell during such sessions, grow moist, unbearably hot, and I would ache for relief, for something to spread me apart, fill me up, and make me whole. I needed it, begged for it, craved satisfaction. Eventually, after suitable suffering, my husband would concede to my wishes, and he and his friends would fulfill my needs. I took them, took them all, in my hands, in my mouth, in my sex, and yes, I even let myself be sodomized, let the men and women who had trained me take their pleasures. In turn I found my pleasure in them. I took them one by one, and in groups, I let them devour my flesh just as I consumed theirs, and I lost myself amidst the heat and musk and sweat of bodies that were not my own. During such sessions, it was not unusual for me to catch sight of my husband, and see the look in his eyes, that raw wanton look, the ecstasy, the pure unbridled desire as he watched me succumb to the pleasure of violation. I had become what my husband had set out to make me, and both of us reveled in that accomplishment, for it was clear that the hunger inside me, the thing that had been missing since the death of my father, had finally been satisfied.

Inevitably, we left New York and returned to Arkham. Allan took his position as Dean of Medicine, and I assumed the life of a lady of leisure, running his household and managing his personal affairs. We were quite well off, and maintained a luxurious townhouse less than a mile from the university. We employed a cook, and her son as a valet, but both left us each evening and did not arrive back until early the next day. In this manner, Allan and I could indulge ourselves without fear of discovery. Each night was a new exploration of eroticism, and soon I began to understand the rough desires that drove my husband, and learned how to please him. I taught myself the use of knots and ropes. After I perfected my technique, I regularly presented Allan with my body, bound and gagged on a table or chair, surrounded by implements with which to spank, choke, and penetrate me at his leisure. Those nights became a luxurious treat for both of us, and on occasion he would make me wait, begging for his touch, as he partook of food and drink, purposefully delaying his pleasure, and my satisfaction. This, then, was my life, with the occasional trip to New York or Boston or even Providence for special parties, where often I was the center of attention. I loved this life, loved how it made me feel, and loved how it made my husband's eyes shine. With each passing month, with each exploit, I fell deeper in love with him, and he with me. We carried on, thrilled by our mutual adoration and perversions.

Our erotic adventures were not without risk or injury, and from time to time bruises and welts, particularly around my wrists and neck, were the cause of much gossip amongst my social circle. I am thankful for the modest modes of dress that have dominated our society for the last few decades, for without such fashions, the concealment of the evidence of our exploits would have been more difficult. We did, however, face other hurdles. As a medical man, Allan was not unaware of the risks associated with casual sexual contact with multiple partners. To alleviate these fears, to reduce the risks, Allan assured me that all of our partners underwent a full medical examination. We also used a variety of prophylactic methods to prevent both disease and pregnancy. Though many of the methods seemed strange, and were often officially decried by proponents of the Comstock Act, my continual good health is proof that such methods are effective.

It was in 1905, just three short years after my marriage, that Allan was taken from me. A plague of typhus had come to Arkham and swept through the city, sparing neither the rich nor poor. Allan sent me away, and I spent the summer of 1905 in a cabin near Aylesbury. Allan tried to stay with me, but his sense of civic duty forced him into action. He organized the hospital and the medical students to combat the outbreak. In this he was aided by the most capable of students, including Herbert West, Daniel Cain, and his personal assistant, Stuart Hartwell. All these men, so much younger than my Allan, worked feverishly against the plague, and Allan was always at their side, but the pace took its toll. Allan, my sweet love, fell victim to overwork, and suffered a cerebral hemorrhage. There was little time to mourn and fewer facilities to provide a proper ceremony or service. He was buried before I even knew he was dead. I did not even get to see his grave until a week after the wake.

Officially, it was shortly after this that I realized I was pregnant. I spread the story that on one of his visits to me in Aylesbury, Allan and I had found the time, and we conceived a child. A child whom I chose to give birth to in that remote cabin in Aylesbury where she was conceived. To all those who would care, you, my daughter, were born on March the fifth 1906.

Furthermore, following your birth it was discovered that Allan's legacy was insufficient to maintain his widow and daughter, and David Griffith came to my rescue. It is said that your stepfather had never stopped loving me; that he loved you as if you were his own daughter, and proved it by giving you his family name. My friend, Amanda, became your aunt, and came to live with us, to be my constant companion while David toiled at the family business. For almost a decade we dwelt in the great house that Allan left to me, and all was well.

Our contented life was shattered when, in May of 1915, David was lost. He was traveling abroad on business, en route to Great Britain, when the HMS *Lusitania* was sunk by a German submarine. At the age of thirty, with a ten-year-old daughter, I had been tragically widowed not once, but twice. The disgrace was too much for me to bear, and together with your spinster aunt, I slowly withdrew from society, choosing to limit my contact to select friends and family. When you came of age, I sent you to The Hall School for Girls, but I remained hidden behind the walls of our estate.

David's story about our love and his death is, I confess, a fabrication, a lie meant to protect us from a society that would never have accepted the truth. I hope that you can.

It is true that, after Allan left me, I found love once more, not with David Griffith, but rather with his sister, my dear friend Amanda. I implore you not to judge our relationship too harshly, she was as much a spouse to me as was my dear Allan, and she loves you as much as I do, cares for you as much as any mother could. The insufficiency of Allan's legacy was a farce as well, an engineered impetus to make David appear gallant. David had suffered badly, from gambling, from bad investments, and his character was in need of rescuing. Amanda and I provided him the perfect manner in which to repair his reputation. We placed him on a strict allowance, coordinated his social calendar with our own, and we lived happily in the web of lies we had spun, always careful to conceal from you, and all others, the truth.

But David became careless, reckless, and foolish. Our arrangement could have lasted indefinitely. He had no need to gamble, but he did, and to excess. One night, after a week of heavy losses, we found his body on the steps of our home, beaten to death. Fearful that any investigation would expose our secrets, we buried him in Billington's Wood.

We bought passage on an ocean liner under David's name, and then found a man to take his place. He had no clue that David was dead, only that he was leaving his own debts behind. Had things gone as we planned, we would have claimed to have lost contact with him, then after years of being missing, declared him dead. The loss of the RMS *Lusitania* was a convenient tragedy, one which resolved things much faster than we ever could have planned.

Such deceits do not yet explain why I have had to leave you, but I assure you that this long explanation lays the basis for the crux of the matter, your birth, and why so many years later, it forces my hand.

Following Allan's death, I returned to an Arkham still recovering from typhus and ripe with rumor. The plague had only recently burned itself out, and much was made of the so-called Plague Daemon, the simian thing that had been the perpetrator of horrid acts of violence and murder. Some laid the whole of the recent pestilence on the beast, suggesting that it had brought the dreaded typhus with it, and now that it had been captured, and locked away in Sefton Asylum, the danger was past. I scoffed at such things, but could not deny other whispers that came to my ears. Many were those who came to offer their condolences for the loss of Allan, and amongst them were a few that suggested that the rumors finding their way out of Sefton could not be true. When I pressed them for details, they blanched and tried to avoid the subject. It was only after the most persistent of demands that the rumors swirling about were revealed to me. The subhuman murderer that had been confined to the asylum, the thing that could not speak, that shrieked in near-constant agony, that did not walk like a man, they said that it bore an uncanny resemblance to none other than my recently departed husband!

I tried to ignore such ridiculousness, but the idea grew in the back of my mind like a corrupting worm. I had not been present at his death, I had not seen his body, and I had not seen him buried. What proof did I have that he was actually gone? These thoughts gnawed at my reason, chewed on it, weakened it bit by bit, until I had no resistance left. In early October I finally gave in, and discretely visited Sefton Asylum. The assistant administrator was cordial and polite; he listened intently to my questions and concerns. He apologized for the rumors that had found their way to me, but he refused my request to see the thing in the cell. I pressed him, appealed to his sense of honor, and then offered him a substantial donation. It was only after I went down upon my knees and performed a task for which I had been well trained that the man relented and conceded to my request.

The thing that was once a man was kept in a padded cell, wrapped in a straitjacket, chained to the wall. The hunched, bestial thing drooled incessantly, and howled and moaned in apparent agony. It was a pitiful monstrosity, and that it was somehow related to the human species was only indicated by the number of fingers on its hands and the manner in which its feet rested on the floor. Its face was all but lost in the shaggy mane of gray hair and thick beard. All that I could see beneath that unkempt hair were the thing's eyes, eyes that I knew well, eyes that could only belong to Allan. This thing, whatever it was, had once been my husband. I ordered the assistant administrator out; he balked at first, but I promised him a significant reward if he complied.

Once we were alone, I called out to the bound creature, which did little more than snarl and snap at me, but I persisted, and after some time, a look of recognition came over him. He calmed, sat back on his haunches, and whimpered pitifully as he grew to understand the state he was in. I went to him, held him in my arms, unbuckled what straps I could, and caressed his damaged body. He was cold, warmer than the room, but colder than a human being has a right to be. Even though he was bereft of speech, he responded to my touch, and although the jacket and chains made it difficult, we found a way to enjoy each other's flesh.

He took me, violently, but not without restraint. He spread my legs, and mounted me. His thick, icy member impaled me, and his buttocks pounded into me faster than they ever had before. I whimpered in delight as his hands tore through my clothing and ravaged my breasts, as he tore at my nipples with his shattered teeth and rough tongue. It had been so long, my despair at his loss had been so great, that to have him back, even in this decrepit form, was in itself a revelation. That he was still able to perform, able to bring me pleasure, was simply too much for me to handle. As his hands closed around my throat, I felt his pace quicken, I wrapped my legs around his body, and together we climaxed, letting loose a howl of preternatural ecstasy that echoed through the halls like some demonic banshee, as we collapsed in satisfaction.

Such a ruckus did not go unnoticed, and within moments what I had done was made plain to all of the staff. I fled through the halls, half naked; the evidence was dripping down my legs, while the thing that was once Allan Halsey roared in frustration. How I made it home, I cannot remember. The next day the director of Sefton Asylum called on me, and despite the exorbitant bribes I had to pay to assure that the staff never spoke of what had occurred, it was made clear that I was never again to visit the institution.

It was not long thereafter that I learned that my spontaneous and unprotected tryst had born fruit. Flabbergasted by my condition, I retreated to the cabin near Aylesbury. More than once I considered using an herbal concoction to put an end to my pregnancy, and equal were the number of times I considered taking my own life. In the end I did neither, and instead enlisted the help of a local midwife named Latimer to aid me. It came as some relief that on the fourteenth of April, 1906 you were born normal, without disfigurement or defect. I returned to Arkham, lied about your date of birth, and with Amanda, raised you the best I could. I thought that any relationship with your father was forever beyond my reach. That apparently was not true.

It had been many years since I had been to Sefton Asylum, and I was not privy to what happened within its walls, but I knew that the thing they called the Plague Daemon, the reanimated form of my beloved Allan, still was imprisoned within. That is, until that fateful night, the fourth of February, 1921. I do not fully understand what happened, nor do I think the police have any better comprehension. What is clear is that on that date, the asylum was visited by an unknown group of individuals who somehow or another were able to convince the director to release one of its patients into their care. Initially reports failed to identify the prisoner, but soon the papers made clear what I had come to suspect. The Plague Daemon was no longer a guest at the asylum; he had been removed, and by all accounts, by men that apparently suffered from the same horrific condition as the monstrosity himself.

I waited, and hoped that he would come home to me, and he did. He came to me, and I welcomed him, grateful for the opportunity to once more satisfy my desires. It has not been easy to hide him from Amanda, but the house is large and Allan can be quiet when he needs to be. Today we leave for the cabin in Aylesbury; from there we depart for parts unknown. I beg you to not attempt to find us. It would not do for us to be returned to the world. Let your father's reputation and mine stand without blemish. I think perhaps someday, when circumstances allow it, I may find it possible to return to you, but not now.

Please understand, your father is controllable, but insatiable, and so am I. His cold touch is like a fire to me, and I ache for each brutal ravaging that he subjects me to, but he is no threat to you; he would never harm you. But his companions, those who share his strange affliction, one that has left them neither dead nor alive, they are not so reasonable, not always controllable. I leave to keep you and Amanda from them and their desires. For the time being they will have to be satisfied with me, with my body alone. I think perhaps I shall be enough to satisfy them, and at last, perhaps, under their cold, hungry bodies, I too shall once again find my own sense of satisfaction.

Yours,

Elizabeth Halsey

CHAPTER 14

# "On the Staff and Members of Porgy's Fish House"
## From the Diary of Megan Halsey
### June 9 1925

It has been more than a year since that day in Arkham when I was given control of my own fortunes, and therefore my own destiny. It is a rare thing, even in this modern age, for a woman to be given the freedom to do as she pleases without answering to some man one way or another. Yet despite the odds here I was, suddenly the mistress of a small financial empire, complete with dowager aunt. Those first few days after I had been granted my inheritance, my life was a whirlwind of spending. Aunt Amanda had let the house go for too many years and I brought in workmen to repair the roof and windows and two others to update the plumbing and electrics. I also brought in a team of cleaners to do what Molly and Julia had in their complacency neglected to do. While this work took a significant sum it barely made a mark in the ledgers. Nor did the monies I spent purchasing a wardrobe suitable to my station, though my accountants did express some concerns that I had purchased a number of outfits from shops normally frequented by men. These included rugged linen trousers and shirts, leather boots and jackets made out of a waterproof canvas material. When I traveled, I wanted to be prepared, and I had no intention of visiting only the more civilized portions of the world.

That is not to say that I did not appreciate the finer things. As a woman reveling in her freedom, I decided I would no longer rely on taxis and the idea of a chauffeur revolted me. This was solved by the purchase of an automobile, a burgundy-paneled Heron Silver Wing, and an instructor to teach me how to handle her. Benjamin Duke was a rather charming man, in a folksy way, born and raised in the backwoods of Hazzard County, Georgia. He had a woman down there and a son named Jesse. He was in Arkham to make money, he was a moonshiner and damn good at it, but all he wanted to do was go home to his darling Jessica Hogg and make a respectable woman out of her.

He was a good driver and a good teacher, and when he discovered that I was also interested in learning how to shoot he helped me pick out guns: two surplus Colt 1911s with mother-of-pearl handles. What can I say, I'm a girl, and I like pretty things. I also like things that make loud noises and can make very large, very angry men fall to the ground and stop moving. I like that, and given what I was planning to do with my life, having a weapon like that was exactly what I needed. Not that I told Duke that. When he asked what I wanted the guns for I told him that I planned on doing some target shooting, after all, isn't that what the rich tend to do with guns?

Ben Duke looked at me and nearly laughed. "In my experience," he said, "I've learned that the rich tend to use guns for a lot of things; shooting skeet doesn't rate high on the list." He never said much else about it after that. He taught me to drive and to shoot, and he never laid a hand on me, never even said anything that could be considered provocative. He never even looked at me cross-eyed. He may have been the most decent man I had ever met; it pained when the state cops caught him driving a load down out of the mountains and then sent him packing back to Georgia with a broken wrist and one less eye.

That had been June, and the first part of July, and I spent the rest of that month and all of August practicing out by Satan's Ledge. I learned how to shoot with one gun in each hand, and how to roll my shoulders to absorb the recoil. It took me a lot of time and money and bullets but I eventually became rather proficient. I wasn't going to win any awards for my marksmanship, but I could do better than just hitting the broadside of a barn. When my holsters finally came in, one for the outside of my thigh, and the other for under my arm, I felt truly invincible, but knew that Ben would warn me about being too cocky. Still, I had a right to be. I was very good with the guns, and it was a talent I suspected I would need if I planned on finding my mother.

It was in that quest to find my missing parent that in early September I climbed into the Heron and drove toward Essex Bay, hunting for the unmarked dirt and gravel road that led into the salt marsh that was the fringe of the estuary. Saltonstall had refused to tell me anything about it, but one of his associates had been less discreet. It took me half the morning, and I went down too many dead ends, but I eventually found the immense gray barn with the tin roof that sat on massive wooden pilings above the high water line. A handful of cars were parked in front, and I could see a bevy of boats moored on the far side. Gulls lined the peaked metal roof, squabbling over territory like widows over a widower. It didn't matter that in an hour or so the roof would be too hot to perch on; right now it was something to squawk about.

I didn't get three steps onto the stairs before a porterhouse steak of a man stepped out of the shadows and warned me off. "This here's a private club, miss. I suggest you get back in your fancy car and go back the way you came."

"A private club," I retorted. "Is this Porgy's Fish House? If so, then I am a member, and I would like to talk to Mr. Porgy."

The walking slab of meat chuckled as I handed him the membership card that I had found amongst my mother's things. "You ain't no member, we ain't used these cards in more than five years." He flipped it over and looked at the name typed on the back, and then looked me in the eye. "Elizabeth Halsey." He let the name roll around on his tongue. "I knew Elizabeth Halsey, and you ain't her. Now get before I have to hurt you." He pocketed the card.

I slipped a hand inside my jacket and felt for one of my Colts. It was cold and heavy, and it made me feel powerful just touching it. "Elizabeth Halsey was my mother, my name is Megan, Megan Halsey-Griffith." I had hoped by using my hyphenated name a sense of authority would be invoked. "If I could, I would like to talk to Mr. Porgy."

Porterhouse huffed, turned, and told me to follow, all the time chuckling to himself. "Mr. Porgy, that's rich, ain't never heard that one before."

The inside of the building was dim, but even with just a few lights burning I could tell it was cavernous. An old man was pushing a broom, while his twin stood stacking glassware behind an ornately carved bar easily a hundred feet long. A man in a suit was in the corner cuddled up with a young woman less than half his age. She was smiling, keeping her eyes locked on his and stroking his ear with her right hand. Off to the side, at one of the larger tables, three men and another young woman sat going over a ledger. Two of the men, both dressed rather casually, flanked the third, who wore a rather smart charcoal suit. Charcoal was bigger than Porterhouse and seemed enraptured by the woman who was making notes in the ledger. She was not much older than me, with her dark hair cut in a bob that accented her round face. She wore a man's pinstripe suit that failed to hide her ample bust. While she wrote with her right hand, she held a cigarette in her left.

Porterhouse sat me down in a chair and told me to wait quietly. He then careened across the floor not so much like a bull in a china shop, but like a bull who had been fed nothing but beer for three days and then shoved into a china shop. I was absolutely stunned that anyone could be so obviously sober and still have so little grace. Perhaps this was why he had been relegated to standing guard outside.

He handed the card I had given him to one of the casually dressed men, and the three of them passed it back and forth, like it was something they had never expected to see again before tossing it onto the table next to the ledger. The smartly dressed woman finished what she was writing and then nonchalantly picked the piece of cardboard up. She looked at it, flipped a few pages in her ledger, confirmed something, and then nodded her head. She never once looked at me, or any of the men that were around her. Porterhouse waved me over and as I crossed the floor he lumbered away.

When I got close enough one of the men spoke. "Don't sit. You have one minute to explain what you're doing here and why we shouldn't take you out in the inlet and make sure you never come back." I don't know which one said it, and it didn't seem to matter.

"Mr. Porgy," I was trying not to stammer. "My name is Megan Halsey-Griffith, I inherited my mother's estate back in March. There was a request for payment of annual dues to Porgy's Fish House. I came to see what exactly I was being invited to join."

Charcoal looked me up and down with big watery eyes. "You want to be a member, what are you, eighteen?"

"Just," I snapped back. I thought they were going to bust a gut, or at least fall out of their chairs in hysterics.

The woman in the pinstripe suit closed her book with a snap and in doing so shut her three compatriots down. "Give us some space, boys." Her voice was smooth and when she spoke smoke poured out of her mouth like molasses from a barrel. She didn't have to ask twice, and as the table cleared she motioned for me to sit.

"My name is Maris Fiske, my father was George Fiske, they called him Porgy, as in Georgy Porgy, this was his place. He's been gone almost ten years now, I run it now, didn't seem like there was a reason to change it, and I much prefer being called Porgy over Maris."

"What's wrong with Maris?"

"Where I come from, up the coast, in Innsmouth, half the girls are named Maris. It's a thing, you know? It's either Maris or Octavia, one or the other; folks up in Innsmouth aren't too creative when it comes to naming their kids." She took a drag from her cigarette and let the cherry burn bright. "Now, what can I do for you?"

"I was wondering what you do here, what my mother was doing here, and why she seemed to keep a membership to a club even after she disappeared."

She smiled. "Porgy's is a social club for men with refined and unusual tastes. We provide dockage for private vessels, we host fishing tournaments, in the fall we go duck hunting, and we have a thousand acres of forest where our members can hunt deer, pheasant, and wild boar, even raccoons if you are so inclined." She took a final drag of her cigarette and then crushed it out. "Do you hunt, Miss Halsey-Griffith?"

"No," I said, "but I would be interested in learning how."

She nodded ominously. "A word of advice, then. Next time, leave the gun behind. The holsters you bought are cut for a man, not a woman, and you're not only walking funny but that bulge in your jacket is making everybody in here twitchy. We're a friendly bunch, you be nice and honest, and we'll be nice and honest. Is that clear?"

"Crystal."

"Good." The way she said it, there were at least three syllables. "Now honestly, why are you here?"

I took a deep breath. "My mother is missing, I intend to find her. I thought perhaps you, well, someone here, might know something, give me some clue as to where she might be."

She shook her head slowly and deliberately. "I wish I could help you, I truly do, but I haven't seen your mother in years. We do sorely miss her; she was very . . . popular with both the club staff and the members."

"This isn't really a sporting club, is it? What really goes on here?"

"Everything I've told you is true."

"But what haven't you told me?"

"Would you like to know?" There was a hint of excitement in her eyes. "You're Liz's daughter, if you want to know, you only have to ask."

I leaned in across the table. "I want to know."

"Then follow me."

We didn't go far. The room she led me to was rich in décor, all satin drapes and velvet curtains. There was a lounge to one side, and it was here that Maris had me sit and then found a spot for herself that was too close for my comfort. The center of the room was occupied by a sumptuous circular bed covered in red satin sheets, turned rich like a dark cherry by the warm light of the candelabra. Lounging there in the flickering light were two bodies, one male and one female, a nude couple, unashamed by their exposed state.

"Alex, Amber, would you be so kind as to entertain us?" It wasn't really a request. "Miss Halsey-Griffith, I must warn you to remain very still. Amber can be quite unpredictable when she is aroused. If you must speak, whisper softly, but only if you must." Her hand was suddenly on my knee.

The man slid back into the light, exposing himself completely; he was a magnificent specimen, with dusky skin, well-defined muscles, dark hair, and piercing black eyes; I though him an Egyptian or perhaps a Syrian, or even perhaps a Spanish Moor. As for his partner, the woman called Amber, she was a most unusual beauty. She was small, perhaps five inches over five feet, with wide hips and shoulders, and small, firm breasts with points that sat unusually high. Her hair was cut short, shorter than that of her partner, and this accentuated her large, wide-set eyes and her broad, flat nose. On her neck, on both sides, behind her jaw and below her small ears, there were large semicircular scars that caught the light and glittered with an alluring beauty.

She was smiling and moving rhythmically; her hands were wrapped around Alex's phallus and were gently rubbing and massaging the growing member. I have already said how attractive Alex was; what I have not mentioned was the sheer size of what sat between his legs. I may not be the best to judge, for admittedly my experience in such matters is limited, but I was simply astounded by the length and girth of the wand of flesh that hung there. What was even more startling, was that under Amber's expert hands it was growing larger, swelling into something akin to a small baseball bat, straight and stiff. Even from a distance I could see the fat pulsating vein that snaked up the side and beat in time with his racing heart.

I watched as she ran her hands over Alex's body, teasing and tempting, drawing him slowly toward the brink of total satisfaction. I watched his legs tense and his back arch; he was suddenly thrusting against Amber's hand, but she was having none of it. With thumb and forefinger she wrapped around the base of him and applied pressure to a critical locale. With her other hand she forced him back down to the bed, calmed his thrusting pelvis, and in mere moments coaxed him away from the edge. He whined in disappointment, but only briefly, for he knew what was to come next.

Amber leaned forward on her haunches and laid her head down in his lap. I watched as she opened her mouth, saw the small, translucent teeth that dwelled there, and then let loose her tongue. It was large, preternaturally so, longer than the member that it flicked and teased, and then coiled around. It squeezed and danced around that stiff pole, drawing him up toward Amber's mouth. I watched as she engulfed the head of his cock, her lips stretched thin. I thought it impossible, for he was so large, so thick, but I could see the bulge of him as he pressed against her cheek from the inside.

I swear I heard something crack as Amber shifted and suddenly pulled back slightly. She arched her back and brought her throat back in line with her mouth, and then surged forward, forcing a few more inches down. On the side of her neck those weird, glittering semicircular scars cracked open and revealed something red and wet inside. Those flaps of skin found their own rhythm and with each beat Amber inched forward, and I could see her throat swell as it filled.

I remembered Maris's warning but couldn't resist asking, "How can she . . . ?" But I didn't know how to finish that question.

"Breathe?" added Maris. "Those slits on her throat are primitive gills, they oxygenate her blood. She doesn't need to breathe. A neat little trick, don't you think?"

Amber leaned forward, shaking her head like an animal and forcing herself down toward the base of her lover's tool. In a single quick thrust she buried her face in the neat thatch of hair that he kept there. I could see the muscles in Amber's throat contract and release, massaging what was inside, driving her lover once more to the brink of ecstasy. He wrapped his legs around her shoulders and drove himself even farther inside, as if that was even possible. His hands clenched down into the sheets and his head arched back, opening his mouth in an agonizing cry of unfettered pleasure. He was thrusting against her face, once, twice, thrice. And then he shuddered, fell back, and lay still.

Alex may have finished, but Amber still had to extract herself, and she did so slowly, taking exacting care to maximize the unendurable pleasure that the now-hypersensitive Alex was suffering. With each motion Alex gasped in terrific and unimaginable pleasure, until at last the whole of Alex's rapidly deflating member flopped out of Amber's mouth and came to a rest on his thigh, still oozing fluid.

In an instant Maris was by Amber's side, using a towel to wipe the spittle and whatever else from her lips and chin. There was a look of joy in Amber's eyes, a look of satisfaction, a look I had never seen before, and it stirred something down inside me. Without warning Maris was suddenly kissing Amber; it was an intimate gesture, more intimate than what I had just witnessed between Amber and Alex, and I turned away, ashamed at violating their privacy. But at the same time that odd feeling deep inside was growing, blossoming, and my mind was suddenly a torrent of confused and contradictory thoughts.

Maris was suddenly back at my side with a small snifter of brandy, and I swallowed it faster than I should have, letting its warmth fill my stomach and spread through my veins and nerves. "You're saying my mother used to . . ."

"Well, not that exactly. Amber and her sisters have certain anatomical gifts that your mother lacked, but yes, she was capable of similar acts. She was a master of the erotic arts."

"She worked for you?"

"Not at first, she was simply a member in the beginning, but after the money ran out, before she married your stepfather. Yes, she worked here."

"My mother was a whore." I was whispering again, embarrassed by the sudden revelation.

"Don't think of it that way. It is, after all, the oldest profession. Women have been doing it for millennia; only in recent years has society suddenly deemed the act unacceptable." She lit a cigarette. "And no, your mother was never one of my girls."

"But you said she worked here."

"But not as one of my girls. I told you she was an artist, an expert. We can't have that kind of skill employed here. None of the other girls would make any money." She was smiling as I squirmed. "Your mother was a teacher, she taught most of the girls here. Hell, she taught Amber how to do that thing with her throat." I saw Amber smile and nod.

The room was suddenly spinning, and almost everything inside was screaming, "*Run!*", but there was a small, tiny voice that said something else, something that leaked out in a whispering cry. "Teach me."

Maris turned away as those words left my lips, but Amber perked up, as did Alex. They both watched as Maris considered my request.

"Teach me." I wasn't whispering anymore.

Maris spun around and had the most delicious grin on her face. "There would be something perversely decadent about undertaking such a project. You are sure, this is what you want?"

I nodded, and bowed my head a little, not in shame, but rather in shy acceptance of the choice I had just made.

Maris lifted my chin and brought her lips to mine. She tasted of cherries, and scotch, and sex. "It will be my absolute pleasure," she said.

It took longer than I thought, but that might have just been me taking advantage of the situation, to linger longer than I needed to. It's the little things that matter, and you should take pleasure wherever, and with whomever, you find it.

# CHAPTER 15

# "The Issue of Dr. Jekyll"
## Found Amongst the Papers of Megan Halsey
## A Report Commissioned by the Bank of England
## November 10 1888

Mr. Klein,

As requested I have met with Doctor George Edward Rutherford concerning the issue of Doctor Jekyll and his estate. This meeting took place on the fourth of November, 1888 in my London office. Present as witnesses were representatives of the Bank of England, Mr. Banks, and Mr. Darling.

Dr. Rutherford is an unusual man, quite large, loud, and condescending, with a huge black beard covering his face and extending well down his chest. He was particularly annoyed at being summoned to meet with me, and bristled when I noted that any failure to keep our conversation completely confidential might besmirch the reputation of our client, or his family, and might therefore require us to pursue legal action. Rutherford took that as an affront and suggested that, given the behavior of our client, his former mentor, he doubted the ability to successfully litigate any such action including libel or slander. Once the unpleasantness of our position was clearly outlined I asked Rutherford for an account of the events of the summer of 1882. Rutherford's narrative of that summer is reproduced below for your files. The transcription is from my own notes as well as those of Mr. Banks and Mr. Darling.

"The summer of 1882, you say? That was the summer my employers and I traveled to the American state of Massachusetts. A small college was hosting a summer series of lectures by visiting professors, and I had been hired to act as assistant to three of them: the medical researcher Doctor Henry Jekyll, philologist Professor Henry Higgins, and the vivisectionist Doctor Jean-Paul Moreau, who, still being notorious amongst the general public for his experiments on animals, joined us incognito. I, as something of a polymath and polyglot, seemed extremely well suited in serving the needs of these three distinct and distinguished researchers.

"Our voyage to New York on board the SS *Arctic* was uneventful and pleasant. Professor Higgins entertained himself by talking with the crew and other passengers and making notes on their dialects. Monsieur Moreau spent much time in the kitchens examining the anatomical structure of whatever things the deckhands brought up out of the sea. Henry, Dr. Jekyll, that is, spent the days reading and outlining a series of experiments in which he planned to expose animals, particularly primates, to a compound of his own design, one he said should have a radical effect on the baser instincts of the animal. It was a relaxing trip and I must say that the staff of the ship was most accommodating.

"We were met in New York by our host, a fussy little man, an engineer of some sort, by the name of Perry. It took us a little more than an hour to clear customs and lay claim to our luggage. The port of New York is an amazing place, massively cosmopolitan, ferociously busy, and I fear it may one day overshadow the great transportation hubs of Europe. Our bags followed us from the port to the station where we boarded a railcar. This final leg of our trip took us north through Boston and then into the countryside beyond. The beauty of Massachusetts rivals that of Wales and Scotland, and the small town that we finally disembarked at was quaint, picturesque, and reminded me of similar places in our own country, such as Denton and Causton. The station in Arkham, for that was the name of the place we finally came to, is old as American cities go, and the architecture reflects the influence of the British settlers. The streets were lined with beautiful elm trees, and in the early June winds they swayed back and forth, creating a lyrical, rustling sound.

"Our quarters were but a short walk from the station, and just blocks away from the campus where the trio of scholars would be lecturing. Doctor Perry had arranged for us an assistant of sorts, someone who would make sure that we could find our way around, make our appointments and our meals. Evangeline West was surprisingly charming, a lithe woman in her midtwenties with blond hair and stunning green eyes. She was well educated, and well versed in all manner of issues and subjects. She was a fabulous conversationalist, and on more than one occasion regaled us with tales concerning her uncle, who, if

I understand things, was a hero of the civil war, and afterward served as an agent reporting directly to the President. Her tales of egomaniacal dwarfs, giant mechanical spiders, and armored steam engines were as fanciful as they were beguiling. Many an evening we four spent enchanted by her tales. Had I known where such things would lead I would have done my best to discourage Miss West, perhaps even asked Perry to find someone else.

"Our lecture schedule at Miskatonic University was light, and it allowed for much socializing and independent work. Professor Higgins became fast friends with a local historian, a Professor Everet L. Watkins, and the two would take daytrips to the various villages in the area, including Witches' Hollow, Bolton, Kingsport, and Innsmouth. I even accompanied them on a weekend trip to the neighboring state of Maine to visit a dreadfully sad place called Derrie.

"Most of my time, however, was spent assisting Moreau and Jekyll. The two had found a way to merge their studies. Jekyll had not been able to obtain the primates he had wanted to experiment on, Arkham being more provincial and less well supplied than London. Instead, Jekyll was using rabbits, of which there was a regular supply. His experiments involved exposing the animals to a chemical reagent delivered via syringe to various organs and structures, including the brain. Jekyll would then watch for any observable reaction. Afterward, the subjects would be turned over to Moreau for dissection and measurement of induced changes.

"It was my responsibility to prepare the reagents and the animals and under the supervision of my seniors administer the dosages. Evangeline, Miss West, recorded notes during each experiment and later transcribed them. Her fortitude in this process was quite surprising. Most individuals of the fairer sex are somewhat squeamish when it comes to the vivisection, but Miss West was not only capable and levelheaded, but singularly unemotional, at least in the laboratory. Gentlemen, I will not muddle about. Miss West was quite unlike any other woman I have ever met. That summer she was vivacious, beautiful, and frankly forward about her desires. When we were not in the labs she would take us dancing. We all went even though it was only Moreau who was really capable of matching her. Even Jekyll was seduced by her charms and took to the floor to join her.

"I had at that time been in Jekyll's employ for less than a year, though I did have occasion to take some coursework with him prior. In that time, I knew that he had occasional liaisons, but he was always discrete, and the exact nature and extent of his interactions with the fairer sex were always ambiguous. The same can be said of Jekyll's relationship with Evangeline West. I can make no comment on the nature or extent of their interaction, for as I have said I was a hired man, paid by all three men. If you wish exact details of the nights that Jekyll and Moreau spent with West, I suggest you contact Doctor Moreau.

"What I can provide are recollections of my direct observations through June and into late August, when we returned to Britain. There was a particularly memorable day in late June; both Moreau and Jekyll were in high spirits, as was Miss West, and there was an inordinate amount of frivolity in the laboratory. This unprofessional atmosphere made working difficult, and by late morning it was clear that no significant amount of work was going to be accomplished. Thus, when Miss West suggested an afternoon picnic, I saw no good reason to oppose the idea. The day was warm but not unbearable and the four of us took our repast in a small field to the west of the college.

"It was at the height of the day that we began to hear a strange and faint resonance, coming from the east. The hum grew louder with each passing second until finally it resolved into a reverberating roar not unlike that of a large freight train. Evangeline, who grew up in the midwestern portion of the continent, took this sign to indicate a tornado, but as we scanned the sky for signs of the devastating twister, we discovered something wholly else. Plummeting in a linear trajectory across the sky was a fireball that was leaving a trail of thick, black smoke in its wake. It was as if some omnipotent deity was using a massive and invisible pen to bisect the sky. Its course took it directly over Arkham, Miskatonic University, and our own locale, and as it did so droves of people came out to look at it. The angle of descent was steep, and as it passed behind the trees I was already making estimates as to its impact location. I was only a few seconds into my calculations when we all felt a low but definite wave of ultrasonic sound moving through the earth. Not long after, we observed a pillar of smoke that rose up in the distance to mark the location of the meteor's impact.

"Motivated by the event, we quickly tracked down Professor Perry and convinced him to allow us to locate the fallen object and collect samples of the thing for study. He agreed, but he was entirely uncomfortable allowing Miss West to travel into the field, and given that we were only visiting scholars, a member of the faculty would have to travel with us. Moreover, Moreau fully admitted that he had little interest in actually collecting the sample, but was more than eager to aid in the experiments. In the end, Perry found a senior member of the geology department who shared our desire, a gregarious man by the name of Axel Lidenbrock. With his assistance we spent the afternoon laying out a search grid, arranging for travel, and gathering up supplies we might need for this local expedition. Lidenbrock and I estimated a probable impact zone and which local farmers and residents might be able to provide us guidance. These plans were quickly disposed of as word came to us of a farmer from the area who had come to town announcing the impact of the meteorite just yards from his home. Noting the man's name, we located his homestead on county maps and determined the shortest route that we could take to the area, fully planning to arrive there before the nine o'clock hour the next morning.

"We took a wagon, driven by Lidenbrock, with Jekyll seated beside him and me in the rear with all of our equipment. It was a warm summer day, the road was well maintained, and the slow journey into the countryside was a welcome change of pace. Lulled by the blue sky, a cool breeze, and the tune that Lidenbrock was constantly whistling, I quickly dozed off, only awakening occasionally when we encountered a rough patch in the road or encountered another wagon. We had been traveling for two hours when we finally came to the farm owned by Ammi Pierce. It was not his land that the fireball had impacted on, but his house marked the path that led to the farm which was our destination. After surveying the way forward, an overgrown and rocky footpath, it became clear that the wagon we had come in was too delicate to proceed. We made arrangements for the horse and soon, accompanied by Pierce and his wife, were traversing the trail on foot.

"The three-mile walk over rugged terrain led us to a set of ramshackle buildings, weathered gray with age. We were greeted by Nahum Gardner, a simple but amiable man, and his wife, Abigail, whom he called Nabby. The couple had three boys, strapping young lads who were quickly dismissed, along with both women, while the professors and Nahum examined the strange object that had embedded itself in the yard near the well.

"It was oblong, one could even say that it was crudely lozenge-shaped, rust-colored and seven feet long by five feet wide, and three to four feet thick. This matched the description reported the previous day, though as with many reports from laymen, the size had been exaggerated. Gardner denied this, saying that it had noticeably shrunk overnight. He pointed to the crater and noted where a gap between the object and the surrounding edge had developed. Gardner also reported that overnight the thing generated a soft greenish glow. This luminescence excited Lidenbrock, who attempted to isolate a section and observe the phenomenon himself by cupping his hands over the surface. He pulled back almost immediately, for the extraterrene substance was strangely, even uncomfortably warm. Intrigued, Lidenbrock called for the geologist's hammer and with a single swift blow gouged a chunk of the material away from the main body. The six-inch-long sample was oddly soft, pliable but tough, like rubber or tar. Lidenbrock declared it wholly unlike any other meteoric compound he had ever heard tell of.

"Borrowing an old pail from the kitchen to carry it, Doctor Jekyll slipped Gardner a dollar, an outrageous sum, or so I thought at the time, and the five of us, three learned men and the Pierces, tramped back over the countryside. At the Pierces' farmhouse, while Ammi tended to the horses and wagon, Mrs. Pierce made us some simple cheese sandwiches and fresh cool water from Chapman's Brook, which ran the length of both the Gardner and Pierce properties. As we were bidding our farewells and Mrs. Pierce was tidying up, she accidently took hold of the pail which held our sample. It took her only a moment to realize her mistake, but instead of setting the bucket back down, she instead peered at it with a most puzzled expression and called for us to join her. The specimen, she claimed, had decreased in size, shrunk since we first obtained it. I could not validate her observation, having little recall of the exact original measurements. Lidenbrock snorted and scoffed at the idea, politely but forcefully asked for the bucket, and then marched out of the house. Jekyll followed without a word, leaving me to apologize for my seniors and thank Mrs. Pierce for the meal.

"Our journey home was uneventful, and with some delay for the return of the cart and supplies we were soon in the laboratory and experimenting on our acquisition. Dr. Moreau and Miss West had set up a series of experiments, and frankly the five of us, including Lidenbrock, were like children with a new toy. Even Higgins, who had expressed no interest in the whole ordeal, joined us briefly and even organized a brigade of sandwiches and drinks as we toiled away into the night.

"As for the specimen itself, it was still uncomfortably warm, and despite liberal applications of refrigerated air, ice, and dry ice, showed no tendency to cool. On the anvil it was highly malleable and showed an unusual elasticity. As Gardner had noted, it was indeed luminescent, and when heated before a spectroscope displayed bands with unfamiliar colors which brought to mind the recent work on the detection of infrared through photography by William de Wivcleslie Abney. Under heat we detected no volatilization, even when we introduced the oxy-hydrogen blowpipe. Taking our lead from Walter Flight, we heated the sample on charcoal but were unable to detect any occluded gases. The sample was magnetic, and therefore clearly metallic in nature, but application of the borax bead test produced wholly negative results, which suggested a range of possible candidate metals. Placing the sample in a crucible, we subjected it to a variety of solvents including water, alcohol, ammonia, ether, caustic soda, carbon disulfide, hydrochloric acid, and nitric acid, to no effect. Only when we immersed the thing in aqua regia did we observe three reactions. The most noticeable reaction was the production of something similar to a Widmanstätten pattern, which is normally produced when applying nitric acid to octahedrite iron meteorites; that such a reaction did not occur during the direct application of nitric acid was in itself a conundrum. The second reaction was a detectable change in mass, which as we watched the sample on the balance, seemed to be slowly but definitely growing steadily less. Finally, the application of aqua regia seemed to engender a change in temperature to the sample which now seemed to be more tolerable. Fearing that we had initiated some kind of catalytic reaction, we placed the sample within a sealed glass beaker and evacuated the gaseous contents. This seemed to stabilize the sample, and as it was well after midnight, we all retired for the evening.

"Much to our chagrin and surprise, the isolation of the sample in the glass beaker did not prevent its slow decay. Indeed, not only had the entire mass vanished, the beaker itself was gone as well. The only physical evidence that remained was a small charred spot on the wooden table. Flabbergasted as we were, the five of us were also intrigued and were quickly theorizing possible explanations for the sample's strange affinity for silicon, bizarre optical properties, and reactions to aqua regia. Lidenbrock suggested that the meteor might be comprised of an element, or compound of an element, previously unknown to science. As Jekyll and Moreau debated the possibility, I noticed Miss West slowly rise up and cross over to the chalkboard. There she began to make a list of all the properties that we had attributed to the sample. Once she was finished, she stepped back and seemed to be thinking intently. This went on for a few moments, and then she once more went back to the board and carefully wrote the name Selwyn Cavor.

"Moreau and I both knew of Professor Cavor by his reputation as a genius in the realm of physics, but what Miss West could be referring to was lost to us. Cavor, at least according to Miss West, had consulted certain volumes in the Miskatonic Library on a project that seemed relevant to our current situation. In trying to resolve certain discrepancies in the vortex theory of gravity, Cavor theorized that there must exist a type of matter that exhibited behavior antagonistic to that of normal matter, and instead of being attracted to a mass, was instead repelled by it. He referred to such a tendency as anti-gravity. West was proposing an advancement of Cavor's theory, a form of matter that was almost entirely antagonistic to normal matter. This so-called anti-matter, when in contact with normal matter would induce a reaction that released energy, perhaps as both light and heat, but because it represented a complete annihilation of both components would leave no waste products.

"As West touched on this last point I realized what she was driving at. She believed that the meteorite we had sampled, the one that still sat in a field outside Arkham, was made of her theoretical anti-matter. Lidenbrock scoffed, but Jekyll and Moreau came to her defense, and soon we were all convinced that Miss West was, if not entirely correct, then at least taking a step in the right direction. However, so intent were we on trying to explain the behavior of our missing sample, we had nearly forgotten all about the source itself. Realizing that time was of the essence we once more divided into two groups. Lidenbrock, Jekyll, and I would return to the Gardner farm and obtain another sample, and begin negotiations for acquiring the entire meteorite. In the meanwhile, Moreau and West would attempt to develop a method for isolating the material and preventing its spontaneous decay.

"Sooner than I would have thought probable we were once more boarding the horses at the Pierce farm, and accompanied by Ammi Pierce, on our way by foot to the Gardner farm. As we walked we explained to Pierce how we had tested the sample, and how it had or had not responded. I could tell that much of this was lost on the man, but his lack of comprehension did not derail us. We trooped down the path, carrying our equipment, our pace quickened by our excitement.

"Nahum Gardner met us as we came upon the house and joined us at the impact site. At the sight of the thing he was as much taken aback as we were. In a day it had shrunk significantly, being now only about five feet long and the earth much caved in around it. It was still uncomfortably hot, and Lidenbrock suggested that it might even be warmer than it had been the day before. While Jekyll spoke to Gardner, I handed Lidenbrock a hammer and chisel. With a single blow, a large gouge appeared in the mass, penetrating five to six inches into the rock. A large chunk perhaps two feet across detached and tumbled to the ground. With gloved hands I recovered it and placed it into a large ceramic jar, which I then sealed with paraffin.

"As I was finishing the bead, Lidenbrock let out a cry of discovery and called us all to his side. In the area exposed by our efforts there was embedded a glossy globule about three inches across. As the sun played across the surface of the newly exposed sphere, a brilliant display of color reflected outward which reminded me of the spectrum we had seen the previous night while testing the now vanished sample. We all watched as Lidenbrock gently tapped the thing and were surprised by the sound that echoed back, which suggested hollowness and a thin, perhaps even brittle, shell. Before anyone could act to stop him, Lidenbrock gave the globule a quick, smart blow of the hammer. There was an audible pop as the spherical jewel burst and I watched for the pieces of shell to rain to the ground. Instead, they simply vanished.

Whatever material the object had been made of, it was apparently only stable when in that particular shape; in this I draw parallels to bubbles of soap and other such thin liquid shells.

"The discovery and loss of that globule spurred us to search for others, and within the hour we had drilled a number of exploratory holes with no results. Disheartened by our lack of discovery, our spirits were lifted when Jekyll revealed that he and Gardner had worked out an agreement that allowed us to return the next day and remove the entire specimen. We left with our new sample and hurried back to Miskatonic University in order to make arrangements for equipment and a heavy truck. As we trundled back onto campus a summer storm was blowing in from the east, bringing rain, wind, and lightning with it.

"That night we divided into three teams, each with a substantial portion of meteorite to work with. Lidenbrock was to repeat many of the tests from the previous night and ensure that the sample behaved homogeneously. Jekyll and Moreau were to pursue a study in which animals were exposed to minute quantities of the material, either intravenously or orally. In the meanwhile, West and I were to subdivide our sample and subject them to multiple treatments in an attempt to retard or cease its slow decay. After some consultation we decided to divide the sample into five pieces and attempt five different preservation techniques. The simplest of our designs involved a casement made out of lead, while our most complicated design involved containers made out of low-grade sapphires wrapped in magnetized wires which would then suspend the material in such a manner that it would not come in contact with any other solid.

"It was in the course of subdividing our sample that West and I discovered a second globule, smaller than the first, only two inches across, but still as dynamic and beautiful as the first. Knowing that this sphere was likely to be as brittle as the last, we extracted it from its matrix using fine tools borrowed from the archaeology department. Once it was clean we transferred it to a porcelain crucible, which we then set into a cabinet for safe keeping. It was only after we had completed our evening of work, trying to preserve the meteoric matrix, that we considered going back to research the multispectral sphere. Unfortunately, by this time we were all too tired to carry out any formal examination and after braving the thunderstorm we all retired well after midnight.

"The next morning, for the third day in a row, a familiar trio of scientists once more made the trip to the Gardner farm, this time accompanied by a heavy truck full of equipment and supplies. To our great disappointment, the great meteorite was gone, only a ragged pit remaining to mark its existence. I suggested that the rain had acted to accelerate the dissolution, but this seemed contrary to our laboratory experiments. When asked if he had seen anything odd the previous night, Gardner was reluctant to speak at first, but eventually revealed that the storm may indeed have had some effect on the object. The stone, it seems, had a tendency to draw the lightning from the storm, for he had seen tremendous bolts rain down on the thing six times in the first hour of the downpour. After that, Gardner lost track, though he admitted the strikes continued throughout the night. Half-heartedly, I dug around in the pit, but found nothing. We took lunch with the Gardners, a rabbit stew, and then bid them goodbye. Our return to Miskatonic University was solemn, the loss weighing heavy on our minds. Only the knowledge that some samples remained in our laboratory, including an intact globule, provided any relief to our disappointment.

"Back at our laboratory, we found ourselves beset by the most boorish little man. Karel Colceag—Higgins identified the man as Romanian in origin—identified himself as a reporter for the local weekly newspaper, the *Arkham Gazette*. His questions concerning the meteorite were at first straightforward and we were happy to supply him with answers. However, as the questioning continued, it seemed plain that Colceag was more interested in exploiting the Gardner family, characterizing them as uneducated and superstitious folk, and trying to manipulate us into making such statements. I cannot stand such men who seek to profit in the documentation of the failings of the less fortunate. It is rare that I use my own stature to dominate others, but in this case I was provoked, and rising to my full height I made it clear to Mr. Colceag that he was unwelcome in our facility and that he should neither write about us nor return for a further interview. This encounter spurred a discussion of how to proceed with publicizing our work. All agreed that we should only publish our findings in respectable scientific journals, and that communication with the press should be avoided at all costs.

"To accomplish this we devised a simple plan in which we provided to the public announcements that were designed to purposefully misinform. We made no mention of the surviving globule, nor that we had subdivided the sample, and neither did we discuss the act of animal testing. We did describe how we had sealed a sample in a lead casement, and after a week, when the fragment within had ceased to exist, we announced that event publicly. As planned, the stories written by reporters, including Colceag, detailed the strange properties of the material and lamented our inability to preserve any bit of the outré visitor. By the second week in July all inquiries into our work had ceased. We did not let it be known that some of our other preservation methods were slightly more successful, and allowed us to formulate a new concept for preserving the globule.

"As I have said, our research into the nature of the alien material took many paths, and while West and I pursued the preservation of samples, and Lidenbrock explored its chemical and physical nature, the path chosen by Jekyll and Moreau was on the possible effects such material would have on the organs and structures of living creatures. These were, in a single word, astounding. The material had a profound effect on the tissues of the subjects, regardless of dosage. At extremely low oral dosages the substance acted as a desiccant, drawing water out of the tissues and cells to such a point that the tissues eventually became dry and gray before becoming exceedingly brittle. It was both astounding and horrible to watch vibrant creatures succumb to forces that in a matter of hours turned them slowly into masses of little more than gray dust. More concerning was that the lost water itself remained unaccountable, as if whatever process was occurring was also acting to destroy the water. Attempts to determine the final fate of the missing mass proved fruitless.

"Strangely enough, while the samples of the meteoric matrix were slowly disintegrating, the strange globule was noticeably expanding, albeit slowly. By the end of the third week of July, all of the meteoric material had dissolved, while the strange globule had swelled to slightly more than four inches in diameter. We treated the globule with care and examined it in the most passive and benign of methods. Unlike the matrix from which it was recovered, it was cold to the touch, and was not luminous. Indeed, tests of reflectivity suggested that the thing actually absorbed light, but only in select wavelengths. Experiments with direct heat produced no measurable change in temperature. This did not mean that there were no measurable changes in the object itself. Indeed, I have already commented on the fact that the object was growing in size, but it was also gaining mass. The surface area of a sphere is a function of the square of its diameter, while the volume of a sphere is a function of the cube of its diameter. The sphere was gaining mass at a rate that was proportional to neither of these, but rather at a rate somewhere between the two. This perplexed us for a bit, but eventually I realized that the rate of mass gain might be properly explained if the mass of the shell were held constant, while the quantity of whatever was held inside was increasing proportionately to volume. Essentially, what we were watching was a balloon made of extra-terrene material being filled with a substance the source and nature of which was unknown. Moreau thought perhaps that the surface material was porous and was drawing gaseous matter from our atmosphere to the interior, but we found no evidence of any currents or vortices around the object to support such an idea.

"By the end of July, the sphere had grown to more than a foot in diameter. All attempts to halt its progression had failed, though we had achieved some success in slowing the expansion by placing it inside a lead chamber in which a vacuum had been created. Removing all light sources apparently helped as well. It was about this time that we began to detect a new property of the sphere that prompted us to ask Professor Higgins to join our research team. The sphere rested inside its chamber on a tripod of ceramic, which itself was set on a slab of lead. At irregular intervals the slab would be subjected to a low-frequency vibration, the source of which was obviously the sphere. As an expert in sounds and sound production we invited Higgins to apply himself to our literally growing issue. Of course, he readily agreed.

"The subsequent events cannot be laid solely on Higgins, or on any one of us. We all agreed to take the globule out of the isolation chamber so as to facilitate the detection and study of the strange harmonics being produced. That those studies lasted for days, and that all of us failed to realize that Higgins had neither slept nor eaten during the time period, is a monumental failure that culminated on August 11th 1882 in what can only be termed a disaster. It was Evangeline West who first noticed the strain Higgins was under, for she had been assisting him nonstop for several hours and in a state of near exhaustion had suggested that they both break for food and a cup of tea. Higgins launched into a tirade, demeaning the poor woman personally, and her gender as a whole, suggesting that her constant prattle was slowly driving him mad, and if she were simply to leave him alone, perhaps he could finally finish deciphering what the damned sphere was trying to tell him.

"For her part, Evangeline was most professional, and immediately left the lab to fetch me and the others. She returned with all of us in tow, perhaps no more than thirty minutes later. Higgins was standing next to the sphere with a large tuning fork raised up over his head with both hands. Jekyll shouted as he came through the door and then sprinted forward. He covered the distance between them in an instant while Higgins himself, in response to the sudden ruckus, spun around to face us. I do not know what Higgins's intention was, that point is moot. What I do know is that the collision between Jekyll and Higgins sent the philologist to the floor and deflected Jekyll onto the table top and crashing into the sphere. The great multicolored ball was knocked into the air and seemed to hover there for a second before it suddenly shuddered violently, and then, with a tremendous, almost comical sound, popped.

"The space once occupied by the sphere was now occupied by a brilliant green luminescence that quickly expanded in all directions to form a kind of thick blanket, or dense fog. So bright was the light given off by this gaseous substance that the others and I had to shield our eyes while we fumbled for protective goggles. Jekyll, who was prone on the table directly beneath the glowing mass, brought his arm up over his face to hide his eyes. West, who had obviously retained more of her rationality than the rest of us, donned a thick pair of protective gloves and then grabbed a large bucket. She dashed forward and, using the handle, swung the bucket through the odd gas, scooping a large portion out and down. I heard her cry out as her hand passed through the substance, but whatever had occurred, it failed to stop her. She kept the bucket moving, slid it and its contents beneath the lead chamber, and sealed it shut.

"Her actions were not without consequence. The main body of the phenomenon turned from green to red and there was a sudden piercing sound that rapidly increased in frequency, like the sound of a train whistle moving toward you. The mass seemed to implode in on itself, condensed, and then surged downward toward Jekyll. It enveloped the poor man and he screamed in pitiful agony, but only briefly. The open orifice was apparently too appealing to whatever force was motivating the strange mass, and it poured down his throat, filling the man with a sickly glow that cycled through some strange alien analog of the spectrum. As it did so, the shrieking claxon subsided and was replaced with a low, almost satisfied, hum.

"In addition to the droning hum there was still another sound, one not unlike the shrieking that had subsided, but of a much lower volume and somewhat muffled. It took me a minute, but I soon realized that the noise was originating from the lead chamber which Miss West was currently securing shut. Lidenbrock was first to act and fled out the door with a wild, fearful look upon his face. I called after him but it had no effect. Moreau staggered over to Jekyll, while I went to attend to Higgins. The poor man had collapsed and was mumbling incoherently in a language I did not recognize. I did a quick examination of the man, and finding no obvious injuries I made sure he was comfortable and then shuffled over to help Moreau.

"Jekyll's body was being wracked by arcs of blue electrical energy, the movement of which in turn caused his body to spasm and jerk Moreau reached out to hold Jekyll down, but as his hand approached the body a spark of energy arced out from Jekyll and threw Moreau several feet back. I moved to help him but he waved me off and directed me to a pair of insulated gloves. I stumbled over, secured them, and then moved toward Jekyll's energized body. The same manner of energy leapt toward my outstretched hand, but the gloves performed as needed and I was able to grab him by the shoulders and pin him to the floor. Moreau obtained another pair of gloves and was quickly able to pin the poor man's feet. By this time West had finished securing the chamber and had unraveled a roll of rubber hose. Together, the three of us bound Jekyll's arms and legs and created a crude stretcher. We cleared a low table at the far end of the laboratory and laid our friend out on it before covering him with a blanket. Once we were assured that he was secured we all collapsed in exhaustion.

"Lidenbrock returned several hours later and apologized for his cowardly behavior. Despite this he remained fearful and was careful to avoid approaching Jekyll's body. Higgins and Lidenbrock assisted West in transferring samples of the strange gas from the lead box and into sapphire containers wrapped in magnetized wire, while Moreau and I examined Jekyll. After several hours of testing and attempts to draw the substance out of Jekyll using passive or noninvasive methods, Moreau and I concluded that more serious methods might be needed. However, all of the ideas we came up with were dangerous, and likely to injure Jekyll if not singly, then successively. What we needed were subjects that were similarly infected by the same material on which we could experiment.

"To this end we took the remainder of the sample in the lead box and placed it inside a glass cabinet with a dozen rabbits. West had prepared four containers with small subsamples of the gas which appeared to be stable, although both luminescent and energized. The rest of the green, cloudy gas was pumped into the cabinet, where it almost immediately flowed violently into the nasal passages of the small mammals. As with Jekyll, the creatures were suddenly wracked with strange energies and suffered severe convulsions. After some consultation we agreed to allow our specimens to undergo at least twenty-four hours of exposure before any attempts to force the gas out of their bodies was made.

"To our astonishment, the exposed animals showed a wholly remarkable response. All twelve animals showed marked changes in morphology, with changes to the head, spine, and all four legs and to the front paws. The overall effect on appearance was disturbing, for the animals now seemed to be more comfortable in an upright bipedal position than as quadrupeds. It was obvious that the animals were in considerable pain, but they were also exhibiting unusual signs of aggressive behavior. Perhaps the most startling transformation was not the sudden restructuring of the front paws into grasping hands, but rather the speed at which the animals developed skill in their use. So adept had the creatures become that we found it prudent to add a lock to the cage latch and remove the key to a safe distance.

"Despite the observed and strange changes in the rabbits, we were thankful that our friend Jekyll was showing no such metamorphosis, at least not outwardly. Our concern over other changes increased suddenly after Higgins joined Moreau in examining the rabbits and recording their measurements. Higgins has an unusual habit of singing while he works—not any song in particular, but rather a spontaneous work created by his own mind concerning whatever is going on at the moment. In his style there was some semblance to the works of Gilbert and Sullivan, such as *HMS Pinafore* and *The Pirates of Penzance*. So complex were his spontaneous productions that they often contained not only lyrics, but also repetitive sections for a chorus. Higgins had this day composed an amusing refrain concerning the life of a laboratory assistant and was now into the fourth or so verse of the thing when he was suddenly joined by a chorus of tiny chirping voices. Voices that startled all of us, for it was apparent that the source was none other than the animals upon which we were preparing to experiment.

"There, in that too-small cage, the poor creatures who had been subjected to an alien substance were swaying back and forth, singing in perfect harmony about the menial tasks that must be carried out in a laboratory, in perfect imitation of Higgins's lyrical presentation. West and I were stunned, as was Higgins, and we ceased whatever tasks we were undertaking to appreciate the pure beauty of the sight and sound of what was occurring. Higgins softly suggested that what we were looking at was a form of mimicry, similar to what can be accomplished by some birds. I cast a dissenting glance in West's direction, for as I listened I noted several slight variations amongst the lyrics originally sung by Higgins. It seemed to indicate some level of cognizance as well as a familiarity with the English language. Such things seemed improbable, but given that these very animals were now exhibiting bipedal motion, hand dexterity, and vocal repetition, how much of a stretch was the development of not only intelligence but language skills as well?

"The question was never to be explored. Moreau was apparently unmoved by the entire display and continued with his work on trying to find a way to drive the gas out of the animals. While we were distracted, the eager vivisectionist had attached electrodes to the cage and with a flip of a single switch sent hundreds of volts of electricity surging through the cage and its inhabitants. The poor rabbits grew rigid for a moment and then seemed to vibrate to some strange frequency. Electricity arced between their ears and between rabbits and I could see thin wisps of smoke trailing into the air. Evangeline turned away and buried her face in my shoulder. There was a macabre grin on Moreau's face, and he seemed to take some horrid satisfaction in the process. I motioned for him to stop, not out of compassion for the animals, but rather for fear that the treatment did not appear to be having an effect, and I did not want to kill all of our test subjects. Instead of turning the power off, Moreau gleefully adjusted it higher, causing the animals to vibrate even faster. The whole thing reached a fever-pitched crescendo when the mouths of the animals suddenly opened and the thick yellow gas began to disgorge. The strangely luminescent vapor poured out of the rabbits and seeped upward out of the cage and into the space above it.

"The miasma hung there in the air, congealing, but at the same time tendrils of the material spun out in several directions, curling through the air like the tentacles of some deep-sea beast. After the last of it had left the cage Moreau turned off the power, letting the now tortured animals collapse to the ground in agony. Several were breathing rapidly, but all in all the beasts seemed to be relatively unharmed. Gently pulling Evangeline with me, I backed away from the strangely moving vapor and both Higgins and Moreau did the same. That the mass possessed some semblance of life and motor force seemed undeniable, for it continued to probe and pull itself through the air in defiance of all obstacles or breezes that plied the laboratory. Slowly, the thing drifted to a point above where poor Jekyll had been laid out. Thick, ropy masses roiled down and enveloped the prone man's head. At first I thought that the mass was going to flow down into Jekyll, but it soon became apparent that the opposite was occurring; the free-floating vapor was actually drawing its other parts out of the infused man. Streamers of gas were flowing up through the air, and in response the mass was growing larger, nearly filling the space between the ceiling and the work area.

"With a tremendous gasp Jekyll's body arched up as the last of the alien creature vacated his system, and then collapsed back to the makeshift bed. From a distance we could see that his breathing was labored, but he seemed to be regaining consciousness. The gaseous entity continued to probe about, and I realized that it was looking for the pieces of itself that we had sealed in sapphire containers. Moreau called for me to open a window and I made my way to the far side of the room with my back against the wall. I struggled with the mechanism, which was stuck from years of disuse, but eventually the rust and grime came loose and the upper pane swung open with a wrenching creak.

"Moreau had attached his electrodes to two metal rods, and using a pair of insulated gloves was carrying the charged poles raised in the air. He plunged one, then the other rod toward the alien fog, and then brought them closer to each other. The things sparked violently and the gaseous entity recoiled out of either fear or surprise. Moreau took a step forward and shifted the position of his rods, herding the radiant vapor toward the open window. The thing tried to move in another direction but Moreau anticipated each feint and countered it expertly. There was something graceful in his movements and attacks, something that reminded me of an expert with a rapier. He was so lithe on his feet, so sure of his movements, so daring in his attacks. Inevitably the extraterrestrial cloud had no choice but to ooze out the open window and into the open air outside.

"All of us were outside and we watched as the thing floated above the university, moving slowly like a cloud, or a rather thick puff of smoke. Whatever it was, it seemed confused to be out in the open and soon the only motion it made was to move farther and farther into the sky. We watched it, watched as it slowly receded from the confines of the earth. It became small, miniscule, and then at last a single solitary pinprick that was swallowed up by the sky.

"We thought the matter closed. Jekyll showed no indication that the intrusion or the removal of the strange gas had caused any permanent damage. He was, however, weak, and required the rest of the month to recover. The recovery process consumed most of Miss West's time, for she spent all of her waking hours attending to his every need. Of the three remaining samples that we had encased in sapphire containers, we drew lots for their dispersal. Jekyll, Moreau, and Higgins each received one of the wire-wrapped stones. By the end of August it was clear that there was an intense bond between Jekyll and West, and we were all quite sure that Jekyll would make some change in his plans, either one way or another. Despite our confidence, none of us mentioned a word of it, and when we departed in early September, Evangeline West was not with us.

It was on the fourth day out of port that a ruckus brought us to the forward deck. The passengers and many of the crew were looking skyward, shielding their eyes from the sun, for there in the sky was an object of significant magnitude. Of course it was not in the sky, but rather beyond our planet in the space between our atmosphere and the sun. Her Majesty's astronomer has called it a comet, and the press christened it the Great Comet of 1882. In Cape Town the Chief Assistant applied a wide variety of filters to his instruments and photographed the thing as it passed in front of the sun and then beyond it before fading into the depths of the void. His observations, duly recorded, testify that the thing was radiant with a light unlike any he had ever seen before. But I, George Edward Rutherford, know that spectrum, and so do my colleagues Henry Higgins, John-Paul Moreau, and Evangeline West, for it was the same strange spectrum that had belonged to the radiant vapor that had issued forth from the mouth of Doctor Henry Jekyll so many days earlier."

When it became clear that Rutherford had finished his account, I consulted with Misters Banks and Darling and we agreed that we needed to be direct. We thanked Dr. Rutherford for his time, and apologized for our brashness but requested that he be forthcoming concerning Jekyll's relationship with Miss West. Was it possible that Jekyll had consummated the relationship, and that Evangeline West had given birth to Jekyll's child?"

At this Rutherford rose up out of his seat, donned his coat and hat, and made his way to the door, pausing only long enough to answer my question. "Evangeline West is the finest, smartest, and most outstanding woman I have ever met. If she has told you that she gave birth to the son of Henry Jekyll, there is no reason to doubt her." He slammed the door as he left, and it was clear that his participation in our investigation was at an end.

Despite the rather circuital response, I do believe that Rutherford has provided us with an answer, or at least one that would hold fast in a court of law. With your approval, I shall draw up papers legally recognizing the son of Evangeline West, born in Arkham, Massachusetts, in 1883, as the issue of Doctor Henry Jekyll, and therefore an heir to his estate. Based on my estimates there are sufficient funds to maintain both the mother and child in a comfortable state, and if carefully marshaled it is likely that the child will be able to attend university, perhaps even becoming as skilled a physician as his father.

As for Jekyll's pocket watch, the one with the sapphire fob, I shall place it in the firm's vault at the Bank of England with instructions that it be released to the child when he reaches the age of majority, but not before. We may have been engaged by Dr. Henry Jekyll, but we must also serve his heir, and be sure that our young charge, Herbert West, reaches his full potential.

Regards,

Gabriel Utterson, Solicitor
17 Tower Hill
London, England
5 November 1888

# Chapter 16

## "The Desires of Herbert West"
### From the Diary of Megan Halsey
### June 18 1926

It was because of Aunt Amanda that I left Arkham in May, and drove south to a place where I could escape from her nagging voice and the incessant chatter of the household staff. The winter of 1925–26 had been particularly cold and long, with freezing temperatures still being recorded into March. April had warmed somewhat, but not enough to allow me to escape from the noisy chatterers that disturbed my own house. I had spent days in the university library, but there is only so much of that one can take, and so I decided to take my leave of the town, and summer elsewhere.

Of course, I should have been searching for my mother, I had after all sworn to do so. Well, perhaps saying I had sworn to undertake that task is an exaggeration, I hadn't even made a promise to undertake that task, indeed my mother's letter had expressly asked me not to look for her. Yet that quest had come to consume me, to drive me, to motivate me to become what can only be described as a lady adventuress, though my actual adventures had been few. I was, if I do say so myself, an Irene Adler or Jane Porter still early in my career, still waiting for the events that would shape my future. That the quest for my mother had gone poorly could be said to have contributed to my melancholy and irritability. And so I made plans to escape, at least for the summer.

I thought perhaps I would book passage on the *Homeric* and spend some time at sea, and then roaming the country lanes of Britain. When I mentioned this, dear Aunt Amanda scoffed and commented that whenever my mother became antsy she would take a place on Long Island in a little town called Blackstone Shoals. I had fond memories

of the place, vague as they were. Some distant cousins had an ancestral home there and one of their offspring had once been a student of
my father's, and I can remember that he had been rather fond of my
mother. Suddenly intrigued, I wrote asking if I could visit for a day or
so. Imagine my delight and surprise when Doctor Maurice J. Xavier
wrote back, saying that he remembered me with abject fondness. He
suggested that instead of a day, I spend several weeks. He was organizing a symposium of sorts, one that would run for the latter part of May
and into June, and hoped that I would come and help lighten the off
hours with a feminine touch.

And so toward the end of May I took the train from Arkham to
Boston, and then from Boston to New York, with the final leg being
from New York to Blackstone Shoals, where Doctor Xavier's butler,
Otto, was waiting to take me through winding roads of Long Island
to the castle-like Cliff Manor, a moldering stone edifice straight out
of some gothic novel. As its name implied, it sat on a ledge overlooking a small spit of ocean called Egg Bay. This charming little cove was
framed by the entirely aptly named peninsulas of East Egg and West
Egg, which despite sharing the sheltering harbor were two towns that
wanted nothing whatsoever to do with each other. East Egg, it seems,
was the home of old families, those with history and breeding, and of
course deep pockets. West Egg was the territory of the nouveau-rich,
upstart industrialists and people who were otherwise set apart, regardless of how much money they had. At least that's how Otto told it.
There had been some scandal a few years back, something concerning
an attempt by a West Egger to steal the wife of a man across the bay. It
had culminated in the death of a woman beneath the wheels of a speeding car. Her husband had sought revenge, and the man from West Egg
had died in a flurry of bullets. No one on either side of the bay liked to
talk about it, but the rest of the island from Queens to Amity Island
did.

Doctor Xavier and his daughter greeted me at the door. Joanne was
a charming fourteen-year-old girl with freckles and pigtails, but as she
spoke, I knew that she carried in her that same independent streak that
burned within me, and that she was frightfully protective of her father.
I casually inquired about her mother and to my embarrassment learned
that she had succumbed to a fever of the brain several years back, leaving

Xavier to care for his daughter as best he could. Watching how Xavier spoke and acted, concentrating solely on his work, I soon came to realize that while he may have been the adult, it was Joanne who was the parent, and it was she who did her best to look after her father.

Xavier was hosting this symposium for the Kilaree Foundation, under the auspices of creating in New York a revolutionary new medical center. The Academy of Surgical Research would be the culmination of Xavier's career, and provide him and his colleagues a chance to teach what they knew to the next generation of surgeons, all the while carrying out research on revolutionary techniques and procedures. As for the invited guests, they numbered in the dozens, and included Xavier's assistant hematologist, Francis Flegg, the wheelchair-bound surgeon Harold Duke, his assistant, the biochemist Preston Wells, the neuro-physicist Edmund Rowitz, and Leslie Haines, whose specialty was the grafting of brain tissues.

While all of these experts intrigued me, the most astonishing amongst them was a man I had already met, a man whom I thought I would never see again. I had met him in a gallery in Boston, the same gallery where I had met the artist Richard Upton Pickman, the man who had so influenced my appreciation of art and artists. Our encounter had been brief, but memorable, for he had almost instantly recognized my name; if not my face. That he was here with Xavier was not entirely unexpected; they had after all been classmates at Miskatonic, and both had studied under my father. But as Xavier had thrived both in Arkham and then in New York, his colleague had pursued less noticeable goals. Rumors had swirled amongst the professional circles of Arkham and most people were pleased that Doctor Herbert West had left Arkham and all of New England to take up residence in New York City.

There had been rumors once that he had died; he had been missing for years, but I as much as anyone knew that such rumors met little. I recognized him immediately; it had been years since that day in Boston, but he hadn't changed. He was still the same strangely attractive man, awkward in an endearing, if somewhat macabre way, with a mop of blond hair framing a gaunt face that tried unsuccessfully to hide behind a pair of wire-frame glasses.

He recognized me as well, and took my hand and kissed it. "Miss Halsey-Griffith, it has been too long. When last we met you were but a slip of a girl, now look at you—a woman in the full blossom of her youth." I felt his hand in mine and I casually caressed the soft flesh that ran between his thumb and forefinger. Ever more forward than I should be, I kissed him on the cheek; he was oddly cool, almost cold, and in an instant I felt those old feelings, the ones that had stirred inside an infatuated schoolgirl, begin to rise up again, and I blushed at the thought that I might actually be able to consummate the fantasies of so many years ago. That night my sleep was restless, filled with thoughts and dreams of the most lurid and titillating kind.

The next day was spent with Joanne and several of the other female guests, wives of various attendees, on the rocky beach that sat below Cliff Manor. It was a rather relaxing day of frolicking in the cool surf and sun. Xavier's maid, Mamie, a young girl just a little older than Joanne, made sure that we had a steady supply of iced tea and lemonade. At noon she brought down a basket of fried chicken and some apple tarts. While we were devouring this feast, which was more than passable fare, we were visited by a gaggle of husbands who descended on us like geese in their suits and dress shoes, ostensibly to check on their wives, but I recognized the old tactic as an opportunity for the men to ogle the women in their bathing suits.

Included in this was Doctor Haines, who took a moment to kneel down next to me and strike up a conversation about nothing in particular. To the casual observer it would have seemed that he was attempting to flirt with me, but as a trained expert in the art of seduction I knew this to be anything but the truth. He was speaking to me, but his eyes rarely made contact with mine, but instead were darting back and forth, lingering over the shapely legs and nape of the precocious Joanne Xavier. I was his unwitting accomplice, camouflage, as he all but salivated over the girl, who was little more than a child. It was all too lascivious for my tastes and I casually stood up and accidentally spilled my drink all over his tailored suit, sending him clomping back up the cliff-side stairs muttering to himself incoherently. Joanne laughed, and then apologized for being so cruel. I explained what had happened and that she should be careful around men like that, and then explained how to spot such deviants in the first place.

That afternoon, with her father's permission, I had Otto drive us into town. I had told him I was taking her shopping for some undergarments, something Xavier seemed relieved to not have to do himself. After Otto had left I rushed her through the purchase of a few pieces and then whisked her away to a small country store filled with various supplies needed for extended visits to the wilds. There I bought a small handgun, and in the range behind the store showed her how to properly use it. She was a natural, although a bit stiff. She had a habit of closing one eye while she aimed, but I soon broke her of that. It may have seemed irresponsible of me, to give a child like that a deadly weapon, but I saw little recourse. Her father was oblivious to the situation of his daughter growing up, and was marching a literal platoon of men through his house, leaving her entirely unsupervised. Something was bound to happen and I wanted Joanne to have a fighting chance when it did.

We returned home in time for a rather inspired dinner of grilled swordfish surrounded by spring vegetables and a soup of roasted squash. Xavier was particularly proud that all of the food had come from local farms, with a professional angler named Quint supplying the fish. The meal and drinks created a quite intoxicating atmosphere; and the conversation amongst learned men and their equally intelligent wives lasted for several hours. Why some men married women who were not their intellectual equal struck me as an exercise in masochism; as that night bore witness. Women and men who hold similar levels of intellect make the most excellent of partners. It was nearly midnight when our host finally rose and announced that he was retiring for the evening. In moments, many of his guests made similar pronouncements and slowly drifted away.

I, however, was invigorated, and by the light of the full moon took a stroll to the edge of the cliff to watch the sea crash on the beach below. There I watched as a lone and furtive figure dashed along the shoreline of West Egg. That figure was plainly Doctor Herbert West, easily recognizable from his blond hair, which caught and reflected the moonlight like a beacon in the night. Intrigued, I careened down the stairs and chased after him. This was not as easy as it sounds. No longer viewing the landscape from above, I could not see my quarry, but he had left clear tracks in the sand. These, however, were rapidly vanishing, being systematically washed away by the waves that were a constant eraser on the metaphoric blackboard of the sandy strip of land. This, I supposed, was why West had run so close to the waterline, so that any evidence of his passage might be quickly washed away. Faced with the potential of losing the trail, I removed my heels and in bare feet broke into a run, splashing through the surf as I stalked the enigmatic Doctor West.

We did not go far, in fact it seemed as if I had traveled only a little more than a mile before West's sandy prints suddenly turned and headed up past the high water mark and onto a vast and ornate patio that lay in the shadow of a house that made Cliff Manor look miniscule in comparison. It had been a magnificent thing once, all too ostentatious for my tastes, but someone had built it as a kind of bauble, a showplace for wealth and power. But as the empty pools, still fountains, and crumbling masonry testified, that wealth and power had faded, leaving their Ozymandian trappings to succumb to devouring time.

Even here West's path was easy to follow, for sandy clumps led from the patio through an open door and into the great hall of the crumbling palace. I followed those sandy breadcrumbs, leaving my own trail of damp footprints. Inevitably, I was led from the hall and into one of the side rooms, which revealed itself to be an immense library with twelve-foot ceilings lined with bookcases that were still filled with shelf after shelf of gilt-edge books. Huge ladders meant to slide around the shelves provided access to the upper levels of the collection. I was dazzled by the enormity of it all and in stunned silence wandered in, my neck craned up, taking it all in. A huge mural of the sun, the light of knowledge, had been painted on the ceiling, and care had been taken to integrate the rays of the sun with the light fixtures that had been embedded within. I found it odd that in a home that was clearly abandoned the lights still worked, but was grateful for the amazing display they revealed. I spun about, taking it all in, reveling in the obvious joy that someone had taken in creating this monument to literature and knowledge. For one instant I forgot what had brought me here, and that brief lapse was enough to turn the tables and change me from hunter to the one being caught.

"It is a grand facade is it not, Miss Halsey?" Herbert West's voice echoed in the vast chamber. He was perched on one of the ladders, his glasses on the tip of his nose, a fat volume bound in leather in his hand.

My pirouette disturbed, I tumbled clumsily to the floor and laughed at my own lack of grace and discretion. I had been caught stalking

Doctor Herbert West, but whom would he tell, he had no more business here than I did. "A facade, Doctor West?"

He waved the book in his arm in a wide arch. "All of this. Oh, it's pleasant enough to look at, but it's not made to last. The wood is substandard, the craftsmanship poor, even the floors are the cheapest of marble polished to a high gloss. These books," he dropped the one he held in his hand and it crashed to the floor, falling open as it split almost in two. "Cheap bindings, and only the lower shelves have actual books. The upper levels are all dummies, bindings filled with cheap unprinted pages. It is, as I have said, a facade, there is nothing of value or substance here. In a decade, maybe two, this grand edifice shall likely collapse in on itself, leaving nothing but rotting timbers and crumbling masonry to mark its passing."

"Then why are you here, Doctor?"

"I could ask the same of you, Miss Halsey, but if you must know I want to know the truth. I've done the research, seen the permits and the invoices. The man who built this place spent a fortune to create it, but where did the money go? This monstrosity could have been built for a fraction of what they said was spent." With careful steps he descended to the floor.

"Why do you care?" I lifted myself up and brushed the dust off my dress.

He strolled over casually. "Once something was stolen from me, and I found it necessary to exact terrible revenge on the thief. I thought the matter closed, but learned too late that my work had been taken once more. It was used, refined, sold on secret markets as if it were some illicit distillation of opium. My life's work was taken from me and used to help fund this man's lavish lifestyle and this decadent and decaying mausoleum. I want to know what he really did with all those riches."

"Does it matter that much to you?" I put a hand on his shoulder.

"It does." He put a hand on my waist. "There is nothing I loathe more than seeing my work stolen and perverted."

I brought my lips close to his ear and whispered. "What do you know about perversion?"

His hand reached down and pulled my dress up. "Let me show you." He found me ready and eager, and I spread myself wide and let him plunge his fingers inside me.

As he did, I let my mouth come to rest on his throat, and with practiced control let my teeth and lips tease the tender flesh of his neck. I heard him moan as I tore open his shirt and raked my hand across his back. He lifted me up, sliding his hand deeper inside and spinning me about. I wrapped a leg around his waist and bit down deep. Aroused and unstable, we stumbled forward and I twisted our entwined bodies so that his back hit the shelf and absorbed the brunt of the impact.

That collision was softer than expected, for the shelf and the books that resided there collapsed under our weight. As Herbert had said, the library was merely a facade, and this section more so than others. The balsa wood shelves and painted-on books splintered and deposited us at the top of a set of stone stairs that overlooked a vast stone chamber, the lights of which flickered and sputtered to life at our mere presence.

I was on top of him now, and we both craned our necks in opposite directions to look out over what was before us. "I think we've found where that money was spent." I announced with a laugh in my voice.

"Indeed." His hands withdrew and he made to move me off him, but I shoved him back down.

"We'll explore what's down there in a few minutes. Right now, there are things that I've been waiting years to do to you." He lay back and let my hands snake down between his legs. "It's your lucky day, Doctor West, in more ways than one."

A half hour later, still sweating from our passions, we were wandering through the cavernous cellars that had been carved out beneath the house. It was a lab of sorts, with the trappings and equipment spanning a number of fields. Some areas were clearly chemical, while others seemed to focus on electricity, and yet others allowed for the examination of biological specimens. Both Herbert and I were stunned; neither of us had ever seen anything like it, and West muttered that it was plain to him that this was where the money had gone.

While it was clear that the funds to create such a place must have been immense, its exact purpose remained unclear. That was until we found the room full of rabbits. They were dead, of course, and had been for a long time; that in itself wasn't unusual, and rabbits were often used as test subjects in experiments. What was odd was the way the animals had been preserved in jars. Hundreds of them lined the shelves and each jar bore a small dated note detailing some defect or the other.

Earlier dates bore horrific defects such as the lack of eyes or other organs, or some other congenital deformity. As I proceeded, the gross defects faded and became replaced with lesser and lesser flaws, until at last the unknown author was left criticizing the pattern and size of the markings on the fur, markings that were astonishingly similar despite the noted difference. Finally, on the last three specimens dated in late 1921, the unknown critic had written the word *perfect* each time.

"Herbert," I called out. "Have you heard of a man named Webber, a professor of experimental plant biology at Cornell?" There was no answer. "He coined a term for organisms derived asexually from a single progenitor, he called them clones. I think someone has been using this lab to create clones of rabbits. Why would you clone rabbits?"

Suddenly the far wall was shaking, a lever was thrown, and it slid to the side, revealing Herbert standing there in front of a vastly larger room still unlit. "You wouldn't," he announced. "Rabbits were just the beginning." The electric lights sputtered to life and disclosed row after row of much larger glass jars, each with a tag, and each containing a human embryo. At least, those closer to me did—in the distance I could see even larger containers. "This is what he was trying to do, this is what he spent the money on. He was trying to clone a human being."

We walked the rows. The embryos gave way to infants, and in time infants gave way to children. It was clear to me that the process had been tested on humans first—well, human cells. As problems in the development of the clone developed, the potential solutions were explored and then refined using rabbits. This process was repeated, until at last perfection in the form of flawless clones was achieved. This had occurred with the rabbits, and as we stood looking at the last glass container, it was clear from the label that success had been had with a human subject as well; but that subject was missing, the tube was empty, and the label with that triumphant word had been slashed through with a bold and defiant line of ink. There were two other containers, both the same size, or at least they had been. The glass had been shattered, the bodies that were presumably once inside were gone, and the paper labels lay stained amidst the glass, decaying into dust.

"A magnificent triumph occurred here," concluded Herbert West.

I nodded. "But then why destroy it?" I wondered.

The answer came from behind us, in a voice that was ancient and cracked as it spoke. "Because a man is not a rabbit." The figure that tottered out of the darkness was frail and small. Age had taken its toll. The man's spine was bent, his hair reduced to a few scraggly wisps. His hands and legs shook with palsy, and even from a distance I could see that his skin was as thin as paper.

I wanted to ask him who he was, but West cut me off. "Mr. Jay Gats—"

"That man is dead!" cried the old man. "A victim of his own childish and wanton desires; I will not honor his memory by taking his name." He paused to take a breath. "If you must, call me James. He may have rejected our birth name, but I shall gladly embrace it."

I waved my hand around. "You did all this?"

He sighed, exasperated. "My predecessor did. Not alone, of course, he had help, the brightest and most advanced minds he could buy. He had a gift for seeing how things might work together, how they might benefit each other. His Kilaree Foundation continues this work to this very day."

"That's the group sponsoring Xavier's work on the surgical academy." I reminded West.

James nodded painfully. "Surgery is just the start. By the time we finish there will be a dozen such institutes; one for each field, researching the various causes of disease and congenital defects and bringing mankind, all of mankind, into a paradise free from infirmity and death. In time, if I last long enough, we might even be able to reverse this travesty that has afflicted me."

West walked over to him and with permission began a cursory examination. "A form of Hutchinson-Gilford syndrome, I presume."

"Premature and accelerated aging," responded James. "Onset after about one year from being decanted. Most likely a side effect of the rapid forced growth needed to bring the body to adulthood."

"Who decanted you?"

"It was automatic. There was a timer that had to be reset every month or so. When my predecessor was killed the mechanism was triggered."

"And the memories, you retained them?"

"Everything from the day the cells were harvested for cultivation."

"And the other two?"

"Destroyed in a fit of depression. Impulsive, I know, but that is one of the dangers of experimenting on one's own self. At least I spared them the horror of being trapped in a body that slowly betrays itself."

West looked around the lab and found a small scalpel and a petri dish. "I just want to take a small skin sample." He scraped some flesh from behind the old man's ear. 'The good news is that I think I can reverse this. I've been experimenting along these lines, and I have had a startling amount of success."

I was surprised, startled, really. "Really?" He nodded, never taking his eyes off his patient.

"What's the bad news?" croaked James.

West lifted the scalpel back to the man's neck. "You won't live to see it." The scalpel cut deep and left a red line across the front of his throat. Blood bubbled up like an overflowing sewer spilling down the front of his shirt in great gouts. I screamed as he crumpled to the ground like a doll discarded by a petulant child. He was clawing at his throat, and horrific gurgling noises were echoing across the floor as blood pooled around the body.

The word "Why?!" filled the room, and it took me a moment to realize that the sound was coming out of my mouth.

He spun around and I could see the madness that had welled up from inside him boiling through his eyes. "My research! Mine! How dare he steal from me. For that alone he deserved to die, but that he took it from me and twisted it for his own devices . . . for that he deserves to suffer." He turned and plunged the scalpel into the back of the already dying man.

"You're a madman!"

"You presume to judge me!" Spittle flew from his lips. "Without me you wouldn't even exist. I made you! What god would humble himself before his own creation?"

I was flabbergasted but eventually stuttered out a coherent sentence. "What do you mean, you made me?"

The madness magnified his arrogance. "Your father was dead, your mother barren. It was I that brought him back, I and my reagent, which acted to return your father from beyond the grave. Without me your mother would never have had the opportunity to couple with your father once more, and she would never have been impregnated." He stalked forward and placed his hands on my shoulders, his lips coming close to mine, close enough to feel his breath as he spoke. "You're as much my creation, my daughter, as you are your father's, or your mother's."

I screamed at such a suggestion and reached for my gun, but it wasn't there. I hadn't worn it to dinner, I had seen no need, and now that I needed it I was without. He threw me to the ground and stood over me. I think that perhaps, if I hadn't just finished sating him an hour earlier, he surely would have taken me by force. Instead he stared at me with those mad eyes and that unkempt hair, as if he were looking into my very soul, as if my physical body wasn't even there. "You would be wise, Miss Halsey, not to contradict me in the future." With that, he left me lying there, surrounded by the fantastic laboratory and the man, or at least the clone of the man, who had built it.

What I did next was perhaps the wisest of all things I had ever done, and perhaps the most foolish as well. It was certainly the most dangerous. I wasn't as arrogant or mad as Doctor Herbert West, I had not come here seeking vengeance, and thus I was more rational. I knew that somewhere in this vast research facility there was a notebook, a manual, something that documented the work that had been done here. It did not take me long to find such papers, and after I bundled them together I left the house that sat empty in West Egg, but not before assuring that its secret basement and the bodies that were hidden within were all consumed in a blazing inferno, fed by the faux library that resided above.

It was nearly dawn when I returned to Cliff Manor, and I was careful to slip around the side and join the other members of the household and the guests as they watched the fire brigade attempt to quell the blaze that filled the sky with smoke and ash. West was nowhere to be found. A note in his handwriting apologized for his sudden departure, but urgent matters called him back to the city. He did not expect to return.

I stayed two more weeks, and found amongst the scientists gathered a man whom I could trust. I shared the notebooks with Doctor Preston Wells, whose knowledge of biochemistry was just as boundless as was his patience in educating me in everything from basic chemistry to the complexities of cellular replication and the methods needed to accelerate such processes, and if need be alter them in other ways. He educated me in the basic principles of what I had found in the basement laboratory, and at the same time I provided Wells with an invaluable direction to take with his own research.

Wells made a pass at me, of course, but I kept things purely professional. I had had enough of medical men for one summer. I had seen in Herbert West the genius that such men harbor, and the madness. I had borne witness to their quest for vengeance, and I suppose the lust that they try to keep hidden and controlled.

I had been a willing participant, a victim and beneficiary of the desires of one such man, a monster who went by the name of Doctor Herbert West.

One such disastrous affair was enough for one summer.

# CHAPTER 17

# "The Monsters of Dunwich"
## From the Diary of Megan Halsey
## November 2 1926

Progress at last! I have seen them, or at least I think I have. It was the last place I would have thought to look, but it should have been the first, if only I had been more diligent earlier on. If only Aunt Amanda weren't so damned frustrating. If only . . . but I get ahead of myself.

It was in the middle part of October and I was still reeling from the events of that summer, and growing increasingly frustrated with my lack of progress in the search for my mother. I say search, but the truth is I had done little more than skirt the periphery of the subject. I had, in the last two and a half years, done little more than entertain myself. It was true that I had acquired certain skills in the sport of driving, in the use of firearms, and in the erotic arts—I even had a working knowledge of the science of reanimation, though I had not yet found a reason to apply that knowledge—but I had done little in the way of actually looking for my mother. So it was with a sense of outrage at my own failures that I eventually picked up a small statuette from my desk and with all of my might threw it against the wall.

The racket brought the household staff, who peered through the door cautiously as I scattered the contents of my desk about, decorating the room in pens and papers and documents. This went on for longer than it should have, and my tantrum was halted by my aunt, who was able to calm me down with a slap to the face. After a good and needed cry we set about cleaning up the mess I had made, and it was then that Aunt Amanda made the comment, the casual offhand remark that gave me my first potential clue to Mother's whereabouts.

We were picking up the papers I had scattered, putting them back in order, and suddenly Amanda was in possession of the letter that my mother had written, the one that told me the truth about herself, my father, and Amanda, and what they had done to my stepfather. I had never let her see it before, never even mentioned it, never even discussed its contents, and now she held it in her hand. Yet as she looked at those pages, it wasn't the words that she commented on. "Well, they don't make paper like that anymore."

I nodded and took the pages from her and went to file them away, out of her sight, when the realization of what she had said dawned on me. "What do you mean?"

She took one of the pages from me and held it up to the light. "These pages have to be older than you are."

I looked at the page she was holding up; there was a small watermark that I could barely make out. "Something Dunwich something and something."

Amanda handed the page back to me. "The Dunwich Paper and Bag Company—hasn't existed in years, not since they closed up the mill. I think your father bought an entire ream of it decades ago, just before he died. Elizabeth used to write her letters on it, whenever she took you to the cabin in Dunwich." For the first time in a decade I embraced my aunt. I thought she was going to scream.

Two days later I was in Dunwich. My mother always called it a cabin, but by any real measure it was just another home, modest by the standards of our family, but in comparison to the houses that were scattered throughout the hills it was a luxurious residence. There were three bedrooms, one of which I had supposedly been born in, a kitchen, a dining room, and a single large room that served as a common room. A porch wrapped around the entire property and connected to three storage sheds and an outhouse. The real joy of the place was the lower level. My grandfather had built the place over the top of a cave, from which a fresh breeze constantly issued. It kept the whole place cool, and provided a dry space in which to store perishables. There was a thick layer of dust, and something had long ago eaten a small hole through the door, but the structure was still intact, and the linens, sealed inside hardwood chests, may have been musty, but they had not fell victim to rodents or bugs. It took a day of cleaning, but the well still had clear water and by nightfall I had made enough progress to call the place tidy.

After a quick and simple meal, I sat on the porch, looking at the stars and listening to the voices of the insects and frogs as they began their evening chorus. The cabin was rather remote, even by Dunwich standards. The nearest neighbor was miles away, and that was merely another hunting cabin, this one owned by a physician by the name of Houghton—who, like so many of the medical men who resided in the Miskatonic Valley, had once been a student of my father—or at least it had been. The night sky led my mind in strange directions, and I wondered how many of his students had known about his predilections, and of those who didn't, what they would say if they learned the truth of what he had been. I wonder what they would say about me if they knew my secret. It was with dark thoughts such as these that I finally let the whip-poor-wills lull me to sleep with their haunting songs.

The next day I took the Heron down to Osborn's General Store in order to stock up on supplies and a few pots, utensils, and tools that needed replacing. While waiting for my order to be filled—it was, after all, rather extensive, for I planned to spend more than just a few days here—I spotted a familiar though unexpected face coming through the door. It had been years since I had seen the hawkish and pale visage of Doctor Roman Lydecker, and never would I have expected to find him so far from the hallowed classrooms of The Hall School.

It seems that he had similarly not expected to see one of his students in this locale either. "Miss Halsey-Griffith, how unexpected, what brings you to Dunwich Village?"

"I could ask them same of you, Doctor. My family has a cabin not far from here." I lied about the rest. "I've come to make some repairs and take in the scenery. Arkham can be so stifling sometimes. Don't you agree?"

He seemed agitated, and his throaty voice cracked as he spoke. "Indeed, I find the wilds of the Dunwich hills invigorating." He adjusted his ever-present cravat. "My friends and I come up here for the sport, hunting and fishing mostly."

"Oh, you like game? I've never acquired the taste myself."

"Yes." He was fidgeting. "If you'll excuse me, I've an urgent issue I need to attend to." I thought he would be placing an order, but instead he dashed out of the store and left me standing there alone, wondering what had just happened.

Though that didn't last long, for as the Doctor left another man came in, one who quickly introduced himself as the local school teacher, Nathan Vreeland, rather dashing in a backwoods kind of way. He had seen the Heron outside, and being something of an automobile enthusiast wanted to meet the owner. He helped me load the supplies into the trunk and, as was to be expected, asked what such an obvious city girl was doing out in the wilds of Dunwich. This time I explained that I was spending time at the family cabin in an attempt to commune with nature and perhaps find myself.

Vreeland chuckled and suggested that perhaps I had read too much Thoreau, but then became suddenly serious. He asked if I had been wandering about the woods, and when I said that I hadn't, but planned to, he become quite concerned. "The woods can be a dangerous place. There are bears and bobcats, even a panther about. It would be best not to be out by yourself."

I thought he was fishing for a way to join me, but when I suggested so he shook his head. "I've got work to do, Miss Halsey, but I know of someone who I think would make a fine guide for you, someone who tends to wanders these hills and knows them better than any hunter." I thanked him for his suggestion, gave him directions to the cabin, and offered what I thought was a fair price for the services of the young man.

Imagine my surprise when the person who showed up early the next morning was neither young nor a man. She came out of the woods, on a path I hadn't even noticed before, and she was a sight to behold. First off she was an albino, pale from head to toe with pink eyes and a mass of unkempt and crinkly hair. She wore a cotton dress that was faded, stained, and torn, and a pair of heavy boots that had seen better days. She carried herself like a little girl, but she was anything but, and I placed her age at around fifty years. As she approached, I saw that her arms and legs were exceedingly thin, though muscular, almost wiry, but her belly seemed disproportionately large, not unlike some men I knew who lounged around an office all day.

She introduced herself as Lavinia Whateley and made it clear that Mr. Vreeland had sent her, and that she understood the task and what she was to be paid. There was something inherently sad about the woman, and in some ways she reminded me of my Aunt Amanda. She lived, she said, with her son, to the south, beyond the swamp, on the far side of Sentinel Hill. In speaking with her I came to realize that she had likely been poorly educated, a victim of her condition and the place where she lived, but given the manner in which she often corrected her grammar and speech I suspected that her situation was in the process of being rectified. I thought perhaps Mr. Vreeland was attempting to reproduce Professor Higgin's famous or infamous Pygmalion Experiment. I explained to Miss Whateley that I would like to explore the environs of Dunwich, and that I would be doing this on a daily basis, even on Sunday. She nodded and indicated that, "Me and me boy ain't . . . my son and I do not attend services. I have no compulsion against working on the Sabbath."

That first day we stayed in the area surrounding the cabin, which Lavinia told me was known as Sulphur Springs, so called for the waters that bubbled up out of the side of Sulphur Mountain and fed the aptly named Sulphur Swamp, the headwaters of the North Fork of the Miskatonic. We could see all of these things from the top of Cromlech Mountain, where a crude stone circle also provided a way of looking down on the meager farms and homes that dotted the area. Lavinia was a wealth of information concerning the various residents, who included the Hutchins, Bishops, Wilsons, and Dunstables. When I noted a small patch with what appeared to be the skeletal remains of a home, Lavinia told me that Toby Dunstable, his wife, and his sister had set fire to it, after the man had complained about Toby poaching on his land.

When I casually asked what Toby's wife's name was, Lavinia said "Mehitabel." When I asked what his sister's name was, she looked at me oddly and said rather slowly the same odd name, "Mehitabel."

I screwed up my face. "Same name?"

"Uh," she muttered, "same person."

It was then that I took a moment to check how much ammunition I was carrying, and if the Colts were in working order.

The next day we headed west over the Divide Ridge and into the Copper Hills. The day after that we went east to the valley that the North Fork had carved through the craggy mountains. We followed the roiling river past the Farr farm and then headed west again along the brook that ran on the south end of the Farr pastures. We cut between a marshy area that Lavinia called Snakes Pond and an oddly shaped mountain that my guide suggested was too steep for us to climb. Such were my days, and I came to greatly enjoy the brisk walks that Lavinia and I took together. She was not much of a conversationalist, but she was knowledgeable about the land and the legends that surrounded it. She was also well versed in what plants, roots, and berries were edible, and on many days we supplemented my rations with rabbit, squirrel, and raccoon stews garnished with wild vegetables and spices. On more than one occasion we were forced to flee, not from bears or panthers, but from folk who didn't appreciate strangers, or who held some grudge against Lavinia or her family. There had been a rash of youthful disappearances, only girls over the age of fourteen. A few of these girls had returned with no memory of where they had been, but with strange marks upon their thighs and buttocks. Despite the lack of proof, such events were laid at the Whateley doorstep and Lavinia's son had been forced to pay out from the family fortune to make such accusations go away. When I asked after the boy's father she became taciturn and had a dour look on her face. After that I was careful never to bring up the issue again.

It was on the last Sunday of the month, the thirty-first of October, that Lavinia surprised me by showing up. She had told me the day before that she was not going with me, for she had intentions to celebrate Hallowmass with her son. When she had told me that she and her son did not attend church services I had assumed that they were simply irreligious; it had not occurred to me that they might maintain a faith different from that of the folk around them. Not that the celebrations of Allhallowtide were so outlandish, it was simply something that the local protestants did not observe. Such differences in faith might be minor, but they were enough to drive wedges between families and result in the kind of animosity I had seen inflicted on Lavinia. At least, that is what I believed then.

As for why she was at my doorstep on this day, the answer was quite confusing: she had been forbidden from going with her son to the Hallowmass. He had apparently become increasingly contemptuous of her to the point where she was almost afraid of him. "There's more about him than I can tell you, Miss Halsey." I could tell she was genuinely upset, and suggested that we treat this as any other day and begin our hike. She smiled and together we set out for one of the few areas that I had yet to explore, the region to the southwest that Lavinia called Harris Glen.

The trek to the small vale that was set between Hale and Wheeler Mountains took most of the day, possibly because this was an area so remote and so sparsely populated that there were few trails in, and even Lavinia had not been down some of them. But that did not mean that they had not been visited recently, for there were signs, trampled brush, broken limbs, and trails of footprints of various sizes, some shod, some not, and some showing a most curious gait as if they were lame or twisted in some manner.

It was following these tracks that led us to the necropolis that lay hidden there. It was a cemetery, as large as I had ever seen, encompassed it seemed by a low rock wall that helped contain the innumerable headstones and monuments and tombs that stood inside. It was to this place, and the wrought iron gate that led inside, that our travels had taken us, and I knew at once that we were about to face a terrible culmination of events. I drew my guns and took a step forward, but then a lone hand fell on my shoulder and stopped me where I stood.

In all our hikes and expeditions over the last few weeks I don't think Lavinia Whateley had touched me once, and now she had felt compelled to reach out and keep me from entering the vast graveyard that stood before me. "Dawn't," she said. "This is auwn evil place. Sumthin' bawd is here." All pretenses of her attempts to better herself were lost to fear. "We shudn't be here."

I heard something move behind the wall, and a shadow fell along the path beyond the gate. I cocked my guns. Something grunted and growled. "A bear," I said, as if I knew about such things.

Lavinia shook her head. "Too noisy for a bear."

"A wild hog, then." I took a step backward. There was another shadow, and a shuffling sound.

"Too big for a hawg." She was pulling my arm. Something unseen creaked open and there was suddenly a scrambling sound, like rats crawling in the walls.

We turned and ran back the way we came, splashing through the creek bed. As we did I heard those ancient gates swing open and a thunderous din filled the air, like the hooves of a dozen horses pounding on the street. Lavinia screamed and ran as fast as her thin legs would carry her, not daring to cast a glance back to what had emerged from that crumbling necropolis.

I, however, could not resist. Like Lot's wife I cast a brief glance over my shoulder and in the rays of the dying sun glimpsed the silhouetted things that boiled and gibbered in our wake. They were only shadows, and those bore some semblance to the anthropomorphic form of man, but were at the same time totally indistinguishable from the terrifying shapes of long-extinct primates that we are taught once dwelt on this planet. They were only remotely men, and it made some perverse sense that they had chosen to reside in that lost boneyard, for I am sure it was the only place that they could feel truly comfortable.

We ran, my partner and I, we careened down that small brook, our hearts pounding, our breath ragged, the fear plain on our faces. We ran until we reached the shallows where the rivulet joined the main body of the Miskatonic River, and we cursed the fact that the only bridge across that dark water was more than five miles downstream. We paused to assess our options and then, after realizing that there was nothing but abandoned farmhouses and ramshackle shacks in either direction, we plunged into the cool waters of the river in a desperate hope that our pursuers would balk at doing the same.

The water was warmer than I expected, but it had a queer thickness to it that made each stroke a battle. The current was present but not too swift and although it seemed as if it took hours to cross that stretch of dark water, it was only minutes later that we were standing on the other shore, shivering and staring back across the way. There were dark figures there, railing and screaming against the injustice that we were on one side and they were on the other. We took a moment to catch our breath and gain our bearings. Then, as we slowly turned to walk down the bank, we heard the first ominous splash. Our heads whipped around just as a second object broke the water, and then there was a third, followed by gargling cries as they moved toward us. They weren't very good swimmers, but that didn't matter—if we didn't get moving they would soon be upon us.

"We should go," whispered Lavinia.

We clambered up the bank and onto the North River Road heading east toward Dunwich village. The road followed the river, and as we fled along it we could see dark and flailing shapes float past, their cries not of fear or requests for help, but meant to terrorize us. I am not ashamed to say that such tactics worked, and more than once I felt myself on the verge of terrified panic. It was only the presence of Lavinia that kept me going, otherwise I would have succumbed to the irrationality of fear and collapsed early on.

As we rounded a curve, our pace slowed by exhaustion, we came to a small road that led due north. There was a farmhouse with a light on and a barking dog. I went to move off the road and approach the farmhouse, but Lavinia stopped me. "They woan't help."

I watched the light go dim and someone hushed the dog. "The village then," I proposed.

She shook her head and started walking north along the side road, which was little more than a dirt path. We were cold and wet and tired, shivering as we plodded forward. "Where are you going?"

Lavinia didn't even look back. "Home," she said dejectedly.

It was pitch dark by the time we reached the foot of Sentinel Hill and I first laid eyes on the Whateley farm. It had been a fine place once, you could see that, but time and neglect had taken their toll and more. It had been a great old house in the Georgian tradition, but that had been years ago; now the old lady was a pale shadow of what she once had been. Unpainted, dry rot had set in. The second story was all boarded up, presumably because the windows had been broken. Lavinia walked up the creaking steps and through the door with confidence, and with no other real options I followed, stumbling inside her home.

*Home* was not a word that I would use to describe what I found inside. The furniture was ancient and threadbare, a broken chair stood in the corner by the fireplace, and huge piles of used lumber lay in stacks along the walls. Lavinia had already lit two oil lamps, but they did little to provide any relief from the gloom. I was still as frightened as I had been outside.

Lavinia saw how terrified I was and did her best to comfort me. She sat me on a chair and knelt down before me. "I'm going to get sumthin for us to eat. You need to stay here, in this room. Yer safe in this room."

And then she left, and I was alone.

The first thing I noticed was the smell. It wasn't constant, but rather came in wafts or waves. It was a rotten smell, a dead smell, not unlike the smell of Kingsport Bay at low tide. I gagged as the stench filled my nose and mouth and retched when I couldn't take it anymore. It was then that I heard the noise. I felt it really, in my bones, in my bladder, in the air inside my lungs. I felt a strange rhythm, a pulsing, that came and went and came again. It was as if I was listening to the breathing of some monstrous titan, and it was then that I realized the stench, that horrible eye-watering reek, came and went just as the subsonic pulse did. In fact it came in time with it, the two were linked, entwined, synchronized. Then I saw the ceiling bow out, it actually bowed out between two of the fat beams that were themselves visibly warped.

I could feel the panic rising up inside me, the room was spinning, and I could feel my eyes darting back and forth around the space, jumping at each little whispering sound. My heart was pounding, my ears ringing, and I was hyperventilating, panting, on the verge of screaming. I opened my mouth and let a small noise pass through my lips. The window by the door exploded and glass shards flew across the room, tinkling down over the furniture.

Lavinia came running back into the room and grabbed me by the hand. "They're here!" She dragged me through the room to the stairs; I thought for certain we were going to go up, to go up to the rooms where something titanic heaved and shuddered. Instead, we went down into a root cellar carved out of the earth. Light from the room above leaked down through the floorboards, letting us watch as the front door was forced open and a dozen anthropoid figures stumbled in. They tore through the furniture, roaming wildly, aimlessly about, destroying everything they touched.

They were making a strange mumbling sound, a gibbering; there were no words, but somehow they seemed to be communicating with each other. Somehow, and this I didn't understand, I could feel what they were feeling, and had a vague concept of what they were going through. They were terrified. As terrified as I was of them, they were equally terrified of me. They felt vulnerable, exposed, and weak. They were afraid of me, of what I could do to them. Suddenly I felt very sorry for them.

When they reached the stairs, Lavinia dug her fingers into my arm. She was whispering nonsense. "They mustn't go upstairs, they mustn't open the door, they mustn't let it out. It's too soon, it isn't time."

I heard feet mount the stairs, shuffling, taking them one by one, the creaking boards letting us know exactly where they were. Step by step they rose up closer and closer to the second floor until at last they reached the landing. I could hear a hand on the doorknob, hear the mechanism turn and the latch slide away. I heard the door slide open, the hinges squealing in protest.

There was a terrible, pregnant silence, and then the screaming started. I closed my eyes. A queer gurgling, bubbling sound filled the room as if some titanic pot had suddenly boiled over. It was all too much and I clamped my hands down over my ears to block out the screaming, that terrible inhuman screaming. I sat there rocking back and forth, and then I felt the warmness on my back, that damp heat that was dripping down onto my face and back. There was blood pouring through the floorboards in gouts. Blood, so much blood.

Lavinia was pulling me, there was a door that led to the outside; we scrambled up and out into the night. You would think escaping from that house would have been a relief, and yet the night provided no comfort. The whole farm was full of the terrifying and incessant calling of thousands and thousands of whip-poor-wills. They flooded the fields with their small feathery bodies and that hauntingly slow and repeated call.

We ran, ran around Sentinel Hill and through the sulfurous swamp and through the creek. We ran as if our lives depended on it. The Heron was waiting for us, and the car carried us through the winding roads of the backwoods until at last we came to the village of Dunwich and crossed the bridge that would lead us back to the main road. It was not until we reached Dean's Corners that we stopped and caught our breath. Lavinia made a phone call and a half hour later the schoolteacher Nathan Vreeland arrived. Together, the three of us drove back to Arkham and took refuge in Griffith House, much to the chagrin of my aunt and household staff.

The next morning we three sat around a table; we didn't talk about what had happened, only about what was going to happen. Mr. Vreeland was going to send Lavinia to Europe, to family he still had in the Netherlands. She would be safe there, and would be free to travel about until he had finished preparing a home for her. He had property in the Pacific Northwest in a place called Sesqua Valley. It would be a fine place to raise the child she was carrying.

I congratulated Mr. Vreeland, who just smiled and said nothing, as did Lavinia. It wasn't until an hour later, when the cab arrived to take them to the train station, that Lavinia spoke once more.

"The child isn't Nathan's, but he'll love it just the same. He'll love it just as I have loved it for the last thirteen years, just as he has loved me. All my children are special, Miss Halsey, in their own way. Didymus may not be as large or as intelligent as his siblings but he has his own talents, he just needs time, time to grow, time to be more than he is now." She kissed me on the cheek. "Thanks to you I think he'll have that time."

The cab drove off and I just sat there, stunned, unable to do anything. Wondering what madness I had rescued from Dunwich and released onto the world. Wondering if there was anything I could do about it. I thought about the Colts, thought about going down to the train station and ending things. But honestly I was too stunned to do anything at all.

In the end I went back inside and tried to figure out what had happened, what I had seen, and what it all meant.

# CHAPTER 18

# Excerpts from the Diary of Megan Halsey
## November 1926—March 1928

*5 November 1926*

Of course I went back. Of course I didn't go alone. I knew that if I were to go to the police, or any other official, I would have been laughed at and written off as a hysterical woman, so instead I turned to old friends. I met with Asenath Waite and Hannah Peaslee on Tuesday for lunch, and then after some discussion we came up with a plan. Ostensibly, we were going up to secure the cabin, but we would take a detour to the ancient necropolis and then stop in at Osborn's to ask some questions.

Asenath had a hired hand whom she could bring along; he was rather a dim-witted, lumbering man, but he was stout, fearless, and good with a gun. We left on Wednesday just after dawn, in the Heron, and reached the cabin just before noon.

The place was just as I had left it. Lunch and the pretense of packing took about an hour and half. As we were leaving I cast an eye to the south and caught sight of a lone figure walking up on Sentinel Hill. Even from a distance I could tell that it was a large man, larger than any man I had ever seen, and from his direction I could hear a strange wailing, a keening, a kind of lonely cry that echoed through the hills and stirred up the birds, sending them into the sky. I shuddered as that murmuration turned and reeled, casting queer shadows over the hills like the hand of some giant god, blocking out the sun.

We had to pass through the village to cross the Miskatonic and make our way back along winding dirt roads and around the low mountains. We drove to within a half mile of where I thought the necropolis was. The spot was marked for us. There were the tracks of at least three heavy trucks that had parked and then turned around in the mud and brush. There was a trail as well, one that had been freshly trampled by the lock of the still-green brush and broken saplings. It didn't take long for us to reach the ancient graveyard, but the trek was essentially useless. There was evidence that a great number of people had been residing amongst the tombs and in the mausoleums, but they had left little of use behind, and nothing that pointed to where they had gone. We must have looked the sight, though; three women and a lumbering man, armed to the teeth, stalking through the crumbling headstones of a long-forgotten cemetery, the wind blowing through our hair and winter coats.

The tracks led back the way we had come, and even as the road improved we could still on occasion see a track with the same tire pattern. It wasn't till we nearly reached the bridge that the road improved enough to obliterate any trace of the trucks. The Heron clambered over the aging wooden bridge and parked in front of Osborn's store. We left Asenath's man with the car while the three of us girls went inside. Even without our guns we must have been something to look at, three young women dressed in city clothes, their makeup and hair done, with fair skin, soft hands, and still in possession of all their own teeth. As we walked in the old men playing checkers in the corner turned their heads and one of them whistled.

"Yew be polite, Jed, or yer missus'll be wonderin why yer not'alloed in the store no more," said the proprietor, the eponymous Joe Osborn. "Now, ladies, what can I do fer yew?"

I smiled and stepped forward but Asenath cut me off. "We were looking for some friends of ours, we were supposed to meet them up the road a ways but it looks like we got the dates wrong. They would have been traveling in a couple of trucks. Have you seen them?"

"A few trucks came through baout two days ago. Big things came in from the pike, went back that way a day later."

"Ayuhh," said one of the old-timers. "Big trucks with an address down in Arkham, seen em ouat here befoare."

"Was there a name on the trucks?" I sputtered my question out before I had a chance to think about what I was saying. Asenath gave me a look as if I was an idiot.

While Osborn realized we were being deceitful, the old man didn't have a clue. "Course they had a name, trucks always have a name now, don't they. Big letters like on the buses that come throuwgh."

He mumbled a little, rummaging around in his memory, "Griffinson Trucking, that was it, that was the name on the trucks—Griffinson."

The look that Osborn gave us made it clear that we were suddenly unwelcome, and we all but ran to the car. We were all quiet until we made it back to the pike and the road noise settled down to a dull hum of the tires on the asphalt.

It was Hannah that spoke first. "Well, that was easy."

"Indeed," responded Asenath, "all we need to do is find this Griffinson Trucking Company."

"And convince them to tell us who their client was, and where they were going." I added.

Hannah was simply agog, staring at us as if we had suddenly said the most stupid of all things. "You won't have to convince them to do anything, they'll tell you anything that you want. All you have to do is ask."

"What are you talking about?" I must have been an idiot not to have seen what Hannah had.

"Griffinson," said Hannah. "Griffith and Son. You don't have to find the trucking company, you own it."

We drove back, laughing at our good fortune and the ease at which this mystery, or at least this piece of it, was going to be solved.

*8 November 1926*

Finally Young and his cronies have been able to figure out who ordered the trucks and where they went. The account was one registered to a small subsidiary company, nearly forgotten by the administration. It was mostly used to manage and store furniture for some of the properties that we owned around Arkham and Kingsport. It was rarely used, because it was rare that we needed to move furniture from one property to the other, but the work order was valid and had worked its way through the system and assigned trucks to three drivers who had shown up at the right place and the right time.

The trucks weren't the only thing that had been requisitioned. There was a ship, a freighter, the *Melindia*—she had been commissioned for two years, not an unusual amount of time, but what had been unusual was the fact that all the itinerary papers were missing. Griffith and Son had leased a vessel to an unknown group for an unknown destination to carry an unknown cargo. It was slipshod management and

Young knew it. He had no excuse, save one, and it was perhaps the only reason that would have excused the lack of safeguarding our corporate property.

All of the documents, the requisitions, the insurances, and the checks, they were all completed and signed by a familiar hand, one that I knew as soon as I saw it. All of this had been signed, sealed, and delivered by my mother!

*5 December 1926*

Molly is dead. She fell down the stairs and cracked open her skull while carrying laundry. Julia is simply devastated, and Amanda is doing her best to console her. I always thought of them as nothing more than servants, it had never occurred to me that there might be something more between them. I apparently have been less than observant concerning the relationships in this house.

*4 January 1927*

Amanda is taking Julia on a trip; they've decided on the Pacific. The itinerary includes San Francisco, Hawaii, Australia, Fiji, and some of the surrounding islands. They leave in two weeks and will be gone almost nine months.

*7 October 1927*

Aunt Amanda has returned, alone. She seems strange, stranger than usual. She will not speak of where Julia is or what has happened. When I press for details she gets this faraway look and begins to sing this dreadfully horrid song. I've heard it before, and I know the words by heart,

> *Ain't she sweet*
> *See her walking down the street*
> *Now I ask you very confidentially*
> *Ain't she sweet?*

It's a nonsense song really, but when Amanda sings it I just shudder and want to run away.

*5 November 1927*

Amanda has demanded that I replace the butcher. She claims that what the man is bringing is not fresh, and is making her sick. It's not true, of course. Since she has returned, her eating habits are abhorrent, as is her hygiene. I may have to ask Doctor Hartwell to intervene.

*10 January 1928*

Word from Young, the *Melindia* was seen by one of the other ships in our fleet. She was in London, and by the look of her she's been there some time. Our captain hired a local man to keep an eye on her, and let us know if she leaves port.

*27 February 1928*

The *Melindia* has apparently left London, bound for Boston. I've asked Young to alert our ships and those of our friends to keep a look out.

*23 March 1928*

She's returned! Not to Boston but farther north. A longshoreman saw her moored off the coast near Crabapple Cove. Young wants me to wait till morning but I simply can't, they could be gone by then. I've packed the Heron and left word for Hannah but I can't reach either her or Asenath, who is probably out with that milksop, Derby. I'm leaving a note for Aunt Amanda. If I drive fast enough I can be there before dawn.

The race is on!

PART FOUR
# Robert Peaslee
## May–September 1928

# CHAPTER 19

# "A Promise to Mary Czanek"
## From the Journal of Robert Peaslee
## May 3 1928

It was just after dawn on the first of May that the phone rang and my self-imposed sabbatical was brought to an end. I had spent weeks going through the papers and belongings of Megan Halsey-Griffith, though she preferred to leave off the hyphenated surname of her stepfather. I had found much to give me an idea of what she had been involved in, and the terrifying truth of her origin, but I was still collating facts in the case of her death. I had meant to spend those first few days in May retracing some of her steps, particularly in Dunwich, where she had encountered those terrifying semi-human things that had chased her from a long-forgotten necropolis to the Whateley home, where something else, something monstrous, had dealt with those ghoulish pursuers. Megan Halsey had not described the thing that had come down the stairs, but for some reason a nerve had been touched. A road trip to Dunwich and then a visit to Griffith and Son were in order.

The phone call ended all that, and slowed my investigation of the death of Halsey-Griffith to a crawl. The Arkham cops were all riled up—there had been a kidnapping. A child of a laundry worker had vanished and the locals were pointing the figure at the local boogeyman, the legendary witch, Keziah Mason. Normally this was the exact kind of thing the Chief would pawn off on me, or another member of the State Police, but the local papers had gotten wind of things and were forcing Nichols to act directly. He had sent a force on a predawn raid to the ravine beyond Meadow Hill, where they encountered a curious gathering of revelers who had gathered around the ancient white stone that had long been the subject of regional superstitions. The officers on site had been unable to capture any of the group, but they had glimpsed one suspect, a huge negro whom they described as easily seven or eight feet tall. The Chief himself had driven out to take charge of the search, and had taken a half dozen bloodhounds with him in hopes of finding little Ladislas Wolejko, or the men who had taken him. They needed me to do some busy work, talk to the mother again, and her boyfriend— the two of them had been cagey with the local detectives. There was a level of distrust between the Polish immigrants and the Arkham police force, and the thought was that maybe they might trust the State Police, meaning me, a little bit more.

Orne's Gangway is a seedy alleyway that runs through a series of dilapidated tenements that house some of the poorest and least-educated residents of Arkham, men and women who labor at the most menial of tasks. Anastasia Wolejko was one of the lowest of these, a washwoman who worked ten hours a day, whose husband had disappeared before the boy was even born. Her boyfriend, Pete Stowacki, had been less than cooperative and had apparently wanted the child out of the way anyway. She kept the child with a neighbor, Mary Czanek, during the day. Rumor had it that Czanek was a gypsy and that Anastasia had wanted Mary to sleep in the child's room, to protect it from being taken by Keziah Mason. Czanek had refused.

All this I learned from the notes provided by the officers who had carried out the previous interviews. But I knew something that they didn't, that it wasn't Wolejko or Stowacki who needed a second look, but rather the woman who watched the child, Mary Czanek. I found her where I expected, at home with ten children of various ages, none of them hers, crying and playing in the crumbling sty that she called an apartment. Something in the kitchen smelled like rotting cabbage and the stench wafted out and permeated not only the apartment, but the alley as well. She was friendly enough, meaning she let me in and pretended to want to talk with me, but her answers in broken English and nonsensical Polish made things difficult. I let it go on for a few minutes and then put a stop to it.

"Mrs. Mary Czanek," I said forcefully, "husband Joseph deceased, body found on the beach in Kingsport back in April of 1920." She was suddenly quiet. "That was your husband, Mrs. Czanek, correct?" She nodded. "That would make you Mary Fowler, Mary Elizabeth Fowler, born in Aylesbury, which is you, correct?"

Suddenly the whole immigrant demeanor was gone. "You know it is." She crossed her arms in front of her chest.

"So, let me get this straight. You're what, the five-times great grand-daughter of the witch Goody Fowler, the sister of Keziah Mason and Abigail Prinn, the three hags that give Arkham the epitaph 'witch-haunted,' is that right?"

"Something like that."

"Do the people round here know that? Do they know you're related to Keziah? Do they know that her blood flows through your veins?"

There was a panicked look in her eyes. "No."

"But you've told them you have powers, you sell them hexes and charms, little bags of bullshit, right."

She nodded reluctantly.

"Mary, this is what's going to happen now." I closed my notebook. "You are going to tell me exactly why you're down here, why you've been down here for more than a decade. You're going to tell me what happened to your husband, Joe, and then you're going to tell me what happened to little Ladislas Wolejko." There were tears welling up in her eyes. "If you don't, Mary, if you dick me around and try any more of this crap I will let everyone down here know exactly who you are, and then, when they come after you, and trust me they will come after you, I'm going to have a front row seat as they take you out and string you up, just like they did to witches back in the day."

She was sobbing, choking on her own gasping breath. "You promise you won't tell?"

I nodded. "I promise. You tell me what I've asked and I'll make sure no one in Arkham knows who you are or what you've done, no one but me."

I just stood there and let her work through it, but finally she told me. She told me everything. She told me about how she had been caught making little spirit bags and how her paternal grandmother had banished her from the family home at sixteen. How she had met Joe Czanek while walking down the Pike on her way to Arkham, and how he took her in and gave her a place to stay, and then a week later turned her out to any guy with five bucks. How Joe had married her just so that he could rape her and not be charged. How she had told him all about the family secrets and the legends of Arkham and Kingsport, and how one night she made sure that he went after a man in Kingsport, one she knew would never let him come home. Then she told me how she began taking care of kids from the neighborhood and how once a year a request was made of her, a request she couldn't refuse. She didn't actually do anything, she just picked the child, marked him or her. That was all. Then she told me where the child had been taken, and what had been done to it. When she had finished she looked at me with those big brown cow eyes full of tears and reminded me of my promise. "You promised you wouldn't tell them, you promised."

And I had, damn me, I had. I didn't believe her, didn't believe it was possible, but it all made sense, twisted, sick sense. I left her and wandered the streets in a daze, reeling from what had been said, and the promise I had made. I walked until nightfall, until the sun had set and the moon had risen. I walked until the only things I could sense were the vague blurs of obstacles in my path and the feel of my shoes beating on the sidewalk. I walked in circles, weaving my way through the city, but not seeing any of it. I crossed bridges and streets and then crossed back. I roamed the town like an accursed spirit searching for a place to haunt. Then, as if I had suddenly realized the truth, I stopped my aimless walking and instead set myself on a distinct path, with a very clear destination. I had a purpose, a goal, an objective, and a course of action. Yet in the short time it took me to reach my destination I discovered I had been thwarted. There were cops outside the Witch House, and the patrolman in charge told me that the college kid that Mary Czanek had named as a suspect, Walter Gilman, was already dead; a rat had eaten its way in through his back and then through his heart. It had burrowed straight through him. He had died screaming in agony.

That's when I knew that Mary Czanek had been telling the truth, and I knew I would have to do something about it.

They found me around midnight, on a hill outside the city. I was sitting there beneath a tree, the body of Mary Czanek smoldering amongst the garbage I had piled around her. They had to carry me away from there before they could put the fire out; even then the gasoline I had doused her in kept things going for a while. The fire department finally had to come and smother the whole thing. There wasn't enough to positively identify the body, and there was no evidence to connect me to her murder. I had made sure of that. They asked me about that, asked me if I knew who she was and what had happened.

"You have any idea what this is about, Peaslee?" the chief asked me point blank.

"No, sir," I whispered, "I've no idea at all." It was a lie, of course, but if I had told the truth they wouldn't have believed me anyhow. Besides, I couldn't tell them the truth, couldn't tell anyone the truth. I had made a promise, a promise that I wouldn't tell anyone what she said or who she was, that no one would hang her like they had hanged witches in the old days. No one knows what she said, no one knows who she was, and she certainly wasn't hanged.

I've kept my promise.

I think I can live with that.

## CHAPTER 20

# "Kingsport Days"
## From the Journal of Robert Peaslee
## May 29 1928

They put me on leave, one day back on the job and I was on leave. The Chief didn't want to see me, not on the job, not in the office, not even in Arkham. I was given strict instructions, things had been arranged, and I was driven to Kingsport where I would stay with my sister, Hannah, at her house. I had free run of the town, but if I was caught anywhere else, the Chief would have me in front of a review board. They took my gun and my badge, gave me twenty minutes to pack my bags. We drove from Arkham to Kingsport in uncomfortable silence. I stared out the window and watched the river pass by. The still waters were soothing to my troubled mind and I lost myself in that fluid darkness, letting it wash over my thoughts and drown away all the madness that had intruded in the last few weeks. That slate gray river lulled me into a contemplative state, and I reflected on the events that had brought me to this point.

My investigation into the death of Megan Halsey had driven me to the edge of obsession, perhaps even further. My relationship with Megan—with Megan's memory, her ghost—had become improper, unhealthy. I had developed feelings for a dead woman. I had met her once, years ago, and had been mildly intrigued, and perhaps even developed a kind of attraction to the girl, but that was all. Now, all these years later, with her journals and notes, her entire life at my fingertips, was it any surprise that the attraction had turned into something more? I had heard of men who had lost their wives, and yet for years afterward still spoke to them, still loved them. I was reminded of the man I had met on the train, Mr. Dennis, who had loved his wife so much he was willing to risk his life to understand her death. Such love for a dead woman—could I feel the same way?

It was not a question of her gender. I had loved women before, though not for years, not since before the war. Women were complicated creatures whom I couldn't understand no matter how hard I tried. Men I understood; their motives and actions were plain, if oft times heavy-handed, but I knew what they wanted and could respond accordingly. Women left me confused. I couldn't discern their motivations. They seemed too whimsical, too capricious, and too unfathomable. No matter how hard I tried I simply couldn't plumb their depths. Megan Halsey was the exception. I knew all about her; knew what she liked to eat, and read, what she liked to wear, and listen to. Megan Halsey was the first woman I had ever truly gotten close to, but only because she was dead. Was that so wrong?

I suppose in a way it was. My relationships with other people, with women and men, were always so forced, so artificial. I observed the behavior of couples I saw and imitated it, but the love they felt for each other, the passion that seemed so real, so vibrant, that made them so alive, I never felt any of that. For anyone, not even Arthur. My brother the analyst would probably blame this on what had happened to our father, and how that had made me reticent to trust anyone ever again. There was some truth to it, I suppose, and that might also explain why I was so strongly drawn to the memory of Megan Halsey. Being dead, Megan could never fail me, never disappointment, never become distant, and never leave me. In some ways she was the perfect person for me to fall in love with. Was it wrong that I loved a dead woman? Even if it was wrong, whom would it hurt? No one would ever know. Who would ever care?

Kingsport is a sleepy little town full of federal architecture and small bungalows overlooking a quaint harbor. It had been a village of shipbuilders and fishermen once, but that was decades ago, and now some great mercantile families survived by renting their own houses out to vacationing tourists; others had opened up restaurants or galleries to show off the work of local craftsmen. There were a few antique and curio shops that showcased the rich seafaring past of the village. A good portion of the harbor had been converted from a working wharf to anchorages for pleasure craft. In the public marina a few enterprising captains ran charter trips for adventurous men who longed to battle against whatever lurked in the depths.

My sister's home was on Bradford Avenue, overlooking the public marina, and only a block from The Hall School, where she worked. It was a small two-bedroom bungalow that had once been a carriage house. It was nothing fancy, but from the front gate I could see the harbor and the islands that framed its mouth. As I walked up the shell rock path, the red, wooden barn door swung open, and my sister, Hannah, was standing there with that look on her face, the same one my mother used to give me when I had done something wrong, and she was more concerned than disappointed.

As caring as ever, Hannah hustled me inside her cottage and settled me in. It was a cozy little place, not quite cramped, but much smaller than I had been accustomed to living at Griffith House. The kitchen was tight and cluttered with a wide assortment of baking supplies, which, judging from the flour strewn about, Hannah used with some regularity. The whole south side of the house was comprised of two modestly sized bedrooms that shared a small bath. There was neither a formal dining room nor parlor, but rather a single space that functioned as both with a set of large windows looking out over the front yard and beyond that the bay. On the north side of the room there was a fireplace and a set of steep stairs that led up to a semifinished attic. Here in this drafty place my sister had set up a kind of rudimentary laboratory in which she experimented in the development of photographs. Hannah had some time ago purchased a camera, a Kodak Brownie 2, and had become a rather adept amateur photographer. It was then that I realized that the numerous framed photographs decorating her walls were the work of my own sister, and presumably captured the architecture, landscape, and inhabitants of Kingsport.

Hannah was quite proud of her work, and had been involved in her hobby for more than a decade, though she had only recently begun developing her own photographs. She had even found a way to turn her passion into a small enterprise. She had gotten into the habit of photographing the staff and students of The Hall School, sometimes as individuals, but mostly as a group image. These she could reproduce and sell to students who wished to have some keepsake of their time. Some students even paid for individual sittings. She had vast binders full of the students and teachers who had been part of the school, stacks of them, of which she was quite proud.

As much as I was pleased that my sister had secured a position and a pastime that seemed to make her happy, I knew that my mother was not. Hannah was in her late twenties and already a widow, having lost her husband, Jack, to an accident in Brooklyn. Mother had hoped for her to remarry, and while she had received several marriage proposals she had turned them all down. Not that my mother was in any position to cast stones. From what Hannah said, Mother's second marriage had collapsed and the divorce was nearly finalized. Hannah blamed my mother's Bohemian lifestyle, her association with the literati of Boston and New York, for her current condition. The fact that her husband had left her to pursue his own career in literature seemed not to quench Hannah's opinion of the reasons behind Mother's latest marital failing. Besides, it seemed that there was a man interested in Hannah, a fellow teacher at the school who had come just this year. His name was Samuel Beckett, and he was from Indiana, where his family ran a dairy farm. They had only been seeing each other for a few months, but apparently Beckett's folksy Midwestern ways were quite charming, at least to Hannah. She promised to introduce me to him some time during the week, after I had settled in.

How exactly does one settle into a prison? True, Kingsport was more comfortable than most institutes of incarceration, and larger, too, but I had been to Paris and London—this seaside town was just too quaint for me. And knowing that I couldn't leave made me chafe. The truth is I could have left anytime I wanted to, but I had work to do in Massachusetts, work that required me to keep my badge, that meant keeping my nose clean and getting back in the good graces of Chief Nichols. So despite my desire to cut and run I resigned myself to an extended stay in the sleepy town of Kingsport.

That did not mean I had to enjoy it.

I immediately fell into a bad habit, of staying up all night long reading and then sleeping late. I was a voracious reader and could often read an entire book in a single day, and was often unsatisfied or disappointed with myself if I didn't accomplish just that. So, late nights reading were followed by late mornings and then slow, leisurely walks around the wharf. Each morning I would head to the south, passing the Coast Guard Station and then the private yacht club, before turning around and heading back the same way, this time not going home, but rather to the small utilitarian building that passed as a library. The lady in charge—I hesitate to call her a librarian for fear of insulting the profession—was a thin, crane-like woman who never once bothered to introduce herself, and seemed to have horrid tastes in books, preferring popular romances by the likes of Twain and Chambers. Given that Kingsport was a resort town, such views on popular fiction were likely to be understandable, but there really is no excuse not to make authors like Watson and Hastings available. There was even a book on the shelves by my mother, a collection of her short stories called *The Unreal Edge and Others*. After locating a book that I thought I would enjoy, I often stopped at a small corner shop that prepared cheap, albeit fine, selections of local fare, and began my book, watching the tide go out and the boats come in. After an hour or so I would take another walk past the station and then wind my way through the streets back home. There I would do a bit of light housework, prepare dinner, and greet Hannah when she came home from school around six in the evening. She balked at this at first, but as I was not working and she was, she resigned herself to the fact that I would be taking over some duties usually assigned to women. As if that division of labor ever made any sense.

This was my routine, our routine, except for Sunday, when the library was closed and Hannah's day at the school was limited to making sure her pupils attended the chapel for morning services. It went on like this for ten days, and I saw no reason to make any change to it, and wouldn't have if it hadn't been for a patch of bad weather one morning that trapped me in the library, along with several others. The sky had been threatening all morning, and I had hoped to beat any cloudburst to the diner, but instead found my exit blocked by a group of three men who ran inside to escape the sudden downpour and vicious biting wind that was blowing in off the bay. They were genial fellows, retirees by the look of things, and from their demeanor on a kind of working holiday, though what work they did together wasn't clear.

Before I could settle into a chair and begin my book, the three men asked if I would join them in a friendly game, to pass the time. "My name is Zachariah Armitage, the man with the bushy hair is Arnold Zeck, and the gentleman in glasses is Alton Oz. Our friends call us the A to Z Club." They were all about my age, and of average appearance with nothing that would distinguish them from the general public.

"Armitage? You aren't related to Henry Armitage, the librarian at Miskatonic University?"

He nodded. "Guilty as charged. He's my father; though don't ask him about me, I'm afraid I'm a bit of a black sheep. He hasn't spoken to me in years."

I smiled. "I haven't spoken to my father in years either. My name is Peaslee, Robert Peaslee." I left off my credentials.

Armitage shook my hand vigorously. "We play Anagrams, Mr. Peaslee. Would you join us?"

I indicated my affirmation and the four of us sat down around a large, round table. Something was said to the librarian, and she stood up in a huff and departed for one of the back rooms.

As Armitage spread the lettered tiles out on the table he explained the rules they played by. "Seven bank tiles each. Four-letter words or more to play. You must draw a letter at the beginning of each turn. You can add what you draw to your bank, but you can only have seven letters in your bank at the end of your turn; any more tiles than that go into the pool. Words can be stolen from other players using your letters or pool letters to rearrange them into new words, or add prefixes or suffixes, but not simple plurals. Most tiles at the end wins." Not dissimilar to how I had played before. "I warn you, Mr. Peaslee, we take the game seriously."

As we drew our tiles Mr. Oz began a conversation. "Tell me, Mr. Peaslee, what brings you to Kingsport?"

I had no desire to tell these men the truth, but there was no need to lie either. "I'm taking some time off from the job, visiting family."

"And what is it you do, Mr. Peaslee?" Arnold Zeck's voice was gravelly but precise.

"I'm not exactly sure how to describe it." I was stalling for time to think. "During the war I was in security, and afterward I sort of fell into a position doing the same kind of thing, only for civilian clients. Let's just say I protect people from things they don't even know they need protecting from."

"Well, that's rather vague," commented Oz as he drew his last tile and indicated that it was Armitage's turn. "What kind of people employ you?"

I opened my mouth to respond but was cut off by Armitage. "Whores," he said, laying out his tiles.

My eyes grew wide. "I beg your pardon?"

He was arranging his tiles on the table. "H-O-R-S-E, horse, five letters."

"Yes, of course. What do you gentlemen do, if I may ask?"

Armitage was gathering new tiles, while Zeck was pondering what to do with his own, leaving Oz to answer me. "I'm in shipping myself, exclusive clientele, all very secretive mind you. Armitage is in bookkeeping, and Zeck deals in insurance."

"Lyre!" shouted Zeck, laying out the four tiles of his word. "I make sure that people can sleep comfortable at night, knowing that their most valued things are safe and secure."

It was my turn; there was nothing in the pool and I looked down at my seven letters in despair:

F Z U W I T E

I had nothing to work with in my hand, but suddenly realized that I could steal a word, thanks to my mishearing what Armitage had said earlier. I reached across the table. "Horse becomes Whores, a simple plural yes, but the S was already in play."

Zeck nodded. "Those are the rules."

While I drew letters, Oz laid out two letters and stole LYRE by turning it into REALLY.

It went on like this for a good hour, during which the rain stopped and the sun burned through the clouds. They asked me to play a second game, but I declined. I had been entertained, but I was rather peckish and desperately needed something to fill my stomach. As I left, I paused and finally asked something that I had wanted to ask all morning. "You know why I'm here gentlemen, but I wonder what brings you three to Kingsport? It is a little early for the tourist season."

Armitage smiled as he gathered the tiles up and dropped them back in the bag. "We're here on business, Mr. Peaslee. You see, there was a ship and a cargo that never made it to port. We've heard rumors that it's been sighted adrift off the coast. Some of the cargo belonged to Oz, and Mr. Zeck provided the insurance. I was the bookkeeper responsible for the inventory. We've come to see if we can find it. Sadly, the local coast guard hasn't been much help."

I nodded and made to leave, but then turned back. "Just to satisfy my own curiosity," I was waving my arms, trying to appear casual. "What was the name of the ship?"

Armitage cinched the bag shut. "She was the *Melindia*, steaming from Great Britain. Do you know her?"

I nodded. "I've heard of her." With that, I left and made my way back to Hannah's house.

The rain started up again just after Hannah returned, and just as my version of grilled steak and spring vegetables was hitting the table. Afterward, we sat in the parlor and talked. It was the first time we had had a simple conversation in a long time. I told her about my day, she dug out her bag of Anagram tiles and offered to play, but I declined. Instead, I decided to take an interest in her hobby, and asked to see her photograph albums.

Most of the work was of the people and buildings and landscapes, or I should say seascapes, of Kingsport. There was a magnificent shot from the top of a tower looking down onto the harbor and the boats that hugged the docks. She had a real penchant for capturing the mood of the village; whether that was in the play between light and shadows that permeated the streets, or in the lines and eyes of its inhabitants, didn't seem to matter. Each photograph told a story, and Hannah seemed all too ready to help expound on those tales.

Eventually we left her artistic work behind and began leafing through her formal portraits of the students and teachers at The Hall School. At every page she would stop and talk about a particular student that she had grown to care about, what their dreams had been and what they eventually ended up doing. Sometimes their lives were exactly what they expected; others had lives filled with nothing but disappointment. Casually we flipped the page and there was a photograph of the school faculty from almost eight years earlier. Hannah had set it up on a timer. She looked so proud to be a member of the faculty, standing there surrounded by the stern faces of the other teachers.

Yet as I looked at those erudite scholars, the face of one seemed strangely familiar. He was a tall man, distinguished looking with a cravat and large decorative pin holding it in place. I had seen him before, I just didn't know where. I asked Hannah about it, pointing at the stone-faced instructor.

"Oh yes, that's Mr. Lydecker, I've talked to you about him before. He was a science instructor—well, still is, technically. He's on sabbatical. Friendly enough man, I suppose, hard to talk to. He was wounded in the war and has a terrible time breathing on occasion."

"Lydecker?"

"Yes, Roman LaChampele Lydecker, he's Canadian, I think—well, French-Canadian."

"Hmm." I didn't know the name, but the face seemed so familiar. It gnawed at the back of my mind. I closed the book and let whatever was bothering me slip away. I was supposed to be relaxing, recovering, not obsessing over a man I had never met.

But I had met him, I was sure of it.

About nine that evening I decided to retire to my room and read. Hannah saw the novel I had borrowed from the library and frowned. "You won't be happy with how that ends," she told me. "I don't know anyone who read *Tamara* and liked the ending. The new issue of *Whispers* is out with stories by Mother, Simon Jacobs, and Randolph Carter."

I was fond of Carter's fantasies so picked it up and flipped through, but I couldn't find anything attributed to the author. "Hannah, there's nothing in here by Carter."

She laughed, "Not under his real name, he's supposed to be missing you know, but he's been publishing regularly under the pseudonym Howard Lovecraft—it's a kind of anagram."

I looked at the table of contents, and sure enough there was a story by an author named Lovecraft, but for the life of me I couldn't see how Howard Lovecraft was even close to an anagram for Randolph Carter. "Are you sure they're the same author?"

"I'll show you," she said, going to the cabinet and getting her bag full of Anagram tiles. It took her a moment, but eventually she had all the tiles she needed and spelled out the supposed pseudonym.

HOWARD LOVECRAFT

"Some of this is easy," she said, and began to rearrange the letters. "Remember the accent, we don't pronounce our Rs properly, we use an H sound."

## OWARD LOV F CARTEH

"Keep in mind that the PH sound is just an F, and we tend to draw out our Os."

## RAVDOOWLF CARTEH

"Hannah," I said, "there's a vague phonetics to it, I'll admit, but you can't replace an N with a V, it doesn't make any sense."

"It doesn't make any sense in English, but Carter was an antiquarian, a classicist, he studied both Latin and Greek. In ancient Greek, the symbol for a lower case N is the letter V."

I stared at the letters that she had rearranged on the table:

## RAVDOOWLF CARTEH

"Who would have thought," I said.

"Actually, Mother worked it out. I think she recognized that Carter and Lovecraft were writing in the same style and went to town proving it."

I took the small digest of stories and wandered back into my room. I never did finish that story, or any of them, really. I was asleep before I was able to turn two pages.

The next morning Hannah was gone before I woke, and I found that she had not put away her photo albums, or put away the letters from the Anagram game. It was as I was picking them up that I saw that portrait again, the one that included the face of a man that looked so familiar, but whom I just couldn't place, the man whom Hannah had called Moreland. His whole name was there on the page:

Roman LaChampele Lydecker

He looked so familiar.

It gnawed at me. It festered and boiled.

Why did he look so familiar?

I sat down at the table and began gathering up the Anagram letters. Then, just as I was about to put the last tile away, it hit me. I had a name. Was it possible, or was I just imagining things? I poured the letters back onto the table and quickly spelled out the name Hannah had attributed to the man in the picture.

ROMAN LACHAMPELE LYDEKER

I pulled a few letters to the side.

ROMAN LACHAMP LYDECKER LEE

I could see the letters moving in my mind even before I moved them with my hand.

ROMAN LYDEKER CLAPHAM LEE

It was coming faster now.

YKER MORELAND CLAPHAM LEE

It was there, I just needed to stretch one letter.

ERYK MORELAND CLAPHAM LEE

Or, as I knew him, Eric Moreland Clapham-Lee—the man whom Doctor Herbert West had resurrected in the trenches, whom I had met in Averoigne, and whose own head he had grasped with one hand and lifted up from his neck. Seeing his name brought his words to mind. "And one day, the Undead shall outnumber the living and they shall rule the world."

I collapsed back into a chair, stunned by the undeniable truth of my revelation. Clapham-Lee was here, had been here in Kingsport for years. Megan had seen him in Dunwich just before she and Lavinia had been chased by slathering things hiding in the cemetery. It couldn't be coincidence. Somehow or another Clapham-Lee was connected to the murder of Megan Halsey, to the monstrous things that had been hiding in that forgotten necropolis. It was all coming together. The only problem was that Megan had seen Clapham-Lee more than a year ago, but Hannah said he was on sabbatical, visiting England. Where was he now? Had he returned, and if so, how and when? Did his arrival result in a confrontation with Megan that had turned fatal?

I needed to get to Dunwich, to find that lost graveyard and see if there were any clues as to where Clapham-Lee and his monstrous brethren had gone. They had shipped out, that was obvious, and according to Megan's notes they had returned on the *Melindia*, the very ship that the A to Z Club was hoping to find and recover their cargo from. I was suddenly frantic, I needed to get back to work and trace Clapham-Lee's movements. Roman Lydecker had to have left some kind of trail—after all, he wasn't trying to hide.

I planned on packing, on catching a bus back to Arkham, on resigning from the force, and then heading to Arkham. That was the plan. If it hadn't been for that damn library book, I would have done just that. I felt guilty leaving it for Hannah to return, and it would only take me a few minutes to walk to the library and back. It would be no time at all. Besides, I was going to disappoint her in a variety of other ways; returning a book was simple.

I saw them before they saw me; they were huddled together, talking feverishly to one another about something I couldn't quite make out. The A to Z Club was walking down the street, heading in the opposite direction. I bid them good morning as we passed each other. If I hadn't done that I might have been ignored, that is how intent and oblivious they were. But I did, and in doing so, caught Armitage's eye.

"Ehh? Oh, Mr. Peaslee. Good morning. Sorry, can't stop." He didn't break his stride. "We're on our way to the Coast Guard Station. The ship's come in."

I waved and took two steps before stopping in my tracks. I turned and called out, "What ship?"

"Our ship," he yelled back. "The one we told you about, the *Melindia*." With each step he was moving farther away from me.

I turned on my heel and dashed after the chattering trio, catching them as fast as I could. "Gentlemen, I think I would like to see this ship of yours, if you don't mind?"

Zeck caught my eye. "Not at all, Peaslee, you might be useful. You don't mind getting a little dirty, do you?"

I thought about what he said, and I may have taken it the wrong way. "Mr. Zeck, I may have been too clean for too long." There was something ironic in my voice. "If I'm going to get where I need to I might have to get more than a little dirty."

The ship that sat in the Kingsport harbor, berthed in the protected area reserved for the Coast Guard, was best described as unfit. That this had been the *Melindia* there was no doubt, for there on her bow, faded and rusted, you could still see the faint outline where her name had once been painted. She had suffered from lack of maintenance and the failure to do any proper upkeep had not only contributed to her rust, but to rivets and bolts being missing, to her ropes being tangled, and for large pieces of her railing having gone missing. Many of her portholes had cracked glass, and the wheel room itself looked as if the windows had not been tended to in years. Worst of all was the great gash on her port side, below the bow, just above the water line. It was a fresh cut, and appeared to have been made when she ran aground, or collided with some unforgiving rock as she approached the mainland.

According to the manifest, more than half the cargo was missing. However, those boxes belonging to and so keen to be recovered by the A to Z Club were still present, and this elicited in Armitage and his colleagues much elation. That elation turned suspect when we actually entered the ship's hold and found the place filled with such a reeking stench that we nearly retched. It was not the remaining cargo that reeked, but rather an odd accumulation of decomposing food and bodily waste that had accumulated in one of the side compartments. It appeared that someone had been using the area as a midden, though why that should occur on a ship where waste could be dumped overboard was perplexing. With handkerchiefs dowsed in cologne wrapped around their faces, the three members of the A to Z Club went about double-checking the status of the cargo while an officer of the Coast Guard looked on, and several dockworkers began preparations for moving what remained.

Being wholly uninterested in the disposition of the remaining cargo, I instead slipped away and began searching casually for any clue as to what had happened aboard the *Melindia*. While my acquaintances were thrilled that their cargo remained in the hold and was salvageable, the implication that the rest of the cargo had been removed did not escape me. Likewise, it seemed apparent that the wound to the hull had likely occurred after the majority of the cargo had been taken off, suggesting that someone wanted no record of the ship reaching port and disgorging whatever it was she held inside. To this end, it seemed likely that not only was the ship considered an acceptable loss, but so was the crew. It was evidence of violence that I was searching for, that and some hint that tied all this back to the murder of Megan Halsey.

It was in the wheel house, a chaotic maelstrom of broken glass, scattered charts, and shattered equipment, that I noticed something odd. I have commented at length on the decrepitude of the ship and its general state of clutter, including the broken railings. Even in the cabin the brass fittings seemed in disrepair, or were tarnished with age, which is why my eye was drawn to a piece of pipe that showed a ring of marks where an ill-fitted wrench had been taken to it. The patina had been scratched, and there were jagged edges where the teeth of the wrench had bit in. I tested it and found that it was loose. With a few quick turns, my eyes constantly casting about to see if I was being watched, I unscrewed the pipe from its fittings and turned it away from the wall. I slipped my finger inside the pipe, but found nothing. In my disappointment I almost forgot, but then as I was fitting the pipe back to the wall I searched the receiving end of the fitting, and was rewarded with the discovery of a significant blockage. Careful not to push it farther in, I gently dragged the item out of its hiding place and revealed a small spindle of papers torn from a notebook. Still fearful that I would be discovered, I slipped the pages inside my coat, replaced the pipe, and returned to the hold.

The A to Z Club was still going through the inventory, but the doors to the hold had been opened and crates were being moved onto the dock. Most people, on finding something as I had, would have departed as quickly as possible, with the intent of finding a safe place to examine in detail the discovered treasure. This, however, tends to draw attention. The wiser course of action, one I had seen carried out by thieves and antique dealers, was to be more casual about things, to linger longer than necessary, and when possible conceal the item of worth amongst a clutter of other things. Once in New York, Vance had discovered a ratty copy of *Tamerlane*, credited to A. Bostonian, which he knew to be a pseudonym of Edgar Allen Poe. Inside, on the frontispiece, the author had inscribed it to a friend. The bookshop owner had marked the volume at only a quarter dollar. Rather than absconding with the volume by itself, he instead piled up several volumes of similar subject and condition, and thus when he approached the clerk nothing in particular existed to catch the man's eye and negate the sale. Thus, I stood around with my friends as they carried out their business, and only an hour or so later took my leave of them. Even then I was careful not to dash down the docks and streets, but rather walked with care. I strolled through the streets of Kingsport as if I had nothing of import to do, making sure I was not followed or observed. It was the most circuitous of routes that brought me back to my sister's house, but once there, I was sure that no one suspected anything was out of the ordinary.

As I sat at the table I unfolded those stiff folded sheets and discovered almost immediately that they represented the first few pages of a log book, hastily torn out and then folded and spindled so as to fit inside the pipe. The handwriting was a scrawling, cramped script that was difficult to read, but as my eyes adjusted with time the contents became clear and I found myself in possession of what appeared to be the logbook of the *Melindia's* first mate.

# CHAPTER 21

# "The Log of the *Melindia*"
## From the Files of the United States Coast Guard, Kingsport
## March 1928

*March 7*

As is traditional, I have bought myself a new logbook to mark the beginning of a new adventure, one that will finally take me home. Oh, how I have missed the verdant and welcoming hills of Massachusetts. It has been six years since I graduated from Miskatonic and joined that ill-fated expedition to Africa in search of Kor. We never even made it out of Zamunda, and it was only through the kindness of the royal family that we weren't thrown into prison for our debts. If you had told me that my engineering degree would have proven useless, and instead my time spent working as a surveyor would lead me first to being a ship's navigator, and then eventually to a helmsman plying the routes between Europe and North Africa, I would have called you mad. Life takes us strange places, and who would have thought that a dead-end trip to Britain's Yorkshire would have led me to an opportunity to travel home.

Whitby, where I came into yesterday via the *Atlas*, is a strange little town, quaint enough, I suppose. It was once a whaling village, and apparently was the source of much of the mourning jewelry fashioned from the nearby deposits of jet. These days it seems to be resting on its laurels and trying to make a go of it as a seaside resort, at least that's what I have discerned as I tried to find decent lodgings. Thankfully, a local firm of solicitors, S. F. Billington and Son, were advertising for a crew for a cargo vessel by name of the *Melindia*. The regular crew and captain had all been discharged a week earlier for gross insubordination and dereliction of duty. Looking at the ship, which is in a right awful state, I can understand why they were discharged. The *Melindia* may be seaworthy, but she shan't win any prizes for looks or cleanliness. I applied for a job as a navigator, and was surprised when they came back and offered me a berth as the first mate. This was apparently because, barring the captain, the rest of the crew were Scots and the captain, being a local man, could barely understand a word of what they said.

That the ship was sailing from Whitby to Kingsport surprised me, for it seemed an odd destination. Billington, the son—the father having passed away some time ago—informed me that the ship had been specifically chartered for such a run by the voyage's sole passenger, a stoic woman by the name of Eliza Hoag, who was also apparently the financial backer as well, and for whom Billington himself worked. She was, it seemed, returning home, not to Kingsport but to Arkham. She had been living in Europe for many years, and had accumulated a significant volume of possessions which she sought to take back to the States with her. Half the hold was full of her accumulation of antiques and oddities, and the other half had been taken up with local carvings and jewelry all comprised of the aforementioned jet. Some young entrepreneur had gotten it into his head that such dreary stuff would be the rage in New England and New York, and had bought crates of it to sell amongst the tycoons of Wall Street, or more specifically their mistresses.

It may be a strange, roundabout way of doing it, but Raclaw Schablotski is finally going home.

*March 8*

Met the captain today, a surly warthog of a man named Barrows who epitomizes everything one thinks of when it comes to captains of garbage scows and tramps. I could smell the liquor on his breath. It is clear to me now that this voyage will be more challenging than I first thought. We leave tomorrow at first light.

*March 9*

Mrs. Hoag is an odd sort. She is, I suppose, what some people call beautiful, tall and willowy with hair that captures and dances in the sea wind. As we left port, steaming east, she was standing on the bow; the light from the morning sun made her into a kind of angel, a silhouetted figurehead come to life. For as beautiful as she is, she is just as melancholy. There is a great sadness about her, the way she looks out into the sea. I've seen that look before amongst men who go to sea and never reach their destination, and I told her so.

"Suicide, Mr. Schablotski?" She looked at me with those large doe eyes. "No, I'm not considering taking my own life, I've seen too much death, lived with too much death." She turned back to the sea. "In my experience death doesn't solve anything, it merely makes things more . . . complicated."

I left her after that, and didn't see her again until the cook rang the bell for supper. When she didn't turn up the captain sent me to look for her. I caught her coming up from the hold. Her hair was out of place and she was cinching the belt on her dress. She was obviously flustered. If we had been on land I would say that I had just caught her leaving a man, but that cannot be: everyone was in the galley or attending to duties above deck. Odd, most odd; if she wasn't meeting a man, what was she doing down there in the hold?

*March 10*

MacLean is missing. He was supposed to relieve me at the helm this morning but he never showed. His bunk hadn't been slept in and no one had seen him since dinner the night before. We searched the whole ship from bow to stern and found nothing, not a trace, not a thing out of place. Well, except for a few crates in the hold that had shifted, but that was to be expected given the rough weather we've encountered. Barrows blames the weather for MacLean's loss, says the man probably fell overboard. It would be more convincing if Barrows wasn't drunk. I've never seen someone drink so much; the farther out to sea we get, the more he drinks. I've tried to find where he hides his bottles but to no avail, not that I think it matters. I suspect that Barrows would be useless even if sober.

*March 11*

The cook has complained that some of his stores have gone missing. Barrows has locked himself in his cabin. Mrs. Hoag has said that this is my concern, and that I am in charge now. I've talked to the crew, tried to make things plain. I think they understood. Five days. By my calculations we'll be in Kingsport in five days. It doesn't seem that long, but out here, on the open ocean, far from land, surrounded by nothing but the rolling gray desert that is the North Atlantic, days seem to stretch to weeks. This far out, even the birds have abandoned us. I hope that God has not.

*March 12*

Barrows is still locked in his cabin, and has been for the last two days. There is a horrible stench leaking out from the vent to his room. The crew is nervous. McNeely says that he saw Mrs. Hoag go into the hold and when he followed a minute later there was no trace of her. He says she must be a ghost. Mrs. Hoag denies this, of course, and accuses McNeely of being as drunk as Barrows. Not unexpectedly, the rest of the crew has sided with McNeely. I've told them to stay away from her, and reminded them that she is paying their wages. I need them to focus on their jobs. We are two men short and from the look of that sky there is a storm on the way.

*March 13*

The storm came up on us just before dawn with sustained winds of at least thirty knots whipping through the wires. I've tried to keep her pointed into the wind, but even so the waves are breaking over the bow and we are being driven east. Barrows is out of his cabin, but not of his own accord. Someone forced the door and dragged him out, I know that much at least. We can't find him. Not that we've been able to conduct a thorough search, the storm has made sure of that. He'll turn up when he gets hungry, when the danger has passed and the work is all done and he's sobered up. Drunks have a habit of doing that.

*March 14*

McIntyre is missing. He was on duty early this morning, but when we went to relieve him he simply wasn't there. Both Barrows and MacLean are still missing. We've searched through the whole ship twice and can't find a trace of any of them. The storm has weakened, but it's still pushing us east. We haven't seen the sun, let alone the sky, in days, no telling where we are. As far as I know we could be dead, and this, this could be hell.

*March 15*
*The Morning*

I found Barrows's head. It was in the meat locker behind a slab of salted pork. The back of the skull had been cracked open and the contents fished out. The edges of the hole looked gnawed on. I didn't show it to the others; I threw it overboard and watched it sink into the dark abyss of the sea.

*The Afternoon*

Besides myself, there's only two of the crew left. The rest, I assume, are dead victims of whatever force has possessed this ship. I thought perhaps Mrs. Hoag would be immune, but even she has vanished. I don't understand, where are they? Where have they all gone? What is happening here?

*The Evening*

The crew is gone. I'm alone in the wheel room. There's a flock of seagulls off the portside. We can't be far from shore. The storm has broken, but it must have pushed us miles off course. The sun is setting in the west, beyond the bow. Mrs. Hoag is there, out on the pulpit. On the deck there are dozens of shadows moving about, kneeling beneath her. Worshipping her. I can hear them, they sound as if they are in pain. There's so many of them. The way they move, it's unnatural. They're coming up the stairs . . . coming for me.

Guess I won't be getting home after all.

# CHAPTER 22

# "A Rainy Day in Dunwich"
## From the Journal of Robert Peaslee
### June 8 1928

Chief Nichols let me come back to Arkham in early June. There was the obligatory dressing down. They had no proof that I had killed Mary Czanek, but my explanation about why I was there and what I had done was flimsy, and too many people had seen me there. The irony wasn't lost on me. Killing Czanek was the exact kind of thing Nichols wanted me around for. I got dirty, he and his boys stayed clean. Between the lines I could see the truth. He was mad that I had gotten caught. He had sent me away to let time and some well-placed cash distract those who might make a stink. It had worked, but officially I was still being reprimanded, and that meant I wasn't going to get back to work until June 11th, which gave me nearly a week to work on the Halsey-Griffith case. I couldn't do anything official, but I figured there was plenty of investigating that I could pull off, if not in Arkham then in Dunwich. I wanted to see Megan's cabin, and the lost graveyard, and if there was time, stop in at the Whateley farm.

I left Arkham on the morning of June 6th, taking the Aylesbury Pike. The drive to Dunwich was slow and tedious, and I found myself lost in the slowly changing vista outside the dusty window. When you leave Arkham, heading west and north along the Aylesbury Pike, following the Miskatonic River, there is a dramatic and abrupt change in the landscape. Less than a mile outside and the farms and small homesteads fade away, the wild and overgrown expanses become more dominant, until at last Billington's Wood—that dark and unwholesome forest that creeps and claws at the road—is all that exists on the western side of the pike. On the other side, the waters of the Miskatonic roil slowly, forming a kind of psychological barrier to whatever lies on the farther shore. It was as if the Miskatonic River was an impassable barrier, an invisible wall that allowed the small farms and hamlets dotting the other side to be seen, but never reached. As I passed the stony remnants of great bridges that had once existed, but had long since been lost to time, the idea that I was someplace else became prevalent. A dark foreboding forest on one side, and a seemingly impenetrable barrier on the other, the Aylesbury Pike was like a long-forgotten trade route through a phantasmal land and the car a lone horse and rider cast out into the wilderness in search of a place to call one's own. I thought of myself as Orpheus, descending into the hell of Dunwich, metaphorically trying to rescue my bride from the clutches of the dead—but Megan was dead, and nothing I did was going to bring her back. The least I could do was find the men or monsters that had killed her and bring them to justice, whatever that meant.

Beyond Billington's Wood, the Miskatonic and the lands around grow wilder, and the pike becomes a ribbon of asphalt, the only sign that civilization even exists in the weed- and briar-choked wilderness. I knew that there were people, ones who lived out here, and on occasion I caught sight of a dirt road, or two sets of grass-choked ruts, or even a footpath that led off into the thicket, but these provided no sense of security. For all I knew, those who lived here were little better than savages. There had been stories, cases I had read about, in which unsuspecting travelers had vanished, or encountered madmen, or cannibals, or even worse. The files on this country were thick with murders and disappearances, presumably linked to moonshiners and smugglers bringing in booze from Canada through the backwoods of Vermont. That was the official theory. Unofficially, there were rumors that something more sinister was going on, that the killing was associated with the various crones, wise-women, and witches who lived in the hills. The whispers went back for generations, and mostly had to do with the various descendants of the three Mason sisters, the women who gave Arkham the epithet *witch-haunted*. M. M. Bartlett, a student of Professor Albert N. Wilmarth, had been through the area a few years back and put together a dissertation on the hill religions of the region entitled *The Witch-Cults of Western Massachusetts*, a volume few people bothered to read, but more should have.

Of all the villages Bartlett had visited, Dunwich had been the one most rife with hill tales and eerie folklore. Bartlett had called the place backward, and as the car rattled into the village I had no reason to doubt the man's opinion. The town center appeared as if it hadn't seen a can of paint in decades, and the clapboards of various buildings had been dislodged and left in disrepair. What had once been a church was now a general store with only the last vestiges of a bell tower collapsing into obscurity. The road had long since turned to dirt and weeds and debris lined the ditches that ran along the side. I hadn't really needed to stop in Dunwich—the route to either of my primary destinations didn't require it—but I wanted to see the place, to get a sense of what it was like, and put Megan's observations into perspective. It was worse than I had thought possible, and rather than engage any of the toothless and unkempt residents I drove off toward the Halsey cabin. I didn't even bother to get out of the car.

The rain started as soon as I pulled up into the dirt patch that served the cabin as a parking space. It was really a nondescript little building, aged, but you could see where work had been done to fix issues. There were branches in the yard and the weeds had grown up in places, but a fine layer of pine needles kept most of the yard clear of vegetation. I used the key that the lawyers had given me when they agreed to let me look into Megan's death. The inside was a little musty, but clean and dry. If anyone had been there since Megan had fled the area there was no sign of it. I spent the next few hours rummaging around the place, going through drawers and closets, checking for secret doors or compartments, but there was nothing to be found except dust and quiet. That was what I noticed most about the cabin: the quiet was pervasive. Unlike Arkham or Paris or any of the other places I had lived, this area was devoid of the sounds of human habitation. It was so removed from humanity that I might as well have been lost at sea or in a desert. If I ever needed a place to hide, this cabin would do quite nicely.

By the time I was ready to leave, the rain had turned the road into a shallow stream with rivulets running around gravel and rocks, turning potholes and depressions into murky pools. It took me twice as long as it should have to get out of the backwoods and onto a main road. The old map which I had liberated from the library in Arkham showed the road to the forgotten cemetery that Megan had discovered, but even then the origins of those graves were unknown, and the place appeared simply as an untitled area marked with a headstone. Knowing where it was made it easy to find, though the drive was neither easy nor quick, and at one point I was forced to abandon the car and begin sloshing through the pools and rain, walking through the wilderness, through the brush-covered hills and tree-filled hollows. It took me more than an hour to finally reach the gates of the graveyard. You could still see the ruts where a truck had once torn up the dirt and then cut cross-country back to the road. There were drag marks as well; they led inside the gates and to a number of the mausoleums and crypts. I had brought a crowbar with me, but I didn't need it; the locks had all been broken out long before.

Inside each tomb the expected contents had been rearranged; the houses of the dead had been used as quarters for the living, or at least the not-so-dead. Broken furniture, old bedding, rotting books and newspapers dominated the evidence that people once lived here. There wasn't much in the way of personal effects. The only thing that seemed out of place was a hand-drawn map of the area with the town and various landmarks marked. Indicated as well were the major roads and footpaths. All of these had been labeled in a small but neat script, but there was another set of marks, unnamed, in a different colored ink. These consisted of small circles scattered across the landscape north of the river—of what they were meant to represent there was no indication. I took the yellowed page, folded it, and put it in my shirt pocket.

I had been hours exploring the necropolis and all I had found was a map of a town I couldn't figure out. The rain was getting worse, and if I was going to spend any time at the Whateley farm I was going to have to get moving. It was as I was leaving that I saw the handprint in the dust. It wasn't fresh; in fact, it was probably months old, but compared to the years of grime that had accumulated it told its own story. The size, the shape, it was a woman's hand, I had no proof of it, no evidence to speak of, but I knew that it was hers. I knew without a doubt that that handprint belonged to Megan Halsey. I knew it in my heart. I reached out and put my hand where hers once had been. I let it rest there for a moment, and then I wiped it away.

I was across the river and heading toward the farm just as the sun was setting, though frankly, given the rain it was hard to tell. I followed the directions that Megan had left in her diary—well, at least some of them. Megan had described something strange residing at the

Whateley farm, something that had presumably destroyed the ghoulish things that had pursued her and Lavinia. According to the map,
the farm wasn't far, and so with little hesitation I decided to make the
trek. I had not intended to actually enter the farmhouse or even the
property, but rather observe it from the road. It was, I suppose, a sort
of reconnaissance mission. A chance to see what it was exactly that was
going on in that farmhouse.

I never made it.

The storm intensified quickly. First there was the wind that whipped
through the trees, tossing their branches to and fro, whipping the farm
fields into frenzy as if they were the open sea itself. I pulled off the
side of the road and watched as the rain swept across the hills and valley like a wall of darkness. With the sudden torrential downpour came
the lightning, which split the sky and dispelled the shadow that had
enveloped the region. It was a queer kind of storm, for the rain seemed
unnaturally heavy, each drop a huge globule, the very impact of which
was jarring, pinging against the car like a hail of rocks. What was even
odder was the silence that came after each bolt of lightning. Instead of
there being a great rolling bass of thunder, there was a crashing wave of
silence that seemed to draw sound out of the very air, out of the valley
itself. Yet despite how strange and terrifying that eerie thundering was,
it wasn't that which frightened me. It was instead the tableau that each
bolt of lightning revealed as it lit up the side of Sentinel Hill and let me
see the figure that was standing there.

That sight terrified me—I don't know why, but it did. It was just a
lone figure standing on the summit, the rain showering down upon it
in great torrents. He held a rope in one hand, and seemed to be using
it to perform tricks like those I've seen in rodeo shows. But this was
different, somehow; the rope was too thick, like those used on ocean
liners, and the lasso impossibly large—the strength it would have taken
to maintain such a thing was beyond the realm of possibility. It terrified
me, straight down to the core, and I turned the car around and careened
down the muddy road to the sound of great rains pinging against its
body. I drove like a madman, not understanding what I had seen, but
some part of my mind had. My subconscious knew something I didn't,
it recognized something and in doing so that ancient reptilian portion
of my brain told me to run. It wasn't long until I was back on the main

road to Arkham, still driving like the devil himself was after me, and I didn't slow down until I was almost halfway back home.

You would think that the backwoods roads would have been empty at that time of night, but as we crossed the river and crawled back onto the main road I saw a man there, walking along the pike—but he wasn't alone, and his companion made me understand. It was then that the last barrier between what my subconscious had recognized and my conscious mind finally fell. The man on the road was holding a rope, a smaller rope, and with a smaller loop for sure, but the image was so similar to that which I had seen on Sentinel Hill. It all made sense now, terrible, horrifying sense. The man on the road, that traveling vagabond, wasn't alone. There, running at his side, with its head in the rope loop, was a dog.

He was nothing more than a man, a man walking his pet with a leash, in the rain.

I pulled off to the side of the road as the realization of things washed over me. I hope the rain drowned out the sound of my screams.

# CHAPTER 23

# "The Violation of Anne Newman"
## From the Journal of Robert Peaslee
### June 16 1928

We would like to think that madness is confined to places like Sefton Asylum, or in the remote and forgotten places like darkest Africa or the frozen Antarctic. We don't think that such things can exist in the heart of our own neighborhoods, our own towns, even in the institutions that we have created to serve us. We don't want such things to be true, but the crawling corruption seeds terror and madness in the most unlikely of places. One only has to look for it, or refuse to ignore it when it comes, even when that call is in the wee hours of a Sunday morning.

Spool House is located on the far side of Aylesbury on the grounds of what was once the Spool family farm. Sometime in the nineteenth century, Anthony Spool had lost his wife and two daughters to a fever and in their memory converted the once-magnificent home into a residence for young women. His son, Hammond, continued the institution, and it was now run by the widow Ada Spool, née Armitage, and her two daughters, Norma and Emma. Spool House had, over the years, become an institution in the valley, and the locals had learned not to bother with the house of wayward women, or else feel the wrath of the Spool family. In turn, what the Spool women had learned was that young ladies who find themselves in the way are often ashamed of their condition, and it takes a supreme effort for them to confide in the staff of Spool House. They needed privacy and seclusion to deal with the things they had done, and come to terms with it, one way or another. Consequently, Spool House and all who worked there discouraged visitors, particularly those with any official capacity. So when one of Mrs. Spool's daughters called and requested an officer of some discretion be sent, it was I that was dispatched and forced to traverse the darkness and solitude of the Aylesbury Pike.

It was just after dawn when I reached the estate that now served as the temporary residence for so many needy girls. In the morning sun the place looked respectable enough, framed with shrubbery and flowers that highlighted the manicured lawn. Paths of crushed rock led to the white columns of a neoclassical house that had been fashionable during the founding of the Republic. Mrs. Spool was a domineering, gray-haired dowager built low to the ground with a wide base, as some women tend to in their age. She offered me coffee and something to eat, mostly because it was the expected thing to do. I declined, for the same reason.

She nodded, and with a kind of finality led me down the halls and stairs of the old house into the lower levels. It was not an uncomfortable place, still warm and clean, but quiet, isolated from the rest of the house and residents. Mrs. Spool led me to a door with a window embedded in it, not unlike those I had seen in the asylums and prisons. She slid back the window and stepped back. With some hesitation I moved forward and then pressed my face to the window. I was unprepared for what I saw.

There in that room was a thing that was only remotely related to humanity. The body was immense, perhaps the size of two heifers, and covered with a dozen or so pairs of fat, pendulous teats. From this grotesque core the shriveled twig-like things that I recognized as limbs waved uselessly in the air; there was no way in which these could be used for locomotion. A head vaguely topped the body, but this, too, was only barely human. There were only wisps of greasy hair, hints of ears, and pale sunken eyes that stared blindly at the door. The mouth was round, and as it opened up in a queer sucking motion I could see that it had no teeth. It opened wide and screamed out in a kind of throaty, bestial voice, "Ia, Ia Shub-Niggurath! Ia Thaquallah! Ia Ia!" As the screams echoed down the hall I slammed the window shut and stepped back in revulsion.

Mrs. Spool led me away in silence and when we finally reached her office offered me something more than coffee. I had not expected her to make such an offer—she had, after all, seemed a teetotaler to me.

This time I accepted her offer and carefully nursed the small glass of scotch, hoping it would calm my nerves. When I had finished about half the glass, Mrs. Spool began to speak.

"Anne Newman came to us back in June of last year. She had been a student nurse at Miskatonic University and had traveled out to Dean's Corners in May to visit family. While on her way back her bus had broken down, and she had been forced to either walk back to the town or make her way back to Arkham. A dedicated employee, Miss Newman had no desire to miss her shift at the hospital and instead of joining the other passengers on the trek back to Dean's Corners she walked alone down that deserted road. She made it to the hospital, but not in time for her shift. She was brought in the back of a farmer's truck. She had been attacked, assaulted the police said, violated said the doctors. She had little memory of her attacker, only a shadowy image of someone impossibly large with hairy arms and a beard like a goat. There were bite marks on her legs, round ones, as if she had been attacked by dozens of hagfish."

"She came to us a few weeks after the attack. We listened to her story, and I must admit we didn't believe her. She bore the signs of being pregnant; a woman's body changes, Detective Peaslee, it transforms, readies itself to give birth and nurse the child it will bring into this world. Anne Newman's hips had widened, her breasts grown full, and her belly distended so much that I would have sworn that she was more than six months pregnant, not the six weeks she claimed. We didn't believe her story, but that didn't matter. We took her in and gave her a place to live while she had her baby. Three days later, when I saw her again, I was amazed, for Anne no longer looked six months pregnant. Instead, she was nine months along, and I no longer doubted what she said."

She paused and seemed to gird herself for what came next. "Seven days after she came to us, seven weeks after she had been attacked, Anne Newman went into labor. It was perhaps the most difficult birth I had ever seen. It lasted eighteen hours, during which Anne screamed the entire time. It wasn't only the pain of labor; as we watched, her body continued to change, to make itself ready for the birth. By the end I think she went mad from the pain. All the agony she had suffered and endured, all that fear had finally accumulated and struck at her psyche in yet another kind of violation. That she went mad was probably for the best. When her child came the midwife ran from the room in terror. I was left alone to deal with the thing that she gave birth to. It was a bloated, tick-like thing, with a miniscule head and thin, goat-like arms and legs. It screamed in agony and in a shrill voice called out that horrific chant you heard downstairs, 'Ia, Ia Shub-Niggurath! Ia Thaquallah! Ia Ia!' I took that thing and with the metal basin I smashed at it until it ceased its foul and incessant bleating."

"I wish it all had ended there, but as the thing Anne Newman had given birth to drew its final breath the mother screamed once more and a second of the things crawled its way out from between her legs. It called out in that horrific bleating and was joined by another one of its brood, and then another, and then another. Twelve things in all wormed their way out of Anne Newman's bloated womb. Twelve mewling, bleating things that called out to some blasphemous parent in an inhuman language crawled out of that poor girl and I lifted up my weapon, the steel basin that had already killed, and I brought it down again and again and again. Eight of those things fell before my wrath that day. Three escaped. The last we captured and imprisoned. It grew at a startling rate, one that required massive quantities of nourishment. In mere days it was larger than a cow."

She paused there, and it was plain that she had reached a point in her tale that she was no longer comfortable with. Though how she had endured the tale to this point I could not say, but I didn't wish for her to suffer anymore. "That thing in the basement," I said, "that thing you've brought me out here to see, the last of the spawn that Anne Newman was cursed with, it has grown too big for you to contain. Is that why I am here, Mrs. Spool? Is that why you've finally called the authorities? Am I here to kill the last of these monsters, the one you couldn't kill yourself?"

It was then that I learned the truth, for Mrs. Spool did finally speak and told me what she had been so reluctant to reveal previously. She told me and then I went down the stairs and into that room. I cradled that thing, that monstrous tick-like thing, as best I could. I sang to it, and I think perhaps for a moment it sang back to me. I like to think I gave it some comfort before I took my revolver and shot it in the back of the head. I like to think that for a moment, it remembered what it was like to be human.

I can still hear Mrs. Spool's voice as she told me the truth, the truth that I had so obviously tried to avoid. "That last spawn died weeks ago, Mr. Peaslee. We couldn't feed it enough of what it needed, it cried constantly, it screamed for its mother. My daughter, Emma, took a knife and stabbed at it until it, too, ceased to move. We had no problem killing those things, Mr. Peaslee. We burned it like the rest of the brood that had come out of poor Anne Newman. Anne Newman, whose body had transformed itself, had changed, had become something inhuman so as to nurse the things that had violated her womb. Anne Newman, who had gone mad, and had ever since ranted and screamed from a mouth that was no longer human the first words she had next heard, the words her horrific children had spoken as they broke free of her gravid body. 'Ia, Ia Shub-Niggurath! Ia Thaquallah! Ia Ia!' Mr. Peaslee, that thing in the basement isn't one of Anne Newman's spawn, it is what she became to give birth and suckle them. That's why we couldn't kill it. That thing is, or at least was, Anne Newman herself!"

CHAPTER 24

# "The Transmogrification
# of Llewelyn Barrass"
## From the Journal of Robert Peaslee
## July 18 1928

### I. What Dr. Willett Didn't Say

It has been five days since I first heard of Corvin Farm. Five days
which have led me into yet another case of the madness that haunts
Arkham and her environs. I wonder if this town has always been witch-
haunted or if the source of all its troubles can be traced to an event that
forever altered its character. In the meantime, I find myself embroiled
in an event that must be hidden from public scrutiny. It was six days ago
that the local authorities were called to the old Corvin farm in Witches'
Hollow. There was an odor, a stench that, despite the distances between
properties, the locals could tolerate no longer. What the locals found
was beyond their capabilities, and thus the State Police were called
and took control the next day. Under normal circumstances I would
have been dispatched to such a scene, but on that particular day I was
already too far to be of assistance, at least directly. I was at the Biltmore
Hotel in Providence when the call came in. I had spent the night after
concluding my business with the local authorities concerning the death
a few years back of Professor Angell. The call came in before I had
finished breakfast, and I was ordered to travel to Conanicut Island to
research the history of the current occupant of Corvin Farm, a man
named Llewelyn Barrass.

It was in late April that Barrass had presented himself to the
Permanent Assurance Company with documents establishing his right
to the Corvin farm. The papers that Barrass bore were of no particular age, and the man admitted they had been produced just a few
weeks before, but something about their content matched instructions
held within the ancient files of the firm, and although the staff was

momentarily stunned, they turned over the keys to the property forth-with, and quickly typed up letters of credit for him to use at the local bank. When Llewelyn Barrass left Arkham and made the short trip to Witches' Hollow he was, by all accounts, a very wealthy man.

Mail at the farm suggested that prior to coming to Witches' Hollow Barrass had been employed by the Whitmarsh Institute, a private hospi-tal on Conanicut Island. It was to this place that Chief Nichols ordered me in a desperate attempt to gather some information about Barrass and how he came to be at Corvin Farm, and perhaps gain a clue as to what precipitated the events that led to the horrors in Witches' Hollow. What those horrors were, I, at this point, hadn't been told. Nichols hadn't been explicit about what had occurred at the farm, but from his tone I knew it was bad, and that he didn't want to talk about details over the phone with the possibility of the hotel operator listening in.

The Senior Physician of the Whitmarsh Institute was a Doctor M. B. Willett, who at first seemed unwilling to discuss much of anything with me, but when I suggested that I could always return with an army of local investigators to paw through his records his tune changed. Dr. Willett informed me that Barrass had been employed at the institute as an orderly for several years and most recently had overwintered at the hospital during a particularly violent snowstorm. During the storm Barrass had been attacked by a patient, a man who himself later escaped from the institute. A search of the island had proved fruitless, and it was assumed that he had tried to swim across the bay to the mainland. Dr. Willett seemed adamant that the man was no longer a threat, and had made the same overtures to staff. Most took him at his word, but Barrass seemed more shaken than the others, particularly over the fact that one of the staff physicians had disappeared as well. A day after the search ended Barrass resigned, and he left the island almost immedi-ately after. A week later he sent a note supplying Corvin Farm as his new address. Beyond these few things, the only information Willett could provide was that Barrass was from Manchester, but his parents were dead. He had a sister in Aylesbury, but he didn't have an address for the woman. He dismissed me after less than half an hour.

On my way out I made a pretense to stop by the kitchen, hoping for a Dewar flask of coffee. There I received not only the coffee, but information as well, for the old cook, Mrs. Davis, was in a talkative mood. She showed me a staff photo which included Barrass, a stout, rough-looking fellow, and I wondered how anyone had ever gotten the drop on him. Mrs. Davis confirmed everything that Willett had told me, but then also provided details he had conveniently left out. Barrass had indeed overwintered through a terrible storm, and a patient had attacked him. They called the man Mr. Pulver, though it was obviously an alias, and he had been a difficult patient, with a specialized diet consisting of raw meat. This requirement was met by a local supply of wild rabbits, though I suspected that in this she was holding something back, but I did not press.

The missing doctor was named Wilson, and he vanished a few days before Mr. Pulver escaped. Barrass had reported that he had seen Wilson intoxicated and wandering about on the beach. It was assumed he passed out and drowned in the bay. As for Pulver, in the days that followed his escape Conanicut Island found itself in disarray, still desperately trying to recover from the storm. Doctor Willett organized a search party, but could only rally three men. The storm and its aftermath had brought enough troubles to the residents of the island. The docks had been damaged by ice, and downed trees had blocked some of the roads. The roof on Bill Goodfellow's workshop had collapsed, and the Fulton farm was missing a half dozen cows. As the villagers were occupied with more pressing matters, Willett's attempts to find Pulver were quickly abandoned. The hospital itself was only slightly upset by the escape of their charge. Pulver had made a mess of his room, and it had taken the junior orderly, Barrass, nearly an hour to sweep up the strange blue powder that coated the floors. Doctor Willett had ordered the material disposed of, but not in the incinerator as normal—rather, it was to be thrown into the bay, scattered from the beach just down the hill from the institute.

Returning back to the mainland, I stared out into Narragansett Bay and wondered what had truly happened in this place. The dark waters churned as the old boat plowed through them, and they seemed too often a convenient way for inconvenient men to vanish; first Dr. Wilson and then Pulver. I had no reason to suspect that their disappearance was linked to whatever happened at Corvin Farm, but in my experience such conclusions were not only easy to reach, they usually proved themselves valid. Once on the mainland I made my way back to Providence and then took the train back to Arkham. I mulled over the possibilities, and found the rhythmic pace of the car conducive to my thoughts. When we finally reached Arkham the conductor loaded me into a cab, and once at home I retreated into a sound and dreamless sleep—but I couldn't help but wonder who Willet's patient truly was, and why he felt the need to hide his identity from me.

## II. What Wilbur Dunlock Saw

The next morning I spent at the office reading the reports and going through the documents submitted by the investigating officers. It seems that the involvement of the police was a result of the weather. June had been an unseasonably warm month and that more than anything was likely what caused the residents of Witches' Hollow to plead with authorities to do something concerning the stench that had begun to emanate from the old Corvin farm. The place had been abandoned for as long as anyone could remember, and despite the fact that it had been well maintained it had an odd reputation. Certainly the occupation of Corvin Farm brought out the gossips in the community, but besides some rather cordial words between Barrass and the local merchants, none made the effort to befriend the man. The area was an insular community and had little use for outsiders. There were still whispers about that damned Potter boy and his family, and the cows that had died a few years back. Few locals wanted those events repeated. Consequently, Mr. Barrass and his companions were left to their own devices, at least until the stench had become unbearable and action was demanded. Afterward, after the health department and the State Police descended on the place en masse, the locals admitted that Mr. Barrass had not been the most desirable of neighbors.

Now that the police were involved, his nearest neighbors, the Scotts, complained vociferously about strange noises, particularly a kind of lamentable howling that was not a dog, and which would often disturb the night for hours on end. Much also was said about the strangers who would be seen at the farm, sometimes dozens at a time, but with no evidence of any vehicle that had brought or taken them away. Barrass and his enigmatic guests were apparently great consumers of livestock from the surrounding farms, including cows, sheep, goats, and pigs. Likewise, one of the local boys often found himself employed to travel into Arkham to bring back crates from specialty shops in Boston, the contents of which were always very vague but seemed to involve obscure cooking implements and rare spices. Indeed, the boy often overheard Barrass and one of his regular guests, a man who identified himself as Dr. Asche, speaking of the need for a variety of minerals, "essential salts" they would say, and then chuckle. The relationship between Barrass and Asche as well as their conversation made young Matt Carpenter uncomfortable, but his family was poor and the money was good so he kept his mouth shut and did as he was asked.

It was the testimony, if one could call it that, of the town drunk, a man in his twenties by the name of Wilbur Dunlock, that most intrigued me. Dunlock had no home of his own, the family farm having been lost to a fire a few years earlier, and as a result had taken to sleeping in unlocked barns. One of his regular haunts was a shed that sat on the Corvin farm, not far from the main house. It was here on that first night after Barrass had arrived that Dunlock was resting. Barrass had brought to the farm a fattened ewe, and Dunlock thought for a moment that he was caught, but instead of leading the animal into the shed, the stranger took the beast into the house. Intrigued, Dunlock crept from his hiding spot and peered through a window into the house.

Dunlock watched and listened as Barrass began chanting in a loud and powerful voice, and with it came a cold wind that blew the door open and set the oil lamps sputtering. A strange gloom seemed to devour the light, and through the window a noxious cloud of dark green vapor seemed to grow. It filled the room and gave off a kind of dim phosphorescence. Dunlock watched as Barrass repeated those strange words, words that burned themselves into Dunlock's memory. He wrote them down for the investigating officer:

EYAH ENG ENGAH
YOG-SOTHOTH
HAH HALGEB
EFAY THRODOG
EWAAAH

Dunlock saw Barrass stagger back toward the open door. Whatever strength he had once had, whatever had held back the fear, it left him and he fell to the floor whimpering and unable to flee. Within the fumes a thickening began to occur; the gas began to coalesce and resolve itself into a kind of disjointed shape. There was something recognizable to it that reminded Dunlock of something he had seen years earlier. It coalesced in that misty gloom, and while it bore the general outline of a man, it was not a strong and upright shape. Instead, it was a broken parody of a man, a thing with uneven legs, a twisted spine, and hunched shoulders. As it solidified into something less than human it let loose the most unearthly of screams, terrifying the ewe into a panic.

The thing in the mist leaped toward the terrified animal and wrapped itself around the beast's body. The hands clawed at the animal's mouth, grabbed the jaws and wrenched them apart. Blood flowed from the broken mouth of the poor animal, propelled by the thing's still-beating heart. The monstrous thing lifted the struggling body above its head and let the hot life of the sheep run down over its body, swallowing what it could and reveling in the sticky, wet warmth of it.

When it was over, when the blood finally stopped flowing, it tossed the drained creature to the side and roared into the air. Dunlock watched as Barrass gasped and then threw himself prostrate onto the floor as the thing that was now at least recognizable as a man screamed out, *I live! Twice men have sent me to the grave, and twice I have returned!*

Whatever had happened next Dunlock couldn't say, for terror finally overcame his drunkenness and he ran from Corvin Farm into the depths of the night. He ran in silence and hid himself within the confines of the local church. Father Strazynski found the man the next day, babbling to himself, reciting the Lord's Prayer over and over again. It took two strong men to drag Dunlock out of the pews and into the churchyard, where he once more ran, though this time it was during the day, and it definitely was not in silence.

### III. The Thing In The Crypt, And What Became Of It

It was just before noon on my second day back, the fourth day of the investigation, when Chief Nichols came to me. He called me Robert, not Peaslee or Detective, just Robert. He always calls me Robert when things are particularly bad, when he needs me to take care of something; to do something that others haven't the stomach for; to ask me to do something he has no right to. This is my task, my job. A natural result of what happened to my father, to my family, and the enmity that has built up in me over the years. I do these things because I can, because no one else can, because no one else should have to. Nichols knows I can't say no, for it is not in my nature to shirk from such things.

Within the hour I was out of Arkham and racing across the country roads that led to Witches' Hollow. It is wild country, though not at all like that which surrounds Aylesbury Pike. The hills are flatter, the forest thinner, and the scrub thicker. It is a sad, lonely place, and it reflects the people who choose to live there. The town itself is little more than a crossroads surrounded by a cluster of gray clapboard buildings that have all but succumbed to the ravages of time. The Corvin farm was a few miles west of the crossroads, and as I approached I was greeted by two armed officers who cleared me to go up to the house. As I drove on, they drove off and I realized I was to be alone to do what must be done.

The farmhouse itself was nothing unusual, although perhaps a poor example of the surviving colonial architecture of the region. The inside was little better and were it not for the multitude of oil lamps the place would have been more gloomy than I would have thought possible. How the officers had found the courage to come up to the house and keep the lamps full I cannot say. It had been two days since the bodies had been found. A full day since those corpses had burned. The stench still lingered. The report had said that all the bodies had been animals— sheep, dogs, cats, calves, even goats. All of them had been desiccated, exsanguinated the doctor had said, drained of all blood, and then tossed aside. There were hundreds of the things buried in a shallow grave. If the weather had stayed cooler they might have gone unnoticed, and simply rotted away beneath the earth, and we would never have known about the things that had gone on in that place, and I would not have had to do the thing I did.

I found the passageway down where Nichols said it was, and the ancient steps of worn granite were as treacherous as I was led to believe. They went down, down deep into the damp earth, into chthonic darkness, into that stygian night that dwells beneath our feet. It was as dark and as cold as the grave, and my lamp did little to pierce that all but tangible pitch. With the darkness came a kind of silence, an absence of sound that filled me with dread and amplified the sound of my own heart into a titanic drum that only I could hear. A lesser man would have turned and fled, but I, who was long ago inured to such terrors, I descended without pause.

A spark broke the darkness and as I made my way forward it grew. It grew until I no longer needed my lamp. The chamber into which I entered was a colossal space, an arched, cavernous catacomb that captured the sound of my heavy footsteps and echoed them back to me from a dozen different directions. The place was scattered with massive rocky monoliths that served as furniture for some strange alchemical laboratory. Bizarre equipment, glassware, and electrics were scattered about the place. For the life of me I thought that I had stumbled into some kind of film set, perhaps for a remake of Edison's *Frankenstein*. A great scroll hung from a column; on it were inscribed words in two columns. One column I recognized as a variation on the words that Wilbur Dunlock had heard chanted by Barrass. The other column bore a similar though different passage. It was a surreal sensation to be in that place, surrounded by the darkness and the earth and the madness of science and sorcery. There was nothing missing from that setting, not even the obligatory monster.

It stumbled out of the darkness, and once more I recognized it from Dunlock's description. It was a simian thing, a parody of a man with misshapen arms and mismatched legs that forced it to limp and slouch toward me. It was a broken thing, hunched and twisted. Its breathing was labored and it wheezed phlegmatically. As it approached I nodded politely and spoke in a calm and rational manner. "My name is Peaslee, Detective Robert Peaslee. I'm with the State Police. At the Whitmarsh Institute they called you Pulver. Can I call you that, or do you prefer something else?" The thing stopped, and turned its head in a strange, animal kind of way. "You are Pulver, are you not?"

The thing chortled in a sad, solemn manner. "Pulver," he wheezed, and seemed to pause. "Yes, I suppose that name could be put to me, at least in part."

It was then that the thing stepped into the light and I could see it for what it truly was. There was a kind of dichotomy in his construction. The legs, the torso, the arms were all twisted, monstrous things with waxy skin with striations of blue and purple and green. That body was a cadaverous thing, fiendish, the product of a diseased and inhuman creator. Yet the horror that chilled me was not that body, but the head that crowned it. For that head was as human as my own. The flesh was white and clear, smooth and unblemished. It was the head of a man, not a monster, and it bore a face that I recognized from the pictures I had seen back on Conanicut Island.

Suddenly things fell into place and I understood, and I knew what had happened, and what had to be done.

The thing in the crypt told me what he could. How Pulver had taught Barrass the incantation that would bring him back from the dead. How he had created documents that would provide access to Corvin Farm and the accounts that went with it. Pulver had dozens of such properties and accounts scattered throughout New England. He promised one to Barrass as long as the man brought him back, restored him to life after he was destroyed. Willett had paid Barrass to throw Pulver's ashes into the bay, but Pulver had promised so much more just to chant a few words over some strange ashes.

It was all too easy, and it all went horribly wrong.

Barrass had failed to sweep up properly, had left some of Pulver's ashes behind, had left impurities in the ashes, had said the words wrong, and Pulver came back as a broken shell of a thing that demanded blood to survive. More blood than Barrass had thought possible, so much blood.

In the laboratory beneath the house Pulver had kept the ashes, the "essential salts" of others, and these he raised to help with his work, to find a way to restore Pulver to his former, more complete form. They worked day and night, experimented with animals and incantations. Graves were robbed and the bodies reduced to powder and then brought back, and then reduced once more. The grains were sifted, sorted, rearranged, and mixed, in the hopes that a composite creature could be created, an amalgam that would return Pulver to his former glory. Yet try as they did, there was nothing but disaster. The resurrected, it seems, were too locked into their patterns, too rigid, unable to accept a blending of bodies and souls. The dead, it seemed, were immutable. They could be brought back from the dead, but they couldn't be transmogrified into anything new. That conclusion brought the breakthrough and the end. To hear that thing in the crypt tell it in that matter-of-fact manner makes it almost seem acceptable, routine, logical, and not the horrific assault on a man that it actually was.

After it was over they brought him back and left him to suffer in the catacombs. His usefulness was at an end. Llewelyn Barrass was no more, only Doctor Asche and his case full of strange powders remained. Asche could have left him that way, but there was something vengeful in the man. He blamed Barrass for the time he had spent in that twisted form, and wanted him to suffer, so he brought him back. He used the formula to raise the dead and brought him back. Barrass knew instantly what had been done. The dead are immutable but the living, to live is to change, and that trait had been taken advantage of.

It took me hours to get that thing up the stairs and into my car. Then, as instructed, I planted the charges and left. As we drove back toward Arkham, the summer night air whipping through our hair, I thought I saw a smile creep across that face. It was a sad smile and it was joined by tears, but whether they were tears of joy or regret I couldn't say, and there was no point in asking. As the charges went off, and Corvin Farm was swallowed by earth and flames, we drove on.

By the time we reached Arkham it was nearly midnight, but I knew that Nichols would still be at the station, waiting for me. I didn't go there. I took my passenger down to the docks, and I helped him stumble and wheeze his way down to the end of a pier that jutted out into the winding Miskatonic River. He held my shoulder as we reached the end of that crumbling wooden platform, and in that grip was all I needed to know.

He stood there by himself, unsteady in the night air as I backed away. He was still a monster, but standing there, committed to what had to be done, he was perhaps the most human of men I had ever seen. He never turned around, never looked back, not even when I began chanting and the wind came up and the clouds rolled in. Great rolls of thunder shattered the night, and heat lightning lit up the heavens as I screamed out those strange words that had decorated the banner in the crypt:

OGTHROD AI'F
GEB'L—EE'H
YOG-SOTHOTH
'NGAH'NH
AI'Y ZHRO

And with that, the thing from the crypt, the composite thing of the incomplete body of the creature they called Pulver and of the orderly who had agreed to serve him, Llewelyn Barrass, turned to dust. It was a pale blue powder, luminescent in a way, and it hung there in the air, in the shape of a man. A broken man to be sure, a man who had made a bargain and been horribly betrayed, but a man nonetheless. It hung there still as death, and then the wind came and blew it all into the Miskatonic River. It seemed to cling together for a time, but then the currents and the roiling eddies broke it apart, swallowed it up, and carried it out to sea.

### IV. An Aftermath and Unanswered Questions

At the station I put out the description of Doctor Asche, or whatever his name was. I knew that it was probably too late, but I had to try. Nichols drove me home and once I was at my door gave me a bottle to crawl into and some days out to sleep it off. But try as I might, I find I cannot sleep, not when there are men like Asche out there, men capable of and willing to do horrible things. They need to be stopped, but I cannot do it alone. This is not a job for normal policemen. Where do I find the men who have the fortitude and the will to oppose them?

It has been two days since I did what had to be done, and this morning I finally have word that a man fitting the description I had given of Doctor Asche had been seen in Providence buying tickets for the train to New York, but that was more than a week ago and none could say where he was bound after that. Nor could they recall the name he had used, though one porter said that the man bore an uncanny resemblance to members of the Ward family. This man Asche, Doctor Asche, was not what he seemed, and I have many questions for Dr. Willett. This time he will supply me with the answers I seek, for I have something to show him—something I think he is quite familiar with.

There is a piece of paper in my pocket with the words on it in a language I do not recognize. Two quatrains, two incantations, one of which I spoke to put an end to Barrass's suffering. Next to it are the words that Wilbur Dunlock heard that serve to bring the dead back to some semblance of life. I will show them to Willett and demand that he explain what has happened, and how it can be done again. These resurrected dead might be put to good use against the things that haunt Arkham.

I read back over what I have written here, and have to wonder if I am really that desperate? Dare I resort to necromancy to put an end to the madness that seems to infect Arkham? Is this what I have been led to?

I have taken that slip and hidden it away in my desk. It seems I am not as desperate as all that—perhaps someday, but not today. I will not create monsters to battle monsters.

At least, not today.

# CHAPTER 25

# "An Inquest into the Death of Wilbur Whateley"
## From the Journals of Robert Peaslee
### September 7 1928

After the first hour I began to wonder what I was doing in the court-room. The inquest into the death was a complete farce. They had no body. Armitage, Rice, and Morgan claimed that they had seen the man lying in the library where the dog had attacked and torn his throat out. I say that Wilbur Whateley was a man, but from what the three university professors had seen, such a classification would have been unlikely. Based on their sworn testimony Wilbur was a hybrid mon-strosity, a chimera, with skin like that of a crocodile, or in some places like that of a snake or lizard. Below the waist, the saurian legs were cov-ered with thick fur and ended in odd, unearthly pads that were neither claws nor hooves. Tentacles with sucking mouths protruded from the thing's waist, and as they were described I thought of the wounds sus-tained by Anne Newman when she was raped. There were also appar-ently vestigial eyes embedded in the hips and behind these was a kind of tubular appendage that could have been a *kind of* mouth or throat. All of this was unsubstantiated by the time the medical examiner had arrived—the thing that had pretended to be a man had shrunken away, sublimated into the very ether. All that remained was a white, viscous material that tests showed bore a vague resemblance to the cartilagi-nous material found in sharks.

There was some discussion of the dog being dangerous; after all, Armitage and the others had admitted that the beast had attacked and killed a man. This was countered with two arguments: one concerned the gun that had been found near to the body, which had obviously been brought in by Whateley to do harm, and therefore it could be construed that the animal was defending itself; alternatively, Armitage argued, there was no evidence that a man had actually been killed, despite his own testimony to the contrary. It was rather circular logic, but I learned quite some time ago that such reasoning was perfectly acceptable in the American judiciary system.

The whole process seemed to be coming to a close when I was suddenly called to testify. To what end, I didn't understand, for I hadn't actually seen anything of value. I only entered the library with the medical examiner, and by then there was only a noxious odor and that white, gelatinous paste on the floor. I prepared myself to keep my answers short and to the point, and explain that I could neither confirm nor deny what the university professors had said.

The first question was unexpected.

"Detective Peaslee, did you know Wilbur Whateley?"

"No. We never met."

"Did you know the victim lived in Dunwich?"

"Yes, sir."

"You've been spending an awful lot of time in Dunwich lately, haven't you, Detective?"

"I'm sorry?"

"I have notes here from several reliable individuals that you've been seen in Dunwich on a regular basis, almost every weekend, since the beginning of June. Is this true?"

"Yes, sir."

"And these visits had nothing to do with Mr. Whateley? You never visited his farm, or saw him in the village?"

"No, sir."

"You're telling this court that in three months of regular visits to Dunwich, you never met the nine-foot-tall freak that was the subject of half the gossip in the village?"

"I didn't frequent the village, sir."

"Well, what exactly were you doing in Dunwich—picking flowers?"

"No, sir. It's a private matter, sir. Family business."

That didn't sit well with Judge Hand. Within the hour I was in the chief's office, learning just how unhappy both he and the judge were with me. I hadn't actually done anything wrong, but my attitude put me in a bad spot, and the visits to Dunwich, which I wouldn't talk about, suggested I was hiding something, something they assumed had to do with Wilbur Whateley. In a way it did—he was the impetus for my preparations—but I didn't have anything to do with his death. It raises an interesting conundrum. Is a man who is preparing to attack another man culpable if he dies by another's hands? It would have to be left for better minds than mine to determine. I certainly wasn't going to volunteer what I had been doing in that long-forgotten graveyard or in the old Halsey cabin, or why my car smelled of moldy earth, or what that queer gray dust that seemed to linger on my clothes was. None of it mattered anymore, anyway. Wilbur Whateley was dead and whatever he had been doing in that old farmhouse was over.

Of this I was certain, for amongst the papers filed with the court were inspections of the Whateley farm and house which affirmed that the ancient and crumbling edifice was empty, and that no one else was in residence on the property. I smiled when I read that the investigators had found little of value on the property and had immediately condemned all the structures that occupied the lands. It was surprising that they suggested that the house and other edifices be burned, but as I read I learned that an unwonted stench seemed to pervade the entire property and that the inspectors had suspected that waste, both animal and human, had been improperly disposed of, making the buildings uninhabitable. That they had not seen or heard anything in the old house brought comfort to me. I concluded that the horrible and invisible monster that had been Whateley's companion that rainy evening in June was no longer there, and I assumed that it had been returned to whatever hellish place it had been called up from. As far as I was concerned, the issue with Wilbur Whateley was closed, and I could go back to looking into the death of Megan Halsey. Unfortunately, the Chief saw things differently.

By September 3rd I was transferred. I wasn't Arkham's problem anymore. All the tasks I had undertaken for them, all the stygian darkness I had fought against, all the little horrors I had dealt with on their behalf, all these were forgotten. I was damaged goods, a blemish as far as the department was concerned, and it was clear to me that if I went quietly there wouldn't be much of an investigation into certain cases that had remained unsolved.

"You seem to like visiting Dunwich, Peaslee," ranted the Chief as he handed me my orders. "Let us see how you like living out there. Effective immediately, you're transferred to the State Police barracks in Aylesbury."

## PART FIVE
# Megan Halsey-Griffith
## May–September 1928

# CHAPTER 26

# "A Note on a Diary Found in an Abandoned Car"
## The Statement of Cedric Hart, Commander
## Massachusetts State Police, Aylesbury Barracks
## September 20 1928

On September 14, 1928, after receiving reports of strange events in Dunwich, five officers of the State Police were dispatched from the barracks in Aylesbury to investigate. Official logs record that they departed the motor pool at 09:45 and reported by radio arriving at a local farm at 11:23. According to locals interviewed later, they left their car at the farm and proceeded by foot crosscountry to an area known as Cold Spring Glen, where the disturbances seemed to be focused. They were never seen or heard from again, and it is assumed they were victims of the conflagration of events that culminated on the evening of September 15—what the tabloids have labeled the Dunwich Horror.

It was, however, on the evening of September 14, with the quintet of officers still missing, that I mobilized the remaining forces and ordered them to Dunwich, including Officer Robert Peaslee, just recently transferred from Arkham. Peaslee left the barracks at 19:17. At 20:36 he used his radio to report the discovery of a car concealed in the thick vegetation along the Eckert Road. His communication with the radio officer indicated that he was stopping to investigate. After twenty minutes the radio officer tried to raise Peaslee, and when he did not respond, a second officer was rerouted to Peaslee's reported location.

Officer Hamilton Phillips reported at 21:52 that he had found Peaslee's vehicle and the abandoned car, but Peaslee was not there. On the driver's seat of the abandoned vehicle was a small diary, selected contents of which follow. Beneath the book was a slip of paper from Peaslee's logbook. It had been torn out hastily and two words, and only two words, had been written. There can be no doubt that it was Peaslee who wrote those words, for they were clearly in his odd and distinctive script, though to Phillips and the rest of the men in the Aylesbury Barracks they meant nothing. Two words that perhaps might shed light on what happened amidst the hills of Dunwich. Perhaps his former colleagues in Arkham, or his sister, they might understand what Peaslee meant when he inscribed into that slip of paper the two words that his hand seemed hesitant to write:

She Lives!

# CHAPTER 27

# "The Rebirth of Megan Halsey"
## From the Diary of Megan Halsey
## May 1 1928

I remember being murdered.

I remember the faces, those terrible faces staring down at me with dead, uncaring eyes as I was pushed off the bridge and into the river. I hit the surface hard, the cold water enveloped me, surrounded me like a blanket of ice. I held my breath as the current pulled me down and slowly put more and more distance between the air and my lungs. It only took a moment for the ache to start, that longing in the jaw, the throat, and the mouth that demands, screams, begs to be fulfilled. I held off as long as I could, swallowing, screaming, and struggling to survive, to live, to have just one more moment. When my resolve finally failed, and my mouth opened and the thick, frigid waters filled my mouth and then my lungs, I opened my eyes and took in the world one last time. I caught a glimpse of the bridge then, with the moon and stars behind it. There was movement, it might have just been a trick of the eye, a wave or ripple passing across the surface of the river, or it might have been a man holding his head over the side of the bridge, making sure that I went under and stayed that way. I closed my eyes and there was nothing but the waters of the river, dark and cold and wet, and I let it sweep me away body and mind.

I remember the darkness, and the whispers in the darkness. That's all they were at first, just whispers, nothing more, faint, like a moth's wings beating against the glass. But with each moment they grew louder, more distinct, the fluttering wings resolved, separated, and became distinct. And then they were gone, replaced with a droning, as if the moth had been replaced by an angry wasp that I, trapped in the darkness, could never see. I was still cold, and the world was still black, but I could hear something and that meant that I had a chance, a chance to live, if I was willing to fight for it.

The angry wasp faded away, and the voices returned. There was a long period of silence and then a new voice spoke and the old voices seemed to mumble and become background noise. Sometime later yet another voice came; this one was softer, kinder, it was somehow familiar. I felt someone touch me; a hand wiped my face clean. I could hear him breathing, feel the heat of his breath as it gently caressed my skin. I tried to cry out, to move, to get his attention somehow, but nothing would work. My hands, arms, and legs seemed paralyzed, still frozen perhaps by the cold, dark waters that I had been immersed in. Not even my eyes would work. In my mind I was screaming, but I could hear nothing but the low voices of other people mumbling incoherently. Then, there was silence.

It wasn't the same as before, it wasn't the absolute silence of the darkness in which I had dwelled for so long that I had lost track of time. It was the silence of the river, a living river with water lapping at the sides of boats, birds calling in the distance, and the occasional fish breaking the surface. There was something calming about those sounds, meditative almost. It centered me somehow, allowed me to focus on the task at hand, and that was coming back to life.

I focused on the simplest of tasks. I needed to gain control of my body, to exert some sort of command over a function, any function, even a single muscle. I focused on opening my eyes. There was nothing at first, but inevitably my left eyelid twitched. It wasn't much, but it was a beginning, and in moments both eyes snapped open and for the first time in what I presumed was days I could see. It was still dark out, but there were enough lights to let me see the man who was standing not far away with his back to me. I tried to call out to him, to somehow get his attention, but to no avail. All of my attempts fell on deaf ears.

No sound came out of my mouth, but it, as well as my eyes, were working, and a moment later I could feel my arms and fingers begin to respond to my commands, but only in the crudest of ways. My arms were trembling and then thrashing about. The spasms spread to my chest and then down to my legs and feet. It was as if a kind of electric shock had been applied to my body. The pain, contracting muscles and what felt like breaking bones, was tremendous. This seizure caught the man's attention and he backed away, muttering the Lord's Prayer, which got louder with each backward step.

As quickly as the pain had come, it subsided, but it left in its wake control over my limbs and with almost no effort I leaped to my feet. I was still unsteady, and my voice was not fully controlled yet. As a consequence I reached out for support, and at the same time opened my mouth and let out the most sorrowful of gurgling moans. The man panicked and out of nowhere there was suddenly a gun in his hand, and it was pointing in my direction. His hand was shaking as I stumbled forward. I saw his hand tighten on the grip and his eye suddenly focus and dilate. Time seemed to slow down, at least for him. I moved like the wind, knocking the gun from his hand and instinctually wrapping my arm around his neck as I twisted around him. There was a sickening snap and he went limp. I dropped him there, almost in the exact same position as I had been in, and then ran.

I ran off the docks and into the streets of Arkham. I ran through the darkness like a madwoman covered in filth, heading for the only place I thought was safe, the place I called home. I sneaked in through the back, shedding the nets and ropes that still clung to my body. They were shreds now, and useless to anyone.

I climbed the stairs in silence and I bathed in the half-light of a single candle. Only when I felt I had removed the grime and filth that had penetrated every bit of me did I dare turn on the lights. I cleaned the bathroom, making sure that there was no trace of the river muck left in the tub. By this time my aunt was up and as I came down the stairs she greeted me in her own peculiar way. She clasped a book to her chest and mentioned something about doing some gardening. The backyard was still a mess, a victim of years of neglect that I hadn't yet had a chance to tend to.

Alone in the kitchen, I suddenly realized I was famished, ravenous, and I devoured monstrous portions of bread, cheese, and vegetables, biting into raw onions as if they were apples or peaches. With each bite I could feel the sustenance being transferred to my body. It was, in a way, addicting, and I gorged myself on whatever could be found to feed the hungers and thirsts that had awakened inside me. When I was finished, the kitchen looked worse than the bathroom had, and needed an equal amount of attention.

It was while I was cleaning up that I began to think about what I had done and what the consequences were likely to be. I had killed a man. There had to be consequences. There were always consequences when you killed. There were even consequences when you brought them back to life. I had learned that the hard way. It was only a matter of time before the body was found and somebody came knocking on my door. That assumed that somebody had recognized me, but that was a safe assumption. I had recognized one of the voices; it was likely its owner had recognized me.

I had to hide. Griffith House would do for a while; there were hidden rooms, left over from the days when the family business had smuggled supplies during the revolution. There was a subbasement not even my mother had known about. I would be safe there until things settled down.

That was weeks ago.

There is someone in the house, someone who comes and goes as he pleases. He is systematically going through our papers, my papers, my life, and my secrets. Sooner or later he will realize that he is not alone here, and then, I don't know what will happen to me. I have to leave here, move someplace else, someplace safer. Griffith House is no longer my home. It's time to move on.

# CHAPTER 28

# "House Calls"
## From the Diary of Megan Halsey
## August 22 1928

It was just after dawn when I reached the house on Derby Street. I had made the journey through the night in order to avoid being seen. I was, after all, a wanted woman, and had been hiding from the police, as well as the man living in my own home of Griffith House, for days. I avoided the front door, and instead surreptitiously entered the grounds of the property and made my way to the back. Through the curtained windows I could see a flickering light that accompanied the calming sounds of someone working in the kitchen. I had vague and cloudy memories of my mother working in that same room, and as I crept up onto the porch and peered through the window I half expected to see her standing there. Instead, I saw the figure of a doughty old woman making pancakes on the stovetop. I recognized her instantly as Mrs. Kreitner, whom, along with her husband, I paid to maintain Crowninshield Manor and this house.

I must have lost my footing, for as I was watching her I slumped against the door, causing a loud bang and startling the old woman. She cried out, ran to the door, and flung it open. I'm not sure what she expected to see, but it certainly wasn't me. There was an audible gasp, followed by a short silence that was finally broken by recognition.

"Miss Megan, they told us you were dead!"

I nodded as I walked into the house, technically my house, and sat down at the kitchen table. "To quote Twain, 'Rumors of my death have been highly exaggerated.'"

"Rumors," whispered the old woman. "T'weren't rumors that brought the lawyers to our door."

Just then, a second figure, that of Mr. Kreitner, came through into the kitchen. "Sheila, who exactly are you talking to at this godforsaken hour?" When he saw me I thought for sure he was going to drop the worn china cup that he was carrying. "It ca-ca-ca-can't be," he stuttered.

"Good morning, Mr. Kreitner," I said to him. "I assure you, your eyes are not deceiving you, and I am not a spirit, nor a phantasm. I am your employer, Megan Halsey-Griffith, and I assure you that despite the police reports and the actions of my lawyers, I am quite alive."

Old Mrs. Kreitner reached out and touched my hand with her own. "She's real, Alex, though chilled to the bone." She stood up. "I'll make some tea—Alex, you fetch the doctor."

"*No doctors!*" I barked, and then for a moment I paused. "No, per-haps a doctor is just what I need." I wrote down a name and address and sent the man on his way, imploring him to be discreet and tell no one of my existence. After he left I turned to his wife. "I'm counting on the both of you. My presence here must be kept secret. What's more is I'll need your support. In my current state I have just a few clothes, and no access to monies of any sort."

"Your mother left behind some of her things when she moved over to Griffith House, I never did have the heart to throw them away. They might be twenty years out of style, but I think they'll fit you, Miss. You do favor her, after all." She paused for a moment. "As for money, Miss, I think we can get you a tidy sum. That is, if you don't mind a bit of fraud, Miss."

"Fraud, Mrs. Kreitner?"

"Well, only against yourself. Mr. Kreitner was planning to do some work on the roof this summer, and has already put in a request for mon-ies in which to buy materials. We could give you those funds, and delay the work until you resolve whatever problem it is that got you mur-dered, and you work out a way to get yourself back amongst the living."

"Can I say, Mrs. Kreitner, that you are taking all this rather in stride, me being not dead and all."

"You call me Sheila, and truth be told my family is Irish and I have five nephews amongst the Republicans. Being temporarily dead is a reg-ular thing amongst that part of the family."

"Thank you, Sheila, now where are those clothes?"

An hour later, I was dressed in one of my mother's old outfits. It wasn't a perfect fit, but nothing a belt or pin couldn't fix. I was waiting in the parlor when Alex Kreitner brought back the man I had sent him for. It had been some time since I had seen him, and it seemed to me he had aged somewhat, but he was still the fine and dapper-looking man I had known since I was a small child. He stood there in the light of the morning sun, holding his medical bag, looking at me without the least bit of surprise on his face.

"Good morning, Miss Halsey-Griffith." He smiled as he spoke.

I put my book down and rose to greet him. "Thank you for coming, Doctor Hartwell. I hope you don't mind, but I must ask you to be discreet and tell no one that I am here, or that I am even alive."

"Of course," he retorted. "But are you?"

"I beg your pardon?"

"Miss Halsey-Griffith, it has been my experience that sometimes the most fundamental things, the things we assume that cannot possibly be wrong, are the ones we should question the most. Do you know why this is?"

"Because this is Arkham."

He nodded. "Because this is Arkham. So I ask you again: are you here, and are you alive?"

I crossed the room and offered him my hand. "Why don't we let you make the final determination of those facts, Doctor Hartwell?"

The good doctor, in violation of all decorum and standards of decency, spent the next hour poking and prodding various parts of my body, drawing blood, taking hair samples, looking in my eyes, nose, and throat, and by any reasonable account doing a thorough job of examining me. He even had me carry out a few makeshift tests of physical strength and endurance. It was perhaps the most interesting and yet most unromantic time I had ever spent with a man. There was rather a lot of hemming and hawing, and a few harrumphs as well. Whatever he had learned about me, it didn't seem to please him.

"Well, the good news, Miss Halsey-Griffith, is that you are not dead."

A snippet of poetry came to mind, "That which is not dead . . ."

"But I would caution you as well. A cursory examination shows that all your vital signs are within normal ranges; a physician of average skill would not notice certain discrepancies."

"Which are?"

"Your senses are peculiarly acute. I think you can see, or at least detect, portions of the spectrum that most people cannot—mostly infrared, but I suspect ultraviolet as well. Your hearing may extend into higher and lower ranges than normal. You're resistant to pain and temperature extremes. Your ability to heal wounds is accelerated; the place where I drew blood hasn't just closed up, it has healed. The strength in your arms, hands, and legs is tremendous, not just for a woman. I need to get your blood under a microscope, but it wouldn't surprise me if certain characteristics were present that were reminiscent of some of my other patients who live not far from here."

"That makes me remarkable, Doctor, not unlike Danner and a few other unique individuals that the press like to report about—not dead."

He placed a few pieces of equipment back into his bag. "No, I wouldn't say you were dead."

I was growing a bit frustrated with the man. "What would you say, then?"

His tone suddenly became officious. "From all outward appearances you are a young woman with a beating heart, breathing lungs, and all the other organs that science says make you human. But I suspect that the biochemical processes that allow those organs to function are very different from those being carried out in the majority of the human population." He guided me back into a chair and held my hand. "What I'm trying to say is that I'm not sure you are human."

"Is that even possible?"

"The functional component of human blood is hemoglobin, which we believe to be an iron-based compound, but in other species it is hemocyanin, a copper-based compound—two different compounds that carry out the same function. You probably still use hemoglobin, but it wouldn't surprise me if there were additional compounds present in your blood that improved efficiencies."

"And you've seen this before?"

"There is a village, the residents of which could be said to have comparable physiologies. I wish I could tell you more, they really are quite fascinating."

"These are the only examples of this you've seen?"

His eyes grew thin and he seemed to be considering something. "There is a procedure I know of, a reagent which is administered to the freshly deceased; it has been known to alter biochemistry in a similar fashion, along with some other, less sociable, side effects."

"Is that what happened to my father?" I finally decided to let Hartwell in on why I asked him here. "After all, you were his assistant when he died."

Hartwell was clearly taken aback, but didn't even take a pause. "Your father was a great man, it was an honor to work with him. What happened later wasn't his fault. I blame someone else entirely."

"Herbert West." I didn't let him speak. "When he resurrected my father and created what has come to be known as the Arkham Terror, he killed your parents and forever sullied the family name of Halsey. He has unleashed a blight, a terrifying monstrous plague that left unchecked might threaten all of humanity."

Hartwell blanched—I had clearly hit a nerve. "What do you mean?"

"I've seen the results of West's experiments first hand. I've also seen exactly how maniacal and irresponsible the man himself is. He's a child who refuses to share his toys. Which wouldn't be so bad if he would learn to clean up after himself."

"While I find your analogy somewhat droll, I can't disagree with it."

"Then we are agreed, you and I will work together and find a solution to the problem of reanimation."

"What exactly are you proposing?"

"If there is a chemical reagent that can reanimate the dead, perhaps there is a similar reagent that can be used to—well, for the lack of a better word—deanimate them. I was hoping, Doctor, that given your experience and hate for West, you might be up to the task."

Doctor Hartwell stood up, straightened his suit, and adjusted his tie. "Miss Halsey, I must admit that I admire what you've conceived here is—well in a word—diabolical. However, while I won't oppose your little endeavor, I can't be part of it, either. I've spent a lifetime pursuing some sense of vengeance against what West did to me and mine. All it has done is taken me down the same path." He turned and took a step toward the door. "A word of advice, my dear: be careful how far you take this little vendetta. If you aren't careful, your quest for vengeance will become stronger and more terrible than you can imagine, perhaps even more terrible than the monstrous plague you seek to snuff out."

I suppose I must have grown irate with the good doctor, for I suddenly stood up and spoke to my guest in a voice that bordered on the uncivil. "Thank you for your opinion, Doctor, but I've seen what West has created lurking out there in the dark, and it has to be dealt with. If you aren't man enough to face them, to do what has to be done to save the world, then to hell with you."

Hartwell opened his mouth to speak, but then apparently thought better of it. He left frustrated, slamming the door and summoning the Kreitners, who were understandably alarmed.

"Are you all right, M-M-Miss?"

I stood staring out the window as Doctor Hartwell walked down the pathway to the street. "I'm fine, Sheila, just fine." I turned to look at the two of them standing there. They weren't exactly the finest of laboratory assistants, but they were all I had; they would have to do. "Is my father's private laboratory still in the basement?"

Mr. Kreitner nodded. "It's a little dusty and some of the rubber seals are probably rotted out, but it's all down there."

"Excellent." I put my hands behind my back and stalked across the room. "We have some work to do, a great deal of work."

It has been months, almost six months to the day, since I came back to Arkham and then came back from the dead. I've been in hiding most of that time, secreted in the home of my father and attended to by the Kreitners. They've been as helpful as they can, but they aren't trained in science or medicine and I've had to do most of the work myself. I haven't been out of this house, out of the laboratory, for more than a few days that entire time.

In June I found myself standing outside Hartwell's house on Crane Street. I stood there in the dark, staring at that house where the thing that was my father had killed two people. Hartwell knew more than he was saying; he could help me, I knew that much. Why he had chosen . . . refused . . . to help me, I didn't know, and didn't understand. I wanted answers, I deserved answers, but I stood there in the light of the streetlamp and never got closer than the sidewalk.

My father's lab proved adequate to my needs, as did his medical books and notes, which furthered my education into areas of human physiology and medicine that my previous studies, those with Herbert West, had not taken me. With nothing else to do, I threw myself into my studies, taking crash courses in anatomy, physiology, biochemistry, and pharmacology. By July I had read more than a hundred books and monographs, and felt that my education had equaled or surpassed that of any first-year intern. I had all the knowledge, all the education. The only thing I lacked was experience in actually treating patients.

And any sort of actual degree.

But I hadn't set myself on this path to get a degree or to treat patients. That had been my father's dream, or so his notes and diaries revealed. Apparently my family has a long history of being physicians, particularly on my grandmother's side. The family had served Bavarian royalty for generations; one illustrious Waldman had once even taught at the University of Ingolstadt. It seems that I came from a long line of noble physicians. Tending to the ill was in my blood, but I wasn't pursuing a noble career in medicine. I was pursuing something else, something that relied on centuries of advances in science, but it wasn't going to be a new medicine or treatment.

I used my own blood. I learned that from Hartwell's hints. I distilled it down, purified the components, and injected it into dead rats that Mr. Kreitner brought me. The initial results were disappointing. My reanimation reagent was more than adequate—the rats came back wrong, violent, and aggressive. More aggressive than any other creature I had ever seen in my life. They mimicked the behaviors I had seen in humans who had been subjected to some version of the reagent, including being cannibalistic, resistant to injury, and remaining mobile even through dismemberment. Major damage to the brain, an ice pick through the skull, was the only sure method of dispatch.

The deanimation reagent wasn't as effective.

In proper doses injected directly into the brain it worked fine. Unfortunately, it took time and almost precise delivery to be effective. Other methods of delivery—I tried darts, sprays, and vaporizers— simply weren't effective. Unless I got the reagent directly into the brain, my concoction just didn't work; putting it in the body, into the blood, just wasn't enough. By the beginning of August I realized that I had to somehow modify the reagent—something was keeping it from reaching the brain.

The problem was that I didn't know how.

My father's books were decades out of date, and I couldn't exactly wander into the medical library at Miskatonic and start doing research. I wouldn't even know where to start to look.

But I knew someone who did.

It took me a time to work up the courage, but one night in the middle of August I found myself on Crane Street looking at Hartwell's house, and I couldn't stay on the sidewalk anymore. With some hesitation I walked up to his door. I stood there for a few minutes, more scared than nervous, but I finally reached out and knocked on the door.

It took only a moment for the man to come to the entryway, but when he finally did swing that door open, the look that was on that face was not the one I was expecting. It wasn't one of surprise or fear, but rather of resignation. He looked at me and at the case I was carrying, nodded slightly, and ushered me inside.

"I've been expecting you," he said as I crossed the threshold.

I let my desperation become apparent. "My deanimation agent works, as long as I inject it into the brain, but it does nothing if I deliver it elsewhere."

We sat down in his parlor. "Lewandowsky's hematoencephalic barrier. Have you read about the dye experiments of Ehrlich and his student, Goldmann?" I shook my head no. "Ehrlich was injecting dye into the bloodstream in an attempt to make fine structures of organs visible. It worked, but failed to stain the brain and central nervous system. His student, Goldmann, injected dyes into the brain, but this failed to spread into the surrounding blood vessels and tissues. This suggests that there is some kind of barrier between the two that keeps some materials, likely including your reagent, from moving from the blood into the brain," Hartwell explained. "If you want your reagent to work you need to find a way to penetrate that barrier."

"Of course I want my reagent to work, why wouldn't I?"

Hartwell stood up, took his glasses off, produced a small handkerchief, and then began to slowly clean the lenses. "We can find a way to penetrate the barrier, to make your deanimation reagent work. I'm thinking about shotgun shells with some of the shot replaced with ampules of your concoction. Headshots that penetrate the skull and allow the reagent to seep into the brain should be sufficient, if rather inefficient."

I stood up in offense. "My reagent is nearly perfect, it's more than 90 percent effective, and I've gotten the response time down to mere seconds. How much more efficient do you want it to be?"

The man had an introspective look as he stared at me. "My father, and his father before him, were butchers. When I was a boy, maybe ten, they took me out to a farm down by Witches' Hollow. We spent the morning hunting for deer so that we could have venison for the shop, and I watched my father shoot a buck, and then I helped him clean and dress the carcass. In the process we took care to remove all the pellets and pieces of broken bone, making sure none of the meat was contaminated."

"Later, after lunch at the farmhouse, we bought a hog from the farmer and my father had it slaughtered. This was the first time I had actually seen this. The farmer took the hog and tied its back feet together, and then strung it up over the branch of a tree. It was screaming, calling, kicking, and bucking, but to no avail. After about ten minutes the pig relaxed, and the farmer walked slowly up behind the whimpering animal and drew a knife across its throat, cutting deep into the flesh. The animal immediately began screaming and kicking, again as its blood drained out like water from a spigot. Almost as an afterthought, one of the farmer's sons brought a basin and set it beneath the animal to collect the blood. It took more than five minutes for the animal to stop squirming, but it seemed longer. Afterward, the farmer and my father gutted and cleaned the animal. We took the carcass, and the farmer kept the organs, head, and feet. It was an additional form of payment, for the work the farmer had done in slaughtering and butchering the animal."

"On the way home I had a question for my father, but it took me almost half the drive to work up the courage. I wanted to know why the hog had been killed with a knife, why it had to suffer, why couldn't it have been shot instead, like we had the buck. He told me something I should have already known. The buck was shot, but it took us longer to clean the meat, and we lost some of it. The hog took longer to die, but the end result was a more complete use of all the parts. Each method was efficient in its own way, but the end results were different."

I stood there, trying to understand his point. "You want me to use a knife to kill the reanimated?"

He laughed a little as he shook his head. "No, Miss Halsey-Griffith. I want you to think about what your end goal is. Despite not being formally trained as a scientist, you've accomplished a great deal. You've come up with a very elegant and scientific solution, but is that what we—you—need here?"

"I don't follow."

"Let me put it another way. Before you perfected your deanimation reagent, how did you put down experimental failures?"

"I used an icepick through the skull."

"So, before we sit down and try to create a weapon that penetrates the skull and delivers your reagent, can we maybe consider that there might be another way, a more brutal and less scientific method?"

"Gunshots directly to the head?"

Doctor Hartwell put his glasses back on. "It has been my experience that the simpler the solution, the better."

"I would need a gun with a significant capacity."

"Well, my dear Miss Halsey-Griffith, there are two things that I have to say about that. The first is that I believe Colonel Thompson and his Auto-Ordinance Company have made great improvements in their weaponry since the war." He smiled and showed me to the front door.

"What was the second thing?"

He opened the door and ushered me out. "Guns and their usefulness in pursuit of your goal are beyond my expertise. Meaning I am of little use to you. Good night, Miss Halsey-Griffith." The door didn't slam in my face, but it might as well have.

# CHAPTER 29

# "The Last Testament of Megan Halsey"
## From the Letters of Megan Halsey
### September 12 1928

Hannah,

I suppose you must be surprised to once more see my cramped hand-writing; after all, I am supposed to be dead, drowned in the Miskatonic back in April. How I survived and where I have been hiding is a tale unto itself, but it is too long and I have limited time before I must once again leave. I thought I would have more time, but this morning's paper brings tales of strange happenings in Dunwich attributed to halluci-nations brought on by bootleg whiskey, but I suspect something else. Again, these are details you are better off not knowing, but I suspect these disturbances are associated with my missing mother, and I am determined to once again brave that weird backwoods wilderness in search of her. In spite of the fact that the last attempt I made nearly cost me my life.

That may be incorrect—I am determined to return to Dunwich and confront the things that dwell there *because* they nearly cost me my life. You know as well as I that I was never satisfied with losing. Nor could I ever let well enough alone. Was it you or Asenath that nicknamed me Princess Vendetta? I had forgotten about that until just now, isn't it strange how things claw their way back out of the mausoleum of mem-ory. That which is not dead . . .

I must ask you to keep the contents of this letter a secret; if my whereabouts for the last few months were to come to light, people who were dear and helpful to me might come under scrutiny, and that would do them a disservice. For much of this time I have taken refuge in the home of my father, hiding there, tended by the caretakers, spending my time formulating a solution to a most perplexing problem, a problem you would be better off not knowing about. But for the last few weeks, things have been much different.

Two weeks ago, in the middle of the night, the caretaker and I left Arkham for a point south of Innsmouth, a rather disreputable place known as Porgy's Fish Club. On seeing the place Mr. Kreitner was loath leaving me there, but I assured him that I would be quite safe in the establishment, despite the unsavory appearances of the clientele. When he still balked at leaving me alone in such a place, I pulled back my jacket and revealed the gun holsters that lay hidden beneath and suggested that these were much better chaperones than he could ever be. It was a position he couldn't argue with, but he still drove off in a huff, the truck leaving a spray of dust and crushed oyster shell in its wake.

Porgy's is advertised as a private club for aficionados of hunting and fishing, but in truth it is a speakeasy and brothel for men with exotic tastes in partners. If I ask you to recall some of the unmentionable skills that Asenath demonstrated for us on more than one occasion you might gain a hint at what decadent delights are available at the place. It is a place outside the law, and as with all such places it has its own methods for enforcing the rule of order, and those methods include not only brutal men but the tools they need as well. This is why I had returned there, to see if I could borrow a few of those tools. The truth is I could use a few of these men as well. For the most part they are lumbering hulks, but there are a few with the brains and I suspect the fortitude to aid me in my task, but as much as I wanted or needed their help I wasn't going to ask. This was a private matter, a family matter, and one that I didn't want anyone else getting hurt or killed over on my behalf. So the tools and nothing else would have to do.

I spent that first night sitting at the bar, nursing a drink and fending off proposals from both directions. Not that I wasn't flattered or interested, but I simply wasn't in the mood. I had come to talk business with the proprietor and until that was done I could think of nothing else. Unfortunately, the proprietor was busy and it was clear that I was going to have to wait until after closing to speak with her. Thankfully, the bartender, knowing who I was, kept me entertained and even made sure I had a small plate of cheese and fruit to keep me satisfied through to the wee hours.

It is an odd thing to watch a bar empty out, and watch the men and women who are charged with operating and caring for both it and its customers go through the process of closing it down. I had seen the practice before, and in this very establishment, but watching it again made me remember the wonder of it all. There is to start an obligatory dimming of the lights, a gentle reminder to patrons that it is time to leave, and a sign for staff to point out to those stragglers who simply won't take a subtle hint and must be physically shown the door. After these issues are dealt with, the lights come back on, and men and women who had seemed so focused on serving customers turn their attentions to the tables and floors, wiping them down and sweeping the debris and refuse from the floors. To the untrained eye it may look as if the cleaning is random and haphazard, but nothing could be further from the truth. Tablecloths are gathered in a very specific order, and as the person tasked with that job works through the room, a second person follows, wiping each table down and scattering various bits to the floor. A third person follows the second with a broom and a dustpan to capture the larger bits. In turn, a fourth person with a push broom follows all of them in order to capture the finer dust and dirt. Only after almost everyone is off the floor does the man with the mop come through and polish everything up. It seems an odd way to divide the workload, but when done right it makes things move in a fast and orderly fashion.

When the time came I was shown back to the office, and sat down to talk business. I explained to the proprietor, a woman whom I considered something of a friend—well, perhaps less than a friend and more than a simple business associate—my situation. I was in trouble with the law, and planning for more. I had little to no cash, but I needed a car and some very special guns. I needed credit and hoped that she would allow me to trade off my reputation and that of my family. She knew I had access to significant funds, or would have at some future point in time. In the end we negotiated and agreed on a price that included lodging, meals, a car, two Tommy guns, and a half dozen drum magazines, as well as a man to teach me how to use them without doing myself an injury. The price was steep, partially because she was the only supplier I could turn to, and also because there was no guarantee that I would be coming back to make good anytime soon.

That is where I must ask you to help me, Hannah.

Attached, you will find documents that in the case of my death function to disperse my holdings. These are, as you know, extensive, and I'm sure that there will be some who will scrutinize them, but I assure you that I have written them such that my lawyers will know they are genuine. I am naming you my executor. You are the only person I trust to carry out my wishes, the vast majority of which are relatively simple. They are detailed in the attached document, but I will summarize them here.

First, as soon as possible, convey to the owner and operator of Porgy's Fish Club the sum of one thousand two hundred dollars, for services rendered.

Second, a trust in the amount of fifteen thousand dollars must be set up to handle claims made under either my name or that of my mother. This is to support either of us in the event that we are alive, but unable to be part of public life. The lawyers will know how to couch the language so as to admit the proper benefactors and deter the unscrupulous.

The remaining balance, including all my monies, houses, and business ventures, are yours to do with as you may. I am the last of the Halseys and Amanda is the last of the Griffiths; our small merchant empire has served us well and is manned by some loyal and savvy people. I urge you to listen to them concerning operations and disposition of our commercial endeavors. If it comes to it I hope that you will see fit to reside in either Halsey or Griffith House, and I urge you to have children. For too long have these homes lacked the pleasurable sounds of children playing in them; I think either place would welcome the return of such noises.

A note on the libraries, which are extensive; Griffith House contains exactly what you would expect, mostly books on history, shipping, and exploration of remote lands and islands, a holdover from when we were more tightly bonded to our shipping interests. The books in the Halsey house are something else entirely, and many can be traced back to the time some ancient Waldman spent in Ingolstadt teaching medicine there. These may have some value and you might consider turning them over to the university.

You have often spoken of your brother Robert's work with the government and the strange goings on he sometimes detailed. I recall him fondly, as a level-headed man whose actions were critical during those strange events in the Catskills. In the basement laboratory of the Halsey house you will find my private notebook detailing my own experiments and studies in the fringes of medical science. This is a small volume bound in green leather with bronze clasps and a lock. It might serve Robert well to have the book and the details of what I have learned.

I trust you with this, Hannah, because I have little choice. Only you and Asenath were ever really friends to me, and Asenath has become so distant of late, ever since the federal government sent men into Innsmouth. I hope you will never have to act on the contents of these pages, but if you have not heard from me by the first day of 1929 then you must assume me dead, or perhaps worse. Either way, I leave the disposition of my and my family's wealth to you. It is perhaps the greatest gift I can give you. Use it wisely and try to forget the darkness and madness that has so haunted my life, since before I was born, really.

Live, Hannah, enjoy life and live.

Perhaps you could do what I could never find the strength to.

## PART SIX
# Robert Peaslee and
# Megan Halsey-Griffith
### September 1928

# CHAPTER 30

# "In the Shadow of Sentinel Hill"
## As Related by Robert Peaslee
## September 14–15 1928

Megan was alive!

I knew that as soon as I saw the first scrap of paper with her hand-writing on it. It took me less than an hour to speed through the notes she left behind; I even tore open the letter addressed to my sister, Hannah, and read that. I must admit that my emotions at the time were mixed. I had, over the last few months, dedicated my life to investigat ing her death, and in the process had suffered detriments to my career. I had seen her body myself, touched it as it lay cold and still on the dock in Arkham—to learn that she was alive was almost too much to believe.

But it was the truth, and the evidence was incontrovertible. I was sitting in her car, reading her words, some of which she had written just days ago. And there in the woods was her trail—at least, I assumed it was hers. The boot prints were small, and whoever had pushed their way from the road into the woods had been small of stature, so it was at least a woman. I may have let my emotional state overwhelm my logic, but it was a leap I was willing to make at the time. Megan was alive and she had driven into the Dunwich area on a mission of vengeance, and if her notes were to be believed then she was armed for bear, ready to go to war.

I was still unclear over exactly what she was involved in, but I had a pretty good idea that it involved a small army of the undead, men who had died and been subjected to the reanimation reagent developed by the mad doctor Herbert West. One of West's subjects had been Eric Clapham-Lee, a doctor himself, who had fallen in combat and been decapitated. West experimented on his fallen colleague, producing a terrifying result, one that I had encountered myself in Ylourgne. Clapham-Lee had for some reason gathered his fellow victims and organized them into a kind of monstrous nomadic tribe, one that had secreted itself in the hills of Dunwich. Megan had encountered them before, a ravening horde of monstrous subhumans that shambled after her and her companion, Lavinia Whateley. Megan and her friend had been saved by something equally as monstrous, something that Megan couldn't describe, something I had glimpsed walking in the rain with Wilbur Whateley. Whatever it had been, it had seemingly vanished after Wilbur had been killed. That Wilbur's own grotesque and inhuman body had vanished as well, dissolving into the very air, added a layer of cosmic terror to the drama I had not only been witness to, but had somehow become part of.

And I had become part of it, an integral part of it. My life was entwined with Megan Halsey's, and hers was entwined with mine. The only problem was that she didn't know it. That needed to change. It was time that Megan and I became reacquainted with each other. I grabbed a few road flares, my gun, and some extra ammunition; after all, I wanted to make a good impression. Armed as best I could be, I set out to follow the trail Megan had left me.

That trail, from the road into the woods, merged with a path not far from the road, one that in general followed Prescott Creek. It was darker in the woods; the trees blocked the moon and stars, making it harder to follow the boot prints that had been left in the soft earth. It was well after midnight and there was an odd wind blowing through the trees, bringing with it a foul scent. It came in wafts and only when the wind came from a specific direction. It was the smell of the river at low tide, of the dump on a hot summer day, of the streets of Paris when the sewers backed up. It was the smell of death and decay and disease and it drifted across the hills of Dunwich in great drafts that made me gag and nearly retch. It was almost palpable. When it moved through the trees I could almost see it, a kind of fog or miasma that seeped and crawled through the undergrowth like a black cat in a dark room, almost invisible unless you knew what to look for.

I learned quickly to avoid that nebulous and malodorous air, and doing so took me off the path and away from Megan's trail, but I picked it up again as I crossed Sumpter Road. Here, the trail turned toward the east, skirting the base of the White Mountain. It was slow going and at times I had to move through the brambles and bushes and undergrowth. It took longer than it should have and to travel just a few miles ended up taking hours. I had been walking, tracking, most of the night, and as the sun rose I could see the queer round shape of Sentinel Hill looming in front of me.

With the dawn came a light drizzle, which made my job more difficult. With each minute Megan's trail was being washed away, being swallowed by the forest floor. With little choice I increased my speed, sloshing through the mud and every third step nearly sliding into a tree or bush. The boot prints were dissolving before my eyes. The raindrops were obliterating them, slowly but surely Megan's footsteps were being erased, and there was nothing I could do about it.

Exhausted and frustrated, I found a sturdy pine and took refuge beneath it. My heart was pounding in my head, and between that and the rain, which had grown from a drizzle to a regular torrent, I could barely hear anything else. Only the distant thunder from the approaching storms, echoing through the hills, reached my ears. At least, I thought it was thunder.

As my heart slowed and the pounding of it in my ears diminished, I realized that only some of what I heard was actually coming from atmospheric disturbances. The low, short, and rapid rumblings were coming not from the sky, but from the small glen that fell between Prescott and Cromlech Mountains and Sentinel Hill. I was, at this point, not far from the Halsey cabin, where I had been spending my off hours for the last few weeks. It was a quiet place, and off the beaten path. The perfect place to experiment and practice, as it were. But those noises weren't anywhere near the Halsey cabin, but much closer, and as I left the tree and headed toward them I recognized the familiar blasting of a pistol being discharged in a rather rapid manner.

The sounds and the realization of what they were rejuvenated me, and I was soon sprinting through the rain-drenched woods, lopping over fallen trunks and branches, desperate to reach the source of gunfire. With each step the sounds of combat grew louder, and the muffled grunts and roars that had been drowned out by the now torrential downpour grew plain to my ears. Those sounds blossomed as I mounted a ridge and there, in the low light, the rain and wind pouring down in buckets, I saw her. She was standing on a log, her legs bent and set to steady herself. A slouch hat covered her head and part of her face. A red trench coat was only partially closed and wrapped around her like a cloak whipping in the wind. A bandolier crossed her chest and I could see that on her back was the butt of a larger gun that I knew had to be one of the Thompsons she had bought. The other Thompson was in her left hand, held low, while in her right hand was a pistol, a Colt 1911. It was the Colt that was firing. Megan Halsey was standing on a log like an avenging angel wrapped in red armor and firing off round after round into the small crowd that stood in the hollow below her.

They were not men, at least not anymore.

By my quick count there were ten of them, not counting another half dozen that Megan had already laid low. They were subhuman things, drooling, hunched, and broken. They clawed at the air, clawed toward Megan like ravenous simian creatures hungry for her flesh. They clawed with broken fingers and gnashed shattered teeth, they clamored over each other like a wave of rats, desperate to feast on the uncorrupted Valkyrie who wielded lightning and thunder and slew them with it. They fell before her, one at a time; slowly but surely, they fell.

She was magnificent to watch. She was a ballerina of brutality, a diva of destruction, a whirling dervish that swept away everything that stood in her way. In England I had seen other people move in this manner, sometimes with walking sticks, sometimes with spears, but always with the same fluidity. They had called it bartitsu, and while they hadn't used guns I could now see how easily such weapons could be added to the art of self-defense. It was beautiful, a wanton waltz that mesmerized me. So entranced was I that I didn't see the one reanimate break off in the opposite direction until it was almost on top of me.

Its breath was fetid and sick and spittle flew from its lips onto my face as it screamed its shrieking cry in my ears. Reflex took over and my gun had only just come out of its holster when I fired and the momentum of the bullet carried my attacker away from me. It hit the ground with a terrific thud, but almost immediately sprang back to its feet. As Megan had discovered, body shots had little permanent effect on the reanimated, but I took careful aim and fired another shot into the thing's brain. It spun backward once more, and then hit the ground with a shuddering spasm. The seizure only lasted for a few seconds, but then the thing ceased its movements and stayed dead.

I stared at it for a moment, before I realized that my shots had acted as a clarion call; not only had Megan ceased firing and looked over in my direction, but all of the monstrous things she was battling had also turned toward my position. Megan was staring at me with a puzzled look. It took her a moment, but only a moment. I suppose I had aged since the last time we had met, but even so, Hannah and I still bore a family resemblance. It took her just a moment to place my face and then I heard her say my name.

"Robert? Robert Peaslee?" There was confusion in her voice, and I could hear it above the falling rain and rustling creatures that stood between us. "Robert Peaslee, what in the hell are you doing here?"

What was I supposed to say? I couldn't rightly just stand there and blurt out the words "I love you," or, "I've spent the last five months reading your secret diaries and private papers and I know you better than anyone else in the world, and I've become infatuated with you." These are not things you say while standing with guns drawn, staring down a horde of reanimated corpses. Flabbergasted and flummoxed, I did the only thing I could do in the situation.

I aimed my gun at the head of the nearest monster and pulled the trigger. This broke the spell and the once-still creatures split their forces and came after each of us. There were only ten of them and together we put them down swiftly and efficiently. In mere moments the hollow was covered with blood and brains oozing from the motionless corpses that had been trying to reach us.

As we stood there, looking at each other across the carnage, our guns smoking, Megan again raised the question. "What are you doing here?"

I paused, panting to catch my breath, to try and tamp down the heat that was running through my blood. "I found your car. I read your papers. I came here to rescue you." It wasn't a lie.

She dropped a cartridge out of her Colt and slid another one in. I took the hint and reloaded myself. "You came here to rescue me?" She waved the Tommy gun at the bodies beneath her. "Does it look like I need help?"

I had to admit she hadn't really needed me. For all my bravado, for all my bluster, for all my apparent courage, Megan Halsey hadn't needed me at all. "No, I suppose not. Megan. I wanted—I needed—I just . . ."

I saw her Colt 1911 rise up into the air. I saw her hand clench around it. I saw it swing in my direction. "Megan, I just wanted to be here, with you."

Her face grew rigid, her eyes narrowed, and suddenly I was staring down the barrel of her gun. "You shouldn't have come, Robert. You really shouldn't have come." I saw her finger tighten. "You have no idea what you've landed in the middle of."

She pulled the trigger.

# CHAPTER 31

# "A Refuge in the Woods"
## As Related by Megan Halsey
## September 15 1928

I fired the pistol and watched as Robert Peaslee dropped to the ground. The shot would never have hit the man, it hadn't been meant to. My aim is good, impeccable I think, and the bullet went exactly where I intended, between the eyes of the reanimated. The creature's head jerked back and then the eyes went dull and it crumpled to the ground in a twitching heap, just feet from where Robert had come to rest. My would-be savior instinctively rolled away, something he had learned in the military, I suppose. His roll took him toward me, and into the small hollow where the reanimated we had just slaughtered lay still and truly dead.

Robert scrambled to his feet and began to climb up the rise. I didn't have time to help him or make sure that his ascent was smooth. I was too busy shooting the undead as they rose up over the hill and swarmed toward us. They came at us single file, making the Tommy gun essentially useless, and I picked them off with my pistol as they stalked up over the mound. It was like watching the dead rise out of the earth, which of course they were actually doing, for the cave they were coming from was just a few yards away, hidden in the underbrush that Robert had passed in front of.

That was the secret of the reanimated: they lived in Dunwich like ants or rabbits, in burrows under the ground. The whole of Dunwich was riddled with them, or so I supposed. I had only been down into the caverns for a few hours, both on this trip and the one before, but I had seen enough. There were dozens of entrances scattered throughout the landscape that led to miles of tunnels, hosting hundreds of the reanimated. Clapham-Lee had gathered them together, West's subjects, his experiments, his successes, his failures, West's victims, and formed a kind of monstrous tribe, a clan of the reanimated. They lived down there in those tunnels; there was an entire village, almost as complex and robust as that which lay above. Beneath the hills of Dunwich was a village of the living dead.

And they had my mother.

I had sneaked my way in through the very entrance through which the monstrous undead minions were now emerging. I had wormed my way through the rent in the earth and crawled through those tunnels, spying on the things that dwelt there. I came armed, but it was not my intent to kill, at least not right away. I wanted to find my mother and rescue her, and then fight my way out if necessary. I didn't get that far. I had wound my way through those stone corridors for over an hour before I had been detected and the alarms raised. They came for me, a slavering horde of broken and bent monstrosities, men and women who should have been dead, but weren't. I retreated, fighting a running battle against the approaching legions as they swarmed out of side tunnels and forced me back. With each minute, with each step, I was forced backward, ever backward, back toward the surface.

While my intrusion had taken more than an hour, my exit took only a fraction of that time. When you aren't trying to be quiet and unseen you can move quite a bit quicker. Of course, the half-human cannibals that were swarming in my wake provided sufficient impetus for me to apply more than a modicum of speed, and I burst onto the surface and into the rain and dawn like a bat out of hell. I sped up the low hill, turned and waited for the first and second waves of terrors to crash out upon me. It was only a moment or so later, after I had dispatched the first wave, that Robert Peaslee burst onto the scene and put himself into the line of fire.

He was clearly unprepared for the situation, and as he clambered up the hill to my side, I fired round after round until he got to his feet and took aim. He stood there for a moment before I realized that he wasn't firing. "Mr. Peaslee, I could use some help here."

There was something in his voice, something I recognized as fear. "Miss Halsey, I think we have a problem." He was looking in the opposite direction, at the sun rising over Sentinel Hill. I followed his gaze. There was something on the hill, something huge and transparent that had been made at least partly visible by the rain. It was a massive thing borne on legs that were both elephantine and insectile. Colossal tentacles sprouted from the thing's back and waved like titanic reeds in the wind. It hurt to look at it in a way I can't explain. I've had foods that I found vile, disgusting either in taste or texture, sometimes both, that have made me retch. Seeing the thing on the hill produced a similar reaction, but you can't spit out or throw up something you've seen.

I turned away and took two more shots. "The thing has finally broken out from the Whateley house."

"Wilbur's brother," shouted Peaslee. "They told me the house was empty. I thought it was dead, banished—something like that."

"Wrong on multiple counts, Mr. Peaslee, and I agree that whatever that thing is we will deal with it, but right now we have more pressing concerns." As I spoke I saw the next wave of undead stream out of the cave, but instead of coming straight for us they went the opposite direction and into the woods. "We're being flanked. We need to find a more defensible position."

Robert fired at something that moved in the woods. "Do you know how to get to your cabin from here?"

"What? Yes, of course." I reloaded. "But the cabin, really? That's our best option?"

"It may be. I've been staying there on weekends, I've got some supplies laid in. Maybe even a few surprises for our friends here."

"Guns, ammunition, a case of incendiary bombs?"

"Not exactly."

"Then what?"

Robert Peaslee grabbed me by the wrist and spun me toward him. He looked me in the eye—his breath was hot, his own eyes burned with a kind of passion. "Reinforcements."

And then we were running.

I was pulling Robert through the woods, across the trails filled with fallen leaves and branches and undergrowth. Behind us, the horde of the undead was in pursuit like some monstrous hydra; every time Robert or I took one down, two more surged over their fallen comrade. All of this occurred while the both of us were doing our best to ignore the strange and terrifying thing that was mounting the apex of Sentinel Hill. We skirted the base of that rise, and as we did so we were subjected to a queer, blasting wind that blew down and carried with it an odd thrumming sound like that of a titanic heartbeat in some colossal vault of a chest. It was not thunder, though as we ran the rain clouds grew darker and condensed into ominous thunderheads that churned from dark gray to black.

As we ran, the mass of things pursuing us grew. Like streams coming together into a river, the undead flowed out of the woods and in a torrent fell in behind us. Robert used my gun, the Tommy gun, to slow down the front of that macabre flood of the living dead. We wound our way through the small strip of dry land that separated Cromlech Mountain from the Sulphur Swamp and then along the North Fork of the Miskatonic River. From there it was only a few hundred yards to the cabin, and as we entered the clearing Robert handed me the Tommy gun and fumbled in his pockets for the keys to the cabin.

The door swung open and we nearly fell inside, and then slammed the door behind us. Robert flipped a switch and I heard the generator come to life, and the lights sputtered on to reveal the cabin in which I had once briefly lived, but it was no longer the place I knew. It was full of tables and shelves, and upon those were bottles and jars and pots, dozens upon dozens of them. They numbered in the hundreds and on each was a small paper tag. As I took the place in I saw that each tag bore a different name: Lee Herber, John Gibbons, Carol Snyder, Les Triplett, Charlie Brooks, Anne Crank, Sam Merritt, Keith Shirley—these were just a few of the names. Each jar bore a name and in each container was the same fine gray ash.

They were names that I didn't recognize, but I had no time to ponder who or what they meant. Robert had sat down at one of the tables and was shuffling through some papers. The place was a veritable alchemist's laboratory. In addition to the labeled jars of ash, on the large central table at which Robert was sitting there were also braziers and tubes and cylinders of various sizes and materials. Not just glass, but also clay and ceramic as well. There were even a few metallic containers. While all of this disturbed me, perhaps the most unsettling thing was the weird and massive sigil that had been inscribed in chalk on the wall. It was a conglomeration of circles and uneven triangles that formed a kind of aberrant pentagram. There was something about those angles, something wrong, something that violated the laws of geometry, of space and of the orderly universe. It was like that thing on the hill—it hurt the eyes to look at.

"Mr. Peaslee, what are we doing here? What have you done? What is all this?"

He waved his hands at me, both in panic and frustration. "Shhh. Please, Megan . . . Miss Halsey, be quiet. I need to concentrate. The incantation must be precise, particularly with this magnitude of subjects."

Peaslee rose from the table with a single page in his hand. He cleared his throat and in a deep and clear voice he spoke these words:

Y'AI'NG'NGAH,
YOG-SOTHOTH
H'EE-L'GEB
F'AI THRODOG
UAAAH!

A cold wind suddenly tore through the floorboards, and the electric lights sputtered like candles. A pungent, odiferous smoke was rising from the various containers scattered about the room. They were clouds of thick, black-and-green vapor that quickly obscured vast portions of the room.

Something hit the door, and then something else hit the outside wall. I ran to the window. Even in the pale light of the storm I could see that the yard was full of the undead. They were pouring out of the forest, swarming like ants toward the house. "They're here!" I screamed.

But Robert didn't respond. He just kept chanting.

Y'AI'NG'NGAH,
YOG-SOTHOTH
H'EE-L'GEB
F'AI THRODOG
UAAAH!

I looked back to the window just in time to catch the swift shadow descending toward the glass. I dropped to the floor just as the window exploded in and a thick and pasty white arm grabbed me by the back of the head. I felt the thick, bony fingers scrape against my skull as they grasped a chunk of my hair and pulled me back toward the window. "Robert!" I screamed. The shattered glass tore into my back and thigh as I was pulled outside and onto the porch.

I hit the wooden decking hard and rolled to my side. Something warm and wet was running down my leg. Hands grabbed me by the arms and shoulders and wrenched me upward. All around me the dead were shambling forward, surrounding me, and surrounding the cabin. My arms were pinned behind me and another hand grabbed me by the hair and forced my eyes up.

The form standing there was in its own way magnificent, statuesque, almost. The man, the myth, the monster, everything that he ever imagined of himself, stood there looking down on me with eyes full of madness. When he spoke, his voice was commanding and breathtaking.

"Megan Halsey-Griffith! I thought for sure we had seen the last of you!" I had known him as my teacher at The Hall School, Mr. Lydecker, but I had since learned the truth. His name was Clapham-Lee, Eric Moreland Clapham-Lee, Herbert West's greatest success, and possibly his greatest failure as well. I did not know the details, but Clapham-Lee claimed to be West's nemesis, his rival, a victim who was assured that someday he would bring down vengeance upon the mad doctor who had created him. "I thought we had killed you, Miss Halsey-Griffith, but you seem to be gifted with an odd talent of turning up and not being dead."

"The same could be said of you." I nearly spat the words out of my mouth. "What have you done with my mother?"

His eyes looked confused, and then suddenly he began to chuckle. "Your mother? Miss Halsey-Griffith, is all this about your mother? I assure you that your mother is perfectly safe."

I wanted to respond to that, and I even think that the first words, "What do you mean . . ." may have left my mouth, but I was interrupted by the cabin door slamming open and Robert Peaslee running out with a pistol in one hand and the Tommy gun in another. He let out a single shot and blew the head off one of the things holding me. As it dropped to the ground I used the surprise to gain the upper hand. I spun out of the grasp of my captors and threw my back against the wall of the cabin. I reached for my spare pistol and drew a bead on Clapham-Lee.

He laughed. "Mr. Peaslee, well, this is a surprise. I've been busy since last we met. I've perfected West's little formula, and I've been using it quite often. I warned you before, Peaslee. The world is going to change. An empire of the reanimated shall rise and supplant that of the living."

Peaslee's voice was tired, weak, but he seemed determined. "We will stop you."

"I think not. I have an army, and no matter how many guns you have, there are just the two of you."

Peaslee shook his head. "No, there are not. You aren't the only one who has been busy. I, too, have perfected my formula, although my results might be a little cruder than yours."

The walls of the cabin burst and something titanic spewed out of the interior. It was smoky at first, then more like ash, and then a moment later it was like flesh, but not the flesh of a single man or woman. It was a construct, a golem of flesh and bone and sinew. A titan made from the bodies of men and women woven together into something devastatingly huge. It strode out of the wreckage of the cabin and into the yard. Casually, it grabbed a support beam and ripped it from its moorings. With an effortless swing it used the pillar of wood as a club and cleared away the dozen or so reanimated that stood in its path. With its free hand it grabbed a few of the fallen and broken forms, and even though they still squirmed and screamed, raised them up and crushed them, letting the black and crimson vital fluids rain down over its own misshapen form. There must have been hundreds of bodies conglomerated there in that flesh golem, with hundreds of mouths, and all of them with smacking lips and darting tongues lapping up what dripped down upon them, like dogs in a slaughterhouse.

"What have you done?" I heard someone say, not realizing at first that it was my own voice.

"He's begun the inevitable." It was Clapham-Lee who spoke, and there was a sadness in his voice. "A war between the undead!"

# CHAPTER 32

# "The War of the Undead"
## As Related by Robert Peaslee
## September 15 1928

The juggernaut of undead tissue waded through the army of the rean-imated like a scythe through a field of wheat, and with each step the homunculus grabbed up a handful of its fallen opponents and squeezed them dry. It was a horrible thing, a gestalt entity of my own creation, and built from the ashes of the undead. Ashes I had harvested myself from that long-forgotten cemetery that Megan had found on her trav-els, which the reanimated had once used for refuge but then abandoned.

I had spent days exhuming the bodies from that ramshackle grave-yard and then converting them to the powder, the essential salts. It had taken me weeks to learn how to pronounce the words, and to then find the way to intertwine the bodies themselves. I had started with just two, and then three, and then it climbed exponentially, until I had scores of the dead entwined together as a massive creature. One that moved as a single entity, thought as a single entity, and fed as a single entity, and it fed constantly. It fed on blood, so much blood.

I don't know why I did it. I had said I wouldn't, but something had set me off. In retrospect, of course, it was a good idea; the colossus of flesh was exactly what I needed to help me wage a war against the reanimated, not to mention the thing that was climbing Sentinel Hill. Once it had been done, once it had been broken to my will, it was easy to keep it bottled up for just such an occasion. Like a loaded gun kept in the closet. Just in case. I suppose that makes me just a little mad, but after everything I had been through, wasn't I entitled to be just a little mad?

While the reanimated fled from the cyclopean thing that was wad-ing through them, I ran toward Megan and took a shot at the enigmatic thing that was the leader of the undead forces around us. Clapham-Lee dodged my bullet easily and retreated around the side of the cabin. I reached Megan a moment later and grabbed her by both shoulders.

"Are you all right?" I asked, noting the tatters of her coat and the blood that stained it.

She nodded. "The glass from the window cut me deep, but I'll be all right in a minute or two." She stared at the hulking thing smashing through the tiny creatures that were assaulting it. "What is that—abomination?"

"You and West and Clapham-Lee have your way of bringing back the dead, I have another."

Megan's mouth was agape. "West and Clapham-Lee were trying to find a way to cure death, to help people . . . it may have become twisted but that was the goal. I only studied reanimation so that I could bring an end to it. I never intended to become a reanimator . . . reanimatrix."

"That's the thing I've learned about life, Megan; no matter what we set out to do, whatever we think we know about ourselves, and what we believe about ourselves and those around us, we always end up doing things, becoming things that we never intended, and never imagined."

"Is that how you justify creating that thing?"

"Justify it, no, but just as you had to study reanimation to learn how to better put the reanimated down, I had to learn about this, study this, create that thing out there." I pointed at the juggernaut. The reanimated were screaming, being torn to bits, as something they didn't understand fed upon them and their deaths.

"Can you control it?" There was a questioning fear in her eyes.

"Briefly," I admitted. The juggernaut swung his club like a hockey stick and sent a pair of reanimated flying into a tree, where they exploded instantly.

"Briefly! What does briefly mean?"

"Six minutes." Two reanimated had sneaked up behind the thing and jumped on to its back. They scrambled up and then plunged makeshift daggers into the space between its shoulders.

"Six minutes! What happens after six minutes? Please tell me it collapses back into dust!"

We caught the attention of something that had once been human, but now looked more like the results of an unholy union between a woman and a chimpanzee. I put it down with a shot from my pistol.

"After six minutes it becomes unstable and breaks down into its component parts."

"That's dust, right?"

"Unfortunately, it's not, it's the dozens of individuals that make it up, individuals that I can't control; individuals that will be very upset with me." The juggernaut was thrashing about, trying to dislodge the things on its back. I fired at something that had crawled up its leg.

"Care to elaborate?"

"The resurrection process is painful, not just physically but spiritually. They were dead, from what I can tell they have no memory of being dead, but they know there is missing time. They know that for some period of time—months, days, years, sometimes even centuries, they didn't exist, and that is an existential crisis that they simply can't deal with. It makes them violent and I tend to be a reminder, a focus of all that confusion and pain." Megan fired at a meatball of a man and dropped him to the ground just inches from us.

"Six minutes?"

"Well, no, actually." I looked at my watch—it was almost eight in the morning. "We have less than four and a half minutes now." The rain was coming down in buckets.

"This is your play now, Mr. Peaslee," yelled Megan over the sound of rain and the cacophony of screams. "You lead, I'll follow."

I turned and looked into that beautiful face with the strange alluring eyes. "You should know that I love you." And then I kissed her. It wasn't a long kiss, it wasn't a short kiss, but it was enough to make my point.

When I finally and reluctantly pulled away, there was an awkward look on her face and her hands darted to my chest and played nervously with my shirt. "Perhaps we should talk about this later? You know, when we're not surrounded by the undead and on the verge of being killed."

"Good point."

I took the Tommy gun and turned, firing into the crowd with short controlled bursts aimed at the head. Megan followed behind me, laying down covering fire on my flanks. It took us a moment, but we soon got into a rhythm with me taking point and firing into large parties, and then Megan either cleaning up or picking off strays.

As for the juggernaut, that thing eventually cleared its back by rolling over and crushing its attackers beneath its immense bulk. They were still there, embedded like dead flies, but they weren't causing any more damage. The juggernaut was back in the game, smashing its way through the attacking horde. The thing seemed unstoppable, but the reanimated minions of Clapham-Lee didn't seem to understand that; they just kept throwing themselves at it, trying to tear it apart, but to little avail. True, they were able to wrench a limb free, or even decapitate a component or two, but these were quickly replaced and the beast marched on, leaving devastation in its path.

Then, without warning, the Tommy gun ran dry. I disengaged the drum and tossed it to the side. "You had another one of these?" I called out to Megan.

"In my knapsack."

"Which is where now?"

"It tore loose when I was dragged through the window. It's probably still in the cabin."

I looked back, thinking the cabin would be quite some distance away, but in reality we hadn't actually moved that far. Our steps had been slow and sure. We had been methodical, not manic, and consequently we hadn't actually gained that much ground. In contrast, the juggernaut had been anything but controlled, and as a result he had actually circled around and wasn't far from where he had exploded through the front of the cabin, leaving the door and windows as little more than wreckage. Wreckage that I could see someone was now picking through.

It was little more than a shadow, but that shadow was unmistakable, unlike all the others, essentially unique in all the world. It stood there in the darkness, holding in its hands its own head, a head that was even now speaking words I could barely hear, but recognized almost immediately. They were words that I had grown to know almost by heart, but had left a copy of behind on the table in case my memory failed, and now they were being spoken and the juggernaut that had turned the tides of battle in our favor was on the verge of being banished. Clapham-Lee was screaming in that throatless, airy voice of his.

OGTHROD
AI'F GEB'L-EE'H

YOG-SOTHOTH
'NGAHING AI'Y
ZHRO

I fired my pistol, but missed. Megan followed suit, but her shots failed to connect as well. Suddenly I was sprinting across the devastated landscape, shooting as I went. This time my bullets found their mark, and Clapham-Lee's body shuddered and recoiled as the slugs hit, but the head kept speaking.

OGTHROD
AI'F GEB'L-EE'H
YOG-SOTHOTH
'NGAHING AI'Y
ZHRO

Then suddenly he was laughing, and I saw why. The juggernaut, my flesh golem, was falling apart, crumbling, dissolving. It was systematically turning back into ash, and in the wind and rain the ash was being washed away into the muddy field where dozens of the reanimated now lay dead, or dying. Their crushed forms were still struggling; still trying to come to terms with what had happened, but for most it was inevitable. There was little to save, which was actually the whole point.

The body of Clapham-Lee was still standing; it staggered a little, but that was all. "Now what shall you do, Mr. Peaslee? I warned you before not to interfere in my plans, but you've done just that. And now it's time to pay the price for your insolence."

I dropped the useless Tommy gun. I felt the weight of the pistol in my hand. There was still a shot left, maybe two. The last of the juggernaut collapsed onto the ground, spilling bodies and parts of bodies across the muddy lawn. They didn't last. The rain pelted the squirming cadavers and bored into them like drills through soft wood. They weren't even screaming anymore. They were just being washed away into nothingness, while all around us the surviving reanimated came shambling back to surround us. "Did you expect me to do nothing?" I shouted back.

"No, Mr. Peaslee, I expected you to . . ." But he never finished that sentence. I had flicked the gun up and taken aim and pulled the trigger twice. The first shot went right into his chest, and when it exited it took a significant amount of meat with it. There had been no second bullet. The gun had only had one shot left after all.

But there had been two shots. I had heard them.

I looked at Megan. She was running toward me, her mouth screaming my name. Out of the corner of my eye I saw the once-imposing form of Major Doctor Sir Eric Moreland Clapham-Lee, ODS, spin to the ground. I tried to stay focused on Megan. Everything had slowed down. There was something wrong with my shoulder—it hurt. It burned. There was pain. And then I saw her.

She was standing in the distance, just at the edge of the wood. She had a revolver pointed in my direction. There was a wisp of smoke at the tip of the barrel. I was breathing hard, my eyes wouldn't focus. Megan became a blur. The woman standing there with the gun came into sharp resolution. I knew her. I had never met her, of course, but I knew her. I had seen her picture every day. I had lived in her house. There was no mistaking those features. Her pictures didn't do her justice. She was as beautiful and radiant as her daughter, the only girl I had ever fallen in love with.

My hand went to my shoulder and I felt the blood pumping out of the hole I had found there. I had been shot. I fell to the ground. I had been shot. I had been with Megan for only about two hours, and both she and her mother had aimed guns at me.

The difference being, Elizabeth Halsey-Griffith, Megan's mother, had actually shot me.

This was one hell of a way to start a relationship.

# CHAPTER 33

# "A Monstrous Choice"
## As Related by Megan Halsey
## September 15 1928

I watched the bullet strike Robert Peaslee in the shoulder and then he crumpled to the ground. Instinctively, I turned to return fire. The gun went off, but as it did a hand grabbed my wrist and sent my shot astray. I threw the small form off me and this time took better aim at my target. Better aim gave me a better look, and there she stood like a dark angel, her dress in tatters whipping in the wind, my mother, Elizabeth Halsey!

And she wasn't alone.

Behind her and to her left stood a man, or at least what had once been a man. It was a man I recognized, even though I had never met him, a man whom I would have known whatever condition he was in, a man whose picture I had seen a thousand times. There, to her left, was my father, the reanimated form of Allan Halsey.

But there was more!

The frail, thin shape that had flung itself out of the forest and knocked my gun hand was not alone. The one creature that had struck me was the size of a small ape, pale and hairless, dressed in only a worn pair of overalls like the two others that stood by the haunting, statuesque forms of my parents. They were ghoulish things, and as I have said, pale, thin, and hairless, with arms and legs like sticks. Their skin was thin and translucent, and I could see the thick blue lines of the veins that pulsated beneath. There was something about these things, their eyes were too large, their heads too bulbous, their limbs too long and thin. I had seen pictures in medical texts of victims of malnutrition and starvation, and here was some resemblance to these creatures, but as much as those photographs had disturbed me, these small monsters unnerved me even more. The one that had struck me was loping across the yard, moving not like any man, but like an animal, like a cat or perhaps even a dog.

I lowered my gun as she stepped toward me and her retinue followed. My father lumbered behind her, but the small creatures—were they children? My God, had Clapham-Lee experimented on children? The small creatures moved cautiously, and kept close to my mother's skirt, like cats around a favored owner. As the one child-thing reached her she raised her hand slightly, and the creature nuzzled it as it reached her and then fell in with its brethren.

"Mother." My voice cracked as I spoke to the woman who had borne me for the first time in years. "Mother, I've come for you, I've come to rescue you."

There was that look, the one she would give me when she realized that I had done something wrong, that I had disappointed her. I suppose all mothers have that look, or another one just like it. I hadn't seen it for years, but there it was, like something that had crawled across her face and taken up residence there. "Megan, Megan my darling daughter, you have to stop this." She swept her hand across the landscape. "All this madness, this death, you have to stop it, you're destroying everything."

"Destroying—destroying everything? I didn't start this, Mother. I came looking for you and they wouldn't let me see you. These monsters attacked me, threw me in the river. They tried to murder me, Mother."

"And yet here you are. Safe and sound, perhaps a little worse for wear, perhaps a little better." That look suddenly adopted a cruel smile. "You've never been tested before, have you, Megan? Never been hurt or sick or in danger? You could no more be killed by drowning than any of my other children."

The three pale things swirled around her and a horrible realization dawned on me. "Those things—they're my siblings?"

"Your brothers, Megan, your brothers. Magnificent, aren't they? The product of the union between your father and myself, with just a touch of reanimation reagent during the third trimester. That's the key, Megan, the reagent injected directly into the womb during gestation. It alters the development, makes the child stronger, faster, more intelligent, more resistant to damage and disease. They have all the same attributes that you do, Megan, just to a greater degree."

"Clapham-Lee experimented on you while you were pregnant?"

There was that look again, that look of disappointment. "Clapham-Lee? Eric? No, he didn't experiment on me, not at all. You've misunderstood completely. The new reagent, the use of it on fetal development, those weren't Clapham-Lee's ideas. He's more interested in reanimation, building his hollow Empire of the Undead. No, this experiment, this leap in human evolution, this was my idea."

All around me, the reanimated, those that were still left, stumbled forward. There couldn't be more than a dozen of them, but Robert and I were trapped, and I knew I was nearly out of bullets. My cache of ammunition, the spare Tommy gun, and the other drum were somewhere in the debris of the cabin.

"Mother, this is wrong," I said.

"No, my child, it isn't. Search inside yourself, you have strengths and abilities that set you above normal human beings, and even above the reanimated. If you try, if you reach in and focus your powers you'll find this to be true. You have the power to control them, to draw them to you, to make them do your bidding. And you were just the first step. Your brothers are the next generation, and they are even stronger. I can only dream of what powers will manifest in those born from the union of my children."

I stood there, wide-eyed, letting her words slowly sink into my brain, and then slowly began to shake my head. There were words on my lips that slowly, ever so slowly became sounds of denial. "No, NO, NO!" I raised my gun, and with control and precision fired three times.

The bullets sped through the air toward their targets. The first hit home and exploded the head of the smallest of my ersatz siblings. The eyes careened out and away like baseballs that had been hit too hard and lost their covers. The body fell to the ground without a sound. The second bullet hit its target as well, this time leaving a gaping hole in the chest of the largest of the pale-skinned ghouls, through which a torrent of blood flowed. The creature turned and opened its mouth to scream, but only a gurgling whimper came out.

My last shot didn't connect—the middle child grabbed my father and spun his massive and lumbering form around, letting him take the shot in the thigh. My father roared in pain and anger. He took a step toward me, but my mother put a hand on his shoulder and stopped him.

All around me, the undead took a step back and I realized that while I knew that I was out of ammo, my mother didn't.

I waved the gun menacingly. "Mother, please, come with me." There was a touch of sadness and futility in my voice. "Leave this place. Leave the dead behind and come home. We can be a family again, just you and me." A tear traced its way down my cheek.

She raised her pistol and fired. It happened so fast I didn't have time to move, but I wasn't her target. Behind me, the bullet blew a hole in the chest of the towering body of Clapham-Lee and took his heart out of his back. The body shuddered and slowly crumpled to the ground. His head rolled off, moaning as it came to rest mere inches from where I stood.

"A gift, Megan. But the last one I shall ever give you. I asked you once, in my letter, to not try and find me. Now I am telling you. Leave us be." She reached out a hand to her last remaining child-thing. "Come, Lazarus." The demonic monstrosity took her hand and pulled her back.

She and all the others drifted backward into the shadows of the forest, but as I stood there, surrounded by the bodies and ashes, the devastation of our battle and the moaning head of Sir Eric Moreland Clapham-Lee, the only thing I could think of were her last words, which were ringing in my head.

"You belong with us, Megan. Someday you'll realize that. We, you, me, and your brother, belong with your father and his kind. We belong with the dead."

# CHAPTER 34

# "Escape from Sentinel Hill"
## As Related by Robert Peaslee
## September 15 1928

It was late afternoon and the rain was still coming down in torrents, and Megan was carrying me down toward Talbot Road. She was letting me lean on her as we clumsily made our way down the muddy track. My breathing was labored, and with every breath waves of pain shot through my chest. Each step was infinitesimally more difficult than the last, but those minute increases were, over time, adding up. It wasn't just the pain. There was a creeping chill, a cold that was clawing its way through my body. It was more than just the wet and the fall temperature; this was a chill that came from the inside and was working its way into my extremities, at least it felt that way. It felt like I was dying.

Instead of heading west on the Talbot Road we took it south, stumbling along about a half mile around the base of Sentinel Hill, until the road finally petered out and became a trail, and then little more than a footpath. The trail ended at a small stream that took us only seconds to cross. On the far side we picked up another footpath, which grew into a trail and then a road, which given where we were could only have been the Whateley Road, which skirted the southwest quarter of Sentinel Hill.

As we crossed one of the tributaries to Bishop's Brook I heard Megan speaking, arguing with someone. It was someone whom I couldn't see, but whose voice seemed strangely, horribly familiar. "He's dying, you know that, don't you?"

Megan seemed to take the opposite position. "He's not dying. He's going to be just fine." There was doubt in her voice. "We'll get down to Dunwich and then over to Aylesbury. They'll have a doctor there."

"Miss Halsey, I am a doctor, and based on how you packed his wound, I suspect that you've had a significant amount of medical training yourself. He's lost too much blood. It's inevitable."

"Shut up."

Suddenly I was looking up the hill, at the sky. There was something there, something forming in the clouds. A kind of congeries of bubbles, like the foam formed where the ocean meets the shore. It was like that, at least in some ways. In other ways it reminded me of the churning that occurs in the vicinity of a ship's propeller.

"Miss Halsey, you can save him. We can save him. That is, if we work together."

I was on the ground, staring up at the peak of Sentinel Hill and the weird atmospheric phenomenon beyond. The bubbles were growing, expanding and stretching, reaching down toward the earth, like tentacles, like streamers of fluidity desperate to reach the earth. The membrane around the vacuole was growing thinner, stretching itself like the skin of a balloon. It had almost reached the peak, where something else was waiting, something massive, something that was screaming in rhythm with the thunder and lightning.

I couldn't make out the words, wasn't even sure if they were words at all, and then I heard those three syllables that I myself had spoken so many times. They were alien words, ancient from time immemorial, and yet they were being screamed. Something, someone, on Sentinel Hill, was calling out that hideous name.

yog-sothoth
Yog-Sothoth
YOG-SOTHOTH!

And then there was darkness. It was an emptiness, a void of sound and light and feeling. One moment I was there, surrounded by the world, and then I was gone and so was the world. There was simply nothing, and I was simply nothing.

The world flooded back into my brain like a torrent from a broken dam. There was light and sound and sensation, and of course there was pain. There was screaming, but it only took me a moment to realize that it was me that was screaming. It was me that was tearing at my own throat as my vocal cords began to rip apart.

I heard Megan speaking, panic in her voice. "He's come back wrong!"

"No," came that other voice, "he's just coming back to life. There is always pain. With birth, there is always pain."

Megan was suddenly by my side, holding me at the shoulders, holding me down. "We have to help him," she implored.

"Let me see him," that voice demanded. Megan's right hand left my shoulder and reached out and picked something up. Something blotted out the light. It took a minute for my eyes to adjust, to see what was in front of my eyes. It was a face, that of Sir Eric Moreland Clapham-Lee. Megan was holding his head by its hair, dangling it in front of me. "He's going to be fine, my dear Megan," said Clapham-Lee. "He's going to be just fine."

On the hill above us the storm was screaming. It wasn't a voice—it was as if the world itself was speaking.

"Eh-ya-ya-ya-yahaah-e'yayayayaaaa . . . ff-ff-ff-FATHER! FATHER! YOG-SOTHOTH!"

A great crack then seemed to shatter the world, a deafening, apocalyptic report that rolled down across the Dunwich hills, though whether it was from the sky or the earth I could not say. That titanic peal was followed by a single bolt of lightning, which struck the very apex of the hill and reduced whatever stood there to rubble. This was followed by a wave of invisible force that swept across the landscape and carried with it a horrific miasma. The forest itself fell before that queer unseen wave, the trees shattered, the underbrush ripped free by its roots, and the grass fell in a frenzy of unknown and unknowable powers. That mephitic power blew Megan off her feet and down into my arms. Clapham-Lee's head was screaming; Megan tucked it between us and let the monstrous wave roll over us.

Afterward, we stood there looking at the devastation that surrounded us. It was as if a great hand had come down and tried to wipe the forest away. The trees had shattered like toothpicks, and the road had been filled with debris; not just trees, but boulders and undergrowth as well. A half mile into our walk there was a truck tire sticking up out of the road. The axle was buried beneath it, and below that was the truck itself.

It took us hours, but we finally made it back to where I had parked my patrol car, next to hers. The papers, Megan's papers, were gone. I set Clapham-Lee's head inside a tool bag that was in Megan's trunk. He objected, of course, but I made it clear that the situation was only temporary, and the alternative was more permanent. I put Megan in the passenger seat and then started the car.

As we drove away, I looked in the rearview mirror and watched as we pulled farther and farther away from my patrol car. As the vehicle grew small and distant I realized my days as a member of the Massachusetts State Police were over. As we turned onto the Aylesbury Pike, Megan put her head on my shoulder. Behind us, the sun was setting, being swallowed up by the Dunwich Hills. The last rays cut into the sky, setting fire to the dark clouds. When Megan's hand found mine I stopped looking back, and started thinking about what Megan and I were going to do tomorrow.

And the day after that, and the day after that.

PART SEVEN
# Aftermath
## From the Case Files of
## Halsey, Peaslee, & Lydecker
## Consulting Detectives

# CHAPTER 35

# "The Foundlings of Dunwich"
## From the Case File of HP&L
## November 8 1928

As the car approached Aylesbury, the occupant of the passenger seat turned to the driver, opened her mouth, and then closed it again without saying a word. Megan Peaslee, whose maiden name was Megan Halsey-Griffith, but who preferred Megan Halsey, was annoyed. She opened her mouth again, and this time spoke. "So that was your first time."

The driver, Robert Peaslee, formerly of the State Police, shrugged. "Technically, yes."

Megan chuckled a little. "You do know you were very good."

"I've had a lot of practice, just not with women." He smiled and reached out his hand for hers. "You weren't bad yourself, very exuberant, energetic."

"You've read my file. You should have known what you were getting yourself into."

"I did—do you find that odd?"

A thoughtful look crossed her eyes. "I'll admit I was unnerved that a complete stranger had read my diary, learned my innermost secrets, and had essentially studied me as if you were passing judgment on my life."

"But?"

"But I did the same to you while you lay in bed recovering. Your notes and files, they tell your story. You think you're writing about other people, about the things you've seen, the things you've fought against, but you're really writing about yourself. In Paris you were almost a bystander, and then you became a victim, a survivor, and then a pawn to be used for other people's purposes. Now you're something else. Some people might call you a dark knight, or a cowboy, maybe even an adventurer. In Japan they have these warriors, masterless samurai, called ronin. They've lost everything, family, home, purpose. They are hopelessly doomed, trapped in a situation that they didn't make, but for which they feel responsible. In the end these ronin are left with nothing but choosing between two immoral outcomes. I think you're like them, a good man in a corrupt world, trying to do what he can."

"And you find this attractive?"

"I think you're like an old gun. You've been used, and there's a touch of rust; you need to be cleaned and serviced, but with a little care you'll probably still keep firing for years to come."

Robert grinned. "That probably depends on who's pulling the trigger. Think you can hit the target?"

Megan made a fist and shook it defiantly. "Like a rock. Clear eyes, steady hands, loaded guns."

"Let us hope that it doesn't come to that," chided Robert.

Meghan thought for a moment. "You said that the last time, and you ended up shooting that kid, what was his name—something Potter?"

"I don't remember, and I didn't shoot him. He died in the explosion that destroyed the Miskatonic University Extension building in Bolton."

"Right, the explosion, of the dynamite, which you drove into the courtyard, and then set off with a shot from your gun, when you realized that you didn't have a fuse."

"You just like to talk about guns."

"No, darling, I just like pulling your trigger."

He took her hand in his. He caressed it lightly and smiled. He wanted to say something, but then thought better of it and let the conversation drift away into silence.

As they sped through Aylesbury, the sun began to settle behind the not-so-distant mountains, and it was early evening by the time they pulled up in front of the neoclassical mansion that had come to dominate the Spool family farm. In the dim light the place looked odious and uninviting. Megan checked underneath her coat and made sure both holsters were unclipped, just in case. Robert threw her hat, letting the wide-brimmed thing float in the air toward her. Together they mounted the stairs. They didn't have to knock. The door opened and the venerable Ada Spool greeted them with a worried look upon her face.

"Thank you for coming, Mr. Peaslee. When the police said you had resigned I was afraid that there was no one who could help us. Thankfully they gave me the number to your office. I'm sorry to bother you, but I just didn't have anyone else to call."

"It's all right, Mrs. Spool. This is what we do." He unbuttoned his coat, but didn't take it off. "May I introduce my associate, Doctor Megan Halsey-Griffith."

Megan took Mrs. Spool's hand. "A woman doctor?" asked the old woman.

"I studied in Britain, at Shrewsbury College. They teach women to be doctors there."

"I see." There was some dissent in her tone. "If you'll follow me."

As the old woman led the way, Robert whispered into Megan's ear, "You're more qualified than half the physicians at St. Mary's."

Megan smiled slyly. "I know that, you know that; she is never going to believe it, even if I had the diploma in my hand."

"This way, please," Mrs. Spool called back to them. The couple rushed to catch up. "We've had some changes since you were last here, Mr. Peaslee." As they walked down the hall, they passed a tricycle and a rather large play doll. "That awful business in Dunwich left so many people dead, or hurt, or homeless. We've taken in many of the older orphans. We've tried to figure out who they are and then find relatives willing to take them in. It hasn't been easy." She stopped at a door and inserted a key. "The children are unruly, uneducated, and obstinate. Some of them can barely read and write. Their enunciation of our language is atrocious. We've had Doctor Henry Willis up to look at them. He may have specialized in surgery, but he's still a fine doctor, particularly when it comes to children."

Megan knew Willis by reputation, a good man who only resorted to surgery as a last resort. "What did Willis say about the children?"

Mrs. Spool looked up as the key turned in the lock. "Parasites," she announced. The door swung open and revealed a rather large dormitory easily holding over fifty beds. "Every single one of the children had a parasite of one kind or another. Lice, mostly, but tapeworms were common as well." She was walking down the aisle that led between the beds. "We found homes for most of them. The boys were easy. The girls took a little longer, but we placed all of them in homes, all except the foundlings."

She paused in front of a wall. "Normally the term 'foundling' is reserved for infants, but these five girls—they were brought in separately, but within days they had clustered together, formed a clique that none of the other girls could join, or even wanted to. Four of the girls were rather unremarkable, typical of the region, but one, the ringleader if you would, she was so strange, so small and frail, but strong willed. She couldn't speak or write, but somehow she made her wants and needs known. At first Willis said that she might be an idiot or a moron, but she was smart as a whip, and didn't like anyone to know it."

"Where are they now?" pressed Megan.

Mrs. Spool was taken aback. "I thought you understood. They're gone, been missing since this morning. We've asked you here to help us find them."

"And the police didn't want to handle this themselves?"

"We didn't want to involve them. We aren't fond of the authorities, at Spool House, and after we saw this we thought that you would appreciate our discretion." Her hand darted out and flipped a switch, turning on the light.

The light splashed out over the wall, illuminating what had lain hidden in the dark. It was a mural, and clearly done by a child, but not one without some artistic skill. It ran fifteen feet from floor to ceiling, and was just as wide. It depicted a pastoral scene, but one tinged with horror. The perspective was odd, but the two investigators soon realized that it was a panoramic view looking down into the various glens and valleys surrounding a steep rise, or small mountain. Yet both Megan and Robert knew exactly what hill that was, there was no mistaking it. This was a scene of the countryside surrounding Sentinel Hill, and not just on any day, but clearly on the day of the Dunwich Horror. There in one quadrant was a gathering of villagers from Dunwich staring up the hill, their eyes filled with apprehension and terror. Partway up the hill labored three old men, with dour faces. One carried an elephant gun, while another carried a large bag. They were a gray trio, determined, but you could see that they were afraid, too. All around them the trees were bent, the brush was flat, and the tall grass seemed to whip into frenzy. In another quadrant was the image of a small cabin surrounded by a swarm of broken and shattered men, with two figures, a man and a woman, fighting them off. The scene was very familiar; the figures were all recognizable, from the besieged couple to the decapitated form holding its own head as it seemed to orchestrate the attack.

"Now you see why we thought you might appreciate that we had not involved the police."

Peaslee stood up and looked at the woman with a sense of incredulity. "Yes, Mrs. Spool. I do appreciate it. Your discretion is appreciated, most appreciated."

"Then I can trust that you will be equally discreet and make sure that any of what happens next will not be linked back to this institution."

Peaslee nodded. "Of course, and of course we will handle this problem on a pro bono basis. If I may, when did they draw this? How did they draw this?"

Mrs. Spool scowled. "That obscenity wasn't there last night when we put the girls to bed. As to how, Mr. Peaslee, I have no idea, but my man tells me that he will need a ladder and at least two days to clean it off." With that, the old woman stalked out of the room, her footsteps echoing in the empty house.

Megan called after her, "Did the girls have names, Mrs. Spool?"

"I'm sure they did," her voice came from the hall, "but I see no way in which they are relevant to the task at hand."

The callous comment left Megan agasp, but Robert called her back to the mural. "You realize that this scene could only have been visualized by someone at the top of Sentinel Hill."

"But there wasn't anyone at the top of the hill. Not even Armitage and his group made it to the top." As soon as she said those words, Megan realized they weren't true. There had been someone at the top of Sentinel Hill. "We need to get to Dunwich."

As the car sped down Aylesbury Pike toward Dunwich with Robert Peaslee at the wheel, Megan expounded on what she thought they had just learned. "It all makes a little more sense, doesn't it? Yog-Sothoth is the Gate and the Key, a binary pair that have to be joined to release their father into the world. That tentacle-like tail with a rudimentary mouth that Armitage described Wilbur having, I don't think that was a tail or mouth at all. I think that was a kind of reproductive organ meant to join him with that thing on Sentinel Hill."

"But Armitage called the thing Wilbur's twin brother."

"Armitage is a librarian, not a biologist or a doctor, not that that matters. There are thousands of animals—birds, reptiles, insects, other invertebrates—in which determining the gender is nearly impossible to the untrained eye; here we're speaking about a human bred with something completely alien, possibly not even from this universe. I wouldn't expect anyone to be able to identify its gender simply by looking at it. It might not even have gender as we know it; that might be our own biology imprinted over its."

Robert took the curve hard, letting the car drift from one side of the road to the other and then bringing it back. "Just one of the girls, Megan, or all five of them?"

Megan thought for a moment, letting the shadows of the trees pass over her face as they raced down the road. "Only one, I think. The others were probably enlisted, entranced somehow. She must need them for something, support perhaps, or perhaps she is like a queen bee and she has enlisted these others as her drones."

"An interesting theory, but don't queens have to be related to their drones?"

"Usually," quipped Megan, "but you've been to Dunwich, I doubt you could find three people who weren't related within twenty miles of that damned village."

The car turned left onto the Dunwich Road and drove the two miles of dirt road to the covered bridge that spanned the East Creek. Twenty minutes and five miles later, the Dunwich Road hairpinned north and east. It became a sinuous track that forced Peaslee to drop his speed for another seven miles, which was only half that distance as the crow flied. The switchbacks gave way to another covered bridge, this time one that crossed the Miskatonic River and deposited the sedan carrying the two investigators into Dunwich proper.

"As you said, the damned village," remarked Robert as he turned east and followed the north bank of the river. Within minutes they were on the decayed dirt track that led north to Sentinel Hill. All around them the evidence of what had happened here just a few weeks ago was apparent; the crowns of great trees had been snapped off, and old and fragile pines had been pushed down. In some places the branches and debris dangled precariously from branches that had been stripped of leaves. All of this was a reminder of the weird force that had been unleashed from the apex of Sentinel Hill, sending a wave of destruction careening away in all directions, like a pebble in a pond. As they drove through the rural farmland, the fallow fields revealed a landscape of barns with missing roofs, homes with missing windows, and piles of timber that had once stood upright, but were now little more than ruins.

It was as they approached what remained of the Whateley farm, in the shadow of Sentinel Hill, that Robert slowed the car. Just then, a shape darted out into the road, forcing Peaslee to slam on the brakes and twist the wheel to the right. They slid through the dirt and came to rest just inches from a rather large tree. Before they could even move to exit the vehicle, the shape, a wild-eyed local man, was there at the door, screaming at them in a whimpering, terrified voice.

"Oh, oh, great Gawd, it's back. They sed it was ded, gawn fuheveh, but they lied, they lied. I saw it marchin' up past what's lefta Noah Whateley's farm, and then up through what's lefta Sentinel Hill. It's there, all like jelly, or a ball of wrigglin' wurms all bound clost togethei. Eyes and mouths bulgin' out everywhere. Dozens o' legs like barrels that spread out as they step. Great belchin' trunks on its back leavin' a trail of black smoke behind it . . . an' that haff face on top . . . the one that looks like Cousin Lavinia . . . Gawd in Heaven she looked daown the hill and she saw me . . . she saw me!"

And then he ran off and the darkness and the woods that surrounded the road swallowed him whole. Megan took her hand off her guns and relaxed. "So, still think we're going to solve this without guns?"

Robert glared at her mockingly and got out of the car. He walked to the trunk and opened it. He rustled around in the compartment before sliding out the stock of a rather large shotgun. Megan watched in amazement as he moved back away from the car and the gun just kept coming. In the end, the whole monstrosity, stock and barrel, was more than five feet long and as thick as her arm.

"What in the hell is that?" she asked.

"Elephant gun."

"And it's in your trunk?"

"In a special compartment that keeps it slung between the seats, just in case."

"So when you said you didn't want to use guns on this case . . ."

"I said I hope we wouldn't have to use guns on this case. After what that wild-eyed local just spouted off, I've changed my mind. Frankly, I wish I had my punt gun."

"How exactly would you get a punt gun to the top of Sentinel Hill?"

"Oh, that's not a problem—I mounted it on wheels."

Megan looked up at the gray and devastated landscape of Sentinel Hill, and laughed.

It was an hour later, and the night had fallen on Dunwich in a shroud. Clouds had rolled in to cover the moon and stars, blanketing the landscape in a thick darkness that was only broken by the weak and distant lights of the distant village. A few weeks earlier the pair would have had to work their way through the trees or follow a game trail to the crest of the hill, but since the disaster, the researchers from Miskatonic had cut a trail and an army of graduate students had covered it with gravel. Throughout the month of October, most of Miskatonic University, both staff and students, had been at work in the Dunwich area as a sort of relief force. They had set up facilities at Dean's Corners, creating makeshift medical facilities, schools, and the like, to take care of the victims of the disaster. Other members of the faculty and their students had scoured the countryside, gathering samples and data. There was talk about setting up a permanent facility to study the aftereffects of the phenomenon; the name Dunwich Institute had been mentioned. But that had been in October and as things had settled into a kind of routine, the teachers and student body had slowly drifted back into Arkham, and the future of any research into the event and the area was now only talked about at the most esoteric of academic levels.

Megan was leading the way while Robert followed a few steps behind, the elephant gun slung over his shoulder. There was no stealth involved in this approach—the noise of their feet on the gravel was simply too much. Their speed was problematic as well; the gun made it impossible to run, so they were at best trotting up the path, and as they did the sound of the gun rubbing against Robert's coat added one more level of noise.

Megan had wanted to say something about all the noise, and about the usefulness of the elephant gun itself, but she held her tongue and instead kept watch for what she was sure was an imminent attack by one member or another of the foundlings. When they actually reached the top without being challenged she was genuinely surprised, but only for a moment. What she saw there on the crest of Sentinel Hill explained why they hadn't been attacked on the way up.

The five girls were there, arranged in a circle around some ancient stone altar, a slab of granite supported by similar megaliths. Weird lines of energy were pouring out of the girls' hands, forming a complex of light just above the altar. Some would have called it a ball or sphere, but Robert could see it was neither of these; it was a conglomeration of geometric shapes, of polyhedrons with innumerable faces all rotating about various vertices, merging and blending with each other in a maddening cacophony of form and facets. It was a mosaic of tessellations that hurt to look at, not because it was too bright, for it wasn't—if anything it was pale, almost invisible in the darkness—but rather because it was a wrong thing. It didn't belong in this universe, it was an impossible construct, with angles that were both obtuse and acute at the same time, or at least that is how it seemed. It was in a way beautiful, but that beauty was fundamentally wrong. Robert wanted to think of it as inherently evil, but that word didn't convey the true nature of what he was seeing. It was a cosmic abomination, a thing that should not have been, an expression of laws and order, of mathematics and geometrics, but ones that weren't part of this universe. It was a vile intrusion into our universe and it needed to be destroyed.

He spun around and dropped to a knee, positioning the oversized gun, aiming it at the shining trapezohedron that was constantly forming and reforming. Megan was entranced by the thing and didn't realize what he was doing. Robert took his time aiming the gun; it was heavier than he thought and his hand was unused to the shape and weight. Robert was trying to make sure that his shot was on target, the object that had been summoned—he was likely to get only one shot. When he had finally shifted it into an optimum position, he called out to his partner.

"Megan, get back," he ordered in a hushed tone.

She cast a glance in his direction, and then her gaze was drawn back to the girls and the thing that was forming between them. She thought she had figured something out. There was one girl, a slight, waifish thing, with violet eyes and a weak chin. It was a Whateley chin, she had no doubt; that thin girl on the far side of the altar was the mistress of the others. If they could take her out, all this might be stopped. It was as she thought these words that the polyhedrons suddenly collapsed and then expanded in size, doubling the volume of the weird geometries. Megan could see something inside, a coastline, the sea crashing against it, a small village in the shadow of a massive cliff. She thought she recognized it, vaguely at least. Then she realized what was happening.

"Robert, shoot, you have to stop them. Shoot!"

As Megan screamed and dove for cover, one of the girls screeched in anger. It wasn't an animal sound, but it wasn't human either. It was a bellowing emptiness that rolled out of the mouth of a child who was too small to be its source. The other girls turned and flew toward Robert—their eyes were black, their mouths open and echoing that horrific sound.

He pulled the trigger.

The round left the barrel at immense speed and with a tremendous roar, tearing through one of the girls, ripping a gaping hole in her chest and then continuing on to impact on that queer polyhedron. Robert didn't have time to see what damage his attack had inflicted; one of the three remaining harpy-like children careened into him and knocked him to the ground. Out of the corner of his eye he saw the other two girls impact on Megan. He rolled with the hit and let the girl's momentum carry her away from him. She hit the ground and in an instant was on her feet and springing back at Peaslee's head. As she flew through the air, Robert swung the gun butt and smashed her across the face. The girl's jaw shattered and she crumpled to the ground, unconscious.

He turned and ran toward Megan, intent on engaging her attackers, but that was not a necessity. Megan had gathered both girls, one under each arm, and with opposite hands let loose with her pearl-handled revolvers. The bodies kicked, then shuddered and joined their sister on the ground at the summit of Sentinel Hill. All four of the furies were on the ground, with blood and gore staining the earth itself. It made Robert sick to look at what he had been forced to do, but he had done it, the guns had done their duty, and the bodies never stood up again.

But the glowing thing that they had summoned was still there, and so was the child that Megan thought of as the Whateley girl. She had taken cover behind the altar and was now clambering up it toward the hole that held an image of a place far distant from where they stood now. That image was rolling now, destabilizing. The girl-thing roared again and dove toward it. In that weird, unearthly light, the girl ceased to be human. There was something else, a kind of shadow that replaced the girl; it was a titanic thing, cyclopean, and entirely unearthly in its appearance. It was as that wild-eyed man had said, like a bunch of worms all squirming together with eyes and mouths everywhere.

Megan was firing her guns, but to no avail—the monstrous child impacted on the polyhedron and the two seemed to meld into each other. The monster stretched and squeezed, shrank and compressed in a thousand different directions. There was a burst of light, like a thousand snowflakes exploding. The conglomeration of shapes and light was bucking wildly, like a child's top as it neared the end of its spin. Then, just like that, the monster was gone, and the whole thing collapsed in on itself.

Megan grabbed Robert, wrenching him off the ground, and threw him down the slope, diving after him. They hit the gravel path hard, but rolled with it, sliding about ten feet down from the crest. Robert tried to stand, but Megan grabbed him and pulled him back down.

There was a flash of light; they say even people in Aylesbury could see it, for it lit up the whole of the Dunwich valley. It was a queer light which cast white shadows and turned everything black, but only for a moment. Then there was an explosion—not an explosion: an implosion. Leaves, dirt, and loose gravel whipped up the side of the hill, forming great trails of debris as the whirligig presumably collapsed. The two investigators lay there for a moment, catching their breath and tending to minor wounds and detritus that had gotten caught in their clothes and hair.

After two or three minutes they climbed back up the hill. The gun was gone, as were the bodies of the girls. The whole top of Sentinel Hill had been scoured clean. Only the megalithic altar remained. As they turned and walked back down the trail, neither of them spoke, and the night was filled with the sound of tired feet on gravel.

At the car, Robert opened Megan's door. "What did you see?"

But she didn't answer.

They drove back to Arkham in silence. At the Griffith House they ate a little food and then went to their separate rooms and slept. Robert emerged on the second morning, and after making himself a hearty breakfast found Megan sitting in the family library. She had a book open on her lap, one that Robert recognized as volume two of Watkins's *History of the Miskatonic Valley*. She was staring at an illustration.

It was a sketch of a family, a stern father stood next to a dour mother who just exuded piousness. In front of them stood three teenage girls, triplets apparently. In the background was a wharf, and beyond that a small village beneath a large cliff. Robert recognized it as Kingsport Head, and realized that the village must have been colonial Kingsport.

"This is what I saw on top of Sentinel Hill. The village of Kingsport, but not as it is now—as it was when this drawing was made. She went back in time."

"You don't know that for sure. There's no way of knowing if that's what she was doing, or even if she made it. Trust me, I know a thing or two about . . . these things."

She turned the book around and pushed it toward him. "Read the caption."

*The Mason Family circa 1953, artist unknown. Captain Roger Mason, his wife Elizabeth (née Talbye), and their daughters Abigail, Hepzibah, and Keziah. Despite the resemblance, only two of the girls are related. The original Keziah Mason had died in 1640 at the age of three. In 1652, following a tremendous storm, a girl child was found on the beach and taken in by the Masons. She was suffering from amnesia, and unable to speak, and Elizabeth Mason gave the mute foundling her dead child's name. It is hard to believe that these three children would grow up to become such sinister figures in Miskatonic Valley history— Abigail Prinn, Goody Fowler, and Keziah Mason—supplying Arkham with the epitaph "witch-haunted".*

"Whatever she was trying to do, I think she did it. I think that girl—Keziah Mason—has set things in motion, that she has some sort of plan. What happened up on Sentinel Hill, the death of Wilbur Whateley, and the Dunwich Horror, that wasn't the end of things—I think that was just the beginning.

Robert took her in his arms and held her as she sobbed. "What are we going to do, Robert, whatever are we going to do?"

He pulled back and held her tear-streaked face in his hands. "I have a plan," he told her. "It's complicated and devious, and a little illegal, but I have a plan."

And then he told her his plan.

That night she slept in his arms, and lying there felt a little easier, knowing what the future held for them both.

# CHAPTER 36

# "Changing of the Guard"
## From the Case File of HP&L
## November 20 1928

Megan and I walked through the dreary streets of Arkham and made our way over to Miskatonic University for my morning appointment. An icy wind had moved in from the north and turned the air of the city frigid. Morning reports said that there was ice on the river. The year seemed determined to end on a bad note. So much had happened, so much horror had been hinted at, hinted at and more, I doubted that Arkham could endure another year like the one that was nearly over. There was hope that something could be done to bring the current round of horrors to a close. Some had an idea to prevent them from ever happening again. This is why we were on our way to see the library staff. We were to speak to learned men who thought that something could be done, and that they were the ones to do it.

Oddly, to meet with the university library staff, I didn't go to the library. There isn't room for them all there. The Old Marsh Library, what they now call the Tabularium, has its main hall mostly filled with files, school archives, and the like, but it can hold one hundred people easily. My plan was to fill it with the entire staff of librarians, their assistants, the clerks, and those members of the campus police assigned to the library. It was a simple request, and it needed to be. Things needed to change, and the powers of this little empire had nominated me to be the one to break the news.

Cyrus Llanfer, the Acting Director while Armitage recovered, met me at the steps and escorted both me and Megan inside. He was a nervous little man who looked at his watch disapprovingly. "You are late, Detective Peaslee." His pace was almost frenetic.

"The cold and wind slowed us down," I lied. "Is everybody here? I don't want to have to go through this again."

Llanfer nodded. "Everyone is waiting, from Armitage all the way down to that annoying little woman down in receiving. What is her name? Stanley." He clucked her name. "Some kind of prodigy: a law degree at twenty-two, but she ditches that to work in the pit. Who does that?" The inside of the building was warm. The old library had its own furnace and the old thing was still in fine working order.

Megan touched my hand. "I'll wait in the reading room."

Llanfer spoke with a condescending tone. "Thank you, Miss Halsey. Be sure not to wander around; there are no clerks or librarians available to help you, and I would hate to see you get lost."

I called out to her. "This will take me an hour, not counting questions." She kissed me on the cheek and I watched as she strutted down the hall while Llanfer took me through the massive double doors of the entrance to what was once the Marsh Library. The room beyond was full of chattering academics. The venerable Doctor Armitage was sitting in a chair off to the side. He looked weak and sad. His actions had thwarted the Dunwich Horror, but while he had been fighting monsters his wife had fallen ill, and eventually passed away. Her funeral had been just two weeks earlier. Behind Armitage was Professor Harper, the former director, who was a little younger than Armitage but not nearly as spry. He was supposedly retired, but still maintained an office and did a little research. Occasionally he served as an academic advisor to graduate students, but only to very promising candidates.

As I scanned through the crowd I recognized several of the more troublesome members of the staff, ones who were not going to take kindly to what I had to say, or what was going to have to be done. Anthony Alwyn and David Sandwin were in the back, smoking. They were odd birds, younger than most of the others, more talented, more curious, excluding Stanley. Llanfer was right; she was a prodigy, just as talented and curious as any, but quite a bit more cautious. I thought that made her less dangerous—Megan thought the exact opposite.

Llanfer took the makeshift podium and tried to quiet his subordinates, but no matter what he did the uncontrolled conversation continued. It wasn't until Armitage rose and tapped the floor with his cane that the normally quiet caretakers of the Miskatonic University Library ceased their babble and gave me their attention. Llanfer fumbled through an introduction and then sheepishly left me to do the talking.

"Ladies and gentlemen, thank you all for coming. Doctors Armitage and Llanfer have asked me to come speak to you today concerning some changes I've recommended regarding access to some of the library's holdings." A murmur went through the crowd. "I understand that this may be antithetical to your work, to the philosophy behind your profession, but I think most of you might have a clue why these changes are necessary."

There was a voice from the back. "I don't, why don't you stop being all mysterious and explain what is going on. There has been too much rumor and gossip of late. We deserve some explanations." It was Goudsward, a junior reference librarian who specialized in geography and genealogy.

"I don't disagree," I responded. "It would take more time than I have to cover things in depth, so I'll just go over the highlights." I took a deep breath. "Back in January, graduate student Walter Gilman and Wilbur Whateley of Dunwich both consulted the Necronomicon, or at least we think they did. In March, Amos Tuttle died, and as part of his bequest to the library his lawyer dropped off a copy of the Necronomicon. Turns out, the one in the case was a very clever copy. In May, a rat ate out Gilman's heart, and three months later Whateley was killed by one of the library dogs. Dr. Armitage will attest that the events in Dunwich were related to the Necronomicon. Shortly afterward, Dr. Llanfer informed me that he had discovered that someone had broken in and again stolen the Necronomicon, or at least so they thought. Dr. Armitage had taken certain precautions and replaced the real book with the copy. The fire down at the Tuttle place may have been because the wrong book had been stolen. Also, some of you might remember Seth Bishop of Aylesbury—he visited quite often from 1919 through 1923. Late last month, he killed Amos Bowden." There was an overwhelming silence in the room, but I had to drive it home. "Some of you worked with Bryant Hoskins, one of the junior librarians under Dr. Llanfer. He was assigned to work on the Tuttle bequest. Hoskins was unsupervised and used his access to read portions of the Necronomicon. He stole two books: the *R'Lyeh Text* and the *Celeano Fragments*. They found him up in his cabin; he's been confined to the county asylum at Sefton. The books he stole have been placed on the locked shelves. We are going to place more books on the restricted shelf."

Goudsward was outraged. "Why? What gives you the right?"

Dr. Cyrus Llanfer rose in defiant response. "There are some things man is not meant to know, and some books man is not meant to read."

A dull roar filled the room, but once again Armitage rose to quell the disruption. This time he spoke and his voice was filled with emotion. "This is not open to debate. Detective Peaslee has outlined a set of procedures and measures that we are going to begin instituting immediately. If you are unhappy with this decision the university will provide you with a month's severance and a letter of recommendation."

As Armitage sat back down, the crowd settled and I was finally allowed to begin discussing how I was going to make sure that the collection was more secure from both the public and unauthorized staff. Faculty and student use would be limited, controlled by a committee of four with two members each from the faculty and the senior library staff. Locks would be installed on doors, and new, locking cabinets would be used. They would have separate keys, which would be assigned to specific curators. The keys would be of a proprietary design; duplication privileges would be limited to the committee of four. The collection rooms themselves would be redesigned. The books would not be allowed to leave dedicated reading rooms. Books would be viewed by appointment only, and only for limited periods of time. Curating staff would not leave the room while a book was out of a cabinet. The transfer of books from a cabinet to the table and back again would be handled by the curators. No one else was to have access to the storage cabinets. Emergency switches for alarms were to be installed in every room.

It took an hour to go through my designs and recommendations, and to answer a handful of questions. The obligatory handshaking and thanks came from Llanfer and Armitage, as well as Harper. A scowl of disapproval was directed my way from Goudsward, and another from Alwyn. Miss Stanley went out of her way to catch my attention, but then changed her mind and shuffled awkwardly away. By the time I made my way out of the room, Megan had been free to do whatever she wanted for more than an hour.

She took my hand and as the hall emptied expertly helped guide me through the crowd of slightly stunned and annoyed library staff. We said nothing, and as the herd left the Tabularium and headed back to the library, we turned in the opposite direction and headed off campus. It was only then that my wife, Megan Halsey, began to smile.

"They really are just a hypocritical lot of pompous old fools, aren't they?" she pondered out loud. "There are things man was not meant to know. What they mean is they want to be able to control the information. They want access to it, and to keep it away from everyone else. My father would have slapped the man."

"It's what they believe." I told her. "At least, it's what Llanfer believes, probably Armitage, too. They truly think that they are incorruptible, that their education and position as librarians set them above everyone else. They've set themselves at the top and by controlling the information they make sure to keep themselves there."

"Until somebody like us sneaks in and takes it away from them."

I smiled back. "How much were you able to destroy?"

"Everything that we were looking for—say what you want about librarians, but they are very well organized. Everything was filed exactly where it was supposed to be: West's thesis, the file on the Whateleys, what they found in the ashes of Hartwell's house, your father's papers, Tillinghast's designs, even the journals of the 1902 Hawks expedition. All of it went into the furnace."

"Well done. You're still comfortable doing this?"

"It has to be done." There was a kind of lament in her voice.

The clock tower chimed and I turned around to look at it. The smoke from the stack above the Tabularium had changed from white to black. I thought about how much we had just destroyed, just a few boxes of papers, and yet so very dangerous. Changes needed to be made. The thought was sobering. Llanfer and Armitage were going to follow my directions. The new security would be put in place. Only a few people would have keys, including myself. Things were going to be different. I would make sure of it. I wouldn't be able to touch the ancient books; they were too high profile, too noticeable. The other things, journals, accounts, notebooks, things that were just piled up waiting to be properly catalogued, these things could be destroyed quite easily.

Let the old men have their black-lettered grimoires and illuminated manuscripts full of legends and ridiculous spells which only hint at what might be. It's the more recent documents that actually tell the truth. This is a new age, with new ideas, and a new morality. Someone must make sure that we don't end up destroying ourselves. There are things man was not meant to know, but is it really up to a bunch of old librarians to control? Perhaps not, perhaps it is time for someone else to take a turn. Why not Detective Robert Peaslee and Megan Halsey? Why not two people who had suffered as a result of that information and those who had used it?

I can think of no one better.

CHAPTER 37

# A Note from the Editor
## January 8 1930

What you have just completed reading is what I believe to be the truth, as much of it as I have been able to garner from the files left behind by my partners, Robert Peaslee and his wife Megan Halsey-Griffith, who prefers only to use half her maiden name. The vast majority of it cannot be confirmed, but some of it can. Robert Peaslee's work in Paris and then in Arkham, his casework and transfer, are all matters of public record. Likewise, Megan's disappearance and sudden reappearance are also easily verified. That she was the body found in the river has been officially noted as an error, and her absence is explained as her being away in Britain, studying.

Documents on file at the courthouse will prove that the firm of Halsey, Peaslee and Lydecker Consultants was formed in October of 1928 and saw brisk business from the onset. Their files on working with the staff at the university library and the events at the Spooner house are just two of the cases the firm handled, but they serve to explain the tenor of the work they were undertaking. I must beg your forgiveness in changing the perspective throughout these documents, but I thought it would add a bit of flair to our tale. I am not an accomplished storyteller, and can only work with the meager gifts I have been granted.

Documenting the events that led to the formation of HP&L and two of their adventures would not have been necessary if the senior members of the firm had not vanished in June of 1929. That the couple went missing shortly after the wedding of Asenath Waite and Edward Derby should be considered purely coincidental. The firm had, in its nine months of activity, undertaken a number of cases, and in the process collected a gallery of individuals and organizations that one would have no choice but to call enemies, not the least of which were various

faculty and staff members of Miskatonic University and more specifically the senior librarians.

But that is an entirely different story.

Yours,

Roman Lydecker
Managing Partner
HP&L Consultants

# Acknowledgements

*Reanimatrix* is an homage to some of my very favorite movies and books, most notably *Laura* by Vera Caspray, which was made into a fine film directed by Otto Preminger, with Gene Tierney and Dana Andrews. *Laura* is about a cop who falls in love with a murder victim, and is one of the inspirations for David Lynch's *Twin Peaks*, which I also must cite as influential on this book. Other inspirations include the films *Auntie Mame* and *Doctor X*, as well as the novels *The Great Gatsby*, *Locus Solus*, *The Big Sleep*, and the entire Philo Vance series. Evident also is my love of Rex Stout's Nero Wolfe books.

This story relies heavily on the excellent work of Chaosium's Keith Herber and others, who documented much of the geography I needed to travel through in their roleplaying supplement *Return to Dunwich*. It is an excellent guide to that rugged and wild terrain full of the strange and unknown.

As this novel took shape, several of the stories appeared in anthologies, and for this I must thank Mike Davis, Brian Sammons, Glynn Owen Barrass, and Jean-Marc L'Officier.

My version may be different, but I must also thank Messrs. Gordon, Norris, Paoli, and Yuzna, and Miss Barbara Crampton for bringing the original Megan Halsey to life on the big screen. Without their pioneering work, mine would not exist.

Pete Rawlik
Hell's Gate Point, Florida
July 25, 2015

# About the Author

Pete Rawlik has been active in all things Lovecraftian since his father read him "The Rats in the Walls" when he was a child, as a bedtime story. For more than two decades he has run Dead Ink, selling rare and unusual books. Rawlik's fiction has appeared in numerous magazines and anthologies. His two novels, *Reanimators* and *The Weird Company*, were both published by Night Shade Books.